We Don't Live Here Anymore

❧

THE NOVELLAS OF

ANDRE DUBUS

CROWN PUBLISHERS, INC.   NEW YORK

To Mark Costello and David Supple,

corpsmen of the nights

This book contains four novellas by the author previously published separately as follows:

"The Pretty Girl" copyright © 1983 by Andre Dubus from THE TIMES ARE NEVER SO BAD; "We Don't Live Here Anymore" copyright © 1975 by Andre Dubus from SEPARATE FLIGHTS; "Adultery" copyright © 1977 by the University of the South. Published subsequently in ADULTERY & OTHER CHOICES by Andre Dubus, copyright © 1977 by Andre Dubus; "Finding A Girl in America" copyright © 1980 by Andre Dubus from FINDING A GIRL IN AMERICA

"Adultery" was first published in the *Sewanee Review*, 85, 1 (winter 1977). Copyright 1977 by the University of the South. Reprinted with permission of the editor.

Copyright © 1984 by Andre Dubus

All rights reserved. No part of this book may be reproduced or utilized in any form or by any means, electronic or mechanical, including photocopying, recording, or by any information storage and retrieval system, without permission in writing from the publisher.

Published by Crown Publishers, Inc., One Park Avenue, New York, New York 10016 and simultaneously in Canada by General Publishing Company Limited by arrangement with David Godine Publisher, Inc.

Printed in the United States of America

Library of Congress Cataloging in Publication Data

Dubus, Andre, 1936–

   We don't live here anymore.

   I. Title.

PS3554.U265W4   1984   813'.54   83-26215

ISBN 0-517-55362-7

10 9 8 7 6 5 4 3 2 1

First Edition

We
Don't
Live
Here
Anymore

OTHER BOOKS BY ANDRE DUBUS

The Lieutenant

Separate Flights

Adultery & Other Choices

Finding a Girl in America

The Times Are Never So Bad

CONTENTS

The Pretty Girl

But because thou art lukewarm,

and neither cold nor hot,

I am about to vomit thee

out of my mouth. . . .

SAINT JOHN, *The Apocalypse*

For Roger Rath
out among the stars

I DON'T KNOW HOW I feel till I hold that steel. That was always true: I might have a cold, or one of those days when everything is hard to do because you're tired for no reason at all except that you're alive, and I'd work out, and by the time I got in the shower I couldn't remember how I felt before I lifted; it was like that part of the day was yesterday, and now I was starting a new one. Or a hangover: some of my friends and my brother too are hair-of-the-dog people, but I've never done that and I never will, because a drink in the morning shuts down the whole day, and anyway I can't stand the smell of it in the morning and my stomach tells me it would like a Coke or a milkshake, but it is not about to stand for a prank like a shot of vodka or even a beer.

It was drunk out last night, Alex says. And I always say: *A severe drunk front moved in around midnight.* We've been saying that since I was seventeen and he was twenty-one. On a morning after one of those, when I can read the words in the *Boston Globe* but I can't remember them long enough to understand the story, I work out. If it's my day off from weights, I run or go to the Y and swim. Then the hangover is gone. Even the sick ones: some days I've thought I'd either blow my lunch on the bench or get myself squared away and, for the first few sets, as I pushed the bar up from my chest, the booze tried to come up too, with whatever I'd eaten during the night, and I'd swallow and push the iron all the way up and bring it down again, and some of my

3

sweat was cool. Then I'd do it again and again, and add some weights, and do it again till I got a pump, and the blood rushed through my muscles and flushed out the lactic acid, and sweat soaked my shorts and tank shirt, the bench under my back was slick, and all the poison was gone from my body. From my head too, and for the rest of the day, unless something really bothered me, like having to file my tax return, or car trouble, I was as peaceful as I can ever be. Because I get along with people, and they don't treat me the way they treat some; in this world it helps to be big. That's not why I work out, but it's not a bad reason, and one that little guys should think about. The weather doesn't harass me either. New Englanders are always bitching about one thing or another. Once Alex said: *I think they just like to bitch, because when you get down to it, the truth is the Celtics and Patriots and Red Sox and Bruins are all good to watch, and we're lucky they're here, and we've got the ocean and pretty country to hunt and fish and ski in, and you don't have to be rich to get there.* He's right. But I don't bitch about the weather: I like rain and snow and heat and cold, and the only effect they have on me is what I wear to go out in them. The weather up here is female, and goes from one mood to another, and I love her for that.

So as long as I'm working out, I have good days, except for those things that happen to you like dead batteries and forms to fill out. If I skip my workouts I start feeling confused and distracted, then I get tense, and drinking and talking aren't good, they just make it worse, then I don't want to get out of bed in the morning. I've had days like that, when I might not have got up at all if finally I didn't have to piss. An hour with the iron and everything is back in place again, and I don't know what was troubling me or why in the first place I went those eight or twelve or however many days without lifting. But it doesn't matter. Because it's over, and I can write my name on a check or say it out loud again without feeling like a liar. This is Raymond Yarborough, I say into the phone, and I feel my words, my name, go out over the wire, and he says the car is ready and it'll be seventy-eight dollars and sixty-five cents. I tell him I'll come get it now, and I walk out into the world I'd left for a while and it feels like mine again. I like stepping on it and breathing it. I walk to the bank first and cash a check because the garage won't take one unless you have a major credit card, which I don't because I don't believe in buying something, even gas, that I don't have the money for. I always have enough money because I don't buy anything I can't eat or drink. Or almost anything. At the bank window I write a check to Cash and sign both sides and talk to the girl. I tell her she's looking good and I like her sweater and the new way she's got her hair done. I'm not making a move; I feel good and I want to see her smiling.

But for a week or two now, up here at Alex's place in New Hampshire, the iron hasn't worked for me. While I'm pumping I forget Polly, or at least I feel like I have, but in the shower she's back again. I got to her once, back in June: she was scared like a wild animal, a small one without any natural weapons, like a wounded rabbit, the way they quiver in your hand and look at you when you pick them up to knock their heads against trees or rocks. But I think she started to like it anyways, and if I had wanted to, I could have made her come. But that's Polly. I've known her about twelve years, since I was fourteen, and I think I knew her better when we were kids than I ever did after high school when we started going together and then got married. In school I knew she was smart and pretty and tried to look sexy before she was. I still don't know much more. That's not true: I can write down a lot that I know about her, and I did that one cold night early last spring, about fifty pages on a legal pad, but all of it was what she said to me and what she thought I said to her and what she did. I still didn't understand why she was that way, why we couldn't just be at peace with one another, in the evenings drink some beer or booze, talking about this and that, then eat some dinner, and be easy about things, which is what I thought we got married for.

We were camping at a lake and not catching any trout when we decided to get married. We talked about it on the second night, lying in our sleeping bags in the tent. In the morning I woke up feeling like the ground was blessed, a sacred place of Indians. I was twenty-two years old, and I thought about dying; it still seemed many years away, but I felt closer to it, like I could see the rest of my life in that tent while Polly slept, and it didn't matter that at the end of it I'd die. I was very happy, and I thought of my oldest brother, Kingsley, dead in the war we lost, and I talked to him for a while, told him I wished he was here so he could see how good I felt, and could be the best man. Then I talked to Alex and told him he'd be the best man. Then I was asleep again, and when I woke up Polly was handing me a cup of coffee and I could hear the campfire crackling. Late that afternoon we left the ground but I kept the tent; I didn't bring it back to the rental place. I had a tent of my own, a two-man, but I rented a big one so Polly could walk around in it, and arrange the food and cooler and gear, the way women turn places into houses, even motel rooms. There are some that don't, but they're not the kind you want to be with for the whole nine yards; when a woman is a slob, she's even worse than a man. They had my deposit, but they phoned me. I told them we had an accident and the tent was at the bottom of Lake Willoughby up in Vermont, up in what they call the Northern Kingdom. He asked me what it was doing in the lake. I said I had no way of knowing because that lake was formed by a glacier and is so deep in places that nobody could know even how far down it was, much less what it was doing. He said *on* the lake, what was it doing *on* the lake? Did my boat capsize? I said, What boat? He had been growling, but this time he barked: then how did the tent get in the fucking lake? I pitched it there, I said. That's the accident I'm talking about. Then he howled: the deposit didn't cover the cost of the boat. I told him to start getting more deposit, and hung up. That tent is out here at Alex's, folded up and resting on the rafters in the garage. This place was Kingsley's, and when his wife married again she wanted to give it to me and Alex, but Alex said that wasn't right, he knew Kingsley would want her to do that, and at the same time he knew Kingsley would expect us to turn it down and give her some money; their marriage was good, and she has his kid, my niece Olivia who's nearly ten now. I was still in school, so Alex bought it.

What I thought we had—I know we had it—in the tent that morning didn't last, and even though I don't understand why everything changed as fast as our weather does, I blame her because I tried so hard and was the way I always was before, when she loved me; I changed toward her and cursed her and slapped her around when every day was bad and the nights worse. There are things you can do in the daytime that make you feel like your marriage isn't a cage with rattlesnakes on the floor, that you can handle it: not just working out, but driving around for a whole afternoon just getting eggs and light bulbs and dry cleaning and a watchband and some socks. You listen to music in the car and look at people in their cars (I've noticed often you'll see a young girl driving alone, smiling to herself; maybe it's the disc jockey, maybe it's what she's thinking), and you talk to people in their stores (I always try to go to small stores, even for food), and your life seems better than it was when you walked out of the house with the car key. But at night there's nothing to distract you; and besides at night is when you really feel married, and need to; and there you are in the living room with all those snakes on the floor. I was tending bar five nights a week then, so two nights were terrible and sad, and on the others I came home tired and crept into the house and bed, feeling like I was doing something wrong, something I didn't want her to wake up and see. Then near the end Vinnie DeLuca was in that bed on the nights I worked, and I found out and that was the end.

I treated her well. I shared the housework, like my brothers and I did growing up. I've never known a woman who couldn't cook better than I do, but still I can put a meal on the table, and I did that, either fried or barbecued; I cooked on the grill outside all year round; I like cooking out while snow is falling. I washed the dishes when she cooked, and sometimes remembered to vacuum, and I did a lot of errands, because she hated that, probably because she went to supermarkets and never talked to anybody, while I just didn't quite enjoy it.

Never marry a woman who doesn't know what she wants, and knows she doesn't. Mom never knew what she wanted either, but I don't think she knew she didn't, and that's why she's stayed steady through the years. She still brings her Luckies to the table. When I was little I believed Mom was what a wife should look like. I never thought much about what a wife should be like. She was very pretty then and she still is, though you have to look at her for a while to see it. Or I guess other people do, who are looking for pretty women to be young, or the other way around, and when they see a woman in her fifties they don't really look at her until they have to, until they're sitting down talking to her, and seeing her eyes and the way she smiles. But I don't need that closer look. She's outdoors a lot and has good lines in her face, the kind of lines that make me trust someone.

Mom wants Lucky Strikes and coffee, iced in summer after the hot cups in the morning, and bourbon when the sun is low. When she has those she's all right, let it rain where we're camping or the black flies find us fishing. During the blizzard of 1978 Mom ran out of Luckies and Jim Beam, and the coffee beans were low; the old man laughs about it, he says she was showing a lot of courage, but he thought he better do something fast or be snowed in with a crazy woman, so he went on cross-country skis into town and came back with a carton and a bottle and a can of coffee in his parka pockets. I tried to stop you, she says when they joke about it. Not as hard as you've tried to stop me going other places, the old man says. The truth is, it was not dangerous, only three miles into town from their house, and I know the old man was happy for an excuse to get out into the storm and work up a sweat. Younger, he wouldn't have needed an excuse, but I think his age makes him believe when there's a blizzard he should stay indoors. He's buried a few friends. At the store he got to in the snow they only had regular coffee, not the beans that Mom buys at two or three stores you have to drive to. He says when he came home she grabbed the carton first and had one lit before he was out of his ski mask, and she had two drinks poured while he was taking off his boots; then she held up the can of coffee and said: Who drinks this? You have a girl friend you were thinking about? He took the drink from her and said I don't have time for a girl friend. And she said I know you don't. They didn't tell us any more of that story; I know there'd be a fire going, and I like to think he was down to his long underwear by then, and he took that off and they lay in front of the fireplace. But probably they just had bourbon and teased one another and the old man took a shower and they went upstairs to sleep.

I hope the doctors never tell Mom she has to give up her Luckies and coffee and bourbon. You may call that an addiction. So what is my pumping iron? What is Polly?

She would say I raped her in June and so would her cop father and the rest of her family, if she told them, which she probably did because she moved back in with them. But maybe she didn't tell them. She didn't press charges; Alex keeps in touch with what's going on down there, and he lets me know. But I've stayed up here anyway. It's hard to explain: the night I did it I naturally crossed the state line and came up here to the boondocks; I knew when they didn't find me at home or at work, Polly would tell them to try here, but it was a good place to wait for a night and a day, a good place to make plans. In the morning I called Alex and he spoke to a friend on the force and called me back and said, Nothing yet. Late that afternoon he called again, said, Nothing yet. So I stayed here the second night, and next morning and afternoon he called me again, so I stayed a third night and a fourth and fifth, because every day he called and said there was nothing yet. By then I had missed two nights of a job I liked, tending bar at Newburyport, where I got good tips and could have girls if I wanted them. I knew that a girl would help, maybe do more than that, maybe fix everything for me. But having a girl was just an idea, like thinking about a part of the country where you might want to live if you ever stopped loving the place where you were.

So I wanted to want a girl, but I didn't, not even when these two pretty ones came in almost every night I worked and sat at the bar and talked to me when I had the time, and gave me signs with their eyes and the way they joked with me and laughed at each other. I could have had either one, and I don't know how the other one would have taken it. Sometimes I thought about taking both of them back to my place, which is maybe what they had in mind anyway, but that wouldn't be the same as having a girl I wanted to want, and I couldn't get interested enough to go through the trouble. Once, before Polly, I went to a wedding where everyone got drunk on champagne. I noticed then something I hadn't noticed before: girls get horny at weddings. I ended up with two friends of the bride; I had known them before, but not much. They were dressed up and looking very good, and when the party broke up we went to a bar, a crowded bar with a lot of light, one of those places where the management figures it draws a crowd with all kinds in it, so one way to keep down fights and especially guys pulling knives is have the place lit up like a library. I sat between them at the bar and rubbed their thighs, and after we drank some more I had a hand up each of them; it was late spring and their legs were moist, squeezing my hands; then they opened a little, enough; I don't remember if they did this at the same time or one was first. Then I got my hands in their pants. The bar was crowded and people were standing behind us, drinking in groups and pairs, buying drinks over the girls' shoulders, and I was stroking clitoris. When I told Alex this he said, How did you drink and smoke? I said I don't know. But I do know that I kept talking and pretending to each girl that I was only touching her. I got the drinking done too. Maybe they came at the bar, but pretty soon I couldn't take it anymore, and I got them out of there. But in the car I suddenly knew how drunk and tired I was; I was afraid I couldn't make it with both of them, so I took the plump one to her apartment and we told her good night like a couple of innocent people going home drunk from a wedding. Then I brought the other one to my place, and we had a good night, but every time I thought of the bar I was sorry I took the plump one home. Probably the girl with me was sorry too, because in the morning I took a shower and when I got out, the bed was made and she was gone. She left a nice note, but it was strange anyway, and made the whole night feel like a bad mistake, and I thought since it didn't really matter who I got in bed with, it should have been the one that was plump. She was good-looking and I'm sure was not lonesome or hard up for a man, but still for the rest of the day and that night I felt sorry when I remembered her leaving the car and walking up the walk to her apartment building, because you know how women are, and she was bound to feel then that her friend was slender and she wasn't and that was the only reason she was going home alone drunk, with juicy underpants. She was right, and that's why I felt so bad. Next day I decided to stop thinking about her. I do that a lot: you do some things you wish you hadn't, and thinking about them afterward doesn't do any good for anybody, and finally you just feel like your heart has the flu. None of this is why I didn't take the two girls this summer back to my place.

What is hard to explain is why, when I knew Polly wasn't going to press charges, I stayed here instead of giving my boss some almost true story. I thought of some he would believe, or at least accept because he likes me and I do good work, something just a few feet short of saying Hey, lookit, I was running from a rape charge. But I didn't go back, except one night to my apartment for my fishing gear and guns and clothes and groceries. Nothing else in there belonged to me.

When I came up here that night I did it, I went to my place first and loaded the jeep with my weights and bench and power stands. So when I knew nobody was after me, all I did was work out, lifting on three days and running and swimming in the lake on the others. That was first thing in the morning, which was noon for everybody else. Every day was sunny, and in the afternoons I sat on a deck chair on the wharf, with a cooler of beer. Near sundown I rowed out in the boat and fished for bass and pickerel. If I caught one big enough for dinner, I stopped fishing and let the boat drift till dark, then rowed back and ate my fish. So all day and most of the night I was thinking, and most of that was about why I wasn't going back. All I finally knew was something had changed. I had liked my life till that night in June, except for what Polly was doing to it, but you've got to be able to separate those things, and I still believe I did, or at least tried to hard enough so that sometimes I did, often enough to know my life wasn't a bad one and I was luckier than most. Then I went to her house that night and I felt her throat under the Kabar, then her belly under it. I don't just mean I could feel the blade touching her, the way you can cut cheese with your eyes closed; it wasn't like that, the blade moving through air, then stopping because something—her throat, her belly—was in the way. No: I felt her skin touching the steel, like the blade was a finger of mine.

They would call it rape and assault with a deadly weapon, but those words don't apply to me and Polly. I was taking back my wife for a while; and taking back, for a while anyway, some of what she took from me. That is what it felt like: I went to her place torn and came out mended. Then she was torn, so I was back in her life for a while. All night I was happy and I kept getting hard, driving north and up here at Alex's, just remembering. All I could come up with in the days and nights after that, thinking about why I didn't go back to my apartment and working the bar, was that time in my life seemed flat and stale now, like an old glass of beer.

But I have to leave again, go back there for a while. Everything this summer is breaking down to for a while, which it seems is as long as I can keep peaceful. Now after my workout I get in the hot shower feeling strong and fresh, and rub the bar of soap over my biceps and pecs, they're hard and still pumped up; then I start to lose what the workout was really for, because nobody works out for just the body, I don't care what they may say, and it could be that those who don't lift or run or swim or something don't need to because they've got most of the time what the rest of us go for on the bench or road or in the pool, though I'm not talking about the ones who just drink and do drugs. Then again, I've known a lot of women who didn't need booze or drugs or a workout, while I've never known a man who didn't need one or the other, if not both. It would be interesting to meet one someday. So I flex into the spray, make the muscles feel closer to the hot water, but I've lost it: that feeling you get after a workout, that yesterday is gone and last night too, that today is right here in the shower, inside your body; there is nothing out there past the curtain that can bring you down, and you can take all the time you want to turn the water hotter and circle and flex and stretch under it, because the time is yours like the water is; when you're pumped like that you can't even think about death, at least not your own; or about any of the other petty crap you have to deal with just to have a good day; you end up with two or three minutes of cold water, and by the time you're drying off, the pump is easing down into a relaxed state that almost feels like muscle fatigue but it isn't: it's what you lifted all that iron for, and it'll take you like a stream does a trout, cool and easy the rest of the day.

I've lost that now: in the shower I see Polly walking around town smiling at people, talking to them on this warm dry August day. I don't let myself think anymore about her under or on top of or whatever and however with Vinnie DeLuca. I went through that place already, and I'm not going back there again. I can forget the past. Mom still grieves for Kingsley, but I don't. Instead of remembering him the way he was all those years, I think of him now, like he's forever twenty years old out there in the pines around the lake, out there on the water, and in it; Alex and I took all his stuff out of here and gave it to his wife and Mom. What I can't forget is right now. I can't forget that Polly's walking around happy, breathing today in her body. And not thinking about me. Of, if she does, she's still happy, she's still got her day, and she's draining mine like the water running out of the tub. So lately after my workout I stand in the shower and change the pictures; then I take a sandwich and the beer cooler out to the wharf and look at the pictures some more; I do this into the night, and I've stopped fishing or whatever I was doing in the boat. Instead of looking at pictures of Polly happy, I've been looking at Polly scared shitless, Polly fucked up, Polly paying. It's time to do some more terrorizing.

So today when the sun is going down I phone Alex. The lake is in a good-sized woods, and the trees are old and tall; the sun is behind them long before the sky loses its light and color, and turns the lake black. The house faces west and, from that shore, shadows are coming out onto the water. But the rest of it is blue, and so is the sky above the trees. I drink a beer at the phone and look out the screen window at the lake.

"Is she still living with Steve?" I say to Alex. A month ago he came out here for a few beers and told me he heard she'd moved out of her folks' house, into Steve Buckland's place.

"Far as I know," Alex says.

"So when's he heading north?"

Steve is the biggest man I know, and he has never worked out; he's also the strongest man I know, and it's lucky for a lot of people he is also the most laid back and cheerful man I know, even when he's managed to put away enough booze to get drunk, which is a lot for a man his size. I've never seen him fight, and if he ever was in one, I know I would've heard about it, because guys would talk about that for a long time; but I've seen him break up a few when he's tending bar down to Timmy's, and I've seen him come out from the bar at closing time when a lot of the guys are cocked and don't want to leave, and he herds them right out the door like sheep. He has a huge belly that doesn't fool anybody into throwing a punch at him, and he moves fast. Also, we're not good friends, I only know him from the bar, but I like him, he's a good man, and I do not want to fuck over his life with my problem; besides, the word is that Polly is just staying with him till he goes north, but they're not fucking, then she'll sublet his place (he lives on a lake too; Alex is right about New England) while he stays in a cabin he and some guys have in New Hampshire, and after hunting season he'll ski, and he won't come back till late spring. Alex says he's leaving after Labor Day weekend. I have nothing against Steve, but Vinnie DeLuca is another matter. So I ask Alex about that gentleman's schedule.

"He's a bouncer at Old Colony. I think they call him a door-man."

"I'll bounce his ass."

"He might be carrying something, you know. With that job."

"Shit. You think anybody'd let that asshole carry a gun?"

"Sure they would, but I was thinking blackjack. Want me to come along?"

"No, I'm all set."

"If you change your mind, I'll be here."

I know he will. He always has been, and I'm lucky to have a brother who's a friend too; I'm so lucky, I even had two of them; or unlucky because now I only have the one, depending on how I feel about things at the time I'm thinking of my brothers. I bring a beer out and sit on the wharf and watch the trees on the east side of the lake go from green to black as the sun sets beyond the tall woods. Then the sky is dark and I get another beer and listen to the lake sloshing against the bank, like someone is walking on it out there in the middle, his steps pushing the water around, and I think about Kingsley in the war. At first I don't want to, then I give in to it, and I picture him crawling in the jungle. He bought it from a mine; they didn't tell us if he was in a rice paddy or open field or jungle, but I always think of him in jungle because he loved to hunt in the woods and was so quiet in there. After a while I swallow and tighten my chest and let out some air. Polly said I was afraid to cry because it wasn't macho. That's not true. I sure the fuck cried when Mom and the old man told me and Alex about Kingsley, there in the kitchen, and I would've cried no matter who was there to watch. I fight crying because it empties you so you can't do anything about what's making you cry. So I stop thinking about Kingsley, that big good-looking wonderful son of a bitch with that look he had on his face when he was hunting, like he could see through the trees, as he stepped on a mine or tripped a wire. By the time I stop thinking about him, I know what else I'll do tonight, after I deal with Mr. De-Luca a.k.a. the doorman of Old Colony.

It is a rowdy bar at the north end of town, with a band and a lot of girls, and it draws people from out of town instead of just regulars, so it gets rough in there. I sit in my jeep in the parking lot fifteen minutes before closing. The band is gone, but the parking lot is still full. At one o'clock they start coming out, loud in bunches and couples. Some leave right away, but a lot of them stand around, some drinking what they sneaked out of the bar. The place takes about twenty minutes to empty; I know that's done when I see Vinnie come into the doorway, following the last people to leave. He stands there smoking a cigarette. He's short and wide like I am, and he is wearing a leisure suit with his shirt collar out over the lapels. He's got a chain around his neck. The cruiser turns into the parking lot, as I figured it would; the cops drive very slowly through the crowd, stopping here and there for a word; they pass in front of me and go to the end of the lot and hang a slow U and come back; people are in their cars now and driving off. I feel like slouching down but will not do this for a cop, even to get DeLuca. The truth is I'm probably the only one in the parking lot planning a felony. They pass me, looking at the cars leaving and the people still getting into cars, then they follow everybody out of the lot and up the road. Vinnie will either come right out or stay inside and drink while the waitresses and one bartender clean the place and the other bartender counts the money and puts it in the safe. It's amazing how many places there are to rob at night, when you think about it; if that's what you like. I hate a fucking thief. Polly used to shoplift in high school, and when she told me about it, years later, telling it like it was something cute she and her pals did, I didn't think it was funny, though I was supposed to. There are five cars spread around the lot. I don't know what he's driving, so I just sit watching the door, but he stays inside, the fucker getting his free drinks and sitting on a barstool watching the sweeping and table-wiping and the dirty ashtrays stacking up on the bar and the bartender washing them. Maybe he's making it with one of the waitresses, which I hope he isn't. I do not want to kick his ass with a woman there. If he comes out with a bartender or even both of them, it's a problem I can handle: either they'll jump me or try to get between us, or run for the phone; but I'll get him. With a woman, you never know. Some of them like to watch. But she might start screaming or crying or get a tire iron and knock the back of my head out my nose.

He comes out with three women. The women are smoking, so I figure they just finished their work and haven't been sitting around with a drink, they're tired and want to go home. A lot of people don't know what a long, hard job that is. I'm right: they all stand on the little porch, but he's not touching any of them, or even standing close; then they come down the steps and one woman heads for a car down on the left near the road, and the other two go to my right, toward the car at the high end of the lot, and he comes for the one straight ahead of him, off to my left maybe a couple of hundred feet. The TransAm: I should have known. I'm out the door and we're both walking at right angles to his car. He looks at me once, then looks straight ahead. Headlights are on his blue suit, and the two women drive down and pass behind him; the other one is just getting to her car, and she waves and they toot the horn, and turn onto the road. I get to the car first and plant myself in front of it and watch his chain. It's gold and something hangs from it, a disc of some kind.

"Ray," he says, and stops. "How's it going, Ray?" His voice is smooth and deep in his throat, but I can see his eyes now. They look sad, the way scared eyes do. His skin is dark and he is hairy and his shirt is unbuttoned enough to show this, and the swell of his pecs. I think of Alex, and look at Vinnie's hands down by his jacket pockets; I'm looking at his face too, and I keep seeing the gold chain, a short one around his neck so the disc shows high on his chest. My legs are shaky and cool and I need a deep breath, but I don't take it; I swing a left above the chain, see it hit his jaw, then my right is there in his face, and I'm in the eye of the storm, I don't hear us, I don't feel my fists hitting him, but I see them; when my head rocks he's hit me; I hit him fast and his face has a trapped look, then he's inside my arms, grabbing them, his head down, and I turn with him and push him onto the car, his back on the hood. There is a light on his face, and blood; I hold him down with my left hand on his throat and pound him with the right. There is a lot of blood on his mouth and nose and some on his forehead and under an eye. He is limp under my hand, and when I let him go he slides down the hood and his back swings forward like he's sitting up, and he drops between me and the grill. He lies on his side. My foot cocks to kick him but I stop it, looking at his face. The face is enough. The sky feels small, like I could breathe it all in. Then I look into the light. It's the headlights of the waitress's car, the one alone; it's stopped about twenty feet away with the engine running and the lights aimed at me. She's standing beside the car, yelling. I look around. Nobody else is in the lot; it feels small too. I look down at DeLuca, then at her. She's cursing me. I wave at her and walk to my jeep. She is calling me a motherfucking, cocksucking string of other things. I like this girl. With the lights off, I back the jeep up away from the club and make a wide half-circle around her to the road, so she can't read my plates. I pull out and turn on the lights.

I take a beer from the cooler on the floor and light a cigarette. My hands are shaky, but it's the good kind. Kingsley taught me about adrenaline, long before he used it over there, when I started first grade, which for boys means start learning to fight too. He said when you start to tremble, that's not fear, it just feels like it; it's to help you, so put it to use. That is why I didn't say to DeLuca the things I thought of saying. When I know I have to fight I never talk. Adrenaline makes guys start talking at each other, and you can use it up; I hold it in till I've got to either yell or have action.

The street is wide and quiet, most of the houses dark. I pass a cemetery and a school. I don't know why it is, but I know of four schools in this town either next to or across the street from a cemetery. I'm talking elementary schools too. Maybe it's an old custom, but it's weird looking at little girls and boys on a playground, and next door or across the street are all those tombstones over the dead. King is buried in one with trees and no school or anything else around but woods and the Merrimack River. The sky is lit up with stars and moon, the kind of night you could drive in with your lights off if you were the only one on the road, just follow the gray pavement and look at the dark trees and the sky and listen to the air rushing at the window. I turn on the radio and get onto 495 north. My knuckles are sore but the fingers work fine. I suck down the beer and get another from under the ice, and it feels good on my hand. I'm getting WOKQ from Dover, New Hampshire. Every redneck from southern Maine to Boston listens to that station. New Hampshire is also a redneck state, though the natives don't know it because they get snow every winter. When King was at Camp LeJeune he wrote to the family and said they could move New Hampshire down there and everybody would be happy except for the heat, which he wasn't happy with either. The heat got to him in Nam too; he wrote and said the insects and heat and being wet so much of the time were the worst part. I think about that a lot; was he just saying that so we wouldn't worry, or did he mean it? Most of the time I think he meant it, which taught me something I already knew but didn't always know that I knew: it gets down to what's happening to you right now, and if you're hot and wet and itching, that's what you deal with. You'll end up tripping a mine anyways, so you might as well fight the bugs and stay cool and dry till then.

Mostly there's woods on the sides of the highway. People are driving it fast tonight. I pull into the right lane, Crystal Gayle is singing sad, and take the exit. I hope Waylon comes on; I'm in a Waylon mood. I cross the highway on the overpass, cars going under me without a sound I can hear over Crystal, and go on a two-lane into the town square of Merrimac, where they leave off the *k*. I don't know why. The square has a rotary and some lights and is empty. I turn right onto 110, two-lane and hilly with curves, and I have to piss. It's not just beer, it's nerve-piss, and I shiver holding it in. Nobody's on the road, and when I turn left toward the lake I cut the lights and can see clearly: the road is narrow with trees on its sides, and up ahead where the road turns left, there are trees too, a thin line of them at the side of the lake. I shift down and turn and back up and turn, and park it facing 110. I take the gasoline can from behind my seat, then piss on the grass, looking up at the cars and smelling the pines among the trees. I carry the gasoline can in my left hand, the side away from the road, and walk on grass, close to the trees. I have on my newest jeans, the darkest I've got, and a dark blue shirt with long sleeves. My fingers try to stiffen, holding the can. That's from DeLuca, maybe the first one, that came up from behind my ass and got his jaw; he saw it but only in time to turn his face from it a little, so all he did was stretch his jaw out for me to hit. He should have dropped his chin, caught it on the head. I hear the lake, then see it through the trees. It's bigger than ours but there are more houses too, all around it, and in summer they're filled. We only have a few houses, on the east and north sides, because it's way out in the boondocks and the west and south sides belong to some nature outfit that a rich guy gave his land to, and all you can do there is hike and look at trees and birds. The road turns left, between the woods and the backs of houses, and I follow it near the trees. A dog barks and some others pick it up. But it's just the bitchy bark of pets, there's not a serious one there, and I keep walking, and nobody talks to the dogs or comes out for a look, and they stop.

All the houses are so close together I won't see Steve's until I'm at it. I know it's on this road and it's brown. King wrote to me and Alex once from there; he didn't want the folks to read it; he wrote about patrols and ambushes. He said *Don't get me wrong, I wish right now I was back there with you guys and a case of Bud in the cooler out on a boat pulling in mackerel. They must be in, about now. But I'll say this: I'll never feel the adrenaline like this again, not even with bluefish or deer or kicking ass. I understand now what makes bankers and such go skydiving on Saturdays.* Then I see Polly's red Subaru and Steve's van, and I freeze, then lower the can to the ground and kneel beside it. I wonder if this is close to what King felt. When I think of the arsenal Steve's got inside, I believe maybe it is. I kneel listening. There's a breeze and the water lapping in front of the house. I listen some more, then unscrew the cap and get up to a crouch and cross the road. I stand behind his van and look up and down the road and in the yards next door. Every yard is small, every house is small, no rich man's lake here, but people that work. Her car and the van are

side by side in a short dirt driveway; on the right, by the corner
of the house, there's a woodpile. I look at the dark windows, then
go for the wood. I'm right under a window, and all I can hear is
the breeze and the water. I move up the side of the house, under
windows, toward the lake. At the front yard I stop, breathing
through my mouth but slow and quiet as I can. There's a tree
that looks like an oak in the yard, then the wharf. He'd got a ce-
ment patio with some chairs and a hammock and a barbecue grill
and table with empty beer bottles on it. I run to the lake side of
the tree and press my back against it; he has a short wharf with
an outboard and a canoe. I look around the tree at the front of
the house. Then I step toward the lake, move out far enough so
I'm past the branches—it's an oak—and I start pouring: walking
backward parallel to the house that I'm watching all the time,
and when I clear it, I turn and back toward the road, watching
Steve's and the house on my left too. The gasoline is loud, back
and forth in the can, and pouring onto the grass.

I back up past their cars and my back is stiff, I'm breathing
short and quiet and need more of it but won't; I make a wide circle around their cars, and take the can cap from my pocket and
drop it there, and go around the house again, the corner with the
woodpile, and I back toward the lake, checking the other house
on my left now, my head going back and forth but mostly forth,
waiting for Steve to stick a Goddamn .30-06 or 12-gauge out one
of the windows, then I'm past the house and feeling the lake behind me and I keep going to the tree and around it, and all I can
smell is gasoline. I empty the can near where I started so the
lines will meet. Then I straighten up and step down off a low
concrete wall to the beach. I go up the beach past three houses,
then out between them to the road, and I cross it and lay the can
in the woods. Then I cross again and stand at the road with her
car and his van between me and the house. I look down till I see
the gas cap. Then I take one match from a book and strike it and
hold it to the others; they catch with a hiss, and I toss them at the
cap: the gasoline flares with a whoosh and runs left and right and
dances around the corners into the breeze, curving every which

way, and I run back into the road where I can look past the house in time to see the flames coming at each other around the house, doing some front-yard patterns like ice skaters where I emptied the can. Then they meet and I am running on the grass beside the road, down the road and around the corner, on the grass in the dark by the woods, to my jeep up there. The key is in my hand.

In the upstairs bedroom she wakes to firelight and flickering shadows on the walls that do not yet feel like her own, and she is so startled out of sleep that she is for a moment displaced, long enough for this summer's fear—that no walls and roof will ever feel like her own—to rise in her heart before it is dissipated by this new fear she has waked to; then she is throwing back the sheet and crossing the floor. Out the front window she looks at sinuous flames surrounding the yard between her and the lake; calling Steve, she goes to the side window and looks down at fire, then into the back room where Steve's mattress on the floor is empty, still made since morning. She steps on and over it, to the rear window overlooking the yard and car and van and the ring of fire. She switches on the stair light and descends, calling; by the bottom step she knows she is not trapped and her voice softens, becomes quizzical. Downstairs is a kitchen, darkened save for the wavering light on the walls, and a living room where he sleeps sitting on the couch, his feet on the coffee table, the room smelling of beer and cigarette smoke.

"Steve?" He stirs, shakes his head, drops his feet to the floor. She points out the wide front window. "Look."

He is up, out the front door, turning on the faucet and pulling the coiled hose across the patio. In places the fire has spread toward the house, but it is waning and burns close to the ground.

"It's all around," she says, as, facing the lake, he moves the hose in an arc; neighbor men shout and she trots to either side of the house and sees them: the men next door with their hoses and wives and children. Steve belches loudly; she turns and sees him pissing on the fire, using his left hand, while his right moves the hose. He yells thanks over each shoulder; the men call back. The fire is out, and Steve soaks the front lawn, then both sides, joining his stream with the others. He asks her to turn it off, and he coils the hose and she follows him to the backyard. The two men come, and their wives take the children inside.

"Jeesum Crow," one says. "What do you figure that was about?"

"Tooth fairy," Steve says, and offers them a beer. They accept, their voices mischievous as they excuse themselves for drinking at this hour after being wakened. They blame the fire. Polly has come to understand this about men: they need mischief and will even pretend a twelve-ounce can of beer is wicked if that will make them feel collusive while drinking it. Steve brings out four bottles, surprises her by handing her one he had not offered; she is pleased and touches his hand and thanks him as she takes it. She sits on the back stoop and watches the men standing, listens to their strange talk: about who would want to do such a thing, and what did a guy want to get out of doing it, and if they could figure out what he was trying to get done, then maybe they could get an idea of who it might be. But their tone will not stay serious, moves from inquisitive to jestful, without pattern or even harmony: while one supposes aloud that teenaged vandals chose the house at random and another agrees and says it's time for the selectmen to talk strict curfew and for the Goddamn cops to do some enforcing, the first one cackles and wheezes about a teenaged girl he watched water skiing this afternoon, how she could come to his house any night and light some fire. They clap hands on shoulders, grab an arm and pull and push. Steve takes in the empties and brings out four more.

Polly goes upstairs for cigarettes and stands at the back window, looking down at them. Steve has slept in here since she moved in; some nights, some days, one of them has stood in the short hall between their rooms and tapped on the door, with a frequency and need like that of a couple who have lived long together: not often, and not from passion, but often enough for release from carnal solitude. She does not want him to join the men in the yard and does not want to be alone in the house; she goes downstairs and sits on the stoop, smoking, and staring at the woods beyond them. She imagines Ray lying under the trees, watching, his knife in his hand. One of the men stoops and rises with something he shows the others. A cap from a gasoline can, they say. Sitting between the house and the men, she still feels exposed, has the urge to look behind her, and she smokes deeply and presses her fingers against her temples, rubs her eyes to push away her images of him softly paddling a canoe on the lake, standing on the front lawn, creeping into hiding in the living room, up the stairs to her bedroom; in the closet there. The men are leaving. They tell her good night, and she stands and thanks them. Steve comes to her, three bottles in his large hand. He places the other on her shoulder.

"Looks like your ex is back," he says.

"Yes."

"Dumb asshole."

"Yes."

Vinnie is a bruise on the pillow, and from a suspended bottle of something clear, a tube goes to his left arm and ends under tape. He is asleep. She stands in the doorway, wanting to leave; then quietly she goes in, to the right side of the bed. His flesh is black and purple under both eyes, on the bridge of his nose, and his right jaw; cotton is stuffed in his nostrils; his breath hisses between swollen lips, the upper one stitched. Polly has not written a card for the zinnias she cut from her mother's garden but, even so, she can let him wake to them and phone later, come back later, do whatever later. When she puts them on the bedside table, his eyes open.

"I brought you some flowers," she says. She looks over her shoulder at the door, then takes from her purse a brown-bagged pint of vodka. Smiling, she pulls out the bottle so he can see the label, then drops it into the bag. He only watches her. She cannot tell whether his eyes show more than pain. She pushes the vodka under his pillows.

"Do you hurt?"

"Drugs," he says, through his teeth, only his lips moving, spreading in a grimace.

"Oh, Jesus. Your jaw's broken?"

He nods.

"Will you hurt if I sit here?"

"No."

She sits on the side of the bed and takes his right hand lying on the sheet, softly rubs his bare forearm, watching the rise and fall of his dark hair, its ends sun-bleached gold. His arm is wide and hard with muscle, her own looks delicate, and as she imagines Ray's chest and neck swelling with rage, a cool shiver rises from her legs to her chest. She reaches for her purse on the bedside table.

"Can I smoke in here?"

"I guess."

He sounds angry; she knows it is because his jaw is wired, but still she feels he is angry at her and ought to be. She finds an ashtray in the drawer of the bedside table, cocks her head at the hanging bottle of fluid, and says: "Is that your food?"

"Saline. Eat with a straw."

"Can you smoke?"

"Don't know."

She holds her cigarette between his lips, on the right side, away from the stitches. She cannot feel him drawing on it; he nods, she removes it, and he exhales a thin stream.

"Are you hurt anywhere else? Your body?"

"No. How did you know?"

"My father called me." She offers the cigarette, he nods, and as he draws on it, she says: "He said you're not pressing charges."

His face rolls away from the cigarette, he blows smoke toward the tube rising from his arm, then looks at her, and she knows what she first saw in his eyes and mistook for pain.

"I don't blame you," she says. "I wouldn't either. In June he came into my apartment with a fucking knife and raped me. I was afraid to do anything, and I kept thinking he was gone.

Really gone, like California or someplace. Because Dad checked at where he worked and his apartment, and he never went back after that night. Even if I knew he hadn't gone, I wouldn't have. Because he's fucking *crazy*."

She stands and takes her cigarettes and disposable lighter from her purse and puts them on the table.

"I'll leave you these. I have to go. I'll be back."

Her eyes are filling. Besides Steve, Vinnie is the only person outside her family she has told about the rape, but his eyes did not change when she said it; could not change, she knows, for the sorrow in them is so deep. She has known him in passion and mirth, and kissing his forehead, his unbruised left cheek, his chin, she feels as dangerous as Ray, more dangerous with her slender body and pretty face.

"I guess it wasn't worth it," she says.

"Nothing is. I'm all broken."

Sometimes, on her days off that summer, she put on a dress and went to Timmy's in early afternoon to drink. It was never crowded then, and always the table by the window was empty, and she sat there and watched the Main Street traffic and the people walking outside in the heat; or, in the rain, cars with lights and windshield wipers on, the faces of drivers and passengers blurred by rain and dripping windows.

She slept late. She was twenty-six and, for as long as she could remember, she had hated waking early; now that she worked at night, she not only was able to sleep late, but had to; she lived at home and no longer felt, as she had when she was younger and woke to the family voices, that she had wasted daylight sleeping while everyone else had lived half a day. There had been many voices then, but now two brothers and a sister had grown and moved away, and only Margaret was at home. She was seventeen and drank a glass of wine at some family dinners, had never, she said, had a cigarette in her mouth, had not said but was certainly a virgin, and early in the morning jogged for miles on the country roads near their home; during blizzards, hard rain, and days when ice on the roads slowed her pace, she ran around the indoor basketball court at the YMCA. She received Communion every Sunday and, in the Lenten season, every day. She was dark and pretty, but Polly thought all that virtue had left its mark on her face, and it would never be the sort that makes men change their lives.

Polly liked her sister, and was more amused than annoyed by the way she lived. She could not understand what pleasures Margaret drew from running and not drinking or smoking dope or even cigarettes, and from virginity. She did understand Margaret's religion, and sometimes she wished being a Catholic were as easy for her as it was for Margaret. Then she envied Margaret, but when envy became scorn she fought it by imagining Margaret on a date; certainly she felt passion, so maybe her sacramental life was not at all easy. Maybe waking up and jogging weren't either; and she would remember her own high school years when, if you wanted friends and did not want to do what the friends did, you had to be very strong. So those times when she envied, then scorned Margaret ended with her wondering if perhaps all of Margaret's life was good because she willed it.

Polly went to Mass every Sunday, but did not receive communion because she had not been in the state of grace for a long time, and she did not confess because she knew that she could not be absolved of fornication and adultery while wearing an intrauterine device whose presence belied her firm intention of not sinning again. She was not certain that her lovemaking since the end of her marriage was a sin, or one serious enough to forbid her receiving, for she did not feel bad about it, except when she wished during and afterward that she had not gone to bed with someone, and that had to do with making a bad choice. She had never confessed her adultery while she was married to Raymond Yarborough, though she knew she had been wrong, had felt wicked as well as frightened; but, remembering now (she had filed for divorce and changed her name back to Comeau), her short affair with Vinnie when the marriage was in its final months was diminished by her sharper memory of Raymond yelling at her that she was a spoiled, fucked-up cunt not worth a shit to anybody, Raymond slapping her, and, on the last night, hitting her with his fist and leaving her unconscious on the bedroom floor, where she woke hearing Jerry Jeff Walker on the record player in the living room and a beer bottle landing on others in the wastebasket. Her car key was in there with him, so she climbed out the window and ran until she was nauseated and her legs were weak and trembling; then she walked, and in two hours she was home. She had to wake them to get in, and her mother put ice on her jaw, Margaret held her hand and stroked her hair, and her father took his gun and nightstick and drove to the apartment, but Raymond was gone in his jeep, taking with him his weights and bench and power stands, fishing rods and tackle box, two shotguns and a .22 rifle, the hunting knife he bought in memory of his brother, his knapsack and toilet articles and some clothes. When she moved from that apartment two weeks later, she filled a garbage bag with his clothes and Vietnam books, most of them hardcover, and left it on the curb; as she drove away, she looked in the rear view mirror at the green bulk and said aloud: "Adiós, motherfucker."

She also did not go to confession because, as well as not feeling bad about her sexual adventures, and knowing that she would not give them up anyway, she did believe that in some way her life was not a good one, but in a way the Church had not defined. Neither could she: even on those rare and mysterious nights when drinking saddened her and she went to bed drunk and disliking herself and woke hung over and regretful, she did not and could not know what about herself she disliked and regretted. So she could not confess, but she went to Mass with her family every Sunday and had gone when she lived alone, because it was one religious act she could perform, and she was afraid that neglecting it would finally lead her to a fearful loneliness she could not bear.

Dressing for Mass was different from dressing for any other place, and she liked having her morning coffee and cigarette while, without anticipating drinks or dinner or a man or work or anything at all, she put on makeup and a dress and heels; and she liked entering the church where the large doors closed behind her and she walked down the aisle under the high, curved white ceiling, and between stained-glass windows in the white walls whose lower halves were dark brown wood, as the altar was and the large cross with a bronze Christ hanging from the wall behind it. When she was with her family, her father chose a pew and stood at it while Margaret went in, then Polly, then her parents; alone, she looked for a pew near the middle with an aisle seat. She kneeled on the padded kneeler, her arms on the smooth old wood of the pew in front of her, and looked at the altar and crucifix and the stained-glass window behind them; then sat and looked at people sitting in front of her on both sides of the aisle. There was a scent of perfume and sometimes leather from purses and coats, tingeing that smell she only breathed here: a blending of cool, dry basement air with sunlight and melting candle wax. As the priest entered wearing green vestments, she rose and sang with the others, listened to her voice among theirs, read the Confiteor aloud with them, felt forgiven as she read *in what I have done and in what I have failed to do,* those simple and general words as precise as she could be about the life, a week older each Sunday, that followed her like a bridal train into church where, for forty minutes or so, her mind was suspended, much as it was when she lay near sleep at the beach. She did not pray with concentration, but she did not think either, and her mind wandered from the Mass to the faces of people around her. At the offertory she sang with them and, later, stood and read the Lord's Prayer aloud; then the priest said *Let us now offer each other a sign of peace* and, smiling, she shook the hands of people in front of her and behind her, saying *Peace be with you.*

She liked to watch them receive communion: children and teenagers and women and men going slowly in two lines up the center aisle and in single lines up both side aisles, to the four waiting priests. Coming back, they chewed or dissolved the host in their mouths. Sometimes a small boy looked about and smiled. But she only saw children when they crossed her vision; she watched the others: the old, whose faces had lost any sign of beauty or even pleasure, and were gentle now, peacefully dazed, with God on their tongues; the pretty and handsome young, and the young who were plain or homely; and, in their thirties and forties and fifties, women and men who had lost the singularity of youth, their bodies unattractive, most of them too heavy, and no face was pretty or plain, handsome or homely, and all of these returned to their pews with clasped hands and bowed heads, their faces both serious and calm. She tenderly watched them. Now that she was going to Mass with her family, she watched them too, the three dark faces with downcast eyes: slender Margaret with her finely concave cheeks, and no makeup, her lips and brow bearing no trace of the sullen prudery she sometimes turned on Polly, sometimes on everyone; her plump mother, the shortest in the family now, gray lacing her black hair, and her frownlike face one of weariness in repose, looking as it would later in the day when, reading the paper, she would fall asleep on the couch; her father, tall and broad, his shirt and coat tight across his chest, his hair thick and black, and on his face the look of peaceful concentration she saw when he was fishing; and she felt merciful toward them, and toward herself, not only for her guilt or shame because she could not receive (they did not speak to her about it, or about anything else she did, not even—except Margaret—with their eyes), but for her sense and, often at Mass, her conviction that she was a bad woman. She rose and sang as the priest and altar boys walked up the aisle and out the front of the church; then people filled the aisle and she moved with them into the day.

She had always liked boys and was very pretty, so she had never had a close girl friend. In high school she had the friends you need, to keep from being alone, and to go with to places where boys were. Those friendships felt deep because at their heart were shared guilt and the fond trust that comes from it. They existed in, and because of, those years of sexual abeyance when boys shunned their company and went together to playing fields and woods and lakes and the sea. The girls went to houses.

Waiting to be old enough to drive, waiting for those two or three years in their lives when a car's function would not be conveyance but privacy, they gathered at the homes of girls whose mothers had jobs. They sat on the bed and floor and smoked cigarettes.

Sometimes they smoked marijuana too, and at slumber parties, when the parents had gone to bed, they drank beer or wine bought for them by an older friend or brother or sister. But cigarettes were their first and favorite wickedness, and they delightfully entered their addiction, not because they wanted to draw tobacco smoke into their lungs, but because they wanted to be girls who smoked. Within two or three years, cigarette packs in their purses would be as ordinary as wallets and combs; but at fourteen and fifteen, simply looking at the alluring colored pack among their cosmetics excited them with the knowledge that a time of their lives had ended, and a new and promising time was coming. The smooth cellophane covering the pack, the cigarette between their fingers and lips, the taste and feel of smoke, and blowing it into the air, struck in them a sensual chord they had not known they had. They watched one another. They always did that: looked at breasts, knew who had gained or lost weight, had a pimple, had washed her hair or had it done in a beauty parlor, and, if shown the contents of a friend's closet, would know her name. They watched as a girl nodded toward a colored disposable lighter, smiled if smoke watered her eyes, watched the fingers holding the cigarette, the shape of her lips around the tip, the angle of her wrist.

So they were friends in that secret life they had to have; then they were older and in cars, and what they had been waiting for happened. They shared that too, and knew who was late, who was taking the pill, who was trusting luck. Their language was normally profane, but when talking about what they did with boys, they said *had sex, slept with, oral sex, penis.* Then they graduated and spread outward from the high school and the houses where they had gathered, to nearby colleges and jobs within the county. Only one, who married a soldier, moved out of state.

The others lived close enough to keep seeing each other, and in the first year out of high school some of them did; but they all had different lives, and loved men who did not know each other, and soon they only met by chance, and talked on sidewalks or at coffee counters.

Since then Polly had met women she liked, but she felt they did not like her. When she thought about them, she knew she could be wrong, could be feeling only her own discomfort. With her girlhood friends she had developed a style that pleased men. But talking with a woman was scrutiny, and always she was conscious of her makeup, her pretty face, her long black hair, and the way her hands moved with a cigarette, a glass, patting her hair in place at the brow, pushing it back from a cheek. She studied the other woman too, seeing her as a man would; comparing her, as a man would, with herself; and this mutual disassembly made them wary and finally mistrustful. At times Polly envied the friendships of men, who seemed to compete with each other in everything from wit to strength, but never in attractiveness or over women; or girls like Margaret, who did nothing at all with her beauty, so that, seeing her in a group of girls, you would have to look closely to know she was the prettiest. But she knew there was more, knew that when she was in love she did not have the energy and time to become a woman's friend, to go beyond the critical eye, the cautious heart. Even men she did not love, but liked and wanted, distracted her too much for that. She went to Timmy's alone.

But not lonely: she went on days when, waking late, and eating a sandwich or eggs alone in the kitchen, she waited, her mind like a blank movie screen, to know what she wanted to do with her day. She saw herself lying on a towel at the beach; shopping at the mall or in Boston; going to Steve's house to swim in the lake or, if he wanted to run the boat, water-ski; wearing one of her new dresses and drinking at Timmy's. That was it, on this hot day in July: she wanted to be the woman in a summer dress, sitting at the table by the window. She chose the salmon one with shoulder straps, cut to the top of her breasts and nearly to the small of her back. Then she took the pistol from the drawer of her bedside table and put it in her purse. By one o'clock she was at the table, sipping her first vodka and tonic, opening a pack of cigarettes, amused at herself as she tasted lime and smelled tobacco, because she still loved smoking and drinking as she had ten years ago when they were secret pleasures, still at times (and today was one) felt in the lifted glass and fondled pack a glimmer of promise from out there beyond the window and the town, as if the pack and glass were conduits between the mysterious sensuous rhythms of the world and her own.

She looked out the window at people in cars and walking in the hot sunlight. Al was the afternoon bartender, a man in his fifties, who let her sit quietly, only talking to her when she went to the bar for another drink. Men came in out of the heat, alone or in pairs, and drank a beer and left. She drank slowly, glanced at the men as they came and went, kept her back to the bar, listened to them talking with Al. For the first two hours, while she had three drinks, her mood was the one that had come to her at the kitchen table. Had someone approached and spoken, she would have blinked at the face while she waited for the person's name to emerge from wherever her mind had been. She sat peacefully looking out the window, and at times, when she realized that she was having precisely the afternoon she had wanted, and how rare it was now and had been for years to have the feeling you had wanted and planned for, her heart beat faster with a sense of freedom, of generosity; and in those moments she nearly bought the bar a round, but did not, knowing then someone would talk to her, and what she had now would be lost, dissipated into an afternoon of babble and laughter. But the fourth drink shifted something under her mood, as though it rested on a foundation that vodka had begun to dissolve.

Now when she noticed her purse beside her hand, she did not think of money but of the pistol. Looking out at people passing on foot or in cars, she no longer saw each of them as someone who loved and hoped under that brilliant, hot sky; they became parts again, as the cars did, and the Chevrolet building across the street where behind the glass front girls spoke into telephones and salesmen talked to couples, and as the sky itself did: parts of this town, the boundaries of her life.

She saw her life as, at best, a small circle: one year as a commuting student, driving her mother's car twenty minutes to Merrimack College, a Catholic school with secular faculty, leaving home in the morning and returning after classes as she had since kindergarten, discovering in that year—or forcing her parents to discover what she had known since ninth grade—that she was not a student, simply because she was not interested. She could learn anything they taught, and do the work, and get the grades, but in college she was free to do none of this, and she chose to do only enough to accumulate eight Cs and convince her parents that she was, not unlike themselves, a person whose strengths were not meant to be educated in schools.

She did not know why she was not interested. In June, when her first and last year of college was a month behind her, she remembered it with neither fondness nor regret, as she might have recalled movies she had seen with boys she did not love. She had written grammatical compositions she did not feel or believe, choosing topics that seemed both approachable and pleasing to the teacher. She discovered a pattern: all topics were approachable if she simply rendered them, with an opening statement, proper paragraphs, and a conclusion; and every topic was difficult if she began to immerse in it; but always she withdrew. In one course she saw herself: in sociology, with amusement, anger, resignation, and a suspended curiosity that lasted for weeks, she learned of the hunters, the gatherers, the farmers, saw herself and her parents defined by survival; and industrialization bringing about the clock that, on her bedside table, she regarded as a thing which was not inanimate but a conscience run on electricity, and she was delighted, knowing that people had once lived in accord with the sun and weather, and that punctuality and times for work and food and not-work and sleep were later imposed upon them, as she felt now they were imposed upon her.

In her other classes she listened, often with excitement, to a million dead at Borodino, Bismarck's uniting Germany, Chamberlain at Munich, Hitler invading Russia on the twenty-second of June because Napoleon did, all of these people and their actions equally in her past, kaleidoscopic, having no causal sequence whose end was her own birth and first eighteen years. She could say "On honeydew he hath fed / And drunk the milk of paradise" and ". . . the women come and go / Talking of Michelangelo," but they, and Captain Vere hanging Billy Budd, and Huck choosing Nigger Jim and hell, joined Socrates and his hemlock and Bonhoeffer's making an evil act good by performing it for a friend, and conifers and deciduous trees, pistils and stamens, and the generals and presidents and emperors and kings, all like dust motes in the sunlight of that early summer, when she went to work so she could move to an apartment an hour's walk from the house she had lived in for nineteen years, and which she forced herself to call *my parents' house* instead of home until that became habitual.

She was a clerk in a department store in town. The store was old and had not changed its customs: it had no cash registers. She worked in the linen department, and placed bills and coins into a cylinder and put that in a tube which, by vacuum, took the money to a small room upstairs where women she never met sent change down. She worked six days a week and spent the money on rent and heat and a used Ford she bought for nine hundred and eighty-five dollars; she kept food for breakfasts and lunches in her refrigerator, and ate dinners with her parents or dates or bought pieces of fish, chicken, or meat on the way home from work. On Sundays she went to the beach.

A maternal uncle was a jeweler and owned a store, and in fall she went to work for him, learned enough about cameras and watches to help customers narrow their choices to two or three; then her uncle came from his desk, and compared watches or cameras with a fervor that made their purchase seem as fraught with possibilities of happiness and sorrow as choosing a lover. She liked the absolute cleanliness of the store, with its vacuumed carpets and polished glass, its lack of any distinctive odors, and liked to believe what she did smell was sparkle from the show-cases. Her gray-haired uncle always wore a white shirt and bow tie; he told her neckties got in the way of his work, the parts of watches he bent over with loupe and tweezers and screwdriver and hand remover. She said nothing about a tie clasp, but thought of them, even glanced at their shelf. She liked them, and all the other small things in their boxes on the shelves: cuff links and rings and pins and earrings. She liked touching them with customers.

She worked on Saturdays, but on Wednesday afternoons her uncle closed the store. It was an old custom in the town, and most doctors and lawyers and dentists and many owners of small stores kept it still. She had grown up with those Wednesday afternoons when she could not get money at the bank or see a doctor or buy a blouse, but now they were holidays for her. She had been in school so much of her life that she did not think of a year as January to January, but September to June and, outside of measured time, the respite of summer. Now her roads to and from work wound between trees that were orange and scarlet and yellow, then standing naked among pines whose branches a month later held snow, and for the first time in her memory autumn's colors did not mean a school desk and homework, and snow the beginning of the end of half a year and Christmas holidays. One evening in December, as she crossed her lawn, she stopped and looked down at the snow nearly as high as her boots; in one arm she cradled a bag of groceries; and looking at the snow, she knew, as if for the first time, though she had believed she had known and wanted it for years, that spring's trickle of this very snow would not mean now or ever again the beginning of the end of the final half-year, the harbinger of those three months when she lived the way they did before factory whistles and clocks.

The bag seemed heavier, and she shifted its weight and held it more tightly. Then she went inside and up two flights of stairs and into her apartment. She put the groceries on the kitchen table and sat looking from the bag to her wet boots with snow rimming the soles and melting on the instep. She took off her gloves and unbuttoned her coat and put her damp beret on the table. For a long time she had not been afraid of people or the chances of a day, for she believed she could bear the normal pain of being alive: her heart had been broken by girls and boys, and she had borne that, and she had broken hearts and borne that too, and embarrassment and shame and humiliation and failure, and she was not one of those who, once or more wounded, waited fearfully for the next mistake or cruelty or portion of bad luck. But she was afraid of what she was going through now: having more than one feeling at once, so that feeling proud and strong and despairing and resigned, she sat suspended in fear: *So this is the real world they always talked about.* She said it aloud: "the real world," testing its sound in the silence; for always, when they said it, their tone was one of warning, and worse, something not only bitter and defeated but vindictive as well, the same tone they had when they said *I told you so.* She groped into the bag, slowly tore open a beer carton as she looked at the kitchen walls and potted plants in the window, drew out a bottle, twisted off the cap, but did not drink. Her hand went into her purse, came out with cigarettes and lighter, placed them beside the beer. She hooked a toe under the other chair, pulled it closer, and rested both feet on it. *I don't believe it. And if you don't believe it, it's not true, except dying.*

What she did believe through that winter and spring was that she had entered the real world of her town, its time and work and leisure, and she looked back on her years of growing up as something that had happened to her outside of the life she now lived, as though childhood and her teens (she would soon be twenty) were, like those thirteen summers from kindergarten until the year of college, a time so free of what time meant to her now that it was not time but a sanctuary from it. Now, having had those years to become herself so she could enter the very heart of the town, the business street built along the Merrimack, where she joined the rhythmic exchange of things and energy and time for money, she knew she had to move through the town, and out of it. But, wanting that motion, she could not define it, for it had nothing to do with place or even people, but something within herself: a catapult, waiting for both release and direction, that would send her away from these old streets, some still of brick, and old brick leather factories, most of them closed but all of them so bleak, so dimly lit beyond their dirty windows that, driving or even walking past one, you could not tell whether anyone worked inside.

On a Wednesday afternoon in May, at a bar in Newburyport, where the Merrimack flowed through marshes to the sea, she sat alone on the second-floor sun deck, among couples in their twenties drinking at picnic tables. She sat on a bench along the railing, her back to the late-afternoon sun, and watched the drinkers, and anchored sailboats and fishing boats, and boats coming in. A small fishing boat followed by screaming gulls tied up at the wharf beside the bar, and she stood so she could look down at it. She had not fished with her father since she started working; she would call him tonight—no, she would finish this drink and go there for dinner and ask him if he'd like to go Sunday after Mass. Then Raymond Yarborough came around the cabin, at the bow, swinging a plastic bag of fish over his left shoulder. One of the men—there were six—gave him a beer. Her hand was up in a wave, her mouth open to call, but she stopped and watched. He had a beard now, brown and thick; he was shirtless and sunburned. She wore a white Mexican dress and knew how pretty she looked standing up there with the sun on her face and the sky behind her, and she waited. He lifted the bag of fish to the wharf and joined the others scrubbing the cleaning boards and deck. Then he went into the cabin and came out wearing a denim work shirt and looked up and laughed.

"Polly Comeau, what are you doing up there?"

She wondered about that, six years later, on the July afternoon at Timmy's; and wondered why, from that evening on, she not only believed her life had changed but knew that indeed it had (though she was never comfortable with, never sure of, the distinction between believing something about your life and that something also being true). But something did happen: when Ray became not the boy she had known in high school but her lover, then husband, she felt both released and received, no longer in the town, a piece of its streets and time, but of the town, having broken free of its gravity, so that standing behind the jewelry counter she did not feel rooted or even stationary; and driving to and from work, or pushing a cart between grocery shelves, were a new sort of motion whose end was not the jewelry store, the apartment, the supermarket cash register, but herself, the woman she saw in Raymond's face.

In her sleep she knew she was dreaming: she was waitressing at the Harbor Schooner, but inside it looked like the gymnasium in high school with tables for prom night, and the party of four she was serving changed to a crowd, some were familiar, and she strained to know them; then her father was frying squid in the kitchen and she was there with a tray, and he said *Give them all the squid they want;* then a hand was on her mouth and she woke with her right hand pushing his wrist and her left prying his fingers, and in that instant before opening her eyes, when her dream dissolved into darkness, she knew it was Ray. She was on her back and he was straddling her legs. She kneed him but he moved forward and she struck bone. He sat on her thighs and his right hand went to his back and she heard the snap, and the blade leaving its sheath; then he was holding it close to her face, his dark-bladed knife; in the moonlight she saw the silver line of its edge. Then its point touched her throat, and his hand left her mouth.

"Turn over," he said.

He rose to his knees, and she turned on her stomach, her back and throat waiting for the knife, but then his knees were between her legs, his hand under her stomach, lifting: she kneeled with her face in the pillow, heard his buckle and snap and zipper and pants slipping down his legs; he pushed her nightgown up her back, the knife's edge touched her stomach, and he was in, rocking her back and forth. She gripped the pillow and tensed her legs, trying to remain motionless, but his thrusts drove her forward, and her legs like springs forced her to recoil, so she was moving with him, and always on her tightened stomach the knife flickered, his breathing faster and louder then Ah Ah Ah, a tremor of his flesh against hers, the knife scraping toward her ribs and breasts, then gone, and he was too; above his breathing and her own she heard the ascent of pants, the zipper and snap and buckle, but no sheathing of the blade, so the knife itself had, in the air above her as she collapsed forward, its own sound of blood and night: but please God oh Jesus please not her gripping the pillow, her chin pressed down covering her throat, not her in the white Mexican dress with her new sunburn standing at the rail, seeing now Christ looking down through her on the sun deck that May afternoon to her crouched beneath the knife—

"Good, Polly. You got a little juiced after a while. Good."

His weight shifted, then he was on the floor. She heard him cut the telephone cord.

"See you later, Polly."

His steps on the floor were soft: he shut the door and in the corridor he was quiet as night. Her grip on the pillow loosened; her hands opened; still she waited. Then slowly and quietly she rolled over and got out of bed and tiptoed to the door and locked it again. She lit a cigarette, sat on the toilet in the dark, wiped and flushed and went to the window beside the bed, where she stood behind the open curtain and looked down at the empty street. She listened for his jeep starting, heard only slow and occasional cars moving blocks away, in town, and the distant voices and laughter of an outdoor party, and country music from a nearby window. She dressed and went down the hall and three flights of stairs and outside, pausing on the front steps to look at the street and parked cars and, on the apartment's lawn and lawns on both sides of it and across the street, the shadowed trunks of trees. She could not hear the sounds of the party or the music from the record player. Then he was dripping out of her and she went up the stairs and sat on the toilet while he pattered into the water, then scrubbed her hands, went out again, down the walk, and turned left, walking quickly in the middle of the sidewalk between tree trunks and parked cars, and looked at each of them and over her shoulders and between the cars for two and a half blocks to the closed drugstore, lighted in the rear where the counter was. In the phone booth she stood facing the street; the light came on when she closed the door, so she opened it and called her father.

She knew his steps in the hall and opened the door before he knocked. He was not in uniform, but he wore his cartridge belt and holstered .38. She hugged his deep, hard chest, and his arms were around her, one hand patting her back, and when he asked what Ray had done to her, she looked up at his wide sunburned face, his black hair and green eyes like her own, then rested her face on his chest and soft old chamois shirt, and said: "He had his knife. He touched me with it. My throat. My stomach. He cut the phone wire—" His patting hand stopped. "The door was locked and I was asleep, he doesn't even *have* a credit card, I don't know what he used, I woke up with his hand on my mouth then he had that big knife, that M*arine* knife."

His mouth touched her hair, her scalp, and he said: "He raped you?"

She nodded against his chest; he squeezed her, then his hands were holding her waist and he lifted her and his shoulders swung to the left and he put her down, as though moving her out of his path so he could walk to the bed, the wall, through it into the third-story night. But he did not move. He inhaled with a hiss and held it, then blew it out and did it again, and struck his left palm with his right fist, the open hand gripping the fist, and he stood breathing fast, the hand and fist pushing against each other. He was looking at the bed, and she wished she had made it.

"You better come home."

"I want to."

"Then I'm going to look for him."

"Yes."

"You have anything to drink?"

"Wine and beer."

When he turned the corner into the kitchen, she straightened the sheets; he came back while she was pulling the spread over the pillows.

"I'll call Mom," he said. He stood by the bed, his hands on the phone. "Then we'll go to the hospital."

"I'm all right."

He held the cord, looking at its severed end.

"They take care of you, in case you're pregnant."

"I'm all right."

He swallowed from the bottle, his eyes still on the cord. Then he looked at her.

"Just take something for tonight. We can come back tomorrow."

She packed an overnight bag and he took it from her; in the corridor he put his arm around her shoulders, held her going slowly down the stairs and outside to his pickup; with a hand on her elbow he helped her up to the seat. While he drove he opened a beer she had not seen him take from the apartment. She smoked and watched the town through the windshield and open window: Main Street descending past the city hall and courthouse, between the library and a park, to the river; she looked across the river at the street climbing again and, above the streetlights, trees and two church steeples. On the bridge she saw herself on her knees, her face on the pillow, Ray plunging, Ray lying naked and dead on her apartment floor, her father standing above him. She looked at the broad river, then they were off the bridge and climbing again, past Wendy's and McDonald's and Timmy's, all closed. She wanted to speak, or be able to; she wanted to turn and look at her father, but she had to be cleansed first, a shower, six showers, twelve; and time; but it was not only that.

It was her life itself; that was the sin she wanted hidden from her father and the houses and sleeping people they passed; and she wanted to forgive herself but could not because there was no single act or even pattern she could isolate and redeem. There was something about her heart, so that now glimpsing herself waiting on tables, sleeping, eating, walking in town on a spring afternoon, buying a summer blouse, she felt her every action and simplest moments were soiled by an evil she could not name.

Next day after lunch he brought her to a small studio; displayed behind its front window and on its walls were photographs, most in color, of families, brides and grooms, and what she assumed were pictures to commemorate graduation from high school: girls in dresses, boys in jackets and ties. The studio smelled of accumulated cigarette smoke and filled ashtrays, and the woman coughed while she seated Polly on a stool in the dim room at the rear. The woman seemed to be in her fifties; her skin had a yellow hue, and Polly did not want to touch anything, as if the walls and stool, like the handkerchief of a person with a cold, bore traces of the woman's tenuous mortality. She looked at the camera and prepared her face by thinking about its beauty until she felt it. They were Polaroid pictures; as she stood beside her father at the front desk, glancing at portraits to find someone she knew, so she could defy with knowledge what she defied now with instinct, could say to herself: *I know him, her, them; they're not like that at all; are fucked up too,* and, her breath recoiling from the odor of the woman's lungs that permeated the walls and pictures, she looked down at the desk, at her face as it had been only minutes ago in the back room. With scissors, the woman trimmed it. She watched the blade cutting through her breasts. The black-and-white face was not angry or hating or fearful or guilty; she did not know what it was but very serious and not pretty.

At City Hall they went to the detectives' office at the rear of the police station. Two detectives sat at desks, one writing, one drinking coffee. They greeted her father, and she stood in the doorway while he went to the desk of the coffee-drinker, a short man wearing a silver revolver behind his hip. Then her father leaned over him, hiding all but his hand on the coffee cup, and she watched her father's uniformed back, listened to his low voice without words. The other detective frowned as he wrote. Her father turned and beckoned: "Okay, Polly."

The detective rose to meet her, and she shook his hand and

did not hear his name. His voice was gentle, as if soothing her while dressing a wound; he led her across the room and explained what he was doing as he rolled her right forefinger on ink, then on the license. There was a sink and he told her to use the soap and water, the paper towels, then brought her to his desk where her father waited, and held a chair for her. It had a cushioned seat, but a straight wooden back and no arms, so she sat erect, feeling like a supplicant, as she checked answers on a form he gave her (she was not a convicted felon, a drunk, an addict) and answered questions he asked her as he typed on her license: *one twenty-six, black* (he looked at her eyes and said: "Pretty eyes, Polly"), *green.* He gave her the card and signed the front and looked at the back where he had typed *Dark* under Complexion, *Waitress* under Occupation, and, under Reason for Issuing License: *Protection.* He said the chief would sign the license, then it would go to Boston and return laminated in two weeks; he offered them coffee, they said no, and he walked them to the office door, his hand reaching up to rest on her father's shoulder. The other detective was still writing. In the truck, she said. "He was nice."

The gun, her father said, looked like a scaled-down Colt .45: a .380 automatic which they bought because it was used and cost a hundred and fifteen dollars (though he would have paid three hundred, in cash and gladly, for the .38 snubnose she looked at and held first; they were in the store within twenty hours of his bringing her home, then driving to Newburyport, to Ray's empty apartment, where he had kicked open the locked door and looked around enough to see in the floor dust the two bars of clean wood where the weight-lifting bench had been, and the clean circles of varying sizes left by the steel plates and power stands); and because of the way it felt in her hand, light enough so it seemed an extension of her wrist, a part of her palm, its steel and its wooden grips like her skinned bone, and heavy enough so she felt both safe and powerful, and the power seemed not the gun's but her own; and because of its size, which she measured as one and a half Marlboro boxes long, and its shape, flat, so she could carry it concealed in the front pocket of her jeans, when she left home without a purse.

They bought it in Kittery, Maine, less than an hour's drive up New Hampshire's short coast, at the Kittery Trading Post, where as a virgin, then not one but still young enough to keep that as secret as the cigarettes in her purse, she had gone with her father to buy surf rods and spinning rods, parkas, chamois and flannel shirts. It was also the store where Ray, while shopping for a pocketknife, had seen and bought (*I had to,* he told her) a replica of the World War II Marine knife, with the globe and anchor emblem on its sheath. It came in a box, on whose top was a reproduction of the knife's original blueprint from 1942. When he came home, he held the box toward her, said *Look what I found,* his voice alerting her; in his face she saw the same nuance of shy tenderness, so until she looked down at the box she believed he had brought her a gift. *I don't need it,* he said, as she drew it from the sheath, felt its edge, stroked its blood gutter. *But, see, we gave all his stuff away.* That was when she understood he had been talking about Kingsley, and she had again that experience peculiar to marriage, of entering a conversation that had been active for hours in her husband's mind. Now she brought her father to the showcase of knives and showed him, and he said: "Unless he's good with it at thirty feet, he might as well not have it at all. Not now, anyways."

Next day, in the sunlit evening of daylight savings time, at an old gravel pit grown with weeds and enclosed by woods on three sides, with a dirt road at one end and a bluff at the other, her father propped a silhouette of a man's torso and head against the bluff, walked twenty paces from it, and gave her the pistol. He had bought it in his name, because she was waiting for the license, and he could not receive the gun in Maine, so a clerk from the Trading Post, who lived in Massachusetts where he was also a gun dealer, brought it home to Amesbury, and her father got it during his lunch hour.

"It loads just like the .22," he said.

A squirrel chattered in the trees on the bluff. She pushed seven bullets into the magazine, slid it into the handle, and, pointing the gun at the bluff, pulled the slide to the rear and let it snap forward; the hammer was cocked, and she pushed up the safety. Then he told her to take out the magazine and eject the chambered shell: it flipped to the ground, and he wiped it on his pants and gave it to her and told her to load it again; he kept her loading and unloading for ten minutes or so, saying he was damned if he'd get her shot making a mistake with a gun that was supposed to protect her.

"Shoot it like you did the .22 and aim for his middle."

He had taught her to shoot his Colt .22, and she had shot with him on weekends in spring and summer and fall until her midteens, when her pleasures changed and she went with him just often enough to keep him from being hurt because she had outgrown shooting cans and being with him for two hours of a good afternoon; or often enough to keep her from believing he was hurt. She stood profiled to the target, aimed with one extended hand, thumbed the safety off, and, looking over the cocked hammer and barrel at the shape of a man, could not fire.

"The Miller can," she said, and, shifting her feet, aimed at the can at the base of the bluff, held her breath, and squeezed to an explosion that shocked her ears and pushed her arm up and back as dust flew a yard short of the can.

"Jesus *Christ.*"

"Reminds me of what I forgot," he said and, standing behind her, he pulled back her hair and gently pushed cotton into her ears. "Better go for the target. They didn't make that gun to hit something little."

"It's the head. If we could fold it back."

He patted her shoulder.

"Just aim for the middle, and shoot that piece of cardboard."

Cardboard, she told herself as she lined up the sights on the torso's black middle and fired six times, but *shoulder* she thought when she saw the first hole, *missed, stomach, chest, shoulder, stom-*

ach, and she felt clandestine and solemn, as though performing a strange ritual that would forever change her. She was suddenly tired. As she loaded the magazine, images of the past two nights and two days assaulted her, filled her memory so she could not recall doing anything during that time except kneeling between a knife and Ray's cock, riding in her father's truck—home, to the studio, to City Hall, to Kittery, home, to this woods—and being photographed and fingerprinted and questioned and pointing guns at the walls and ceiling of the store, and tomorrow night she had to wait tables, always wiping them, emptying ashtrays, bantering, smiling, soberly watching them get drunk, their voices louder than the jukebox playing music she would like in any other place. She fired, not trying to think *cardboard,* yielding to the target's shape and going further, seeing it not as any man but Ray, so that now as holes appeared and her arm recoiled from the shots muted by cotton and she breathed the smell of gunpowder, and reloaded and fired seven more times and seven more, she saw him attacking her and falling, attacking her and falling, and she faced the target and aimed with both hands at head and throat and chest, and once heard herself exhale: *"Yes."*

Two weeks later her father brought her license home, but he had told her not to wait for it, no judge would send her to jail, knowing she had applied, and knowing why. So from that afternoon's shooting on, she carried it everywhere: in her purse, jeans, shorts, beach bag, in her skirt pocket at work and on the car seat beside her as, at two in the morning, she drove home, where she put it in the drawer of her bedside table and left her windows open to the summer air. At Timmy's on that sunlit afternoon in July she rested her hand on it, rubbed its handle under the soft leather of her purse. She knew she was probably drunk by police or medical standards, but not by her own. Her skin seemed thickened, so she could feel more sharply the leather and the pistol handle beneath it than her fingers themselves when she rubbed them together. For a good while she had been unaware of having legs and feet; her cheeks and lips were numb; sometimes she felt an elbow on the table, or the base of her spine, or her thighs when they pressed on the chair's edge, then she shifted her weight. But she was not drunk because she knew she was: she knew her reflexes were too slow for driving, and she would have to concentrate to walk without weaving to the ladies' room. She also knew that the monologue coming to her was true; they always were. She listened to what her mind told her when it was free of the flesh: sometimes after making love, or waking in the morning, or lying on the beach for those minutes before the sun warmed her to sleep, or when she had drunk enough, either alone or with someone who would listen with her; but for a long time there had been no one like that.

Only three men were at the bar now. She brought her glass and ashtray to it, told Al to fill one and empty the other, and took two cocktail napkins. She paid and tipped, then sat at the table and wiped it dry with the napkins, and waited for Steve. At ten to five he came in, wearing a short-sleeved plaid shirt, his stomach not hanging but protruding over his jeans. Halfway to the bar he saw her watching him and smiled, his hand lifting. She waved him to her and looked at his narrow hips as he came.

"Steve? Can I talk to you for a minute?"

He glanced over her at the bar, said he was early, and sat. Even now in July, his arms and face looked newly sunburned, his hair and beard, which grew below his open collar, more golden.

"You're one of those guys who look good everywhere," she said. "Doing sports outside, drinking in a bar—you know what I mean? Like some guys look right for a bar, but you see them on a boat or something, and they look like somebody on vacation."

"Some girls too."

She focused on his lips and teeth.

"You're always smiling, Steve. Don't you ever get down? I've never seen you down."

"No time for it."

"No time for it. What did you do today, with all your time?"

"Went out for cod this morning—"

"Did you catch any?"

"Six. Came back to the lake, charcoaled a couple of fillets, and crapped out in the hammock. What's wrong—you down?"

"Me? No, I'm buzzed. But let me tell you: I've been thinking. I'm going to ask you a favor, and if its *any* kind of *hass*le, you say no, all right? But I think it might be good for both of us. Okay? But if it's not—"

"What is it?"

"No, but wait. I'm sitting here, right? and looking out the window and thinking, and I've got to leave home. See"—she leaned forward, placed her hands on his wrists, and lowered her voice—"I'm living with my folks because I had a nice apartment and I liked being there, but last month, last month Ray broke in one night while I was sleeping and he held a knife on me and raped me." She did not know what she had expected from his face, but it surprised her: he looked hurt and sad, and he nodded, then slowly shook his head. "So I moved in with my folks. I was scared. I mean, it's not as bad as some girls get it, from some stranger, like that poor fifteen-year-old last year hitchhiking and he had a knife and made her *blow* him; it was just Ray, you know, but still—I've got a gun too, a permit, the whole thing." He nodded. "It's right here, in my purse."

"That's the way it is now."

"What is?"

"Whatever. Women need things; you're built too small to be safe anymore."

"Steve, I got to move. But I'm still scared of having my own place. I was thinking, see, if I could move in with you, then I could do it gradually, you know? And when you leave in the fall I could sublet, I'd pay the whole rent for you till you get back, and by then—when do you come back?"

"Around April."

"I'd be ready. Maybe I'd move to Amesbury or Newbury-port. Maybe even Boston. I don't know why I said Boston. Isn't it funny it's right there and nobody ever goes to live there?"

"Not me. Spend your life walking on concrete? Sure: move in whenever you want."

"Really? I won't be a problem. I can cook too—"

"So can I. Here." He reached into his pocket, brought out a key ring and gave her a key. "Anytime. Call me before, and I'll help you move."

"No. No, I won't bring much: just, you know, clothes and cassette player and stuff. My folks won't like this."

"Why not?"

"They'll think we're shacking up."

"What are you, twenty-five?"

"Six."

"So?"

"I know. It'll be all right. It's just I keep giving them such a bad time."

"Hey: *you*'re the one having the bad time."

"Okay. Can I move in tonight? No, I'm too buzzed. Tomorrow?"

"Tonight, tomorrow. Better bring sheets and a pillow."

"I can't believe it." He looked at the bar, then smiled at her and stood. "All worked out, just like that. Jesus, you're saving my life, Steve. I'll start paying half the rent right away, and look: I'll stay out of the way, right? If you bring a girl home, I won't *be* there. I'll be shut up in my room, quiet as a mouse. I'll go to my folks' for the night, if you want."

"No problem. Don't you even want to know how much the rent is?"

"I don't even *care*," and she stood and put her arm around his back, her fingers just reaching his other side, and walked with him to the bar.

Polly's father comes down the slope of the lawn toward the wharf and I'm scared even while I look past him at the pickup I heard on the road, then down the driveway, and I look at his jeans and shirt; then I'm not scared anymore. For a second there, I thought Polly or maybe Vinnie had pressed some charges, but it all comes together at once: he's not in a cruiser and he's got no New Hampshire cops with him and he's wearing civvies, if you can call it that when he's wearing his gun and his nightstick too. I

decide to stay in the deck chair. He steps onto the wharf and
keeps coming and I decide to take a swallow of beer too. The
can's almost empty and I tilt my head back; the sun is behind me,
getting near the treetops across the lake. I'm wearing gym shorts
and nothing else. I open the cooler and drop in the empty and
take another; I know what my body looks like, with a sweat glis-
ten and muscles moving while I shift in the chair to pull a beer
out of the ice, while I open it, while I hold it up to him as he stops
spread-legged in front of me.

"Want a beer, John?"

I don't know what pisses him off most, the beer or *John;* his
chest starts working with his breath, then he slaps the can and it
rolls foaming on the wharf, stops at the space between two
boards.

"You don't like Miller," I say. "I think I got a Bud in there."

He unsnaps his nightstick, moves it from his left hand to his
right, then lowers it, holding it down at arm's length, gripping it
hard and resting its end in his left hand. This time I don't shift: I
watch his eyes and pull the cooler to me and reach down through
the ice and water. I open the beer and take a long swallow.

"*As*shole," he says. "You want to *rape* somebody, *as*shole? You
want to set fucking *fires?*"

I watch his eyes. At the bottom of my vision I see the stick
moving up and down, tapping his left hand. I lower the beer to
the wharf and his eyes go with it, just a glance, his head twitching
left and down; I grab the stick with my left hand and let the beer
drop and get my right on it too. He holds on and I pull myself
out of the chair, looking up at his eyes and pushing the stick
down. My chest is close to his; we stand there holding the stick.

"What's the gun for, John?" I've got an overhand grip; I
work my wrists up and down, turning the stick, and his face gets
red as he holds on. I don't stop. "You want to waste me, John?
Huh? Go for it."

I'm pumping: I can raise and lower the stick and his arms and
shoulders till the sun goes down, and now he knows it and he
knows I know it; he is sweating and his teeth are clenched and his

face is very red with the sun on it. All at once I know I will not hurt him; this comes as fast as laughing, is like laughing.

"Go for the gun, John. And they'll cut it out of your ass." I walk him backward a few steps, just to watch him keep his balance. "They can take Polly's nose out too."

"Fucker," he says through his teeth.

"Yes I did, John. Lots of times. On the first date too. Did she tell you that?" He tries to shove me back and lift the stick; all he does is strain. "It wasn't a date, even. I came in from fishing, and there she was, drinking at Michael's. We went to her place and fucked, and know what she said? After? She said, Once you get the clothes off, the rest is easy. Now what the fuck does *that* mean, John? What does that *mean?*"

I'm ahead of him again. Before he gets to the gun my left hand is on it; I swing the stick up above my head, his left hand still on it; I unsnap the holster and start lifting the gun up against his hand pressing down; it comes slowly but it never stops, and his elbow bends as his hand goes up his ribs. When the gun clears the holster he shifts his grip, grabs it at the cylinder, but his fingers slip off and claw air as I throw it backward over my shoulder and grab his wrist before the gun splashes. I lift the stick as high as I can. He still has some reach, so I jerk it down and free, and throw it with a backhand sidearm into the lake. He is panting. I am too, but I shut my mouth on it.

"Go home, John."

"You leave her alone."

He is breathing so hard and is so red that I get a picture of him on his back on the wharf and I'm breathing into his mouth.

"Go get some dinner, John."

"You—" Then he has to cough; it nearly doubles him over, and he turns to the railing and holds it, leans over it, and hacks up a lunger. I turn away and pick up the beer I dropped. There's still some in it; I drink that and take one from the ice, then look at him again. He's standing straight, away from the rail.

"You leave her alone," he says. "Fire last night. What are you, crazy? DeLuca."

"DeLuca who?"

He lifts a hand, waves it from side to side, shakes his head.

"I don't care shit about DeLuca," he says. "Let it go, Ray. You do anything to her, I'll bring help."

"Good. Bring your buddies. What are friends for, that's what I say."

"I mean it."

"I know you do. Now go on home before that club floats in and we have to start all over."

He looks at me. That's all he does for a while, then he turns and goes up the wharf, wiping his face on his bare arm. He walks like he's limping, but he's not. I get another beer and follow him up the lawn to his pickup. By the time he climbs in and starts it, I'm at his window. I toss the beer past him, onto the seat. He doesn't look at me. He backs and turns and I wait for gravel to fly, but he goes slowly up the driveway like the truck is tired too. At the road he stops and looks both ways. Then the beer comes out the window onto the lawn, and he's out on the blacktop, turning right, then he's gone beyond a corner of woods.

Last night waiting tables she was tired, and the muscles in her back and legs hurt. She blamed that afternoon's water skiing, and worked the dining room until the kitchen closed, then went upstairs to the bar and worked there, watching the clock, wiping her brow, sometimes shuddering as a chill spread up her back. She took orders at tables, repeated them to the bartender, garnished the drinks, subtracted in her mind, made change, and thanked for tips, but all that was ever in her mind was the bed at Steve's and herself in it. At one o'clock the Harbor Schooner closed, and when the last drinkers had gone down the stairs, the bartender said: "What'll it be tonight?" and she went to the bar with the other two waitresses, scanned the bottles, shaking her head, wanting to want a drink because always she had one after work, but the bottles, even vodka, even tequila, could have been cruets of vinegar. She lit a cigarette and asked for a Coke.

"You feeling all right?" he said.

"I think I'm sick," and she left the cigarette and carried the Coke, finishing it with long swallows and getting another, as she helped clean the tables, empty the ashtrays, and stack them on the bar.

She wakes at two o'clock in the heat of Labor Day weekend's Sunday afternoon, remembers waking several times, once or more when the room was not so brightly lit, so hot; and remembers she could not keep her eyes open long enough to escape the depth of her sleep. Her eyes close and she drifts downward again, beneath her pain, into darkness; then she opens her eyes, the lids seeming to snap upward against pressing weight. She grasps the edge of the mattress and pulls while she sits and swings her legs off the bed, and a chill grips her body and shakes it. Her teeth chatter as she walks with hunched shoulders to the bathroom; the toilet seat is cold, her skin is alive, crawling away from its touch, crawling up her back and down her arms, and she lowers her head and mutters: "Oh Jesus."

She does not brush her teeth or hair, or look in the mirror. She goes downstairs. There are no railings, and she slides a palm down the wall. She drinks a glass of orange juice, finds a tin with three aspirins behind the rice in the cupboard, swallows them with juice, and phones the Harbor Schooner. Sarah the head waitress answers.

"Is Charlie there?"

"No."

"Who's tending bar?"

"Sonny."

"Let me talk to him."

She ought to tell Sarah, but she does not like to call in sick to women; they always sound like they don't believe her.

"I'm sick," she says to Sonny. "I think the flu."

He tells her to go to bed and take care of herself, and asks if she needs anything.

"No. Maybe I'll come in tomorrow."

"Get well first."

"I'll call."

She takes the glass and pitcher upstairs, breathing quickly as she climbs. The sun angles through her bedroom windows, onto the lower half of the bed. There are shades, but she does not want to darken the room. She puts the pitcher and glass on the bedside table, lies on the damp sheet, pulls up the top sheet and cotton spread, and curls, shivering, on her side. Her two front windows face the lake; she hears voices from there, and motors, and remembers that she has been hearing them since she woke, and before that too, from the sleep she cannot fight. It is taking her now; she wants juice, but every move chills her and she will not reach for it. She stares at the empty glass and wonders why she did not fill it again, drinking would be so much easier, so wonderfully better, if she did not have to sit up and lift the pitcher and pour, so next time she drinks she will refill the glass because then it won't be so hard next time, and if she had a hospital straw, one of bent glass. Vinnie was last week with the tube in his arm and the bandages, but in memory he is farther away than a week, a summer; last night is a week away, going from table to table to table to bar to table to table and driving home, hours of tables and driving. Her memory of making love with Vinnie is clear but her body's aching lethargy rejects it, denies ever making love with anyone, ever wanting to, so that Vinnie last spring, early when the rivers began to swell with melting snow, is in focus as he should be: not loving him then she made love because, it seems to her now, he was something to do, one of a small assortment of choices for a week night; and she remembers him now without tenderness or recalled passion.

When she wakes again she is on her left side, facing the front windows, and the room's light has faded. The chills are gone, and she is hungry. There is ham downstairs, and eggs and cheese and bread, and leftover spaghetti, but her stomach refuses them all. She imagines soup, and wants that. But it is down the stairs and she would have to stand as she opened and heated it, then poured it into a cup so she could climb again and drink it here; she turns onto her right side and waits, braced against chills, but they don't come. Evening sunlight beams through the side window, opposite the foot of her bed, which is now in the dark spreading across the floor and dimming the blue walls. As though she can hear it, she senses the darkness in all the downstairs rooms, and more of it flowing in from the woods and lake. There are no motors on the water. Voices rise and waft from lawns touching the beach. She switches on the bedside lamp, pushes herself back and up till she sits against the pillows, and pours a glass of orange juice. She drinks it in three swallows, refills the glass, then lies on her back, closes her hot eyes, thinks of Ray, of danger she cannot feel, and lets the lamp burn so she will not wake in the dark.

For a while she sleeps, but she is aware that she must not, there is something she must do, and finally she wakes, her head tossing on the pillow, legs and arms tense. She reaches for the drawer beside her, takes the gun, holds it above her with both hands; she pulls the slide to the rear and eases it forward, watching the bullet enter the chamber. She lowers the hammer to half-cock and pushes up the safety. She turns on her side, slips the gun under the pillow, and goes to sleep holding the checkered wood of its handle.

She wakes from a dream that is lost when she opens her eyes to light, though she knows it was pleasant and she was not in it, but watched it. The three windows are black. Steve is looking down at her, his smell of beer and cigarettes, his red face and arms making her feel that health, the life even, are chance gifts to the lucky, kept by the strong, and she was not to have them again.

"Sorry," he says. "You want to go back to sleep?"

"No." Her throat is dry, and she hears a plea in her voice. "I'm sick."

"I figured that. Can I do anything?"

"I think I want to smoke."

He takes cigarette papers from his shirt pocket, a cellophane pouch from his jeans.

"No, a cigarette. In my purse."

He lights it and hands it to her.

"Could I have some soup?"

"Anything else?"

"Toast?"

"Coming up."

He goes downstairs, and she smokes, looking at the windows; she cannot see beyond the screens. Neither can her mind: her life is this room, where her body's heat and pain have released her from everyone but Steve, who brings her a bowl of soup on a plate with two pieces of toast. He pushes up the pillows behind her, then pulls a chair near the bed.

"I'm leaving in the morning."

"What time is it?"

"Almost one."

She shakes her head.

"That way I beat the traffic."

"Good idea."

"I can leave Tuesday, though. Or Wednesday."

"You're meeting your friends there."

"They'll keep."

"No. Go tomorrow, like you planned."

"You sure?"

"It's just the flu."

"No fun having it alone."

"All I do is sleep."

"Still. You know."

"I'll be all right."

"What'll you do about the ex?"

"Maybe he won't come back."

"Don't bet on it."

"My father went to see him."

"Yeah? What did he say?"

"Who, Ray? I don't know."

"No, your dad."

"He told him if he harassed me again, he'd take some people out there and break bones."

"Thing about Ray is he doesn't give a shit."

"He doesn't?"

"Think about it."

"He gives a shit about a lot of things."

"Not broken bones. That little gun you got: if he comes, fire a couple over his head."

"Why?"

"Because I don't think you could use it on him, and you might just leave it in the drawer. Then there's nothing you can do. So think about scaring him off."

"I'd use it. You don't know what it's like, a man—what's the *mat*ter with him?"

He shrugs and takes the bowl and plate.

"Think two shots across the bow," he says and stands; then, leaning over her, he is huge, blocking the ceiling and walls, his chest and beard lowering, his face and breath close to hers; he kisses her forehead and right cheek and smooths the hair at her brow. She watches him cross the room; at the door he turns and says: "I'll leave this open; mine too. If you need something, give a shout."

"You've got a nice ass," she says, and smiles as his eyes brighten and his beard and cheeks move with his grin. She listens to his steps going down, and the running water as he washes her dishes. When he starts upstairs she turns out the lamp. In his room his boots drop to the floor, there is a rustle of clothes, and he is in bed. He shifts twice, then is quiet. She sits against the pillows in the dark; and wakes there, Steve standing beside her, the room sunlit and cool. The lake is quiet.

"You're going?"

"It's time."

"Have fun."

"Sure. You want breakfast?"

"No."

She takes his hand, and says: "I'll see you in April, I guess. Good hunting and all. Skiing."

"If you don't find a place, or you want to stay on in spring, that's fine."

"I know."

"Well—" His thumb rubs the back of her hand.

"Thanks for everything," she says.

"You too."

"The room. Good talks. Whatever."

"Whatever," he says, smiling. Then he kisses her lips and is gone.

In early afternoon she phones the Harbor Schooner and tells Charlie, the manager, that she is still sick and can't make it that night but will try tomorrow. She eats a sandwich of ham and cheese, makes a pitcher of orange juice, and brings it upstairs. She reaches the bed weak and short of breath. Through the long hot afternoon she lies uncovered on the bed, asleep, awake, asleep, waking always to the sound of motorboats, the voices of many children, and talk and shouts of laughter of men and women. When the sun has moved to the foot of the bed and the room is darkening, she smells charcoal smoke. She turns on the lamp and lies awake listening to the beginning of silence: the boats are out of the water, most of them on trailers by now; she hears cars leaving, and on the stretch of beach below her window, families gather, their voices rising with the smells of burning charcoal and cooking meat. Tomorrow she will wake to quiet that will last until May.

She closes her eyes and imagines the frozen lake, evergreens, the silent snow. After school and on weekends boys will clean the ice with snow shovels and play hockey; she will hear only burning logs in the fireplace, will watch them from the living room, darting without sound into and around one another. She will have a Christmas tree, will eat dinner at her parents', but on Christmas Eve she could have them and Margaret here for dinner before midnight Mass. She will live here—she counts by raising thumb and fingers from a closed fist—eight months. Or seven, so she can be out before Steve comes back. Out where? She shuts her eyes tighter, frowning, but no street, no town appears. In the Merrimack Valley she likes Newburyport but not as much since she started working there, and less since Ray moved there.

Amesbury and Merrimac are too small, Lawrence is mills and factories, and too many grocery stores and restaurants with Spanish names, and Haverhill: Jesus, Haverhill: some people knew how to live there, her parents did, Haverhill for her father was the police department and their house in the city limits but in the country as well, with the garden her mother and father planted each spring: tomatoes, beans, squash, radishes, beets; and woods beyond the garden, not forest or anything, but enough to walk in for a while before you came to farmland; and her father ice-fished, and fished streams and lakes in spring, the ocean in summer. Everyone joked about living in Haverhill, or almost everyone: the skyline of McDonald's arch and old factories and the one new building on the corner of Main Street and the river, an old folks' home and office building that looked like a gigantic cinder block. But it wasn't that. The Back Bay of Boston was pretty, and the North End was interesting with all those narrow streets and cluttered apartments of Italians, but Jesus, Boston was dirtier than Haverhill and on a gray winter day no city looked good. It was that nothing happened in Haverhill, and she had never lived outside its limits till now, and to go back in spring was going downhill backward. A place would come. She would spend the fall and winter here, and by then she would know where to go.

She looks at the walls, the chest with her purse and cassette player on its top, the closed door of the closet; she will keep this room so she'll have the lake (and it occurs to her that this must have been Steve's, and he gave it up), and she'll hang curtains. She will leave his room, or the back room, alone; will store in it whatever she doesn't want downstairs, that chair with the flowered cover he always sits in, and its hassock, the coffee table with cigarette burns like Timmy's bar; she will paint the peeling cream walls in the kitchen. For the first time since moving in, she begins to feel that more than this one room is hers; not only hers but her: her sense of this seems to spread downward, like sentient love leaving her body to move about the three rooms downstairs, touching, looking, making plans. Her body is of no use to her but to move weakly to the bathroom, to sleep and drink and, when it will, to eat. Lying here, though, is good; it is like the beach or sleeping late, better than those because she will not do anything else, cannot do anything else, and so is free. Even at the beach you have to—what? Go into the water. Collect your things and drive home. Wash salt from suit, shower, wash hair, dry hair. Cook. Eat. But this, with no chills now, no pain unless she moves, which she won't, this doesn't have to end until it ends on its own, and she can lie here and decorate the house, move furniture from one room to another, one floor to another, bring all her clothes from her parents' house, her dresser and mirror, while outside voices lower as the smell of meat fades until all she smells is smoke. Tomorrow she will smell trees and the lake.

She hears a car going away, and would like to stand at the window and look at the darkened houses, but imagines them instead, one by one the lights going out behind windows until the house becomes the shape of one, locked for the winter. She is standing at the chest, getting her cigarettes, when she hears the people next door leaving. *Do it,* she tells herself. She turns out the bedside lamp, crouches at a front window, her arms crossed on its sill, and looks past trees in the front lawn at the dark lake. She looks up at stars. To her right, trees enclose the lake; she cannot see the houses among them. Water laps at the beach and wharf pilings. She can see most of the wharf before it is shielded by the oak; below her, Steve's boat, covered with tarpaulin, rests on sawhorses. Her legs tire, and she weakens and gets into bed, covers with the sheet and spread, and lights a cigarette, the flame bright and large in the dark. She reaches for the lamp switch, touches it, but withdraws her hand. She smokes and sees the bathroom painted mauve.

For a long while she lies awake, filling the ashtray, living the lovely fall and winter: in a sweater she will walk in the woods on brown leaves, under yellow and red, and pines and the blue sky of Indian summer. She will find her ice skates in her parents' basement; she remembers the ponds when she was a child, and wonders how or why she outgrew skating, and blames her fever for making her think this way, but is uncertain whether the fever has made her lucid or foolish. She is considering a snow blower for the driveway, has decided to buy one and learn to use it, when he comes in the crash of breaking glass and a loud voice: he has said something to the door, and now he calls her name. She moves the ashtray from her stomach to the floor, turns on her side to get the gun from under the pillow, then lies on her back.

"Polly?" He is at the foot of the stairs. "It's me. I'm coming up."

He has the voice of a returning drunk, boldly apologetic, and she cocks the hammer and points the gun at the door as he climbs, his boots loud, without rhythm, pausing for balance, then quick steps, a pause, a slow step, evenly down the few strides of hall, and his width above his hips fills the door; he is dark against the gray light above him.

"You in here?"

"I've got a gun."

"No shit? Let me see it."

She moves her finger from the trigger, and pushes the safety down with her thumb.

"It's pointed at you."

"Yeah? Where's the light in here?"

"You liked the dark before."

"I did? That's true. That little apartment we had?"

"I mean June, with that fucking knife."

"Oh. No knife tonight. I went to the Harbor Schooner—"

"Shit: what *for?*"

"—So I goes Hey: where's Polly? Don't she work here? Sick, they said. To see you, that's all. So I did some shots of tequila and I'm driving up to New Hampshire, and I say what the fuck? So here I am. You going to tell me where the light is?"

His shoulders lurch as he steps forward; she fires at the ceiling above him, and he ducks, his hands covering his head.

"Pol*ly.*" He lowers his hands, raises his head. "Hey, Polly. Hey: put that away. I just want to talk. That's all. That was an asshole thing I did, that other time. See—"

"Go away."

Her hand trembles, her ears ring, and she sits up in the gun-powder smell, swings her feet to the floor, and places her left hand under her right, holding the gun with both.

"I just want to ask you what's the difference, that's all. I mean, how was it out here with Steve? You happy, and everything?"

"It was *great*. And it's going to be better."

"Better. Better without Steve?"

"Yes."

"Why's that? You got somebody moving in?"

"No."

"But it was good with Steve here. Great with Steve. So what's the difference, that's what I think about. Maybe the lake. The house? I mean, what if it was with me? Same thing, right? Sleep up here over the lake. Do some fucking. Wake up. Eat. Swim. Work. How come it was so good with Steve?"

"We weren't *mar*ried."

"Oh. Okay. That's cool. Why couldn't it be us then, out here? What did I ever do anyways?"

"Jesus, what is this?"

"No, come on: what did I do?"

"Nothing."

"Nothing? I must've done something."

"You didn't do anything."

"Then why weren't you happy, like with Steve? I mean, I thought about it a lot. It wasn't that asshole DeLuca."

"You almost killed him."

"Bullshit."

"You could have."

"You see him?"

"I brought him flowers, is all."

"See: it wasn't him. And I don't think it was me either. If it was him, you'd be with him, and if it was me, well, you got rid of me, so then you'd be happy."

"I *am* happy."

"I don't know, Polly."

She can see the shape and muted color of his face, but his eyes are shadows, his beard and hair darker; his shoulders and arms move, his hands are at his chest, going down, then he opens his shirt, twists from one side to the other pulling off the sleeves.

"Don't, Ray."

Flesh glimmers above his dark pants, and she pushes the gun toward it.

"Let's just try it, Polly. Turn on the light, you'll see." He unbuckles his belt, then stops, raises a foot, holds it with both hands, hops backward and hits the doorjamb, pulls off the boot, and drops it. Leaning there, he takes off the other one, unzips his pants, and they fall to his ankles. He steps out of them, stoops, pushing his shorts down. "See. No knife. No clothes." He looks down. "No hard-on. If you'd turn on a light and put away that hogleg—"

He moves into the light of the door, into the room, and she shakes her head, says No, but it only shapes her lips, does not leave her throat. She closes her eyes and becomes the shots jolting her hands as she pulls and pulls, hears him fall, and still pulls and explodes until the trigger is quiet and she opens her eyes and moves, leaping over him, to the hall and stairs.

In the middle of the night I sit out here in the skiff and I try to think of something else but I can't, because over and over I keep hearing him tell me that time: *Alex, she's the best fuck I've ever had in my life.* I don't want to think about that. But I look back at the house that was Kingsley's and I wish I had put on the lights before I got in the boat, but it wasn't dark yet and I didn't think I'd drift around half the night and have to look back at it with no lights on so it looks like a tomb, with his weights and fishing gear in there. I'll have to get them out. It looks like we're always taking somebody's things out of that house, and maybe it's time to sell it to somebody who's not so unlucky.

He bled to death, so even then she could have done something. I want to hate her for that. I will, too. After he knew he loved her, he didn't talk about her like that anymore, but it was still there between us, what he told me, and he knew I remembered, and sometimes when we were out drinking, me and some-body and him and Polly, and then we'd call it a night and go home, he'd grin at me. What I don't know is how you can be like that with a guy, then shoot him and leave him to bleed to death while you sit outside waiting for your old man and everybody. This morning we put him next to Kingsley and I was hugging Mom from one side and the old man hugging her from the other, and it seemed to me I had two brothers down there for no rea-son. Kingsley wouldn't agree, and he wouldn't like it that I don't vote anymore, or read the newspapers, or even watch the news. All Ray did was fall in love and not get over it when she got weird the way women do sometimes.

So I sit out here in the skiff and it's like they're both out here with me. I can feel them, and I wish I'd see them come walking across the lake. And I'd say, Why didn't you guys do something else? Why didn't you wait to be drafted, or go to Canada? Why didn't you find another girl? I'd tell them I'm going to sell this—and oh shit it starts now, the crying, the big first one, and I let it come and I shout against it over the water: "I'm going to *sell* this fucking *house,* you *guys.* And the one in *town,* and I'm moving in with *Mom* and the *old man;* I'm going to get them to sell *theirs* too and get the fuck *out* of here, take them down to *Flor*ida and live in a *con*do. We'll go fishing. We'll buy a boat, and fish."

We Don't
Live Here
Anymore

Pity is the worst passion of all:

we don't outlive it like sex.

—GRAHAM GREENE, *The Ministry of Fear*

Come see us again some time;

nobody's home but us,

and we don't live here anymore.

— *a friend, drunk one night*

1

THE OWNER of the liquor store was an Irishman with graying hair; he glanced at Edith, then pretended he hadn't, and said: "There's my ale man."

"Six Pickwicks," I said. "And a six-pack of Miller's for the women."

"You hardly find a woman who'll drink ale."

"That's right."

We leaned against the counter; I felt Edith wanting to touch me, so I stepped back and took out my wallet. Hank had wanted to pay for all of it but I held him to two dollars.

"Used to be everybody in New England drank ale. Who taught you? Your father?"

"He taught me to drink ale and laugh with pretty girls. What happened to the others?"

I was watching Edith enjoying us. She is dark and very small with long black hair, and she has the same charming gestures that other girls with long hair have: with a slow hand she pushes it from her eye; when she bends over a drinking fountain, she holds it at her ear so it won't fall into the basin. Some time I would like to see it fall: Edith drinking, lips wet, throat moving with cool water, and her hair fallen in the chrome basin, soaking.

"World War II. The boys all got drafted before they were old enough to drink in Massachusetts, see? So they started drinking beer on the Army bases. When they came home they still wanted beer. That was the end of ale. Now if one of your old ale drinkers dies, you don't replace him."

Outside under the streetlights Edith took my arm. In front of the newsstand across the street a cop watched us get into the car, and in the dark Edith sat close to me as I drove through town. There were few cars and no one was on the sidewalks. On the streets where people lived most of the houses were dark; a few blocks from my house I stopped under a large tree near the curb and held Edith and we kissed.

"We'd better go," she said.

"I'll bring my car to the Shell Station at twelve."

She moved near the door and brushed her hair with her fingers, and I drove home. Terry and Hank were sitting on the front steps. When I stopped the car Edith got out and crossed the lawn without waiting or looking back. Terry watched me carrying the bag, and when I stepped between her and Hank she looked straight up at me.

We talked in the dark, sitting in lawn chairs on the porch. Except Hank, who was always restless: he leaned against the porch rail, paced, leaned against a wall, stood over one of us as we talked, nodding his head, a bottle in one fist, a glass in the other, listening, then breaking in, swinging his glass like a slow hook to the body the instant before he interrupted, then his voice came, louder than ours. In high school he had played halfback. He went to college weighing a hundred and fifty-six pounds and started writing. He had kept in condition, and his walk and gestures had about them an athletic grace that I had tried to cultivate as a boy, walking home from movies where I had seen gunmen striding like mountain lions. Edith sat to my right, with her back to the wall; sometimes she rested her foot against mine. Terry sat across from me, smoking too much. She has long red hair and eleven years ago she was the prettiest girl I had ever seen; or, rather, the prettiest girl I had ever touched. Now she's thirty and she's gained a pound for each of those eleven years, but she has gained them subtly, and her only striking change is in her eyes, blue eyes that I fell in love with: more and more now, they have that sad, pensive look that married women get after a few years. Her eyes used to be merry. Edith is twenty-seven and her eyes are still merry, and she turned them bright and dark to me as I talked. When Hank and Edith left, we walked them to the car, hugging and pecking them goodnight as we always did; I watched Edith's silhouette as they drove away.

"Come here," Terry said. She took my wrist and pulled me toward the back door.

"Come where."

"In the kitchen. I want to talk to you."

"Would you let go of my wrist?"

She kept pulling. At the sidewalk leading to the back door I stopped and jerked my arm but she held on and turned to face me.

"I said let go of my wrist," and I jerked again and was free. Then I followed her in.

"From now on we're going to act like married people," she said. "No more of this crap." I went to the refrigerator and got an ale. "Just like other married people. And no flirting around with silly adventures. Do you understand that?"

"Of course I don't. Who could understand such bullshit."

"You're not *really* going to play dumb. Are you? Come on."

"Terry." I was still calm; I thought I might be able to hold onto that, pull us out of this, into bed, into sleep. "Would you please tell me what's wrong?"

She moved toward me and I squared my feet to duck or block, but she went past me and got ice from the refrigerator and went to the cabinet where the bourbon was.

"Why don't you have a beer instead."

"I don't want a beer."

"You'll get drunk."

"Maybe I will."

I looked down at my glass, away from her face: in summer she had freckles that were pretty, and I remembered how I used to touch her in daylight, a quick kiss or hug as I went through the kitchen, a hand at her waist or shoulder as we walked in town;

that was not long ago, and still she reached for me passing in the house, or touched me as she walked by the couch where I read, but I never did; in bed at night, yes, but not in daylight anymore.

"Why don't we talk in the morning. We'll just fight now, you've got that look of yours."

"Never mind that look of mine."

The pots from dinner were still on the stove, the plates were dirty in the sink, and when I sat at the table I brushed crumbs and bits of food from the place in front of me; the table was sticky where I rested my hands, and I went to the sink and got a sponge and wiped the part I had cleaned. I left the sponge on the table and sat down and felt her fury at my cleaning before I looked up and saw it in her eyes. She stood at the stove, an unlit cigarette in her hand.

"You and Edith, all these trips you make, all these Goddamn errands, all summer if someone runs out of booze or cigarettes or wants Goddamn egg rolls, off you go, you and Edith, and it's not right to leave me with Hank, to put me in that position—"

"Now wait a minute."

"—something's going on, either it's going on or you want it to—"

"Just a minute, wait just a minute—two questions: why is it wrong for Edith and me to go get some beer and Goddamn ale, and what's this position you're in when you're alone with Hank, and what is it you're *really* worrying about? Do you get horny every time you're alone with Hank and you want Daddy to save you from yourself?"

"*No,* I don't get horny when I'm alone with Hank; I only get horny for my Goddamn husband but he likes to be with Edith."

"We've been married ten years. We're not on our honeymoon, for Christ's sake."

Her eyes changed, softened, and her voice did too: "Why aren't we? Don't you love me?"

"Oh hell. Of course I do."

"Well what are you saying, that you love me but we've been married so long that you need Edith too, or maybe you're already having her? Is that it, because if it is maybe we should talk about how long this marriage is going to last. Because you can move out anytime you want to, I can get a job—"

"Terry."

"—and the kids will be all right, there's no reason for you to suffer if marriage is such a disappointment. Maybe I've done something—"

"Terry."

"What."

"Calm down. Here." I reached across the table with my lighter and she leaned over to light her cigarette, cupping her hands around mine, and under her flesh like a pulse I could feel her need and I wanted at once to shove her against the stove, and to stroke her cheek and tousle her hair.

"Terry, you said those things. Not me. I have never wanted to leave you. I am not suffering. I'm not tired of you, and I don't need Edith or anyone else. I like being with her. Like with any other friend—man or woman—sometimes I like being alone with her. So once in a while we run an errand. I see nothing threatening in that, nothing bad. I don't think married people have to cling to each other, and I think if you look around you'll see that most of them don't. You're the only wife I know who gets pissed at her husband because he doesn't touch her at parties—"

"The other husbands *touch* their wives! They put their *arms* around them!"

"Hank doesn't."

"That's why she's so lonely, that's why she likes to tag along like your little lamb, because Hank doesn't love her—"

"Who ever said that?"

"Hank did." Her eyes lowered. "Tonight while you two were gone."

"He said that?"

"Yes."

"Why?"

"I don't know, he just said it."

"What were you doing?"

"Well we were talking, how else do you tell people things."

"When people talk like that they're usually doing other things."

"Oh sure, we were screwing on the front porch, what do you care?"

"I don't, as long as I know the truth."

"The *truth*. You wouldn't know the truth if it knocked on the door. You won't even admit the truth about yourself, that you don't really love me—"

"Stop that, Terry. Do not say that shit. You know why? Because it's not true, it's never been true, but when you say it like that, it is. For a minute. For long enough to start a *really* crazy fight. Do you understand that?"

She was nodding, her cheeks looking numb, her eyes frightened and forlorn; then I felt my own eyes giving her pity, washing her cheeks and lips with it, and when I did that her face tightened, her eyes raged again, and too quick for me to duck she threw her drink in my face, ice cubes flying past my head and smacking the wall and sliding across the floor. I rose fast but only halfway, poised with my hands gripping the edge of the table; then I looked away from her and sat down and took out my handkerchief and slowly wiped my face and beard, looking out the back door at the night where I wanted to be, then I brushed at the spots on the burgundy sweat shirt she had brought home for me one day, happily taking it from the bag and holding it up for me to see. Then I stood up and walked quickly out the back door, and she threw her glass at me but too late, the door was already swinging to and the glass bounced off the screen and hit the floor. Somehow it didn't break.

I crossed the lawn, onto the sidewalk that sloped down with the street; a half block from the house I was suddenly afraid she was coming, I felt her behind me, and I turned, but the sidewalk was empty and lovely in the shadows of maples and elms. I went on. If there was a way to call Edith and she could come get me. But of course no. I could go back and get my car, the keys were in my pocket, I could start it and be gone before Terry came running out with a Goddamn knife, if I drove to Edith's and parked in front of the house and looked up at the window where she slept beside Hank she would know, if I waited long enough watching her window she would know in her sleep and she would wake and look out the window at me under the moon; she would tiptoe downstairs and hold me on the damp lawn. I came to a corner and went up another street. "Edith," I whispered into the shadows of my diagonal walk, "oh Edith sweet baby, I love you, I love you forever." I thought about forever and if we live afterward, then I saw myself laid out in a coffin, the beard and hair lovely white. I stopped and leaned against a car, dew on its fender cool through my slacks. Natasha and Sean and I looked at Terry in her coffin. I stood between them holding their small hands. Terry's smooth cheeks were pale against her red hair.

When she told me she was pregnant she wasn't afraid. She was twenty years old. It was a cold bright Thursday in January, the sky had been blue for a week and the snow in Boston was dirty and old. We went to a bookstore on Boylston Street and bought paperbacks for each other, then we had steamers and draft beer in a dim place with paintings of whale fishing and storms at sea and fishing boats in harbor on the walls. For some reason the waiters wore leather tunics. In those days Terry always seemed happy. I can close my eyes any time and remember how I loved her and see and feel her as she took my hand on the table and said: "After today I'll be careful about eating, and if I promise not to get fat and if I get a job, can I keep our baby?"

Now I started walking home. We were, after all this, the same Jack and Terry, and I would go to her now and touch her and hold her; I walked faster, nodding my head yes yes yes. Then going into the dark living room I felt her in the house like the large and sharpened edge of a knife. She was asleep. I crept into the bedroom and lay beside her, at the edge of the bed so we didn't touch.

Natasha and Sean woke Terry early for breakfast but I stayed in bed, held onto sleep through the breakfast voices then their voices outside, while the sun got higher and the room hotter until it was too hot and I got up. I went straight to the shower without seeing anyone. While I was drying myself she tapped on the door.

"Do you want lunch or breakfast?"

Her voice had the practiced sweetness she assumed when she was afraid: strangers got it, and I got it after some fights or when she made mistakes with money. For an instant I was tender and warm and I wanted to help her with a cheerful line (Oh, I'll have you for breakfast, love; just stick a banana in it and hop in bed); but then sure as time is a trick I was sitting in the kitchen last night, and the bourbon and ice were flying at me.

"I don't know," I said. Through the door I could feel the tone of my voice piercing her. "What do you have?"

"Just cereal if you want breakfast. But if you want lunch I could get some lobsters, just for you and me; the kids don't like them anyway."

"No, I have to hurry. I'm taking the car in."

Linhart, I said to my face in the mirror. *You are a petulant son of a bitch. Why don't you drag her in here and whip her ass then eat lobster with her.* She was still waiting outside the door; I pretended not to know, and went about drying myself.

"I could go to the fish market and be back and have them done in thirty minutes. Forty to be safe."

"I have to get the car there at twelve."

"You *have* to?"

"If I want the work done, yes."

"What's the work?"

"Oil and grease."

"That doesn't take long."

"They're busy, Terry. They want it at twelve or not at all. They don't care how badly you want a lobster. But if you want one, get it now before I leave."

"I don't want one by myself."

"What, you mean it won't taste good?"

"Oh, you know what I *mean,*" in that mock-whine you hear

from girls everywhere when they're being lovingly teased. I started brushing my teeth.

"Cheerios or Grape Nuts?"

"Grape Nuts."

She went away. When I came dressed to the kitchen the table was set neatly for one: a red straw place mat, a deep bowl which had the faint sparkle of fresh washing, a spoon on a napkin, a glass of orange juice. She was upstairs with the vacuum cleaner. Over in the sink were the children's breakfast dishes, unwashed; beneath them were last night's dishes.

Terry is the toy of poltergeists: washer, dryer, stove, refrigerator, dishes, clothes, and woolly house dust. The stove wants cleaning and as she lifts off burners the washing machine stops in the wash room; she leaves the stove and takes another load of dirty clothes to the wash room; it is a white load, bagged in a sheet, lying on the kitchen floor since before breakfast. She unloads the washing machine and, hugging the wet clothes to her breasts, she opens the dryer; but she has forgotten, it's full of clothes she dried last night. She lays the wet ones on top of the dryer and takes out the dry ones; these she carries to the living room and drops in a loose pile on the couch; a pair of Sean's Levi's falls to the floor and as she stoops to pick it up she sees a bread crust and an orange peel lying in the dust under the couch. She cannot reach them without lying on the floor, so she tells herself, with the beginnings of panic, that she must do the living room this morning: sweep, dust, vacuum. But there are clothes waiting to be folded, and a new load going into the dryer, another into the washer. Going through the kitchen she sees the stove she has forgotten, its crusted burners lying on greasy white porcelain. In the wash room she puts the wet clothes into the dryer, shuts the door, and starts it, a good smooth sound of machine, the clothes turning in the dark. In fifty minutes they will be dry. It is all so efficient, and standing there listening to the machine, she feels that efficiency, and everything seems in order now, she is in control, she can rest. This lasts only a moment. She loads the washer, turns it on, goes back to the kitchen, averts her eyes from the stove and makes for the coffee pot; she will first have a cup of coffee, gather herself up, plan her morning. With despair she sees it is not a morning but an entire day, past cocktail hour and dinner, into the night: when the dinner dishes are done she will have more clothes to fold and some to iron. This happens often and forces her to watch television while she works. She is ashamed of watching Johnny Carson. The breakfast dishes are in the sink, last night's pots are on the counter: hardened mashed potatoes, congealed grease. She hunts for the coffee cup she's been using all morning, finds it on the lavatory in the bathroom, and empties the cold coffee over the dishes in the sink. She lights a cigarette and thinks of some place she can sit, some place that will let her drink a cup of coffee. There is none, there's not a clean room downstairs; upstairs the TV room is clean enough, because no one lives there. But to climb the stairs for a sanctuary is too depressing, so she goes to the living room and sits on the couch with the clean clothes, ignores the bread crust and orange peel whispering to her from the floor. Trying to plan her work for the day overwhelms her; it is too much. So she does what is at hand; she begins folding clothes, drinking coffee, smoking. After a while she hears the washer stop. Then the dryer. She goes to the wash room, brings back the dry clothes, goes back and puts the wet load in the dryer. When I come in for lunch, the living room is filled with clothes: they are in heaps on chairs, folded and stacked on the couch and floor; I look at them and then at Terry on the couch; beyond her legs are the bread crust and orange peel; with a harried face she is drinking coffee, and the ash tray is full. "Is it noon already?" she says. Her eyes are quick with panic. "Oh Goddamnit, I didn't know it was that late." I walk past her into the kitchen: the burners, the dishes. "Jesus Christ," I say. We fight, but only briefly, because it is daylight, we aren't drinking, the children will be in from playing soon, hungry and dirty. Like our marriage, I think, hungry and dirty.

While I ate the Grape Nuts, Natasha and Sean came in, brown arms and legs and blond hair crowding through the door at once, the screen slamming behind them. Natasha is nine; she is the love child who bound us. Sean is seven. Looking at them I felt love for the first time that day.

"You slept late," Sean said.

"That's because you were up late, you guys were fighting," Natasha said. "I heard you."

"What did you hear?"

"I don't know—" She was hiding whatever it was, down in her heart angry words breaking into her sleep. "Yelling and swear words and then you left."

"You left?" Sean said. He was simply interested, not worried. He lives his own life. He eats and sleeps with us, comes to us when he needs something, but he lives outside with boys and bicycles.

"All grown-ups fight from time to time. If they're married."

"I know," Sean said. "Where's Mom?"

I pointed to the ceiling, to the sound of the vacuum cleaner.

"We want to eat," he said.

"Let her work. I'll fix it."

"You're eating," Natasha said.

"I'll hurry."

"Is that your lunch?" Sean said. "Grape Nuts?"

"It's my supper."

I asked what they had done all morning. It was hard to follow and I didn't try; I just watched their loud faces. They interrupted each other: Natasha likes to draw a story out, lead up to it with history ("Well see, first we thought we'd go to Carol's but then they weren't home and I remembered she said they were going—"). Sean likes to tell a story as quickly as he can, sometimes quicker. While they talked, I made sandwiches. It was close to noon but I lingered; Natasha was stirring Kool-Aid in a pitcher. In twelve minutes Edith would be waiting at the Shell station, but I stood watching them eat, and I hoped something would change her day and she wouldn't be there. But she would. An advantage of an affair with a friend's wife was the matter of phone calls: there was nothing suspicious about them. If Edith called and talked to Terry I'd know she couldn't see me this afternoon. I asked the children if they wanted dessert.

"Do we have any?" Natasha said.

"We never have dessert," Sean said.

I looked in the freezer compartment for ice cream, then in the cupboard for cookies, sweets to sweeten my goodbye, and there were none. Sean was right: we never had desserts because I didn't like them and Terry liked them too much; she controlled her sweet tooth by having nothing sweet in the house.

"I'm sorry," I said. I knew I was being foolish but I couldn't stop. "I'm a stupid daddy. I'll bring some dessert home with me."

"Where are you going?" Natasha asked.

"To get the car worked on," my voice jumping to tenor with the lie.

"Can I go?" Sean said. He had a moustache of grape Kool-Aid.

"Me too," Natasha said.

"No, it takes a long time, then I'm going to run with Hank."

"We don't mind," Natasha said. "We'll watch you."

There is not one God, I thought. There are several, and they all like jests.

"No you won't," I growled, and went at her with fingers curled like talons, then tickled her ribs; her sandwich dropped to her plate, she became a fleshed laugh. "Because after we run we're going to a bar and drink beer. It's what mean old men do."

They were laughing. Now I could leave. Then Terry came downstairs, one of my old shirts hanging out, covering her shorts.

"I want us to start having desserts."

"What?"

"Yay!" Sean said. "Desserts."

"We never have desserts," Natasha said.

Terry stood looking at us, smiling, confused, ready to joke or defend.

"We're depriving the kids of a basic childhood experience."

"What's that?"

"Mother's desserts."

"Jesus."

I wished she were the one going off to wickedness; I would stay home and make cookies from a recipe book.

"Well, I'm off."

I kissed their Kool-Aid mouths, touched lips with Terry, and went out. She followed me to the screen door.

"Did you get enough to eat?"

"Sure. Not as good as lobster," talking over my shoulder, going down the steps, "but cheaper anyway."

She didn't answer. In the car I thought adultery is one thing, but being a male bitch waging peripheral war is another, this poison of throwing gift-lobsters at your wife's vulnerable eyes, drying up her sweetness and hope by alluding to the drought of the budget. Which was also a further, crueler allusion to her awful belief in a secular gospel of good news: we were Americans, nice, healthy, intelligent people with nice, healthy, intelligent friends, and we deserved to eat lobsters the day after a fight, just as we deserved to see plays in Boston and every good movie that came to town, and when I told her there was no money she was not bitter, but surprised. She was also surprised when the bank told her we were overdrawn and she found that she had forgotten to record a check, or when someone wrote her about a bill that lay unopened in her desk.

When I got to the Shell station Edith was parked across the street. I told the man to change the oil and grease it.

"I'll go run some errands with the wife," I said, thumbing over my shoulder at Edith. "Then I'll come pick it up."

He looked across the street at Edith.

"Keys in the car?"

I slapped my pockets.

"Yes."

I wondered what twelve months of daylight would do to adulterers. In daylight it seemed everyone knew: the fat man in the greasy T-shirt nodding at me as I told him twenty weight and a new filter and grease, the women who drove by and glanced at me as I waited to cross the street, and the little suntanned boy, squinting up at me, pulling a wagon with his tricycle on the sidewalk beside her car. I got in and said: "He knows too."

"Who?"

"That kid. He knows where we're going."

She drove through the city. Its built on the Merrimack, which is foul, and the city itself is small, ugly, and has the look of death, as a man with cancer does. The industry was shoes, but the factories have been closing. On the main street the glass-fronted stores, no matter their size, all have the dismal look of pawn shops or Army surplus stores. But urban renewal has started: on the riverbank they have destroyed some old gray wooden buildings; in their place a shopping center will be built, and then as we stop at the red light and look toward the river we shall see instead the new brick buildings with wide glass windows, and specials posted on the glass of the supermarket, and the asphalt parking lot with cars, shopping carts, and unhappy women. Our city is no place for someone who is drawn to suicide.

When Edith got to the divided highway I twisted around and opened the ice chest on the floor in the back. Already we had a ritual like husband and wife: it was for me to begin the drive by opening two beers, lighting two cigarettes. Today she had added something: two Löwenbräus, two Asahis, and two San Miguels angled up at me in the ice.

"She brings such presents," I said, and kissed her cheek.

"Cold presents from a cold woman."

An opener was in the glove compartment, under one of her scarves that was red and soft like pants in my hand. The Asahis opened with a pop. Edith glanced in the rear-view mirror, swallowed, then took the lighted cigarette from my fingers.

"I think I'll change to Luckies," she said, smiling.

"Sure, do that. Why not just let him babysit for us."

We avoided naming them: we said he, she, him, her.

"He'd be glad to."

"Well *she* wouldn't, sweetheart."

I told her about the fight; the sun was warm on my face and arm at the window, the air smelled of trees and grass, we were driving in rolling wooded country under a blue sky, and I was too happy to care about last night. I told it quickly.

"I think he wants to make love to her," she said.

"Why?"

"Why? Because she's pretty and he likes her and he hasn't had any strange since Jeanne. Why do you think?"

"I mean why do you think he wants to?"

"The way he looks at her. And the way he looked when we came back from getting beer last night."

"Guilty?"

"Sheepish. Does that bother you?"

"Not me."

"Good. We can babysit for each other," smiling, her eyes bright.

"She blooms, she blooms," I said. "And in May you were so hurt."

"In May I was alone."

I am surrounded by painful marriages that no one understands. But Hank understands his, and I think for him it has never been painful; the pain was Edith's, and she came to me with it in May, at a party. When she asked me to go outside I knew she had finally caught Hank, and because she is small and her voice soft I saw her as vulnerable, and I felt she lacked the tough spirit to deal with adultery. First I found Terry in the kitchen so she wouldn't miss me, then start looking about to see which woman was missing too. I told her where I was going and she understood too that Edith had finally caught on; she looked at me with that veiled excitement we feel in the face of other people's disasters. In the backyard, away from lighted windows, Edith and I sat side by side on a picnic table.

"You probably already know this, I guess Terry does too and everybody else: about Hank and that phony French bitch that somebody brought to our Christmas party—"

"Jeanne."

"And they crashed that party." She touched my shirt pocket for a cigarette. "I forgot my purse inside. Bumming cigarettes, that's how I first got suspicious: he'd come home with Parliaments, I guess they lay around in bed so long he smoked all his, and now I don't know what to do, I can't stand to see him naked, I keep thinking of—shit: I ought to divorce him, I could do that but I don't really want to, but why shouldn't I? When he doesn't love me."

She stopped. My arm was around her; I patted her shoulder, then squeezed her against my side. There was a time in my life when I believed I could help people by talking to them, and because of that I became a confidant for several people, most of them young girls who were my students. People told me about marriages, jobs, parents, and boyfriends, and I listened and talked a lot and never helped anyone at all. So now if someone comes to me I offer what I know I can give: the friendship of a listening face. That night I held Edith and listened and said very little. After a while she jumped down from the table and walked toward the shadows of the house. She was wearing a white dress. I was about to call to her when she stopped and stood smoking with her back turned. Then she came back to the table.

"You're good to me."

"I haven't helped you any."

She stood looking up at me. I got down from the table and held her, pressing her face to my chest and stroking her hair, then we kissed and she squeezed me tightly, her hands moved on my back, and her tongue darted in. We stood a long time kissing in the shadows.

"Come see me."

"Yes."

"Monday afternoon."

"Are you sure?"

"Yes. Yes, I want you to. Come at one."

Next day was Sunday, and all day while the sun was up I didn't believe Edith, and I didn't believe what I had felt holding her, but after dinner in the night I went for a walk and I believed all of it again, and that night in bed I lay awake for a long time, like a child before a birthday. After my twelve o'clock class Monday I drove to Edith's. When she opened the door I knew from her face that she had been waiting.

Now the place we were going to, the place we always went to after the first afternoon in her house, was a woods off a highway in New Hampshire: down a wide, curving dirt road, dry and dusty, then she parked in the shade and I opened two San Miguels, got the blanket from the back seat, and we climbed a gentle slope, brown pine needles slippery underfoot. I timidly held her hand. I prefer adultery to be a collision: suddenly and without thinking alone with a woman, an urgent embrace, buckles, zippers, buttons. Walking up through the trees gave me time to watch Terry taking the lunch dishes from the table, stacking them on the counter by the sink, and with a distracted, troubled face starting to wash the dishes from three meals. At the knoll's top I lay the blanket under pines and a tall hemlock and heard behind me the buttons of her shorts; I turned and, kneeling, pulled the shorts down her warm brown legs. She took her shirt off and reached back for the clasp of her brassiere; then she lay on the blanket and watched me until I was naked, lying beside her with the sun shining over the crown of a gray birch onto my face.

"What'll we do in winter," she said.

"In the car, like kids."

"If we have a winter."

I kissed her eyes and said: "When fall comes we'll make love in the car and when winter comes we'll fog the windows and make love wearing sweaters and in spring we'll be back here on this blanket on this hill."

"Promise me."

"I promise."

Then I was alone thinking of a year of deceiving Terry and Hank and the others whom you don't and can't watch out for because they're faceless and nameless, but they're always watching you. I could feel Edith knowing what I was thinking.

"I promise."

"I know you do. No, lie down, love. I want to be on top. There. Hello, love."

I reached up for her breasts and watched her face, eyes tightly shut, lips parted, and the long black hair falling across her right cheek, strands of it in her mouth, and she tossed her head, neck arching, and the hair fell back over her shoulder. Then I shut my eyes, and my hands dropped from her breasts and kneaded the earth. For a while we were still, then I opened my eyes to the sun and her face.

"I don't want to move yet," she said. "I want to sit here and drip on you." Already I could feel it. "Can you get the beer?"

I reached behind me and gave her a bottle and watched her throat as she swallowed. I raised my head to drink from mine.

"You're much faster now," she said.

On that afternoon in May we went to the guest room, downstairs at the rear of the house, and after an hour I gave up. We had our shirts on and I was wearing socks.

"Are you sure you can't?" she said.

"I keep listening for Sharon to come down or Hank to walk in."

"You're sure that's all it is?"

"That's plenty enough."

We went outside and sat on lawn chairs in the sun. After a while Sharon woke up and came out and played with Edith's feet. I said I would see her tomorrow, at the shopping center north of town, just over the New Hampshire line; then I went home happy and Terry said: "You must have had a good day in class." I avoided her eyes until she turned back to the stove, then I looked at her long red hair and like singing I thought: *I will love them both.* I said I would go take a shower, and I went to our bedroom: the bed was unmade and a pair of her Levi's and a shirt were on the floor, and I had to step over the vacuum cleaner to get into the bathroom, where two wet towels lay on the floor but no clean ones in the closet, and I yelled at her: "Could I have a Goddamn towel!" That night I read in the living room until she was asleep, and next afternoon Edith and I found this road and woods and hill, and that time it wasn't Sharon and Hank I saw with my eyes closed but Terry at home, and Edith kept working with me until finally I came in spite of thinking, it was like some distant part of me coming, like the semen itself had decided it was tired of waiting, and it spurted out just to give us all a rest. For two or three weeks I was like that, then all at once one day I wasn't, as though even guilt and fear could not survive the familiarity of passion.

Now Edith lay beside me and we drank beer going tepid and smoked lying naked in the sun.

"Don't let it get sunburned," she said. "You'll get caught."

"Poor limp thing."

"I'll keep the sun off."

"No. I can't."

"Yes you can."

"I'm an old man."

"You're my young lover. Your stomach's growling; have you eaten lunch?"

"Grape Nuts. I slept late."

"You should live with me. I'd feed you better than that."

"It's what I wanted. She feeds me what I want."

"You taste like me."

A squirrel darted up the hemlock. After a while I said, "Wait." I stroked her arm, then tugged it, and she moved up beside me. I was on her, in her, taking a long time, the sun on my back, sweating against her belly, listening to the monologue of moans.

"Did you?" I said.

"Yes. I want you to."

Her tongue-moistened fingers went up to my nipples. She had taught me I had those.

"Oh love," she said.

"Again?"

"I think so. Yes. God, yes."

She took me with her and I collapsed on her damp belly and breasts and listened to the pounding of her heart.

"It felt like spurting blood," I said.

"Did it hurt?"

"I couldn't tell."

"My young lover."

"I'm starving."

"You have to run first."

"Maybe I'll cop out."

"No, you have to be strong, taking care of two women. Would you like to live with me?"

"Yes."

"I'd like to live with you. We should all rent one big house."

"And who'd mop up the blood?"

"There wouldn't be any blood."

"She'd cut my throat."

I got up and dressed and went down to the car for the Löwenbraüs, then back up the slope treasuring my hard climbing calf muscles; now I wanted to run. She was dressed, lying on her back, her hands at her sides, eyes closed, face to the sun.

"I wonder how we'll get caught," she said.

"He'll smell you when I undress."

"I mean Terry. If he caught us I wouldn't care, I wouldn't stop unless you wanted to. You probably would. You'd be embarrassed."

"Maybe not."

"You would. You keep trying to fit me into your life, but it's hard for you, and if you got caught you'd throw me out. But you're part of my life: you're what allows me to live with Hank."

"Am I a what? I don't want to be a what." I held up the Löwenbraü. "This is one. It's what's going to make me belch for the first mile."

"You're my lovely what."

"Good old Jack, just part of the family."

"Sure. You make me a good wife. If I didn't love you I'd have to love someone else. We married too young—"

"We all did."

Once at a party Terry was in the kitchen with Edith and two other wives. They came out grinning at the husbands: their own, the others. They had all admitted to shotgun weddings. That was four years ago and now one couple is divorced, another has made a separate peace, fishing and hunting for him and pottery and college for her; and there are the Allisons and the Linharts. A deck-stacking example, but the only one I know.

"He needs us, Sharon and me, but he can't really love anyone, only his work, and the rest is surface."

"I don't believe that."

"I don't mean his friendship with you. Of course it's deep, he doesn't live with you, and best of all you're a man, you don't have those needs he can't be bothered with. He'd give you a kidney if you needed one."

"He'd give it to you too."

"Of course he would. But he wouldn't go to a marriage counselor."

"You funny girl. After a long carnivorous fuck you talk about a marriage counselor. Who *are* you, sweetheart?"

"My name is Edith Allison and I'm the leader of the band. I wanted to go to a marriage counselor so he'd talk. Because he wouldn't talk just to me. He wanted everything simple: he'd been screwing Jeanne, now he'd stopped, and that was that."

"What more did you want?"

"You know what I wanted. Remember me back in May? I still believed in things. I wanted to know where we were, what Jeanne meant. Now that I have you I know what she meant: that he doesn't love me. You love the person you're having the affair with. But it doesn't matter now, I can live with him like that, on the surface. He'll be busting out again soon. He's been hibernating with that novel since he broke off with Jeanne. Before long he'll look around and blink and screw the first thing that walks into his office."

"Jesus. I hope somebody goes in before I do."

"He'd probably do that too."

"Now, now: bitchy bitchy."

"Well, he screws his wife once in a while, so why not another man."

"He screws you? Frigid like you are?"

"I try hard."

"I hear you can go to St. Louis and screw for that man and woman who wrote the book. The one about coming."

"Really?"

"Sure. They watch you and straighten out your hang-ups."

"Let's you and I go. I'd like them to watch us. We'd make them hot."

"You might get rid of your guilt. Do you good."

"Why spoil my fun? Maybe you'd learn to come more."

"What would a wee dirty lass like you have told a marriage counselor?"

"I was trying to keep from being a wee dirty lass. I'm glad now I didn't. What are you doing?"

"Touching you."

"Isn't it getting late?"

"I don't know."

"Can you again?"

"I don't know."

We left our shirts on, a wrong move: they reminded us that time was running out. My back hurt but I kept trying; Edith didn't make it either, and finally she said: "Let's stop." Our shirts were wet. We gathered up the bottles, the cigarettes, the blanket. In the car she made up her face.

"What'll you do with the bottles?" I said.

"I think I'll burn candles in them at dinner. And if he notices—which he wouldn't—I'll tell him they're souvenirs from this afternoon. Along with my sore pussy."

"He'll see them in the garbage. You know, when he empties it or something."

She started the car and grinned at me, almost laughing.

"And then what, Charlie Chan?"

"He'll wonder why in the hell you drank six bottles of imported beer this afternoon."

"Well, he doesn't deserve honesty, but a few clues might be nice."

"Sometimes I think—"

It was possible she wanted him to catch her; you have to keep that in mind when you're making love with a man's wife. But I didn't want to talk about it.

"Sometimes you think what?"

"Sometimes I think I love you even more than I think I do. Which is a lot."

"Which is a lot. Impotent as you are, you try hard."

She turned the car around and drove slowly and bouncing out of the woods. At the highway she stopped and put on sunglasses.

"Light me a Lucky," she said. "My last one till——?"

I thought of the acting and the lies and, right then, if she had said we must stop seeing each other, I would have been relieved.

"I don't know, I'll call you."

As she drove onto the highway both of us pretended we weren't eyeing the road for friends' cars. My damp shirt and chest cooled in the air blowing through the window.

"My pecker aches."

"I'm going to keep the sitter another hour and take a nap."

"Let me give you some money for her."

"Another time. Mother sent me some."

"The empties are in the chest."

"I'll go by the dump."

Summer school was in session, and walking downtown you'd see college girls licking ice cream cones. Once I was teaching *Goodbye, Columbus* and a blonde girl with brown eyes like a deer stopped me at the door before class and said: "Mr. Linhart, what is oral love?" She was licking a lollipop. I looked away from her tongue on the lollipop and said fellatio; when she asked what that was I mumbled in the heat of my face that she ought to ask a girl. It took me a couple of hours to know she was having fun with me. After that I tried to talk to her but she had only wanted that fun; she had a boyfriend who waited every day in the hall outside our classroom, and seeing them holding hands and walking down the hall I felt old and foolish. That was three years ago, when I was twenty-seven.

On summer afternoons there were no classes, and the buildings were empty. Most days when I climbed the three flights of stairs in the old, cool building Hank would be working with his back to the open door; he'd hear me coming and he'd turn smiling, stacking and paper-clipping the manuscript. "Hi," he'd say, his voice affectionate like he was talking to a woman or a child. There are several men I love and who love me, all of us married, passive misogamists, and if we did not have each other to talk to we would probably in our various ways go mad. But our love embarrasses us; we show our affection in reverse: *Where you been, you sonofabitch? Look at that bastard, he wouldn't buy a round for Jesus Christ*—But Hank only did that if it made you feel better.

"Hi," he said.

"You can't write, you fucker, so let's go run."

"One Goddamn page."

"In four hours?"

"Three hours and forty-six minutes. Let's go."

I started walking downstairs before he asked what I had done with my day. Walking over to the gym he was quiet. By the flagpole he lit a cigarette, then flung it to the sidewalk, crumpled his pack and threw it hard, like an outfielder; it arched softly, red and white in the sun.

"You just quit."

"Goddamn right."

"Which time?"

"For the last time."

"You won't make it."

"You watch. They're pissing me off. They're trying to kill me."

"They have no souls."

"Exactly."

"So they're not trying to kill you."

"Not the cigarettes. I mean the fuckers that make 'em."

There were tennis players in the locker room. We had lockers next to each other and I glanced at him as he pulled up his jockstrap then gym shorts.

"Jesus, don't you ever get fat?" I said.

"I'm fat now."

He pinched some tight flesh at the back of his waist.

"Bullshit," I said.

I rarely believed that Edith preferred my flabbier waist and smaller cock. But sometimes I believed it and, when I did, I felt wonderful.

"You smell like beer, man."

"I had a couple."

"I'll carry you in."

"Watch me go, baby."

On the clipped grass behind the gym we did push-ups and sit-ups and side-straddle hops, then started jogging on a blacktop road that would take us into the country.

"Five?" I said.

"I oughta do ten. Run off my Goddamn frustration."

"A page a day's not bad."

"Shit."

It was a hot, still day. We ran easily, stride for stride, past the houses where children waved and called to us and women looked up from their lawns or porches. I belched a couple of times and he grinned and punched my arm. Then the houses weren't close together anymore, the country was rolling and we climbed with it, pounding up the blacktop, not talking as we panted up hills, but going down or level we talked: "Goddamn, there's that lovely orchard." "Hold your breath, mothuh, here comes the hog stench." "Jesus, look at that cock pheasant." Then he was all right, he had forgotten his work, he was talking about shooting pheasants in Iowa, walking through frozen cornfields, the stalks lying brown in the sun. We ran to the top of a wooded hill two and a half miles from the gym and started back, still stride for stride: it would be that last two hundred yards when he'd kick. We ran downhill through sudden cool shade between thick woods; in fall the maple leaves turned orange and yellow and scarlet, and it was like peeping at God. Then on our left the woods stopped, and the hog smell lay on the air we breathed as we ran past the cleared low hills and the barn, chickens walking and pecking in front of it, then past the hog pen and the gray shingled house. A white dog came out from under the porch, barking; he had missed us on the way up, and now he chased us until he was almost at our legs, then we looked back at him and yelled "Hey white dog!" and he trotted away, looking back at us over his shoulder, sometimes stopping to turn and bark. Running has taught me that most dogs are cowards. But there used to be a Doberman pinscher living on this road: he loped after us so quietly that we never knew he was there until we heard his paws on the road and we'd yell and turn on him and crouch to fight, watching him decide whether he wanted to chew on us. He always looked very detached; that's what scared us. Then he'd trot back down the road, dignity intact; we were glad when last year he moved away. All the other dogs were like the white one at the farmhouse. Past the farm there were trees again, pines motionless in the still air, and then to the right, up a long green hill, the apple orchard.

"You're a little screwed up this summer," Hank said.

"Do I look it?"

"Yep."

"Should've taught summer school."

"Maybe not."

"Thought I wouldn't this year. Needed a break, I thought. Now I need the money."

"Need the work more."

"Bothers me. You'd think a man would do something. All that time. Read. Even think. Noble fucking pursuits. I run errands. Makes me wonder what'd happen if I didn't have to make a living."

"You'll never find out."

"Good. Probably mean suicide. Man ought to be able to live with himself. Idly. Without going mad. Women do it."

"Not so well."

"Work is strange."

"All there is."

"This. This is good."

"Best of all."

We stopped talking and right away my head was clear and serene, I was lungs and legs and arms, sun on my shoulders, sweat seeping through the red handkerchief around my forehead, dripping to my eyes, burning, and I flicked it away with a finger. At the houses near the college he moved ahead of me, a pace or two. I caught him and ran beside him for a while, then he kicked and was gone; I stretched my legs, arms swinging, breath in gasps, and watched his back ten then twenty yards away as he sprinted past the gym and slowed and walked, head going up and down for air, hands on his hips. I walked beside him. He didn't smile at beating me, but I felt a smile as though in his rushing breath.

"Competitive bastard," I said.

Then he smiled, and I believed then he knew I was making love with Edith and he was telling me he knew, saying, *You see Edith can't touch me and you can't either, what matters here is what matters to me and what matters to me is I will write and I will outrun you and I will outlive all of you too, and that's where I am.*

He didn't smoke, either. After the shower, a long time of hot water on the shoulders and legs and back muscles, then warm then cool, we drank Heineken draft in tall frosted mugs. We were alone in the bar, then a thin bald man came in carrying wrapped fish. Adjacent to the lounge was the dining room, where people ate fish from the sea and looked out at the dirty Merrimack; if you walked out of the lounge, across the hall, you went into the fish market. Before starting to drink, Hank and I had gone in and stood in the smell of fish, looking at the lobsters in a tank. I thought of Terry, but not with guilt; I had loved and run and sweated that out of me. I stood shifting my weight from one leg to another so I could feel the muscles, and I breathed my own clean smell with the salt water and fish, and resolved not to smoke for an hour, to keep the sharp sense of smell I always had after running restored innocence to my lungs; and I loved and wanted to embrace Edith and Hank and Terry, who in their separate ways made my life good. I felt at the border of some discovery, some way I could juggle my beloveds and save us all. But I didn't know what it was.

The man with the fish sat to our left, put his fish on the bar, and ordered a Schlitz. Betty was tending bar; she was a middle-aged blonde who had lived all her life in this town. She sat on a high stool near the taps and talked to the fish man. He looked at the Heineken sign over the mirror and asked if that was imported beer; she said yes it was. He said he'd never heard of it and she told him oh yes, it was quite popular, it sold ten to one here.

"Schlitz," Hank said, so they couldn't hear. "Some people like it better inside the horse."

"Did you see her before she left?"

"Yeah, I saw her." He gave me the foxy smile I got after he beat me running.

"To tell her goodbye?"

"Remember when I went to New York to see my agent?"

"Ah. I didn't know you could lie so well."

He held out two dollars to the woman.

"We'll have a round, and give my friend on the end a Heineken."

The fish man looked over at us.

"Well, thank you. Thank you very much."

"Beats that horse piss Schlitz is bottling."

Betty grinned. The fish man was embarrassed and he started to say something, maybe about Schlitz, then he just watched her filling the mug; when he tasted it, he said: "Well, by golly, it does have something to it, doesn't it?"

He and Betty talked about beer.

"I've never spent the night with anyone but Terry."

"Same old thing. Sleep, dream, wake up in the morning; piss; brush your teeth."

"Have a cigarette, lover."

"Hell no. Every time I want one I'm going to hold my breath for sixty seconds and think of the Marlboro man and the Winston assholes and all the rest of them, and that'll do it."

"All right, I won't till you do. But you won't be able to stand Edith. I quit once for three days and Terry smelled like an ash tray."

"Not *all* over. It was a good scene, though, in Boston. Hotel, took her to the airport in the morning, sad loving Bloody Marys. Then up in the air. Gone. Me watching the plane. Thinking of her looking down. Gone. Back to France. Maybe I'll go see her someday."

"You love her, huh?"

"I was fucking her, wasn't I?"

"I guess it was tough breaking it off, her right down in Boston."

"Jack." Grinning. "What made you think I broke it off? Why would I do a stupid thing like that?"

"Well, when the shit hit the fan Edith said you broke it off."

"Course she said that. It's what I told her."

"Have a beer, you sly son of a bitch."

I held up two fingers to Betty and she slid off the stool.

"Wait," the fish man said. "I'll get this one for the boys, and—lemmee see—" he pulled out a pocket watch from his khakis, peered down in the red-lighted dark "—yeah, Betty, I'll have one more, then I'll be getting home and put my fish in the oven." Hank cocked his head and watched him. "Don't get it started, the wife'll come home and start looking around, wanting to know where's the dinner."

"I don't blame her," Betty said.

"Oh sure. She works all day too, and I get home a little earlier, so I put the dinner on."

She gave us the beer and we raised our mugs to him and said thanks. He raised his, smiled, nodded, sipped. He picked up his fish, turning it in his hands, then lowered it to the bar.

"If I'm going to fry it I can start later, but when I'm baking like with this one, I need a little more time." He looked through the door at two men going into the dining room. "Someday I'm going to come in here and get me one of those fish platters. I'll be about ready for one, one of these days."

Hank was watching him.

"Did you ever want to leave with her?" I said.

"Why?"

"You said you loved her."

"I still do. You're nineteenth century, Jack."

"That's what you keep telling me."

"It's why you've been faithful so long. Your conscience is made for whores but you're too good for that, so you end up worse: monogamous."

"What's this made for whores shit?"

"The way it used to be. Man had his wife and kids. That was one life. And he had his whore. He knew which was which, see; he didn't get them confused. But now it's not that way: a man has a wife and a girlfriend and they get blurred, you see, he doesn't know where his emotional deposits are supposed to be. He's in love, for Christ sake. It's incongruous. He can't live with it, it's against everything he's supposed to feel, so naturally he takes some sort of action to get himself back to where he believes he's supposed to be. Devoted to one woman or some such shit. He does something stupid: either he breaks with the girl and tries to love only his wife, or he leaves the wife and marries the girl. If he does that, he'll be in the same shit in a few years, so he'll just have to keep marrying—"

"Or stay monogamous."

"Aye. Both of which are utter bullshit."

"And you think that's me."

"I think so. You're a good enough man not to fuck without feeling love, but if you're lucky enough for that to happen, then you feel confused and guilty because you think it means you don't love Terry."

I looked him in the eyes and said: "Have you been talking to my mistress?"

"Mistress pisstress. I've been talking to *you* for three years. I've been watching you watching women."

I believed him. If he knew about Edith and me, it was because he'd guessed: they had not been talking.

"Am I right?" he said.

"I worry about Terry, that's true. Just getting caught, I mean. I worry about love affairs too: the commitment, you know."

"What's commitment got to do with a love affair? A love affair is abandon. Put the joy back in fucking. It's got to be with a good woman, though. See, Jeanne knew. She *knew* I'd never leave Sharon and Edith. Commitment. That's with Terry. It doesn't even matter if you love Terry. You're married. What matters is not to hate each other, and to keep peace. The old Munich of marriage. You live with a wife, around a wife, not through her. She doesn't run with you and come drink beer with you, for Christ sake. Love, shit. Love the kids. Love the horny wives and the girls in short skirts. Love everyone, my son, and keep peace with your wife. Who, by the way, is not invulnerable to love either. What'll you do if that happens?"

"That's her business."

"All right. I believe you."

"You should; it's true."

"So why are *you* so uptight?"

"I'm not, man. What brought all this on, anyway?"

"I didn't like that look of awe in your face. When I said I spent the night with Jeanne, and never broke up with her. I love you, man. You shouldn't feel awe for *any*thing I do. I don't have more guts than you. I just respond more, that's all. I don't like seeing you cramped. Chicks *like* you, I *see* it, Jack. Hell, Edith gets juiced up every time you call the house. Other day Sharon said she wanted a jack-in-the-box, I thought Edith would fall off the couch laughing. Wicked laugh. Lying there laughing."

"Jack-in-the-box," I said, smiling, shaking my head.

He slapped my shoulder and we drained our mugs and left. "Take care," I said, passing the fish man. "See you boys." He raised his mug. Going out the door Hank turned left, toward the dining room; I waited while he talked to the hostess, nodding, smiling, reaching for his wallet. He gave her four dollars and waved off the change.

"What was that about?"

We walked to the front door and I started to go outside, but turned instead and went into the fish market.

"I bought him a fish platter."

I went to the lobster tank, and an old man in a long white apron came from behind the fish counter.

"He'll be gone before it's ready," I said.

"Told her to give him a beer too. He won't waste a beer. By the time he's done, there it'll be."

"All right: cool." I turned to the old man. "How much are you getting for lobsters?"

"As much as we can," winking, laughing, then a wheeze and a cough.

The chicken lobsters were a dollar seventy-nine a pound; she loved to eat, she'd say *mmmm,* sucking the claws, splitting open the tail. I asked for two and didn't watch him weigh them or ring them up. I couldn't; it was like when they call you in to pay for your crime: your father, your boss: the old humiliation of chilled ass and quickened heart. They were four dollars and fifty-two cents. I did not think about the bank balance until I bought the wine. On the way to Hank's I stopped at the liquor store and bought Pinot Chardonnay, Paul Masson: two-fifty. Seven dollars. Two on beer. Nine. I went next door into the A&P; Hank was waiting in the car, listening to the Red Sox in a twi-nighter. Eight at the service station: seventeen. I bought half pints of strawberry, chocolate, and vanilla ice cream, a bunch of bananas, a can of chocolate syrup, a jar of cherries, a pressurized can of whipped cream, but no nuts, there were only cocktail nuts, salted things. My children didn't know what a banana split was; I had told them the other day how the boys and I used to eat them after a movie, and if I could spend seven on Terry and me then certainly they deserved—was love no more than guilt? I have a girl so Terry should have a lover. We get lobster and Pinot Chardonnay so the kids should have this junk. The banana splits cost four dollars and twenty-eight cents. A twenty-one-dollar day, only two on something I wanted: the beer with Hank. Now I could slide back the door in my mind, look at the bank balance written there: forty-three dollars and eighty cents. I had glanced at it yesterday, I hadn't really wanted to see, but it sprang like a snake and got in my head and stayed there. Eight days before payday and a week's groceries still to buy. What now? Stop drinking, Stop smoking? So we could sit stiff and tight-faced night after night, chewing blades of grass, watching the food and milk and gas all going down down down. We had tried that once, for six weeks: nothing but red wine, a dollar and a quarter a half gallon. Nothing happened. The bourbon and gin and beer money never turned up; it jumped into the cash register at the supermarket, the service stations, it went to the utilities and telephone gangs, the landlord, it paid for repairs on a bad car, it went to people who sold bad shoes to children and to people who sold worse toys. It just kept going, and days before payday it was gone; when the last milk carton was empty, Terry put powdered milk in it and didn't fool the kids, and every day there was more space in the refrigerator and cupboard, and each day I woke wanting payday to come and hating the trap I was in: afraid of death and therefore resisting the passage of time, yet now having to wish for it.

"I spent twenty-one bucks today. What's the score?"

"Sox, 2–1. Top of the third. You broke?"

There were driving lanes in the big parking lot, but people drove through the parking spaces too; they drove in circles, triangles, squares, trapezoids, and other geometric figures, and I had to look in all directions at once.

"Not for a couple of days."

"Here." He took out his wallet.

"No, man. That's not why I said that."

"Jesus, I know that. How much you need?"

"I can't."

"Come on. Some day you'll come through for me."

"I need about forty *bucks,* man. I'll go to the bank."

He was holding out two twenties and Reggie Smith was catching a fly ball on the warning path.

"Edith got a check from Winnetka."

"It won't last for shit if you support me too." Thinking of the imported beer, the babysitter.

"We needed two hundred, so she asked for three and her mother sent five."

"*Five?* No shit: you mean there are people in the world who can write a check for five hundred dollars and not break into tears? I'll pay it back a little at a time, okay?"

"Sure. Buy me a bottle some time. Buy me one round of *beer* some time, you cheap cocksucker."

At his house he said to come in for a quick one. I was worried about the ice cream but he reached back and took it from the bag, so I followed him in. She was at the stove. She smiled at us over her shoulder; she had changed her shorts and shirt and had a red ribbon in her black hair. She looked as if she'd changed souls. She stirred a pot of something and looked in the oven while Hank put up the ice cream and opened two ales and a beer. Then she sat at the table and asked Hank for a cigarette.

"I quit."

"Good luck, baby."

I gave her one of mine, and took one too.

"Oh, a Lucky," she said.

"See what you did. As long as he was with me he didn't smoke."

"I like to corrupt."

"You looked like a girl from the forties just then," I said. "Or early fifties. Taking the tobacco off your tongue. Except their fingernails were painted. You'd see that red fingernail moving down their tongues, and I used to love watching them."

"Why?" Hank said.

"I don't know. I think it was watching a woman being sensual. You were a little hard on that fish man."

"I know. Didn't seem so funny once I got in the car."

"What fish man?"

I watched her listen to the story and I thought how she didn't know Hank and Jeanne hadn't ended till she went back to France. And whether he guessed or not he could never know what she was like out there on the blanket. Now she was just an attentive young wife, listening to her husband, her eyes going from him to Sharon with her coloring book on the floor. Still they had a marriage. He was talking to her about his day. She had got that money for them. Her dinner smelled good, and her house was clean. I felt it was my house too, and I remembered what I was like before I loved her, during that long time when I wasn't in love; I need to be in love, I know it is called romantic, it isn't what they call realistic, I am supposed to settle into the steady seasons, the ticking Baby Bens, of marriage.

"Hank, that was cruel."

"I know. But he had no balls. Cooking, for Christ sake."

At my back door I smelled spaghetti sauce. She was ironing in the kitchen and I looked past her at the black iron skillet of sauce on the stove. I didn't give her a chance to ask me how the day had been; I saw the question in her face as she looked up from ironing and reached for her drink at the end of the ironing board. Edith had not been drinking when Hank and I got there, and I wondered if other wives drank before their husbands came home.

"This guy gave me some lobsters," I said, as the screen door shut behind me. "I saved his daughter from drowning and he gave me all he had."

"Oh let me *see.*"

"She hurried around the ironing board and took the bag and looked in. I put the wine in the freezer compartment.

"Wine too?"

"Sure. And some stuff for the kids."

I gave her the supermarket bag.

"Oh look," peering in, taking out the jar of cherries, the whipped cream, the chocolate syrup. "What a nice daddy."

She took the ironed clothes on hangers upstairs, then put the ironing board and basket of waiting clothes in the wash room. I got the ball game on the radio and sat at the kitchen table with the *Boston Globe* while she looked for her big pot and found it and put it on the stove. I skimmed the news stories I couldn't believe while I told her Hank had written only a page, he had quit smoking, we had had a good run, drunk some beer, and he had loaned me forty dollars. She was happy about the money, but she said very seriously we must be sure to pay him back, ten dollars a payday till it was done. All this time I was following the ball game and getting through the news about Nixon and the war, getting to those stories I could believe: a man winning a tobacco spitting contest; a woman and her son drowning, taken into the sea by waves on the coast of Maine; the baseball news. I could also believe all stories about evil. I was accustomed to lies from the government and the press, and I never believed them when they spoke with hope or comfort. So I believed all stories of lies, atrocity, and corruption, for they seemed to be the truth that I was rarely told and that I was waiting for. I knew that my vision was as distorted as the vision of those who lied, but I saw no way out. When I finished the paper, I started to tell Terry about the fish man, but with the first word already shaping my lips, I stopped.

In a marriage there are all sorts of lies whose malignancy slowly kills everything, and that day I was running the gamut from the outright lie of adultery to the careful selectivity which comes when there are things that two people can no longer talk about. It is hard to say which kills faster but I would guess selectivity, because it is a surrender: you avoid touching wounds and therefore avoid touching the heart. If I told her the story, she would see it as a devious way of getting at her: the man's cooking would be the part of me she smothered; Hank's buying the seafood platter would be my rebellion. And she would be right. So I treated our disease with aspirins, I weaved my conversation around us, and all the time I knew with a taste of despair that I was stuck forever with this easy, lying pose; that with the decay of years I had slipped gradually into it, as into death, and that now at the end of those years and the beginning of all the years to come I had lost all dedication to honesty between us. Yet sometimes when I was alone and away from the house, always for this to happen I had to be away from the house, driving perhaps on a day of sunlight and green trees and rolling meadows, I would hear a song from another time and I could weep (but did not) for the time when I loved her every day and came up the walk in the afternoons happy to see her, days when I never had to think before I spoke. As we ate lobsters and drank wine we listened to the ball game.

And later, after the spaghetti dinner that wasn't eaten, we made love. We had watched the children, who were impatient for banana splits and so ate only a little and that quickly, sucking spaghetti, spearing meatballs, their eyes returning again and again to the door of the freezer compartment, to Terry slicing bananas, punching open the can of chocolate syrup. They were like men late for work eyeing the clock behind a lunch counter. They loved the banana splits, ate till I feared for their stomachs, then I went with a book to the living room couch, and Terry put the meatballs and spaghetti sauce in the refrigerator to be warmed again another day.

When she got into bed I pretended to be asleep but she touched my chest and spoke my name until I looked at her.

"I went a little crazy last night," she said. "I'm sorry."

"Okay."

"I shouldn't have got drunk."

She found my hand and held it.

"Forget it," I said.

"I've got to grow up."

"Who ever told you grown-ups weren't violent?"

"Not with their husbands."

"Read the papers. Women murder their husbands."

"Not people like us."

"Sailors' wives, is that it? Construction workers?"

"I don't mean that."

"Maybe some people have enough money so they don't have to kill each other. You can have separate lives then, when things go bad. You don't have to sweat over your beer in the same hot kitchen: watching her fat ass under wilted blue cotton, her dripping face and damp straight hair. Pretty soon somebody picks up a hammer and goes to it. Did Hank make a pass?"

"Yes."

"He did?"

"I said yes."

"Well?"

"Well what."

"What did he do?"

"None of your business."

"All right, then: what did *you* do?"

"Nothing."

"Come on."

"He tried to kiss me on the porch, so I went inside."

"Where?" Grinning at her. "Here?"

"To the *kit*chen. To get a beer."

"And he followed you in and—"

"Said he loved me and kissed me and said he didn't love Edith. Then I felt dirty and we went outside and sat on the front steps."

"Dirty. Because he said that about Edith?"

"Yes. She's a sweet girl and she doesn't deserve that, and I don't want any part of it."

"But until he said that, you felt all right."

"We can stop this now. Or do you want to know whether his nose was to the left or right of mine?"

"Do you remember?"

"We were lying on the floor and he was on my right, so I'd say his nose was to the left of mine."

"Lying on the floor, huh? Goodness."

"I'd squatted down to get a beer from—Oh shut up."

"I was only teasing."

"You were doing more than that. You're glad he kissed me."

"Let's say I'm not disturbed."

"Well I am."

She got out of bed for a cigarette and when she came back I pretended to be asleep and listened to her smoking deeply beside me. Then she put out the cigarette and started touching me, the old lust on quiet signal, and I mounted her, thrusting the sound of bedsprings into the still summer night, not a word between us, only breath and the other sound: and I remembered newly married one morning she was holding a can of frozen orange juice over a pitcher and the sound of its slow descent out of the can drove us back to bed. I could feel her getting close but I still was far away, and I opened my eyes: hers were closed. I shut mine and saw Edith this afternoon *oh love;* then I thought *she is thinking of Hank, behind those closed eyes her skull is an adulterous room,* and now he was here too and he had given me the forty dollars and it was Hank, not I, Hank who was juggling us all, who would save us, and now we came, Hank and Terry and Edith and me, and I said, "Goodnight, love," and rolled over and slept.

2

ON A MOONLIT summer night, in a cemetery six blocks from my house, lying perhaps among the bones of old whaling men, in the shadow of a pedestaled eight-foot bronze angel, Hank made love to my red-haired wife.

At midnight I had left them on the front porch. Edith had the flu, and Hank had come over late for a nightcap; it was the day after payday and I gave him ten dollars which he didn't want to take. We drank on the front porch, but I was tired and I watched them talking about books and movies, then I went to bed, their voices coming like an electric train around the corner of the house, through the screen of my open window. I slept. When I woke my heart was fast before I knew what it knew. I lay in silence louder than their voices had been, and listened for the creak of floor under a step, the click of her Zippo, a whisper before it died in the air. But there was only silence touching my flesh, so they weren't in the house; unless making love in the den or living room they had heard my heart when I woke and now they were locked in sculpted love waiting for me to go back to sleep. Or perhaps they were in the yard and if I went outside I would turn a corner of the house and smack into the sight of her splayed white legs under the moon and the white circle of his wedging ass.

The clock's luminous dial was too moonlit to work: with taut stealth I moved across the bed, onto Terry's side, and took the clock from the bedside table: two-twenty. I waited another ten minutes, each pale gray moonlit moment edged with expectancy, until I was certain it was emptiness I heard, not their silence. And if indeed they were listening, I would cast the burden of cunning on them: I rolled over and dropped my feet thumping to the floor, and walked to the bathroom next to my room and turned on the light. I flushed the toilet, then went through the other door, into the kitchen, the dining room, the living room, and stepped onto the front porch. The night was cool and I shivered, standing in my T-shirt so white if they were watching. His car was parked in front. Their glasses were on the steps. I picked them up: lime and gin-smelling water. Then I went to bed and waited, and I saw them under the willow tree in the backyard, the branches hanging almost to the grass, and I asked myself and yes, I said, I want the horns; plant them, Hank, plant them. I wanted lovely Edith now there with me and twice I picked up the phone and once dialed three numbers, but she would be asleep with her fever and there was nothing really to tell yet, I didn't really know yet, and after that I lay in bed, quick-hearted and alert, and waited and smoked.

At ten minutes after three he started his car. I ran tiptoeing to the living room window as his car slowly left the curb and Terry stood on the sidewalk, smoking; she lifted a hand, waving as Hank drove down the street. He blinked his interior light, but I couldn't see him, then his car was dark, just tail lights again, and then he was gone and the street was quiet. She stood smoking. When she flicked the cigarette in the street and started up the walk, I ran back to the bedroom. She came in and crossed the living room, into the dining room and bathroom. She stayed there a while: water ran, the toilet flushed, water ran again. Then in the kitchen she popped open a beer and went to the living room; her lighter clicked, scraped, clicked shut. When she finished the beer she plunked it down on the coffee table and came into the bedroom.

"Where've you been?"

She got out of her clothes and dropped them on the floor, and lies cracked her voice: "I woke up and couldn't get back to sleep so I went out for a walk."

She went naked to the living room and came back shaking a cigarette from her pack and lit it and got into bed.

"Terry."

"What."

"You don't have to tell me that. I woke up at two-twenty." She drew on her cigarette. Still she had not looked at me.

"You bastard. Did you ever go to sleep?"

"Yes."

"I wish I could believe that."

"I was tired."

"You could've brought me to bed."

"You could've come with me."

She threw back the sheet and blanket and got out of bed and went fast, pale skin and flopping hair, out of the room. She came back with a beer and got into bed and covered up and bent the pillow under her head so she could drink.

"I'm lonely, that's why. I'm a woman, I'm sorry, I can't be anything else, and I need to be told that and I need to be made love to, you don't make love with me anymore, you fuck me; I sat on the steps with him and he held my hand and listened to me talk about this shitty marriage because all you ever see is the house, you don't see me, and he said let's go see the bronze angel, we've never seen it in the dark, and I was happy when he said that and I was happy making love—"

So she had really done it, and I lay there feeling her wash down me, from my throat, down my chest, my legs, then gone like surf from the sea, cold like the sea.

"—and I lay afterward looking up at her wings and for the first time since leaving the porch I thought of you and for a moment under her wings I hated you for bringing me to this. Then that went away. I wanted to go home and seal up the split between us, like gluing this shitty old furniture, I wanted to clap my hands for Tinker Bell, do something profound and magic that would bring us back the way we used to be, when we were happy. When you loved me and when I never would have made love with someone else. And all the way walking home I wanted to hurry and be with you, here in this bed in this house with my husband and children where I belong. And right now I love you I think more than I have for years but I'm angry, Jack, way down in my blood I'm angry because you set this up in all kinds of ways, you wanted it to happen and now it has and now I don't know what else will happen, because it's not ended, making love is never ended—"

"Are you seeing him again?"

"No."

"Then it's ended."

"Do you think making love is like *smo*king, for Christ sake? That if you quit it's *o*ver? It's not just the act. What's wrong with you—it's feeling, it's—"

She drank, then sat up and drank again, head back for a long swallow, then she lit a cigarette from the one she was smoking.

"It's what," I said.

"Promises."

"You promised to see him again?"

"I didn't say anything. Opening my legs is a promise."

"But he must have said something."

"I wish you could hear your voice right now, the way it was just then, I wish I had it taped and I'd play it for you till you went to a shrink to find out why your voice just now was so Goddamn oily. You *like* this. You *like* it. Well hear: it took us a long time to get to the cemetery because we kept stopping to kiss and when we did walk it was slow because we had our arms around each other and his hand was on my tit all the time and when we got to the angel we didn't look at her, not once, we undressed and got down on the ground and we fucked, Jack, we fucked like mad, and I was so hot I came before he did; the second time I was on top and it was long and slow and I told him I loved him and you, you poor man, you sick cuckold, look at your face—Jesus Christ, what am I married to?"

"Will you stop?"

"Why should I? You ought to be knocking my teeth out now. But not you. You want to watch us. Is that it? Is that what you want, Jack?"

I sat up and was swinging at her but stopped even before she saw it coming, and my hand opened and I pointed at her eyes, the finger close, so close, and I wanted to gouge with it, to hit, to strangle, the finger quivering now as I tried not to shout beneath the children's rooms, my voice hoarse and constricted in my throat: "Terry, you fuck who you want and when you want and where you want but do not do *not* give me any of your half-ass insights into the soul of a man you've never understood."

Then she was laughing, a true laugh at first or at least a smile, but she lay with her head back on the pillow, throat arched, her shoulders and breasts shaking, and prolonged it, forced it cracking into the air, withering my tense arm, and I got out of bed so I would not even touch the sheet she lay on.

"Oh God: half-ass insights into the—what? The soul of a man I've never understood? Oh my. You poor baby, and it's so simple. You think you're a swinger, free love, I can fuck whoever I want, oh my how you talk and talk and talk and it all comes down to that one little flaw you won't admit: you're a pervert, Jack. You need help. And I'm sorry, I really am, but there's nothing I

can do about it. I made love with Hank tonight and he wants to
see me tomorrow—or this afternoon really—and when I finish
this beer I'm going to sleep because the kids'll be up soon and
you're not known for getting them breakfast—"

"I'll do it. Forget it, I'll do it."

"Fine. Do that. That's one thing you can do. You can't help
me with my other problem any more than I can help you with
yours. See, I'm a big girl now and I knew what I was doing tonight and I don't know if I can very well say tomorrow—
today—well gee Hank that was last night but this is now and gee
I just don't want to anymore. I mean even you with all your
progressive and liberal ideas will have to admit that even adultery
has its morality, that one can cop out on that too. So I have
things to figure out."

"Yes." I started leaving the room. "Do what you can."

"Oh, that's good." I stopped at the door but didn't look back.
"That's what all my good existential friends say whenever I want
advice: Just do what you can. Well, I will, Jack, I will."

I went to the kitchen and drank an ale and when Terry was
asleep I went to bed.

Next morning I woke first, alert and excited, though I had
slept only four hours. Everything was quiet except birds. I got up
and dressed, watching Terry asleep on her back, mouth open; I
stepped over her clothes on the floor, and going through the living room picked up her beer can and brought it to the kitchen. In
the silence I could feel the children sleeping upstairs, as if their
breathing caressed me. I went outside: the morning was sun and
blue and cool air. I drove to a small grocery store and bought a
Globe and cigarettes. Then I drove to a service station with a pay
phone and parked but didn't get out of the car. It was only five
minutes of nine on a Sunday morning, and they would be
asleep. Or certainly Hank would. But maybe she wouldn't, and I
drove to their street: all the houses looked quiet, theirs did too,
and I went past, then turned around in a driveway and started
back, believing I would go on by; then I stopped and walked up

their driveway to the back door and there she was in the dim kitchen away from the sun, surprised, turning to me in her short nightgown, a happy smile as she came to the door and pushed it gently so the latch was quiet. I stepped in and she was holding me tight, and I stroked her soft brushed hair and breathed her toothpaste and soap.

"Are you all right now?"

"The fever's gone. Was it fun last night?"

"They made love."

She moved her head back to look at me and say, "Really?"; then she was at my cheek again. "She told you?"

"She didn't want to, but I knew, I had waked up. They went to the bronze angel."

"Are you jealous?"

"No." She was holding me, rubbing her cheek on my chest. Her kitchen was clean. "They might see each other today. If they do, we can get together."

"We'll have the kids and they'll have the cars."

"Shit."

Water started boiling; she let me go and turned off the fire. Then she was back.

"How are you?" I said.

"Still weak, that's all. I told you the fever's gone."

"I mean about them."

"Fine. I think it's fine. He'll be asleep for a long time."

"He might wake up."

"We'd hear him, we'd be right under the bedroom. He always goes to the bathroom first."

"Sharon," I said.

"She'll sleep too."

We started for the door; she stopped and put instant coffee in two cups and poured water. Then we crept through the house to the guest room.

When I left, after drinking coffee that was still warm enough, Sharon was coming downstairs. Before getting into the car I squinted up at the bedroom where Hank slept.

At home I didn't go in; I sat on the back steps to read the sports page. I could smell Terry's cigarette, then I heard her moving and she came outside in her robe, hair uncombed, and sat beside me and put a hand on my shoulder. I nearly flinched.

"I was scared," she said. "When I woke up and you weren't there. I thought you had left."

"I did. To get cigarettes and a paper."

"What took so long?"

"Driving around looking at the bright new morning."

"Is it?"

I looked up from the paper and waved a hand at the trees and rooftops and sky.

"Blink your eyes and look at it."

"Your beard's beautiful in the sun. It has some blond and red in it."

"I got that from you and the kids."

"I thought you had left me."

"Why should I?"

"What I said."

"That's night talk."

"I know it. Just as long as you know it. I was being defensive because I was scared and when I'm scared I get vicious."

"Why were you scared?"

"Because I have a lover."

"Is that what you've decided?"

"I haven't decided anything. I made love with Hank so I have a lover, no matter what I do about it. You really don't care?"

She had the right word: care. So I must get her away from that. The way to hunt a deer is not to let him know you're alive.

"I care about you. It's monogamy I don't care about."

"You've said that for years. I've waked up with that whispering to me for years. But a long time ago you weren't that way."

"A long time ago I wasn't a lot of ways."

"I couldn't let you do what I'm doing."

"Are you doing anything?"

"I don't know yet."

"But you want to."

"If I knew that I'd know something."

"Why don't you know it? I know it."

"How?"

Her hand was still on my arm; I was scanning box scores.

"You stayed out there with him because you wanted to and I think you came home planning to see him today and tomorrow and tomorrow and tomorrow, but when you found out I knew about it then it got too sticky. Just too bloody sticky. To all in one night leave monogamy and then have to carry it out with your husband knowing about it, staying with the kids while you—"

"Oh stop," her voice pleading, her fingers tightening on my shoulder. "Shhh, stop."

"Isn't that so?"

"I don't know. I mean, sure I wanted to, and I like Hank very much; in a way I love him, and I love you and nothing's changed that, what's with Hank is—" she squeezed my shoulder again and looking at the paper I heard the fake smile in her voice "— it's friendly lust, that's all. But it might not be marriage, living like this."

"We're married. You and I are married. So it has to be marriage."

"It might not be for long."

"I wish Boston were a National League town. You mean you're afraid you'll run off with him?"

"*No. My God* no. There are all sorts of ways for a marriage not to be a marriage."

"You're just afraid because it's new."

"If I kept on with Hank you'd want a girl. You'd feel justified then. Maybe even with Edith, and wouldn't *that* be a horror."

"Seems strange to me that while you're deciding whether or not to make love with a man you call your lover, you're thinking most about what *I'll* do."

"That's not strange. You're my husband."

"It is strange, and it's beneath you. This is between you and Hank, not me."

She took a pack of cigarettes from the carton I'd bought and sat smoking while I read.

"Are you hungry?" she said.

"Yes."

"Pancakes and eggs?"

"Buckwheat. Are the kids up?"

"No. I think I'll take them to the beach today. Do you want to go?"

"I want to watch the game."

"I think I'll tell him no."

"Is that what you want?"

"I don't know. I'm just scared."

"Because I know about it?"

"Because there's something to know."

She went inside. I read the batting averages and pitching records, then the rest of the paper, listening to her washing last night's pots and dishes. Then she started cooking bacon and I sat waiting, smelling and listening to the bacon, until I heard Natasha and Sean coming downstairs. We ate for a long time, then Terry lit a cigarette and said, "Well," and went to the bedroom and shut both doors. I could hear her voice, but that was all. Natasha and Sean were upstairs getting dressed; when Terry came back to the kitchen she went to the foot of the stairs and called them and said to put on bathing suits. "We're going to the beach!"

"The beach!" they said. "The beach!"

"How did you get it done?" I said.

"He answered. He'd said he would. I asked how Edith was and he told me."

"That was a signal?"

"Yes."

"Poor Hank. And what if you had decided to see him?"

"I wouldn't have called."

She had been smoking a lot all morning. Now she started making a Bloody Mary.

"Do you want one?"

"No. How's Edith?"

"All right. Her fever's gone."

For some years now I have been spiritually allergic to the words husband and wife. When I read or hear husband I see a grimly serene man in a station wagon; he is driving his loud family on a Sunday afternoon. They will end with ice cream, sticky car seats, weariness, and ill tempers. In his youth he had the virtues of madness: rage and passion and generosity. Now he gets a damp sponge from the kitchen and wipes dried ice cream from his seat covers. He longs for the company of loud and ribald men, he would like to drink bourbon and fight in a bar, steal a pretty young girl and love her through the night. When someone says wife I see the confident, possessive, and amused face of a woman in her kitchen; among bright curtains and walls and the smell of hot grease she offers her husband a kiss as he returns from the day sober, paunchy, on his way to some nebulous goal that began as love, changed through marriage to affluence, is now changing to respectable survival. She is wearing a new dress. From her scheming heart his balls hang like a trophy taken in battle from a young hero long dead.

I wheezed again with this allergy as I stood on the lawn and watched Terry and Natasha and Sean drive off to Plum Island. They had a picnic basket, a Styrofoam cooler of soft drinks and beer, a beach bag of cigarettes and towels, and a blanket. They left in a car that needed replacing. This morning's lovely air was now rent apart by the sounds of power mowers. One was across the street, two blocks down to the right; the man behind it wore a T-shirt and shorts and was bald. The one to the left was on my side of the street, behind shrubs, and I only saw him when he got to the very front of his lawn, turned, and started back. I sat on the grass and chewed a blade of it and watched the bald man. I wondered what he was thinking. Then I thought he must be thinking nothing at all. For if he thought, he might cut off the engine that was mowing his lawn and go into the garage and jam the garden shears into his throat.

Yet once in a while you saw them: they sat in restaurants, these old couples of twenty and twenty-five and thirty years, and looked at each other with affection, and above all they talked. They were always a wonder to see, and when I saw them I tried to hear what they said. Usually it was pleasant small talk: aging sailors speaking in signals and a language they have understood forever. If I looked at most couples with scorn and despair, I watched these others as mystified as if I had come across a happy tiger in a zoo; and I watched them with envy. *It can be faked,* Hank said once. We were in a bar. The afternoon bartender had just finished work for the day, his wife was waiting for him in a booth, and they had two drinks and talked; once they laughed aloud. *There are two kinds of people,* Hank said. *The unhappy ones who look it and the unhappy ones who don't.*

Now I went inside and upstairs and turned on the ball game. Hank's marriage wasn't a grave because Hank wasn't dead; he used his marriage as a center and he moved out from it on azimuths of madness and when he was tired he came back. While Edith held to the center she had been hurt, and for a few days when she started guessing that Hank was not faithful I didn't like being with them: you could smell the poison on their breaths, feel the tiny arrows flying between them. Now she had a separate life too and she came home and they sat in the kitchen with their secrets that were keeping them alive, and they were friendly and teasing again. It was as simple as that and all it required was to rid both people of jealousy and of the conviction that being friendly parents and being lovers were the same. Hank and Edith knew it, and I knew it. I had waked happy, believing Terry knew it too, and now after her one night she was at the beach with the children, and we were husband and wife again. I sat watching the game. Far off, as though from the streets behind the black and white ball park, I could hear the power mowers.

After dinner Terry came to the living room where I was reading on the couch. Upstairs the children were watching television.

"Hank came to the beach."

"He found you? On a hot Sunday at Plum Island? My God, the man's in love."

"He says he is."

"Really?"

"Oh, I know it's just talk, it's just a line—he wants to see me tonight." She was smoking. "I wish I hadn't last night. But I did and it doesn't seem really right to say yes and then next morning say no, I mean it's not like I was drunk or something. I knew what I was doing. But I'm scared, Jack." She sat on the couch; I moved to make room, and she took my hand. "Look at me. What do you *really* think? Or really feel. You're not scared of this? People screwing other people?"

"No, I'm not scared."

"Then why am I? When I'm the one who—Jesus."

"What did you feel at the beach?"

"Guilty. Watching my children and talking to him."

"Did you tell him you'd meet him?"

She lowered her eyes and said, "Yes."

"And now you don't feel like it because it's embarrassing to leave the house when I know where you're going. If I didn't know, you'd have got out with some excuse. Does Hank know that I know?"

"I didn't tell him. It just seemed too much, when we're all together. Won't you feel strange? When you see him tomorrow?"

"I don't think so. What are you going to do tonight?"

"I'm going to think about it."

She went to the kitchen. I listened to her washing the dishes: she worked very slowly, the sounds of running water and the dull clatter of plate against plate as she put them in the drainer coming farther and farther apart so that I guessed (and rightly) she had done less than half the dishes when I heard her quickly cross the floor and go into the bathroom. She showered fast, she must have been late, then she opened the bathroom door to let the steam out. Late or not, of course she spent a long while now with the tubes and brushes and small bottles of her beauty, which was natural anyway and good, but when people came over or we went out she worked on it. I had always resented that: if a car pulled up in front of the house she fled to the bathroom and gave whoever it was a prettier face than she gave me. But I thought, too, that she gave it to herself. She closed the bathroom closet, ran the lavatory tap a final time, and came out briskly into the bedroom; lying propped on the couch, I looked over the Tolstoy book; she had a towel around her, and I watched her circling the bed, to our closet. She was careful not to look at me. On the way to the mirror she would have to face me or turn her head; so I raised the book and read while she pushed aside hangered dresses, paused, then chose something. I felt her glance as she crossed the room to the full-length mirror. I tried to read, listening to the snapping of the brassiere, the dress slipping over her head and down her body, and the brush strokes on her hair. Then I raised my eyes as she stepped into the living room wearing her yellow dress and small shiny yellow shoes, her hair long and soft, and behind the yellow at her shoulders it was lovely. When I looked at her she opened her purse and dropped in a fresh pack of cigarettes, watching it fall. She had drawn green on her eyelids.

"Well—" she said.

"All right."

"I'll do the dishes when I get back."

"No sweat."

She looked at me, her eyes bright with ambivalence: love or affection or perhaps only nostalgia and, cutting through that tenderness, an edge of hatred. Maybe she too knew the marriage was forever changed and she blamed me; or maybe it wasn't the marriage at all but herself she worried about, and she was going out now into the night, loosed from her moorings, and she saw me as the man with the axe who had cut her adrift onto the moonless bay. My face was hot. She turned abruptly and went upstairs and I listened to her voice with the children. She lingered. Then she came downstairs and called to me from the kitchen: "The movie should be over around eleven." I read again. I could have been reading words in Latin. Then the screen opened and she was back in the kitchen, my heart dropping a long way; she went through the bathroom into the bedroom, the car keys jingled as she swept them from the dresser, and my heart rose and she was gone. After a while I was able to read and

I turned back the pages I had read without reading; I read for twenty minutes until I was sure Hank was gone too, then I went to the bedroom and phoned Edith.

" 'Ivan Ilyitch's life was most simple and most ordinary and therefore most terrible.' "

"Who said that?"

She wasn't literary but that didn't matter; I loved her for that too and anyway I didn't know what did matter with a woman except to find one who was clean and peaceful and affectionate and then love her.

"Tolstoy. Our lives aren't so simple and ordinary."

"Is she gone too?"

"A movie. That's what she tells me so the kids can hear repeated what she told them. A new twist to the old lying collusion of husband and wife against their children. But she also told me the truth."

"He's going to see some Western. He says they relax him and help him write next day. I hate Westerns."

"I love them. There's one on the tube tonight and I'll watch it with the kids."

"We'll have to do something about these cars."

"Maybe a car pool of sorts."

"Dear Mother, please buy me a car so I can see my lover while Hank sees his."

"Is she really that rich?"

"She's that rich. I miss you."

"Tomorrow. Eleven?"

"I'll go shopping."

"I'll go to the library."

"You use that too much. Someday she'll walk over and see if you're there."

"She's too lazy. Anyway, if things keep on like this maybe I can stop making excuses."

"Don't count on it."

"Being a cuckold's all right, but it's boring. Get a sitter and take a taxi."

"Go watch the movie with your children."

Terry hadn't put her beauty things away; they were on the lavatory and the toilet tank, and I replaced tops on bottles and put all of it into the cabinet. I went to the foot of the stairs and called.

"What!" When their voices were raised they sounded alike; I decided it was Sean.

"Turn to Channel Seven!"

"What's on!"

"Cowbodys, man! Tough hombre cowboys!"

"Cowboys! Can we watch it!"

"Right!"

"All of it!"

"Yeah. All of it!"

"Are you gonna watch it!"

"I am! I'll be up in a while!"

I got a pot out of the dishwater and washed it for popcorn. Once Sean called down that it had started and I said I knew, I knew, I could hear the horses' hooves and I'd be up evermore ricky-tick. There were Cokes hidden in the cupboard so the kids wouldn't drink them all in one day. I poured them over ice and opened a tall bottle of Pickwick ale and got a beer mug and brought everything up on a tray.

"Hey neat-o," Natasha said.

"Popcorn!"

I pulled the coffee table in front of the couch and put the tray on it.

"Sit between us," Natasha said.

Sean hugged me when I sat down.

"We got a good Daddy."

"Now Mom's watching a movie and we're watching a movie," Natasha said.

"What movie did Momma go to?"

"I believe a Western."

"You didn't want to go?"

"Nope. I wanted to see this one. He's going to hit that guy soon."

"Which guy?"

"The fat mean one."

"How do you know?"

"Because if he doesn't hit him we won't be happy."

When the movie was over, I tucked them in and kissed them and went downstairs to Tolstoy and the couch; as I read I kept glancing at my watch and at midnight I thought how she never uses the seat belt, no matter how many times and how graphically and ominously I tell her. I kept reading and I remembered though trying not to Leanard in Michigan: he had married young and outgrown his wife and he hated her. When he was drunk, he used to say Nobody hates his wife as much as I hate mine. And one night drinking beer—he was a big weight-lifting man and drank beer like no one I've ever known—he said I've thought of a way a man can kill his wife. You take her for a ride, you see, and you have a crash helmet with you and it's just resting there on the seat between you, she wonders what it's there for, but the dumb bitch won't say anything, she won't say anything about anything and the world can fall down and still she'll just blink her Goddamn dumb eyes and stare and never let you know if there's anything burning behind them, then you get out on some quiet straight country highway and put that son of a bitch on your head and unbuckle her seat belt and hold onto that son of a bitch and floorboard into a telephone pole and throw the crash helmet way the fuck out into the field—

I wished the movie hadn't ended and I was still upstairs watching it with the children; the TV room was a good room to be in, the cleanest in the house because it was nearly bare: a couch, two canvas deck chairs, the TV, and a coffee table. A beach ball and some toy trucks and cars were on the floor. The secret was not having much life in the room. It was living that defeated Terry: the rooms where we slept and ate and the living room and dishes and our clothes. The problem was a simple one which could be solved with money, but I would never make enough so that I could pay someone to do Terry's work. So there was no solution. Two years ago Terry had pneumonia and was in the hospital for a week. Natasha and Sean and I did well. Everyone made his own bed and washed his own plate and glass and silver, and we took turns with pots; every day I washed clothes, folded them as soon as they were dry, and put them away; twice that week I vacuumed the house. All this took little time and I never felt harried. When Terry came home, I turned over the house to her again, and the children stopped making their beds and washing their dishes, though I'd told her how good they had been. We could do that again now, and I could even have my own laundry bag and put my things in it every night, wash my clothes once a week and wash my own dishes and take turns with the pots, I could work in the house as though I lived with another man. But I wouldn't do it. If Terry had always kept house and was keeping it now, then I could help her without losing and I would do it. But not the way she was now.

In Michigan when I was in graduate school, she found us an old farmhouse in the country for a hundred a month, and for a while she was excited, I'd come home and find the furniture rearranged, and one afternoon she painted the bathroom orange. The landlord had paid for the paint, and for two buckets of yellow for the kitchen; he was an old farmer, he lived down the dirt road from us, he liked Terry, and he told her when she finished the kitchen he'd buy paint for the other rooms. Whatever colors she wanted. For a few days she talked about different colors, asked me what I thought the bedrooms should be, and the halls, and then a week went by and then another and one day when I was running down the road Mr. Kenfield was at his mailbox and he asked me how the painting was coming. I called over my shoulder: "Fine." That afternoon we painted the kitchen. I was sullen because I should have been studying, and we painted in near silence, listening to the radio, while Natasha watched and talked. When we were done I said: "All right, now tell Kenfield you're too busy to paint the other rooms. At least now when he comes for coffee he'll see the yellow walls. And if he pisses he'll see the orange ones. Now I'm going upstairs to do my own work."

All through graduate school that's what she kept doing: my work. When I brought a book home she read it before I did, and when my friends came over for an afternoon beer and we talked about classes and books and papers, she sounded like a graduate student. Once I daydreamed about her soul: she and Rex and I were sitting at our kitchen table drinking beer, and I watched her talking about *Sons and Lovers* and I remembered her only a year ago when I was a lieutenant junior-grade and she was complaining about the captain's snotty treatment of reserve officers, deriding the supply officer's bureaucratic handling of the simplest matters, and saying she wished there were still battleships so I could be on one and she could go aboard. And in that kitchen in the farmhouse in Michigan I daydreamed that Rex and I were ballplayers and now it was after the game and Terry had watched from behind the dugout and she was telling us she saw early in the game that I couldn't get the curve over, and she didn't think I could go all the way, but in the fifth she saw it happen, she saw me get into the groove, and then she thought with the heat I'd tire, but after we scored those four in the seventh—and he *didn't* tag him, I *know* he didn't—she knew I'd go all the way— And she kept talking, this voice from behind the dugout. And from behind the dugout she came up to my den where I worked and brought a book downstairs and later when I came down at twilight, blinking from an afternoon's reading, I'd find her on the couch, reading.

A couple of years ago in this house in Massachusetts, she put Sean to bed on the same dried sheet he had wet the night before; I noticed it when I went up to kiss the children goodnight. That was two days after I had gone to the basement and found on the stairs a pot and a Dutch oven: the stairway was dimly lit, and at first I thought something was growing in them, some plant of dark and dampness that Terry was growing on the stairs. Then I leaned closer and saw that it had once been food; it was covered with mold now, but in places I could see something under the mold, something we hadn't finished eating. I got the tool or whatever I had gone down for, then I went to the living room; she was sitting on the couch, leaning over the coffee table where the newspaper was spread, and without looking at her—for I couldn't, I looked over her head—I said: "I found those pots." She said: "Oh." I turned away. I have never heard her sound so guilty. She got up and went down the basement stairs; I heard her coming up fast, she gagged once going through the kitchen, and then she was gone, into the backyard. Soon I heard the hose. I stood in the living room watching a young couple pushing a baby in a stroller; they were across the street, walking slowly on the sidewalk. The girl had short straight brown hair; her face was plain and she appeared, from that distance, to be heavy in the hips and flat-chested. Yet I longed for her. I imagined her to be clean; I pictured their kitchen, clean and orderly before they left for their walk. Then Terry came in, hurrying; from where I stood I could have seen her in the kitchen if I'd turned, but I didn't want to; she went through the kitchen, into the bathroom, and shut the door; then I heard her throwing up. I stood watching the girl and her husband and child move out of my vision. After a while the toilet flushed, the lavatory tap ran, she was brushing her teeth. Then she went outside again.

For two days we didn't mention it. Every time I looked at her—less and less during those two days—I saw the pot and Dutch oven again, as though in her soul.

But when I kissed little Sean and smelled his clean child's flesh and breath, then the other—last night's urine—I went pounding down the stairs and found her smoking a cigarette at the kitchen table, having cleared a space for herself among the dirty dishes; she was reading the *TV Guide* with a look of concentration as though she were reading poetry, and in that instant when I ran into the room and saw her face before she was afraid, before she looked up and saw the rage in mine, I knew what the concentration was: she was pushing those dishes out of her mind, as one sweeps crumbs off a table and out of sight, and I saw her entire life as that concentrated effort not to face the dishes, the urine on the sheets, the pots in the dark down there, on the stairs. I said low, hoarse, so the children wouldn't hear: "And what *else*. Huh? What *else*." She didn't know what I was talking about. She was frightened, and I knew I had about three minutes before her fright, as always, turned to rage. "What *else* do you hide from behind *TV Guides?* Huh? Who in the hell *are* you?"

"What didn't I do?" She was still frightened, caught. She pushed back her chair, started to rise. She gestured at the dishes. "I'll do these as soon as I finish my—" and we both looked at the ash tray, at the smoldering cigarette she could not have held in her fingers.

"It's not what you didn't do, it's *why*. I can list a dozen whats every day, but I can't name one reason. *Why* do I live in the foulest house I know. Why is it that you say you love me but you give me a shitty house. Why is it that you say you love your children but they go unbathed for days, and right now Sean is lying in last night's piss."

"I forgot."

"Goddamnit," and I was nearly whispering, "that's your *TV Guide* again, you're hiding, you didn't forget anymore than you forgot those pots—"

"Will you stop talking about those pots!"

"Shhh. I haven't mentioned them since I found them."

"They've been in your eyes! Your Goddamn nitpicking eyes!"

And she fled from the room. I stood listening: her steps slowed at the top of the stairs, calmly entered Sean's room, and then she was talking, her voice sweet, motherly, loving. Sean jumped to the floor. After a while Terry came down with the dirty sheet; she went through the kitchen without speaking, into the wash room; I heard her taking wet clothes from the washer to the dryer, then putting a new load in the washer. She started both machines. So she had forgotten the clothes in the washer too, was behind on that too; yet neither of those was true. She hadn't forgotten, and she wasn't merely behind. She was . . . what? I didn't know. For a moment I had an impulse to go through the entire house, a marauding soldier after her soul: to turn over the ironing basket and hold before her eyes the shirts I hadn't seen in months; to shine a flashlight under the children's beds, disclosing fluffs of dust, soiled pajamas, apple cores; to lift up the couch cushions and push her face toward the dirt and beach sand, the crayons and pencils and pennies—over every inch of every room, into every cluttered functionless drawer (but no: they functioned as waste baskets, storage bins for things undone). I wanted to do that: take her arm and pull and push her to all these failures which I saw, that night, as the workings of an evasive and disordered soul.

I left the kitchen as she entered it from the wash room. I went on the front porch for a cigarette in the dark. It was fall then, and for a while I was able to forget the house. The air was brisk but still, and I was warm enough in my sweat shirt; I walked down to the end of the block and back, smelling that lovely clean air. Then I went back into the house. As soon as I stepped in, it all struck me: it was there waiting, jesting with me, allowing me the clean walk in the air, the peace, only to slap me when I walked in.

I stayed in the living room with a book. After two pages I laid it aside and looked for one that would serve as well as the autumn night had; I found one, and after two pages I was right, there was neither house nor Terry. The book was *Saturday Night and Sunday Morning,* and I saw myself in the book, a single man drinking gin and loving a married woman. I thought of the sleeping children above me and was ashamed; but I also felt the slow and persuasive undertow of delight.

Then I heard her singing in the kitchen. She was washing the dishes now; beyond her, from the closed wash room, came the rocking of the washer, the hum of the dryer. I didn't want her to sing. She sings alone in the kitchen when she's angry, brooding.

So I knew then I wouldn't be able to keep reading the book; she would do something. I read faster, as though speed would force a stronger concentration, would block her out. I was able to read for nearly an hour. It took her that long to clean the kitchen; the washer and dryer had stopped, but she hadn't removed the dry clothes and put the wet ones in the dryer. So when she came into the living room, a bourbon and water in her hand, all fright and guilt gone now, her face set in that look of hers that makes me know there are times she could kill me, I looked up at her, then stood and looked scornfully not at her face but past her, and said in a low, cold voice that I would go put the clothes in the dryer.

"Wait. I want to talk to you."

We stood facing each other.

"We can talk while the clothes are drying."

"No. Because I'm not ready to fold the others. And don't look at me like that, I'll fold them, Goddamnit."

I sat down, got out of the position of being squared off, got out of range.

"I'm tired of being judged. Who do you think you are anyway? Who are you to judge me? I *did* forget Sean had wet last night. If you got them up one morning out of every thousand, if *you* loved them as much as you say you do—oh, that was shitty, accusing me of not loving my children, it's the way you always fight, like a catty, bitchy woman—lying inn*uen*dos—if *you* ever got them up you'd know he hadn't wet for four or five days before that, so I wasn't used to—"

"Three days. He's been telling me every morning."

"All right: three. Anyway, I forgot." She had finished her cigarette; she found another on the bookshelf. "And I *did* forget those pots. I cooked in them the night you had the party."

"What night I had the party?"

"Whatever Goddamn night it was. When you were—" she mocked a child's whine "—so depressed—you and your fucking self-indulgent bad moods—"

"What *night* are you talking about?"

"When you called up your *friends* to have this impromptu Goddamn party."

"They're your friends too."

"Oh sure: me and the boys. They bring their wives over because they have to; I get to talk to the wives. It's *your* party, with *your* friends, in *my* Goddamn house I'm supposed to keep clean as Howard *John*son's."

"You know my friends like you. We were discussing the pots. The famous pots on the stairs."

"You supercilious shit." I smiled at her. "I cooked in them

that night, and you were in your funky mood, and you had to call Hank and Roger and Jim and Matt, I didn't even have time to clean the Goddamn kitchen, and I put those pots on the stairs, I was going to wash them when everybody went home but they stayed half the Goddamn night—"

"I recall you dancing."

"So I forgot them that night, I probably got drunk, I don't know, and the next day I wasn't thinking about dirty *pots.* I just don't go around thinking about pots! And I forgot them until you found them. And that's the absolute God's truth!"

She went to the kitchen and came back with a fresh drink and stood looking at me.

"I hate to say this, baby," I said. "But you're full of shit. I can believe you forgot them that night, what with drinking and dancing. Although I don't see why you couldn't have washed them while those quote friends of mine unquote wandered in— other women do that, you know—I realize you probably had to put your face on and so forth before they came, but after they came I think you could have got someone to talk to you in the kitchen for ten minutes while you washed a Dutch oven and a pot—"

"Ten minutes!"

"Fifteen, then."

"A lot you know. Would my husband have sat with me? Hell no, he's busy flirting—"

"Oh, stop that crap. Now: I can even believe that you forgot them next morning. But I cannot and will not cater to your lie by trying to believe that you forgot them for the weeks they've been down there—"

"It hasn't been weeks."

Now her voice didn't have that shrill edge; it was quieter, sullen, and cunning.

"While you were describing your ordeal of merging the problem of two dirty pots with the problem of enjoying a party, I was scratching around through my file of memories—I have this penchant for nostalgic memories, you know—and what I come up with is this: the party was on Friday, the twenty-first of September; today is the twentieth of October; those pots were there about a month. Are you going to stand there drinking my booze and tell me that you did not miss those pots for one month? Or, for one month, descend the basement stairs?"

Then she was throwing things: first the glass, exploding on the wall behind me; I got up from the chair and ducked the copper ash tray, but she got my shoulder with her lighter. I started toward the kitchen, where the car key hung on a nail; she got in front of me and choked me with both hands. "You crazy bitch—" I shoved hard and she fell back against the table, bumping her hip. She came after me but I was gone, slamming the door, leaping from the top step and running across the lawn to the car. I heard the screen door opening then I was in the car, locking all four doors and jabbing the key twice then into the slot and as I turned it and the car started she grabbed the door handle; I accelerated and was gone.

I went to Plum Island and got out and walked on the beach. The moon was out and on the water, and a cold wind blew out to sea. I walked until I was too cold and Terry was gone, my head clear, I was only shivering and walking. Sometimes I stopped and faced the water, taking deep breaths, the wind pushing at my back. Then I drove to a bar where fishermen and men who worked with their hands sat drinking beer with their big wives. I sat at the bar, turning the stool so my back was to the color television, and after two glasses of ale I thought surely she must hate me, and I felt good, sitting there in her hatred. I knew what she felt when she came at me with her bright, tearful eyes and shrill voice and reaching, choking hands: she wanted my death. And sitting in the bar, watching the couples, I liked that.

I remembered the night I had called my friends to come over and drink; I had been sitting on the lawn toward evening, drinking beer and watching the children play; then they came to me and sat on the grass at my feet and I stroked their heads like dogs, and talked to them, and when Terry came out I was telling them a story, making it up as I went along, and I put them in the story: When Natasha and Sean Were Cowboys, it was called; they were comic and heroic, mostly heroic, they endured blizzards, they raised a baby cougar, they captured an outlaw. While I told the story, Terry barbecued pork chops. I felt serene and loving but somehow sad. And it was that sad love that made me, when the children were in bed, call Hank and Matt and Roger and Jim.

Then sitting at that bar, watching the couples who looked past and over me at the movie or variety show or whatever, I remembered clearly the lawn, the children, the story, and my mood, and I remembered eating dinner on the lawn too: barbecued pork chops, baked beans, green salad, garlic bread—I sat in the bar seeing my paper plate in the sunset evening on the lawn, back in September. The baked beans. I saw my fork going into the pile of beans on my plate; and I remembered later, in the kitchen, Sean and I standing over the Pyrex dish and finishing the last of the beans. She had cooked on the grill and in a Pyrex dish.

She had lied. Though at first I thought she had only been mistaken. Because I hate lies so, and I didn't want to believe she would lie. But finally I told myself no: no, she lies. For the story was too good: my mood, my party, had caused her to forget her work. When confronted with the mold and stench of those pots, the urine on the sheets, she reached back for the one night she could use for an excuse.

So she avoided work and she lied. Then what does she want? I thought. What on earth does she want? And right away I knew: to be beautiful, charming, intelligent, seductive, a good cook, a good drinker, a good fuck. In short, to be loved by men and admired by women. A passive life. A receptive life.

I remember once the landlord's daughter came by, a girl of sixteen; she wanted to go into the attic, she thought she left her bicycle pump there. It was a Saturday afternoon; I answered the door and when she told me what she wanted, I thought: *A bicycle pump. My pitiful wife is to be done in by a bicycle pump.* Because the house looked as though it were lived in, not by a family, but a platoon of soldiers holing up before moving on. We had had a party the night before. She had at least moved the party mess to the kitchen, where it still was, along with the breakfast and lunch dishes; on the table, the countertop, in the sink; the kitchen floor was sticky with spilled booze; every bed was unmade; and so on. I let the girl in, and called Terry to show her to the attic; then I went out and got Sean and we rode our bicycles along the Merrimack. When we got back, Terry was standing at the sink, washing dishes.

That night *Uncle Vanya* was on NET. By then our house was in reasonable order, and Terry sat drinking beer and watching the play. Laurence Olivier played Doctor Astrov, and when he said: "She is beautiful, there's no denying that, but . . . You know she does nothing but eat, sleep, walk about, fascinate us all by her beauty—nothing more . . . And an idle life cannot be pure . . ." I wanted to glance at Terry but did not. She sat and watched and when it was over said, "Jesus," and weaved upstairs to bed. Next afternoon we were supposed to go hear Cannonball Adderley at Lennie's; I had put the money aside on payday; we were going with Hank and Edith, but all morning and through lunch she said she wasn't going, her life had reached a turning point, the landlord's daughter (*oh her face!* she said; *she was so hurt, and so—scornful!*) and *Uncle Vanya* were too much, she would work, she would work, she would start right now by paying for being a slob, she would not go hear Cannonball Adderley. I told her she was being foolish, that if she were serious her house would need a long, thorough cleaning, and that she might as well wait for Monday morning, the traditional day for taking on a load of shit. But she wouldn't go. So I went, and told Hank and Edith that Terry was turning over leaves. I didn't have to say more; they like mysteries. Cannonball was playing at four. I got home about eight. The children were in bed, the kitchen was clean, and in the living room Terry was asleep in the warm hum of her portable hair dryer. The house was neither dirtier nor cleaner than when I left. I never asked how she spent the afternoon. I guessed she did normal surface cleaning, and spent a lot of time with the children; it's what she does when she feels

guilty. For three days after that she made all the beds as soon as
we got up in the morning; on the fourth day, without a word
about *Uncle Vanya* or girls looking for bicycle pumps, or Cannonball Adderley, her slow momentum stopped, like a bicyclist
going up a steep hill: she got off and walked the bike. Everything
went back to below normal.

In that bar on the night she gripped my throat, really gripped
it—and for how long would she have squeezed if I hadn't been
able to push her away? she had right away shut off my wind-
pipe—in that bar, I saw something: I saw her sitting with the *TV
Guide* among those dishes, with that look of concentration which
was real, yes, but it wasn't concentrating *on* something, it was
concentrating away from her work. She was saying no. And I
thought: Why, that's her word: No. It is what she said to the life
that waited for her each morning, perched on the foot of the bed.
She simply refused to live it, by avoiding work, by lying about it,
and by—yes: I believed it: violence. It wasn't me she hated, me
she wanted to kill: it was the questions I raised. Yet I couldn't
really separate my questions from me any more than I could separate Terry from her house. She is what she does, I tell her; and I
suppose, for her, I am what I ask. And that is why, I thought,
our quarrels usually ended violently: because she could not or
would not answer my questions about pots on the stairs and Sean
lying in last night's piss. So she hit me.

And now tonight she was out with Hank and I remembered
the day I found the pots and went up to the living room and told
her and she went downstairs; I remembered how I stood at the
window and watched the couple pushing their baby in a stroller;
the girl was, as I have said, rather plain, and her breasts were a
little too small, and her hips a little too wide, but I stood watching her, and that is what I wanted and what I have refused all the
years to admit I wanted: a calm, peaceful life with that plain,
clean girl pushing her stroller in the sunlight of that afternoon.

3
❦

SHE CAME HOME long after midnight, an hour and twenty minutes into a new Monday, coming through the back door into the kitchen, where I sat drinking bourbon, having given up on Tolstoy, sitting and sipping now. She stood just inside the door, looking at me, shaking her head: "Not this way, Jack. Not after ten—" Then her eyes filled, her lips and cheeks began to contort, she bit off her voice and went to the refrigerator for ice. I stood, to go to her; but then I didn't move. I stood near the wall and watched her make the drink; her back was turned, her head lowered, the hair falling on both sides of her face, and I saw us as in a movie and all I had to do now was cross the room and take her shoulders and turn her and look into her eyes, then hold and kiss her. *We can try again,* I would say. And: *Yes, darling,* she would say: *Oh yes yes.* I stood watching her. When she turned, her eyes were dry, her cheeks firm.

"I've been drinking alone in DiBurro's, for the first time in my life, alone in a bar—"

"What happened?"

"Never mind what happened. I've been thinking about love, and I want to tell you this, I want to tell you these things in my heart, but I don't want to see your face. Your cold, guilty face." She sat at the table, facing the back door; I leaned against the wall, waiting. "All right then: I'll move." She turned her chair so she was profiled to me. "Don't worry, you'll get rid of me someday, but not like this, not this sordid, drunken adultery, do you know—no, you wouldn't because you never look at me—do you know that I drink more than any woman we know? I'm the only one who gets drunk as the men at parties. I'm the only one who starts drinking before her husband comes home. So you'll get rid of me anyway: I'll become a statistic. Because, you see, I don't keep a Goddamn Howard Johnson's for you, because I read a lot and, you know, think a lot, and I read someplace that booze and suicide claim many of us, us housewives; did you know that? No other group in the country goes so often to the bottle and the sleeping pill. I guess that's how they do it, with pills. Although as a child I knew a woman who played bridge with my mother, she shot herself one afternoon, a tiny hole in the temple, they said—from a tiny pistol, Daddy said, a woman's gun—she had been in and out of hospitals like others were in and out of supermarkets—maybe there's not much difference, they're both either a bother or terminal—and she was convinced she had cancer. That's what the ladies said, my mother and her friends, but they weren't known for truth, on summer afternoons they had chocolate Oreos and Cokes and talked of little things, said trump and no-trump and I pass; I used to walk through and see their souls rising with the cigarette smoke above their heads. Oh yes, they would rather believe relentless old cancer was eating the bones or liver or lungs of their dead friend than to believe one of the zombies in their midst had chosen one sunny afternoon to rise from the dead. She's the only suicide I've known. And I've only known one alcoholic, unless I'm one, which I'm not. I drink a lot at parties and on nights like this one when my husband sends me off to fuck his friend. I don't drink at lunch or early afternoon, but at ten in the morning a real lush will talk to you smelling of booze, a nice, pleasant enough smell but awfully spooky when the sun's still low and the dew hasn't burned off the grass, like in high school Sue's mother was an alcoholic, she was rich and lovely so maybe it was all right, she didn't really need to function much anyway. She always smelled of booze, she was usually cheerful and friendly, and you never saw her glass until five o'clock, at the cocktail hour. So much for statistics."

She went to the sink and poured another bourbon.

"Don't you want to stop that?"

She turned with the ice tray in her hands.

"Give me a reason, Jack."

I looked at her for a moment, then I looked around the room and down into my glass. She poured the drink and sat at the table and I watched the side of her face.

"A man must have done those statistics," she said. "They sound like a fraud. Because he was treating housewife like a profession, like lawyer or doctor or something, and that's wrong, he's including too many of us; if he had done the same thing with men, just called them all husbands, you can bet they'd have the highest rate. Most of them I know are pretty much drunks anyway, and they commit suicide in all sorts of cowardly ways; sometimes in the bank I wait in line and watch the walking suicides there, the men on my side of the counter and the other, those lowered eyes and turned-down lips and fidgety glances around like God might catch them dying without a fight. So they should classify us if they must classify us by our husbands' jobs: how many pharmacists' wives are too drunk to cook at night? How many teachers' wives slit their fucking throats? But that wouldn't be accurate either. We are an elusive sex, hard to pin down. Though everyone tries to. I know: I have red hair. She has that red-headed temper, Daddy used to say. I was thinking about him tonight. Once when I was ten he took me fishing. We stood barefoot on the sand and cast out into the surf for flounder. The fishing rod was very long; I had to hold it with two hands and I shuffled forward with my side to the sea, and the rod was behind me almost dragging in the sand, then I arced it high over my head and the line went out, not as far as his but better than I had done before, and he said it: "That's better." I reeled in praying I'd hook one, please dear God for one sweet fish. Wasn't that absurd? To think the luck of catching a fish would make me somehow more lovable? Because then it'd follow that to be unlucky was to be unlovable, wouldn't it? And I must have believed that, as a child. And while I was drinking alone tonight I thought maybe I still believe that. But of course luck isn't an element in my life now. I don't fish or play cards; but there's always skill. So should I expect my cooking and screwing to make me more lovable? Maybe. I suppose a man can't be expected to love a woman who fails in the kitchen and the bed. I'll admit that—even though I believe conversation and companionship are more important—but I'll admit that first a man has to be well fed and fucked. "Only God, my dear, could love you for yourself alone and not your yellow hair." What if I cooked badly? Or were paralyzed and couldn't screw? Because maybe then you do hate me for my house, because it's dirty sometimes—"

"I don't hate you." She looked at me: only for a moment, then she turned away and finished her drink and rose for another. "Terry—"

"How would you know if you hate me? You don't even know me. You say, 'You are what you do.' But do you really believe that? Does that mean I'm a cook, an errand runner, a fucker, a bed maker, and on and on—a Goddamn *clean*ing woman, for Christ sake? If you—*you*, you bastard—" looking at me, then looking away "—lost all discipline, just folded up and turned drunk and was fired, *I'd* love you, and I'd get a job and support us too. Maybe no one else would love you. You'd be a different man, to them: your friends and your students. But not to me. I'd love you. I'd love you if you went about at night poisoning dogs. So what is it that I love? If action doesn't matter. I love you—" looking at me, then away "—I love Jack Linhart. And I say you're more than what you do. But if you love me for what I do instead of for what I am—there *is* a difference, I *know* there is— then what are you loving when I screw Hank? Because if you love me for what I do then you can't want me to be unfaithful because if I screw somebody else it's because I love him, so either you don't love me and so you don't care or you don't know me and you just love someone who looks like me, and what you like to do is add to my tricks. Screw Hank. Shake hands. Sit, roll over, play dead, fetch—loving me like a dog. Because I'm not like that, I simply love a dog, I had dogs, four of them, they all disappeared or died or got killed, like everything else around here, like me, and I just *loved* them: fed them and petted them and demanded no tricks. No fucking tricks! But not you." She stood up and looked at me. "Am I right? You don't love me, you love the tricks? Is that true? My stupid spaghetti sauce, the martini waiting in the freezer when you come home in the afternoons, the way I for Christ's sweet sake look and walk and screw?"

"I love Edith," I said, and looked her full in the face; probably I didn't breathe. Her face jerked back, as if threatened by a blow; then she was shaking her head, slowly at first then faster back and forth, and I said: "Terry, Terry, yes: I love her. I don't love you. I haven't for a long time. I don't know why. Maybe no one ever knows why. I'm sorry, Terry, but I can't help it, I—"

"Nooooo," she wailed, and she was across the room, dropping her glass, tears now, shaking her head just below my face, pounding my chest, not rage but like a foiled child: she could have been striking a table or wall. "No, *Jack*. No, *Jack*—" Then she shoved me hard against the wall and I bounced off and pushed her with both hands: she fell loudly on her back, her head thumped the floor, and I crouched with clenched fists, looking down at her frightened face and its sudden pain. She rolled on one side and slowly got up.

"Come on," I said. "Come take it."

She looked at my face and fists, then shook her head.

"No. No, you're right: I've hit you too much. You're right to push me down. I've hit you too much."

She went to the sink and stood with her back to me, bent over the counter with her head on her arms, one fist in a light rhythmic beat; after a while she turned. Tears were on her cheeks and she sniffed once and then again.

"All right. I won't cry and I won't hit you. Edith. So Edith then. All right. Jesus." She looked around for her glass. I moved to pick it up from the floor, but she said, "Oh fuck you," and I straightened again. She took a glass from the cupboard and poured a long drink; the ice tray was empty. She went to the refrigerator and put the glass on top of it and opened the freezer compartment, then stood holding the door and looking in at the trays and vapor and frozen juice cans, and I thought then she would cry; but she didn't, and after a while she banged out an ice tray and went to the sink and ran water on the back of the tray and pulled the lever but the ice didn't come out; then she squeezed the dividers with her hands, then jerked back, dropping the tray and shaking a hand: "I hate these Goddamn cutting ice trays." She ran hot water again and worked the lever and got some cubes. Then she stood leaning against the stove, facing me across the table.

"That fucking bitch whore Edith. My fucking friend Edith. So up Terry. Alone then. I should have known. I did know. I knew all the time. I just wouldn't let myself know that I knew. How long have you been screwing her?"

"May. Late May."

"Yes. I thought so. I thought so tonight going to meet Hank and I thought so while we high school screwed in the car, I saw you, the way you look at her like you haven't looked at me in years, and I saw you screwing her and when Hank finished I told him I wanted to be alone, just to take me back to DiBurro's where my car was. Did you love me until you fell in love with Edith?"

"No." I shook my head. "No. I guess that's why I lo—"

"Don't say it! I don't have to keep hearing that. I—" She lowered her head, the hair covering her eyes, then she went to her purse on the table and got a cigarette and lit it at the stove, holding her hair back behind her neck. When she turned to face me she looked down at the gold wedding ring on her finger, then she twisted it as though to pull it off, but she didn't; she just kept turning it on her finger and looking at it.

"We must have had a lot of people fooled. A lot of people will be surprised. My boyfriend." She let her ring hand fall. "I'm thirty years old, I've lost my figure—"

"No, you haven't."

"Don't, Jack. I've lost my figure, I'm not young anymore, I don't even want to be young anymore, I've become just about what I'll become—" I could not look at her: I went to the refrigerator needing motion more than I needed ale, and got a bottle and opened it and went to the door and stood half-turned, so my back wasn't to her but my face wasn't either. "But there was a time when I wanted to be young again, I never told you that, I didn't see any reason to load you down with it. I remember once nursing Sean when he woke in the night in Ann Arbor, I had the radio on in the kitchen turned down low and listening to music and watching Sean, and of course I loved him but I was almost halfway through my twenties and I'd been married all that time. Then *La Mer* came on the radio and all at once I was back five years, the year before I met you, the summer I was nineteen and all of us used to go to Carolyn Shea's house because it was the biggest and her parents were the best, her mother and father would come and talk to us in the den where the record player was, she was just a little patronizing to the girls but not to the boys, only because she was a woman; but he wasn't patronizing to anyone at all. The boys would come over: Raymond Harper and Tommy Zuern and Warren Huebler and Joe Fleming, and sometimes they'd bring cherrystones, or steamers, and Mr. Shea would help them open the cherrystones and if they brought steamers Mrs. Shea would steam them and we'd sit in the kitchen with beer or wine. We were there all the time, all that summer, and no one was in love with anyone, we all danced and went to movies and the beach, and all that summer we played *La Mer*. When it came on the radio that night in Ann Arbor I thought of Raymond getting knocked off a destroyer at night and they never found him, and Tommy got fat and serious, and Joe became an undertaker like his father, and Warren just went away; and Leslie had an abortion, then married someone else and went to live in Nebraska, and Carolyn married a rich jerk from Harvard Law, and Jo Ann married a peddler and turned dumb to survive, and then there was me nursing my baby in Ann Arbor, Michigan, and I started to cry, loud and shaking, and I thought you'd hear and think Sean had died and I clamped my teeth shut but I couldn't stop crying because I knew my life was gone away because you didn't have a rubber with you because we'd never made love before—and isn't that tender and sweet to think of now?—and I was foolish enough to believe you when you said you wouldn't come inside me, then foolish enough not to care when I knew you were about to and I went to bed that night with Natasha alive in me and next morning when I woke I knew it. Then you got rubbers but every time I knew it didn't matter; I gave up hope, but I thought if I was lucky anyway, I'd start dating others. I would make love with you but I would date others. I was twenty years old. So now you say you don't love me. You love Edith." Her lower lip trembled, then she spun around, her back to me, and slapped the counter with both hands. "I won't cry. You bastard, you won't make me cry. I've given you my *liiife*." She wiped her eyes once, quickly, with the back of a hand and faced me again. "Oh, how I *hate* your Goddamn little girl students you bring in here to babysit, those naïve, helpless little shits, what I'd *give* for their chance, to be young and able to finish college and *do* something. I could be in New *York* now, I could be *any*where but *no*. I had to get *mar*ried. I should have aborted—" Her voice lowered to almost a whisper, and she stopped glaring at me and looked somewhere to my side, her eyes fixed on nothing, just staring: "I thought of it. I didn't get the name of an abortionist but I did get the name of a girl who'd had one, just by manipulating a conversation I got that done, but I didn't go on. Not because I was scared either. What I was scared of was being knocked up and getting married to my boyfriend. That's what you were: my boyfriend. But no, not Terry, she wanted to do the right thing. So I did. And now Natasha's here and so of course I'm glad I didn't kill her. After you see a child and give it a name you can never think about abortion. But I've wasted my life. I knew it all the time but I didn't let myself, I was going to make the best of it, I was going to keep on being a girl in love. All right, then. You're having an affair with Edith and you love her and you don't love me. All right. I won't cry and I won't hit you. When are you leaving?"

"I don't know."

"You might as well go today."

"I guess so."

"Is Edith leaving?"

"We've never talked about it."

"Oh, you must have."

"No."

"So you might be like the coyote."

It was a joke we'd had from the Roadrunner cartoons; one of us trying something fearful and new was like the coyote: poised in midair a thousand feet above a canyon and as long as he doesn't look down he won't fall.

"It doesn't matter," I said. "I wouldn't take her from Hank anyway, if he wants her."

"So it's not her: it's me. Well Jesus. I've been telling you and telling you you don't love me. But I never really meant it. I never believed it at all. Was it the house?"

"I don't know."

"No. I guess you can't know, any more than I can know why I still love you. Jack?" Her lip trembled. "Don't you love me even a little?"

I looked above her, over the pots on the stove, at the wall. Then I closed my eyes and shook my head and said: "No, Terry." Then without looking at her I left. I went to the bedroom and undressed in the dark and got into bed. I heard her in the kitchen, weeping softly.

Sometimes I slept and all night she did not come to bed and all night I woke and listened to her. For a while she stayed in the kitchen: she stopped crying and I went to sleep listening to her silence, and when I woke I knew she was still there, sitting at the table under the light. I had not been heartbroken since I was very young; but I could remember well enough what it was like and I wished Terry were leaving me, I wished with all my heart that she had come to me one afternoon and looked at me with pity but resolve and said: *I'm sorry but I must go*—I wish I were now lying in bed grieving for my wife who had stopped loving me. I rolled one way and then another and then lay on my back and breathed shallow and slow as though sleeping, but I couldn't; I felt her sitting in the kitchen and I felt her thinking of me with Edith and me divorced laughing on a sunny sidewalk with some

friend, and I felt her heart's grieving, and then I was nearly crying too. I sat up, slowly shaking my head, then lit a cigarette and
lay on my back, listening to her silence, then my legs tightened,
ready to go to her, but I drew on the cigarette and shook my
head once viciously on the pillow and pushed my legs down
against the mattress. Then I heard her taking pots from the
stove: footsteps from the stove to the sink, and the sound of the
heavy iron skillet lowered into the dry sink, footsteps again and
this time the higher ringing sound of the steel pot and then
higher again of the aluminum one. She began scraping one of
them with a knife or fork or spoon. She knocked the pot against
the inside of the plastic garbage can and started scraping another.
Then she washed and dried them and hung them on the peg-
board. She ran water into the sink and I lay staring into the night
as she washed the dishes. She washed them quickly, then she was
moving about and I guessed she was circling the table, wiping it
clean, and after that the stove. Still she was moving with quick
steps, into the laundry room and out again, to the sink, and she
lowered a bucket into it and turned on the water; I swung my
feet to the floor and sat on the edge of the bed. When she started
mopping the floor I went to the kitchen. She knew I was there at
the doorway but she didn't look up: she was bent over the stroking sponge mop, her head down, toward me; water had splashed
on the front of her yellow dress; she was mopping fast, pushing
ahead of her a tiny surf of dirty water and soap. Finally she had
to stand straight and look at me. Her forehead was dripping, her
hair was stringy with sweat, and I could not imagine her with
Hank a few hours earlier.

"Come to bed."

"No. I want to clean my house. I've been a pig and I've
beaten you and thrown things at you. I know it's too late for you
but maybe not for me, maybe I can at least be good for my
babies. Or maybe you'll miss them and want to come back and
the house will be clean. Couldn't you just stay and keep screwing
Edith? Couldn't you be happy then?"

"You don't want that."

"No, I guess not." Mopping again, bent over. "I don't know. Maybe I could change. Go to bed, love; I want to clean my house."

I slept lightly. Sometimes I heard Terry moving about the house, and I felt the night leave and the day grow lighter and warmer; at one warm and light time I heard a vacuum cleaner beneath my dreams. When I heard the children's voices I woke up; but I would not open my eyes. I lay on my side and listened to their voices. After a while I heard Terry upstairs, in Sean's room above me. She was walking from one spot to another; then she pushed furniture across the floor. I opened my eyes and looked into the living room: Natasha was standing in the doorway.

"You should see the house."

"What's she doing upstairs?"

"She just fed us and cleaned up our mess and now she's doing the upstairs."

Sean called from the kitchen. "Is that Daddy you're talking to?"

I winked at Natasha.

"Is that true you don't love Mom?" she said.

"Who told you that? The morning paper?"

"I heard Mom last night."

"Oh? Who was she talking to?"

Sean came in, carrying a full glass of orange juice; he held it out in front of him, his forearm extended, and watched it while he stiffly walked to the bed.

"Thanks, chief," I said, and kissed him.

"I couldn't hear you," Natasha said. "Just Mom."

"Are you getting divorced?" Sean said.

"Wow. You really know how to wake a fellow up."

Upstairs the vacuum cleaner went on. I imagined what Terry had got from under the bed.

"Natasha said you were leaving."

"That's an idea. Where should I go? Join the Mounties?"

"I want to live with you," Sean said.

"I'm not going to choose," Natasha said.

"Ah me. You shouldn't listen to drunk grown-ups fighting, sweetheart. It's always exaggerated."

"Mom said you were leaving and you love Edith and you screwed her."

"Do you know what that means?"

"Yes."

"What?" Sean said. "What what means?"

"Nothing," I said, looking at him and feeling Natasha's eyes on me. "Just grown-up foolishness." I looked at Natasha. "Let's get on our bikes."

"You haven't eaten yet."

"Let's go to the river," Sean said.

"We'll stop someplace where I can eat and you two can have something to drink."

I told them to get the bikes out while I dressed. When they were gone, I called Edith to tell her I couldn't meet her. Hank answered.

"I can't run today," I said. "I'm sick. The flu. Tell Edith I have the flu and maybe she'll feel guilty for spreading it to her friends."

White clouds were piled in the sky, and from the southwest gray was coming. I led Natasha and Sean in single file down our street, to the river. From our left the air was turning cooler and the gray was coming. We stopped at a small grocery store and got a quart of apple cider and stood on the sidewalk, drinking from the bottle and looking across the blacktop at the dark river.

"Is it true about you and Edith?" There was in her eyes a will to know, a look of deep interest; nothing more.

"Is what true?" Sean said. He was down there, below our voices and souls, looking at the river.

"It is and it isn't," I said to Natasha's eyes. "I don't know if I have the wisdom to explain it to a little girl I love."

She took a quarter from her pocket and gave it to Sean.

"Go buy us something to eat."

He hurried into the store.

"Where'd you get that?"

"My allowance."

"I'll explain as well as I can," I said. I watched her eyes. "I don't want to abort it." They hadn't changed.

"What's that mean?"

"To kill something before it's fully developed. Like a party you're planning. Or a baby inside the mother."

"Oh."

Now I remembered Terry lowering her voice: *I should have aborted;* even in her raging grief the old instinct of an animal protecting her young was there. Then I looked at the river and the lush woods on the other side, turning bright green as the gray and black moved faster over us; at the horizon the last puffs of white and strips of blue were like daylight under a tent wall; I turned from Natasha because there were tears in my eyes, not for her because she was strong and young and there was hope, but for Terry and her trembling lip: *Jack? Don't you love me even a little?* I am afraid of water; but looking out at the river I wanted suddenly to be in its flow, turning over once, twice, with the current; going down with slow groping arms, and hands opening and shutting on cool muddy death, my hair standing out from my head as I went bubbling down to the bottom. I shuddered, as much with remorse as fear. Then my wish was over. I stood alive again and breathed the rain-scented air and I knew that I would grow old with Terry.

"Mother and I have made mistakes," I said. She was standing at my side, almost touching; I kept my eyes on the woods across the river. Sea gulls crossed my vision. "You must trust us to make things better for everyone. Your mother and I love each other. She's a good and wonderful woman, and don't worry about anything you heard last night, people are all sorts of things, and one mistake is only a small part of a person, Mother's very good, and Edith is very good, and—"

"And so are you," she said, and slipped her hand into mine and I couldn't go on.

The sky was completely gray now and it watched us ride home; we put our bikes in the garage and crossed the lawn and as we climbed the back steps it began to rain. We stood in the darkened kitchen and watched it coming down hard and loud. Sean was touching my leg. I tousled his hair, then turned on the light. The room changed: when it was dark and we had looked out at a day as dark as our kitchen, I had felt we were still out there in the rain, the three of us, somewhere by the river and trees; I could live in that peace, from one fresh rain-filled moment to the next, forever. Now with the light we were home again; our bodies were lightly touching but the flow, the unity, was gone. We were three people in a troubled house. I touched them and went to the bedroom. Terry was putting my clothes in a suitcase. She looked clean and very tired; she had showered and changed clothes. She tried to smile, failed, tried again, and made it.

"Was it awful?" she said.

"Was what awful? Why are you doing that?"

"I thought that's where you went. To tell the kids."

I pushed the suitcase to make room, and lay on the bed; I would not look at her.

"Unpack it," I said.

"Why? Couldn't you tell them?"

"I don't want to."

"I'll call them in and we'll both tell them."

"I mean I don't want to leave."

She stepped closer to the bed and I was afraid she would touch me.

"You really don't?"

"No."

"Is it the kids? I mean I know it's the kids but is it just the kids? You could see them, you know. Whenever you wanted. And I'd never move away, I'd live here as long as you teach here—so if it's just telling them, we can do it and get it over with, these things are always hard, but we can do it—"

"It's not that." I shut my eyes. "Unpack the suitcase."

Across the bed I felt her pain and hope. I kept my eyes shut and listened to her moving from the bed to the closet and hanging up my clothes. Then she came around to my side of the bed and sat on the edge and put a hand on my cheek.

"Hey," she said softly. "Look at me."

I did.

"It'll be all right," she said. "You'll see. It'll be all right again."

She slept the rest of the afternoon, then woke to cook dinner; during dinner she and the children talked, and sometimes I talked with the children, but mostly I listened to their voices and the rain outside the window. After cleaning the kitchen Terry went back to bed and slept late next morning; then she called Edith and asked her to go to lunch.

"Do you have to?" I said.

She stood in the kitchen, in a short skirt and a bright blouse and a raincoat, looking pretty the way women do when they meet each other for lunch.

"I've loved her," she said. "I want to keep loving her."

The rain had stopped for a while, but now it was coming down again. They were a long time at lunch; the children were bored, so I let them watch a movie on television. It was an old movie about British soldiers in India; I explained to the children that the British had no business being there, then we were all free to enjoy watching the British soldiers doing their work. They were all crack shots and awfully brave. The movie hadn't ended when Terry came upstairs and, smiling happily, said: "Don't you want to come down?"

"Just for a minute. I want to see the rest of this."

I followed her downstairs and put on some water for one cup of tea. Her face was loving and forgiving and I could not bear to look at her, I could not bear the images of her in warm collusion with Edith; for I could see it all: we would gather again in living rooms, the four of us, as though nothing had happened. And perhaps indeed nothing had.

"She wants you to see her tonight." Her cheeks were flushed, her eyes bright, and she smelled of bourbon. "She's going to tell Hank, she's probably told him by now, she said he won't mind—"

"I know."

Bubbles were forming beneath the water in the pot. I held the cup with the tea bag and waited.

"I told her about Hank and me, right away, as soon as I'd told her I knew about you two, and it's all right, I told her it was like her with you, because she wasn't trying to steal you or anything, it was to save herself, she said, and—"

"I don't want to hear it."

"You don't?"

"No. I don't know why. I just don't."

The water was boiling, and I poured it into the cup.

"I'm sorry," I said. "I'm sure it was a fine afternoon with Edith."

"It was." I looked at her. She was watching me with pity. "It was wonderful."

I went upstairs. Going up, I could hear the rifles cracking. That night I went to see Edith and Hank. They were drinking coffee at the kitchen table; the dishes were still there from dinner, and the kitchen smelled of broiled fish. From outside the screen door I said hello and walked in.

"Have some coffee," Hank said.

I shook my head and sat at the table.

"A drink?" he said.

"Aye. Bourbon."

Edith got up to pour it.

"I think I'll take in a movie," Hank said.

Edith was holding the bottle and watching me, and it was her face that told me how close I was to crying. I shook my head: "There's no need—"

But he was up and starting for the back door, squeezing my shoulder as he passed. I followed him out.

"Hank—"

He turned at his car.

"Listen, I ought to dedicate my novel to you." He smiled and took my hand. "You helped get it done. It's so much easier to live with a woman who feels loved."

We stood gripping hands.

"Jack? You okay, Jack?"

"I'm okay. I'll be laughing soon. I'm working on the philosophy of laughter. It is based on the belief that if you're drowning in shit, buoyancy is the only answer."

When I got back to the kitchen, Edith was waiting with the drink. I took it from her and put it on the table and held her.

"Hank said he'd guessed long ago," she said. "He said he was happy for us and now he's sad for us. Which means he was happy you were taking care of me and now he's sorry you can't."

I reached down for the drink and, still holding her, drank it fast over her shoulder and then quietly we went to the guest room. In the dark she folded back the spread and sheet; still silent and standing near each other we slowly undressed, folding clothes over the backs of chairs, and I felt my life was out of my hands, that I must now play at a ritual of mortality and goodbye, the goodbye not only to Edith but to love itself, for I would never again lie naked with a woman I loved, and in bed then I held her tightly and in the hard grip of her arms I began to shudder and almost wept but didn't, then I said: "I can't make love, I'm just too sad, I—" She nodded against my cheek and for a long while we quietly held each other and then I got up and dressed and left her naked under the sheet and went home.

Like a cat with corpses, Terry brings me gifts I don't want. When I come home at night she hands me a drink; she cooks better than any woman I know, and she watches me eat as though I were unwrapping a present that she spent three months finding. She never fails to ask about my day, and in bed she responds to my hesitant, ambivalent touch with a passion I can never match. These are the virtues she has always had and her failures, like my own, have not changed. Last summer it took the house about five weeks to beat her: she fought hard but without resilience; she lost a series of skirmishes, attacks from under beds, from closets, the stove, the vegetable bin, the laundry basket. Finally she had lost everything and since then she has waked each day in her old fashion which will be hers forever: she wakes passively, without a plan; she waits to see what the day will bring, and so it brings her its worst: pots and clothes and floors wait to be cleaned. We are your day, they tell her. She pushes them aside and waits for something better. We don't fight about that anymore, because I don't fight; there is no reason to. Except about Edith, she is more jealous than ever; perhaps she is too wise to push me about Edith; but often after parties she accuses me of flirting. I probably do, but it is meaningless, it is a jest. She isn't violent anymore. She approaches me with troubled eyes and says maybe she's wrong but it seemed to her that I was a long time in the kitchen with—I assure her that she's wrong, she apologizes, and we go to bed. I make love to her with a detachment that becomes lust.

Now that it is winter the children and I have put away our bicycles, oiled and standing side by side in the cellar, the three of them waiting, as Sean says, for spring and summer. We go sledding. The college has a hill where students learn to ski and on weekends it is ours; Natasha and Sean always beg Terry to come with us and she always says no, she has work to do, she will go another time. I know what it costs her to say this, I know how she wants to be with us, all of us going shrilly down the hill, and then at the top a thermos of chocolate for the children and a swallow of brandy for mama and papa. But she knows that with the children I'm happy, and she always says she will go another time. We sled and shout for a couple of hours until we're wet and cold, and when we come home with red cheeks Terry gives us hot chocolate.

Last week Hank sold his novel, and Saturday night he and Edith gave a party to celebrate. At noon that day Hank and I ran five miles; the sky was blue then; later in the afternoon clouds came and by night snow was falling. When I went up to his office he had finished writing (he has started another novel) and his girl was there; she is nineteen, a student, and she has long blonde hair and long suede boots and the office smelled of her cigarette smoke. Hank has not started smoking again. He is very discreet about his girl and I think only Terry and I know; we don't talk about it, Terry and I, because she can't. I know it bothers her that she can't, I know she wishes she were different, but she isn't. Edith knows too, about Hank and his girl; they don't lie to each other anymore.

"It's not love," she said that night at the party. We had gone to the front porch to breathe and watch the snow. "It's marriage. We have a good home for Sharon. We respect each other. There's affection. That's what I wish you could have: it's enough. It's sad, watching you two. She loves you and you never touch her, you don't look at her when you talk. Last summer, after we stopped seeing each other, I went to the zoo that week, I took Sharon to the zoo; and we went to see the gorilla: he was alone in his cage, and there were women with their children watching him. They're herbivores—did you know that? They're gentle herbivores. I don't like zoos anyway and I shouldn't have gone but it was such an awful week, finding out how to live this time, I'd been through that in May and then there was you and then in July there wasn't, so I took Sharon to the zoo. And I looked in the gorilla's eyes and he looked so human—you know?—as if he *knew* everything, how awfully and hopelessly and forever trapped he was. It's not like watching a flamingo. He was standing there looking at us looking at him, all the young mothers in their pants and skirts the colors of sherbet and the jabbering children. Then he reached down like this and shit in his hand. He was watching us. He held up the handful of shit—" and she held her hand up, shoulder-high, palm toward me "— and then he brought it to his mouth and licked it. His eyes were darting from side to side, watching us. They were merry and mischievous, his eyes. Then he licked it again. Around me the mothers were gasping and some of the children were laughing; then they all hurried away. Murmuring. Distracting their children. But I stayed, and he looked at me like he was smiling and then he showed me his shit again and then he licked it and then he showed it to me again; he almost looked inquisitive; but by then I was squeezing Sharon's hand and looking in his eyes and I was crying, standing there weeping on a sunny afternoon in front of a gorilla, and he watched me for a while, curious at first, and then he lowered his hand with the shit and we just stood looking at each other, he was looking into my eyes, and he knew that I knew and I knew that he knew, and if he could have cried he would have too. Then I left. And after a few weeks when I was able to see someone besides myself I'd see you and I'd think of that trapped gorilla, standing in his cage and licking his own shit. And I wanted to cry for you too—not just me, because I love you and can't touch you, can't be alone with you, but I wanted to cry for you. And I did. And I still do. Or at least I feel like it, I cry down in my soul. Oh Jack—are you trying at all?"

"There's nothing to try with."

I could not look at her eyes, for I wanted to hold her and there was no use in that now. I moved to the window and looked in; from the couch Terry looked up and smiled; she held the smile when Edith moved into her vision and stood beside me. I turned from the window. Around the streetlight the falling snow was lovely. Terry had stopped watching us after the smile; she was talking ardently with Hank and Roger, and I thought poised like that—a little high on bourbon, talking, being listened to, being talked to—she was probably happy. I raised my glass to the snow and the night.

"Here's to the soul of Jack Linhart: it has grown chicken wings and flaps near the ground." I drank. "I shall grow old and meek and faithful beside her, and when the long winter comes—" I drank "—and her hair is white as snow I shall lay my bent old fingers on her powdered cheek and—"

"I love you."

"Do you still?"

"Always."

"And live with Hank."

"He's my husband and the father of my child."

"And he's got a Goddamn— All right: I'm sorry. It's bitterness, that's all; it's—"

"I don't care if he has a girl."

"You really don't?"

"Some women take up pottery, some do knitting."

"Oh."

"Yes."

"I guess I didn't want to know that."

"I'm sorry."

"Jesus. Oh Jesus Christ, I really didn't want to know that. Course there's no reason for you not to have someone, when I can't, when I—Jesus—"

I went inside and got drunk and lost track of Terry until two in the morning, when she brought my coat. I told her I was too drunk to drive. In the car I smelled her perfume, and I thought how sad that is, the scent of perfume on a rejected woman.

"Edith has a lover," I said.

"I know. She told me a month ago."

"Do you know him?"

"Do you want to?"

"No."

"We don't anyway."

"Why didn't you tell me?"

"I didn't want to talk about it. I think it's sad."

"It makes her happy."

"I don't believe it."

"Oh, you can't tell."

"Please don't," she said. She was leaning forward, looking into the snow in the headlights. "I know you don't love me. Maybe someday you will again. I know you will. You'll see, Jack: you will. But please don't talk like that, okay? Please, because—" Her voice faltered, and she was quiet.

While she took the sitter home I sat in the dark living room, drinking an ale and looking out the window. In the falling snow I saw a lover for Terry. I went to bed before she got home and next morning I woke up first. The sky had cleared and the snow was hard and bright under the sun. While I drank tomato juice in the kitchen Natasha and Sean came downstairs.

"Get dressed," I said. "We'll go buy a paper."

"We should go sledding," Sean said.

"All right."

"Before breakfast?" Natasha said.

"Why not?"

"We've never gone first thing in the morning," Sean said. "It'll be neat."

"Okay," Natasha said. "Is Mom awake?"

"No."

"We'll write her a note."

"Okay. You write it. And be quiet going upstairs."

"We will," Sean said, and he was gone up the stairs.

"What should I write?"

"That we're going sledding at nine and we'll be back about eleven, hungry as hell."

"I'll just say hungry."

I got my coat and filled its pockets with oranges, then went outside and shoveled the driveway while they dressed warmly for the cold morning.

Adultery

... love is a direction
and not a state of the soul.

SIMONE WEIL, *Waiting on God*

for Gina Berriault

1

WHEN THEY have finished eating Edith tells Sharon to clear the table then brush her teeth and put on her pajamas; she brings Hank his coffee, then decides she can have a cup too, that it won't keep her awake because there is a long evening ahead, and she pours a cup for herself and returns to the table. When Sharon has gone upstairs Edith says: "I'm going to see Joe."

Hank nods, sips his coffee, and looks at his watch. They have been silent during most of the meal but after her saying she is going to see Joe the silence is uncomfortable.

"Do you have to work tonight?" she says.

"I have to grade a few papers and read one story. But I'll read to Sharon first."

Edith looks with muted longing at his handlebar moustache, his wide neck, and thick wrists. She is lighting a cigarette when Sharon comes downstairs in pajamas.

"Daddy quit," Sharon says, "Why don't you quit?"

Edith smiles at her, and shrugs.

"I'm going out for a while," she says. "To see a friend."

Sharon's face straightens with quick disappointment that borders on an angry sense of betrayal.

"What friend?"

"Terry," Edith says.

"Why can't she come here?"

"Because Daddy has work to do and we want to talk."

"I'll read to you," Hank says.

Sharon's face brightens.

"What will you read?"

"Kipling."

" 'Rikki-Tikki-Tavi'?"

"Yes: 'Rikki-Tikki-Tavi.' "

She is eight and Edith wonders how long it will be before Sharon senses and understands that other presence or absence that Edith feels so often when the family is together. She leaves the table, puts the dishes and pots in the dishwasher, and turns it on. She is small and slender and she is conscious of her size as she puts on her heavy coat. She goes to the living room and kisses Hank and Sharon, but she does not leave through the front door. She goes to the kitchen and takes from the refrigerator the shrimp wrapped in white paper; she goes out the back door, into the dark. A light snow has started to fall.

It is seven-thirty. She has told Joe not to eat until she gets there, because she wants to cook shrimp scampi for him. She likes cooking for Joe, and she does it as often as she can. Wreathed in the smells of cooking she feels again what she once felt as a wife: that her certain hands are preparing a gift. But there were times, in Joe's kitchen, when this sense of giving was anchored in vengeful images of Hank, and then she stood in the uncertainty and loss of meaningless steam and smells. But that doesn't happen anymore. Since Joe started to die, she has been certain about everything she does with him. She has not felt that way about anyone, even Sharon, for a long time.

The snow is not heavy but she drives slowly, cautiously, through town. It is a small town on the Merrimack River, and tonight there are few cars on the road. Leaving town she enters the two-lane country road that will take her to Joe. She tightens her seat belt, turns on the radio, lights a cigarette, and knows that none of these measures will slow the tempo of her heart. The road curves through pale meadows and dark trees and she is alone on it. Then there are houses again, distanced from each other by hills and fields, and at the third one, its front porch lighted, she turns into the driveway. She turns on the interior light, looks at her face in the rearview mirror, then goes up the shoveled walk, her face lowered from the snow, and for a moment she sees herself as Joe will see her coming inside with cheeks flushed and droplets in her long black hair. Seeing herself that way, she feels loved. She is thirty years old.

When Joe opens the door she feels the awkward futility of the shrimp in her hand. She knows he will not be able to eat tonight. He has lost thirty pounds since the night last summer when they got drunk and the next day he was sick and the day after and the day after, so that finally he could not blame it on gin and he went to a doctor and then to the hospital where a week later they removed one kidney with its envelope of cancer that had already spread upward. During the X-ray treatments in the fall, five days a week for five weeks, with the square drawn in purple marker on his chest so the technician would know where to aim, he was always nauseated. But when the treatments were finished there were nights when he could drink and eat as he used to. Other nights he could not. Tonight is one of those: above his black turtleneck the pallor of his face is sharpened; looking from that flesh his pale blue eyes seem brighter than she knows they are. His forehead is moist; he is forty years old, and his hair has been gray since his mid-thirties. He holds her, but even as he squeezes her to him, she feels him pulling his body back from the embrace, so she knows there is pain too. Yet still he holds her tightly so his pulling away causes only a stiffening of his torso while his chest presses against her. She remembers the purple square and is glad it is gone now. She kisses him.

"I'm sorry about the shrimp," he says. "I don't think I can eat them."

"It's all right; they'll keep."

"Maybe tomorrow."

"Maybe so."

The apartment is small, half of the first floor of a small two-story house, and it is the place of a man who since boyhood has not lived with a woman except housekeepers in rectories. The front room where they are standing, holding each other lightly now like dancers, is functional and, in a masculine disorderly way, orderly; it is also dirty. Fluffs of dust have accumulated on the floor. Edith decides to bring over her vacuum cleaner tomorrow. She puts her coat on a chair and moves through the room and down the short hall toward the kitchen; as she passes his bedroom she glances at the bed to see if he rested before she came; if he did, he has concealed it: the spread is smooth. She wonders how he spent his day, but she is afraid to ask. The college is still paying him, though someone else is teaching his philosophy courses that he started in the fall and had to quit after three days. She puts the shrimp in the refrigerator; always, since they were first lovers, when she looks in his refrigerator she feels a tenderness whose edges touch both amusement and pathos. The refrigerator is clean, it has four ice trays, and it holds only the makings of breakfast and cocktail hour. Behind her he is talking: this afternoon he took a short walk in the woods; he sat on a log and watched a cock pheasant walking across a clearing, its feathers fluffed against the cold. The land is posted and pheasants live there all winter. After the walk he tried to read Unamuno but finally he listened to Rachmaninoff and watched the sun setting behind the trees.

While he gets ice and pours bourbon she looks around the kitchen for signs. In the dish drainer are a bowl, a glass, and a spoon and she hopes they are from lunch, soup and milk, but she thinks they are from breakfast. He gives her the drink and opens a can of beer for himself. When he feels well he drinks gin; once he told her he'd always loved gin and that's why he'd never been a whiskey priest.

"Have you eaten since breakfast?"

"No," he says, and his eyes look like those of a liar. Yet he and Edith never lie to each other. It is simply that they avoid the words cancer and death and time, and when they speak of his symptoms they are looking at the real words like a ghost between them. At the beginning she saw it only in his eyes: while he joked and smiled his eyes saw the ghost and she did too, and she felt isolated by her health and hope. But gradually, as she forced herself to look at his eyes, the ghost became hers too. It filled his apartment: she looked through it at the food she cooked and they ate; she looked through it at the drinks she took from his hand; it was between them when they made love in the dark of the bedroom and afterward when she lay beside him and her eyes adjusted to the dark and discerned the outlines and shapes of the chest of drawers against the wall at the foot of the bed and, hanging above it, the long black crucifix, long enough to hang in the classroom of a parochial school, making her believe Joe had taken with him from the priesthood a crucifix whose size would assert itself on his nights. When they went to restaurants and bars she looked through the ghost at other couples; it delineated these people, froze their gestures in time. One night, looking in his bathroom mirror, she saw that it was in her own eyes. She wondered what Joe's eyes saw when they were closed, in sleep.

"You should eat," she says.

"Yes."

"Do you have something light I could fix?"

"My body." He pats his waist; he used to have a paunch; when he lost the weight he bought clothes and now all his slacks are new.

"Your head will be light if you take walks and don't eat and then drink beer."

He drinks and smiles at her.

"Nag."

"Nagaina. She's the mother cobra. In 'Rikki-Tikki-Tavi.' Would you eat some soup?"

"I would. I was wondering first—" (His eyes start to lower but he raises them again, looks at her) "—if you'd play trainer for a while. Then maybe I'd take some soup."

"Sure. Go lie down."

She gets the heating ointment from the medicine cabinet in the bathroom; it lies beside the bottle of sleeping pills. On the shelf beneath these are his shaving cream, razor, after-shave lotion, and stick deodorant. The juxtaposition disturbs her, and for a moment she succumbs to the heavy weariness of depression. She looks at her hand holding the tube of ointment. The hand does not seem to be hers; or, if it is, it has no function, it is near atrophy, it can touch no one. She lowers the hand out of her vision, closes the cabinet door, and looks at herself in the mirror. She is pretty. The past three years show in her face, but still she is pretty and she sips her drink and thinks of Joe waiting and her fingers caress the tube.

In the bedroom Joe is lying on his back, with his shirt off. The bedside lamp is on. He rolls on his belly and turns his face on the pillow so he can watch her. She lights him a cigarette then swallows the last of her bourbon and feels it. Looking at his back she unscrews the cap from the tube; his flesh is pale and she wishes it were summer so she could take him to the beach and lie beside him and watch his skin assume a semblance of health. She squeezes ointment onto her fingers and gently rubs it into the flesh where his kidney used to be. She is overtaken by a romantic impulse which means nothing in the face of what they are facing: she wishes there were no cancer but that his other kidney was in danger and he needed hers and if only he had hers he would live. Her hands move higher on his back. He lies there and smokes, and they do not talk. The first time she rubbed his back they were silent because he had not wanted to ask her to but he had anyway; and she had not wanted to do it but she had, and her flesh had winced as she touched him, and he had known it and she had known that he did. After that, on nights when she sensed his pain, or when he told her about it, she rose from the bed and got the ointment and they were silent, absorbing the achieved intimacy of her flesh. Now his eyes are closed and she watches his face on the pillow and feels what she is heating with her anointed hands.

When she is done she warms a can of vegetable soup and toasts a slice of bread. As she stirs the soup she feels him watching from the table behind her. He belches and blames it on the beer and she turns to him and smiles. She brings him the bowl of soup, the toast, and a glass of milk. She puts ice in her glass and pours bourbon, pouring with a quick and angry turning of the wrist that is either defiant or despairing—she doesn't know which. She sits with him. She would like to smoke but she knows it bothers him while he is eating so she waits. But he does not finish the soup. He eats some of the toast and drinks some of the milk and pretends to wait for the soup to cool; under her eyes he eats most of the soup and finishes the toast and is lifting a spoonful to his mouth when his face is suffused with weariness and resignation which change as quickly to anger as he shakes his head and lowers the spoon, his eyes for a moment glaring at her (but she knows it isn't her he sees) before he pushes back from the table and moves fast out of the kitchen and down the hall. She follows and is with him when he reaches the toilet and standing behind him she holds his waist with one arm and his forehead with her hand. They are there for a long time and she doesn't ask but knows he was here after breakfast and perhaps later in the day. She thinks of him alone retching and quivering over the toilet. Still holding his waist she takes a washcloth from the towel rack and reaches to the lavatory and dampens it; she presses it against his forehead. When he is finished she walks with him to the bedroom, her arm around his waist, his around her shoulder, and she pulls back the covers while he undresses. The telephone is on the bedside table. He gets into bed and she covers him then turning her back to him she dials her home. When Hank answers she says: "I might stay a while."

"How is he?"

She doesn't answer. She clamps her teeth and shuts her eyes and raising her left hand she pushes her hair back from her face and quickly wipes the tears from beneath her eyes.

"Bad?" Hank says.

"Yes."

"Stay as long as you want," he says. His voice is tender and for a moment she responds to that; but she has been married to him for eight years and known him for the past three and the moment passes; she squeezes the phone and wants to hit him with it.

She goes to the kitchen, the bathroom, and the living room, getting her drink and turning out lights. Joe is lying on his belly with his eyes closed. She undresses, hoping he will open his eyes and see her; she is the only woman he has ever made love with and always he has liked watching her undress; but he does not open his eyes. She turns out the lamp and goes around the bed and gets in with her drink. Propped on a pillow she finishes it and lowers the glass to the floor as he holds her hand. He remains quiet and she can feel him talking to her in his mind. She moves closer to him, smelling mouthwash and ointment, and she thinks of the first time they made love and the next day he bought a second pillow and two satin pillowcases and that night showing them to her he laughed and said he felt like Gatsby with his shirts. She said: Don't make me into that Buchanan bitch; I don't leave bodies in the road. Months later when she went to the hospital to see him after the operation she remembered what she had said. Still, and strangely, there is a sad but definite pleasure remembering him buying the pillow and two satin pillowcases.

Suddenly he is asleep. It happens so quickly that she is afraid. She listens to his slow breath and then, outstretched beside him, touching as much of the length of his body as she can, she closes her eyes and prays to the dark above her. She feels her prayers do not ascend, that they disseminate in the dark beneath the ceiling. She does not use words, for she cannot feel God above the bed. She prays with images: she sees Joe suffering in a hospital bed with tubes in his body and she does not want him to suffer. So finally her prayer is an image of her sitting beside this bed holding his hand while, gazing at her peacefully and without pain, he dies. But this doesn't touch the great well of her need and she wishes she could know the words for all of her need and that her statement would rise through and beyond the ceiling, up beyond the snow and stars, until it reached an ear. Then listening to Joe's breathing she begins to relax, and soon she sleeps. Some time in the night she is waked by his hands. He doesn't speak. His breath is quick and he kisses her and enters with a thrust she receives; she feels him arcing like Icarus, and when he collapses

on her and presses his lips to her throat she knows she holds his
entire history in her body. It has been a long time since she has
felt this with a man. Perhaps she never has.

2

ALL SHE HAD ever wanted to be was a nice girl someone
would want to marry. When she married Hank Allison she was
twenty-two years old and she had not thought of other possibilities. Husbands died, but one didn't think of that. Marriages died
too: she had seen enough corpses and heard enough autopsies in
Winnetka (the women speaking: sipping their drinks, some of
them afraid, some fascinated as though by lust; no other conversation involved them so; Edith could feel flesh in the room,
pores, blood, as they spoke of what had destroyed or set free one
of their kind); so she knew about the death of love as she knew
about breast cancer. And, just as she touched and explored her
breasts, she fondled her marriage, stroked that space of light and
air that separated her from Hank.

He was her first lover; they married a year earlier than they
had planned because she was pregnant. From the time she missed
her first period until she went to the gynecologist she was afraid
and Hank was too; every night he came to her apartment and the
first thing he asked was whether she had started. Then he drank
and talked about his work and the worry left his eyes. After she
had gone to the doctor she was afraid for another week or so;
Hank's eyes pushed her further into herself. But after a while he

was able to joke about it. We should have done it right, he said—gone to the senior prom and made it in the car. He was merry and resilient. In her bed he grinned and said the gods had caught up with him for all the times he'd screwed like a stray dog.

When she was certain Hank did not feel trapped she no longer felt trapped, and she became happy about having a child. She phoned her parents. They seemed neither alarmed nor unhappy. They liked Hank and, though Edith had never told them, she knew they had guessed she and Hank were lovers. She drove up to Winnetka to plan the wedding. While her father was at work or gone to bed she had prenatal conversations with her mother. She spoke of breast-feeding, diet, smoking, natural childbirth, saddleblocks. Edith didn't recognize the significance of these conversations until much later, in her ninth month. They meant that her marriage had begun at the moment when she was first happy about carrying a child. She was no longer Hank's lover; she was his wife. What had been clandestine and sweet and dark was now open; the fruit of that intimacy was shared with her mother. She had begun to nest. Before the wedding she drove back to Iowa City, where Hank was a graduate student, and found and rented a small house. There was a room where Hank could write and there was a room for the baby, as it grew older. There was a back yard with an elm tree. She had money from her parents, and spent a few days buying things to put in the house. People delivered them. It was simple and comforting.

In her ninth month, looking back on that time, she began to worry about Hank. Her life had changed, had entered a trajectory of pregnancy and motherhood; his life had merely shifted to the side, to make more room. But she began to wonder if he had merely shifted. Where was he, who was he, while she talked with her mother, bought a washing machine, and felt the baby growing inside her? At first she worried that he had been left out, or anyway felt left out; that his shifting aside had involved enormous steps. Then at last she worried that he had not shifted at all but, for his own survival, had turned away.

She became frightened. She remembered how they had planned marriage: it would come when he finished school, got a job. They used to talk about it. Hank lived in one room of an old brick building which was owned by a cantankerous and colorful old man who walked with the assistance of a stout, gnarled, and threatening cane; like most colorful people, he knew he was and he used that quality, in his dealings with student-tenants, to balance his cantankerousness, which he was also aware of and could have controlled but instead indulged, the way some people indulge their vicious and beloved dogs. In the old brick house there was one communal kitchen, downstairs; it was always dirty and the refrigerator was usually empty because people tended to eat whatever they found there, even if the owner had attached a note to it asking that it be spared.

Edith did not cook for Hank in that kitchen. When she cooked for him, and she liked to do that often, she did it in her own apartment, in a tiny stifling kitchen that was little more than an alcove never meant to hold the refrigerator and stove, which faced each other and could not be opened at the same time. Her apartment itself was narrow, a room on one side of a house belonging to a tense young lawyer and his tenser young wife and their two loud sons who seemed oblivious to that quality which permeated their parents' lives. Neither the lawyer nor his wife had ever told Edith she could not keep a man overnight. But she knew she could not. She knew this because they did not drink or smoke or laugh very much either, and because of the perturbed lust in the lawyer's eyes when he glanced at her. So she and Hank made love on the couch that unfolded and became a narrow bed, and then he went home. He didn't want to spend the night anyway, except on some nights when he was drunk. Since he was a young writer in a graduate school whose only demand was that he write, and write well, he was often drunk, either because he had written well that day or had not. But he was rarely so drunk that he wanted to stay the night at Edith's. And, when he did, it wasn't because liquor had released in him some need he wouldn't ordinarily yield to; it was because he didn't want to drive home. Always, though, she got him out of the house; and always he was glad next morning that she had.

He had little money, only what an assistantship gave him, and he didn't like her to pay for their evenings out, so when they saw each other at night it was most often at her apartment. Usually before he came she would shower and put on a dress or skirt. He teased her about that but she knew he liked it. So did she. She liked being dressed and smelling of perfume and brushing her long black hair before the mirror, and she liked the look in his eyes and the way his voice heightened and belied his teasing. She put on records and they had drinks and told each other what they had done that day. She was pretending to be in her first year of graduate school, in American history, so she could be near Hank; she attended classes, even read the books and wrote the papers, even did rather well; but she was pretending. They drank for a while, then she stood between the hot stove and the refrigerator and cooked while he stood at the entrance of the alcove, and they talked. They ate at a small table against the wall of the living room; the only other room was the bathroom. After dinner she washed the dishes, put away leftovers in foil, and they unfolded the couch and made love and lay talking until they were ready to make love again. It all felt like marriage. Even at twenty-seven, looking back on those nights after five years of marriage, she still saw in them what marriage could often be: talk and dinner and, the child asleep, living-room lovemaking long before the eleven o'clock news which had become their electronic foreplay, the weather report the final signal to climb the stairs together and undress.

On those nights in the apartment they spoke of marriage. And he explained why, even on the nights of Iowa winter when his moustache froze as he walked from her door around the lawyer's house and down the slippery driveway to his car, he did not want to spend the night with her. It was a matter of ritual, he told her. It had to do with his work. He did not want to wake up with someone (he said *someone*, not *you*) and then drive home to his own room where he would start the morning's work. What he liked to do, he said (already she could see he sometimes confused like to with have to) was spend his first wakeful time of the day alone. In his room, each working morning, he first made his bed and cleared his desk of mail and books, then while he made his coffee and cooked bacon and eggs on the hot plate he read the morning paper; he read through the meal and afterward while he drank coffee and smoked. By the time he had finished the paper and washed the dishes in the bathroom he had been awake for an hour and a half. Then, with the reluctance which began as he reached the final pages of the newspaper, he sat at his desk and started to work.

He spoke so seriously, almost reverently, about making a bed, eating some eggs, and reading a newspaper, that at first Edith was amused; but she stifled it and asked him what was happening during that hour and a half of quiet morning. He said, That's it: quiet: silence. While his body woke he absorbed silence. His work was elusive and difficult and had to be stalked; a phone call or an early visitor could flush it. She said, What about after we're married? He smiled and his arm tightened her against him. He told her of a roommate he had, when he was an undergraduate. The roommate was talkative. He woke up talking and went to bed talking. Most of the talk was good, a lot of it purposely funny, and Hank enjoyed it. Except at breakfast. The roommate liked the share the newspaper with Hank and talk about what they were reading. Hank was writing a novel then; he finished it in his senior year, read it at home that summer in Phoenix, and, with little ceremony or despair, burned it. But he was writing it then, living with the roommate, and after a few weeks of spending an hour and a half cooking, reading, and talking and then another hour in silence at his desk before he could put the first word on paper, he started waking at six o'clock so that his roommate woke at eight to an apartment that smelled of bacon and, walking past Hank's closed door, he entered the kitchen where Hank's plate and fork were in the drainer, the clean skillet on the stove, coffee in the pot, and the newspaper waiting on the table.

So in her ninth month she began worrying about Hank. What had first drawn her to him was his body: in high school he had played football; he was both too light and too serious to play in college; he was short, compact, and hard, and she liked his poised, graceful walk; with yielding hands she liked touching his shoulders and arms. When he told her he ran five miles every day she was pleased. Later, not long before they were lovers, she realized that what she loved about him was his vibrance, intensity; it was not that he was a writer; she had read little and indiscriminately and he would have to teach her those things about his work that she must know. She loved him because he had found his center, and it was that center she began worrying about in her ninth month. For how could a man who didn't want to spend a night with his lover be expected to move into a house with a woman, and then a baby? She watched him.

When he finished the novel, Sharon was two and they were buying a house in Bradford, Massachusetts, where he taught and where Edith believed she could live forever. Boston was forty minutes to the south, and she liked it better than Chicago; the New Hampshire beaches were twenty minutes away; she had been landlocked for twenty-four years and nearly every summer day she took Sharon to the beach while Hank wrote; on sunny days when she let herself get trapped into errands or other trifles that posed as commitments, she felt she had wronged herself; but there were not many of those days. She loved autumn—she and Hank and Sharon drove into New Hampshire and Vermont to look at gold and red and yellow leaves—and she loved winter too—it wasn't as cold and windy as the midwest—and she loved the evergreens and snow on the hills; and all winter she longed for the sea, and some days she bundled up Sharon and drove to it and looked at it from the warmth of the car. Then they got out and walked on the beach until Sharon was cold.

Hank was happy about his novel; he sent it to an agent who was happy about it too; but no one else was and, fourteen months later, with more ceremony this time (a page at a time, in the fireplace, three hundred and forty-eight of them) and much more despair, he burned it. That night he drank a lot but was still sober; or sad enough so that all the bourbon did was make him sadder; in bed he held her but he was not really holding her; he lay on his side, his arms around her; but it was she who was holding him. She wanted to make love with him, wanted that to help him, but she knew it would not and he could not. Since sending his novel to the agent he had written three stories; they existed in the mail and on the desks of editors of literary magazines and then in the mail again. And he had been thinking of a novel. He was twenty-six years old. He had been writing for eight years. And that night, lying against her, he told her the eight years were gone forever and had come to nothing. His wide hard body was rigid in her arms; she thought if he could not make love he ought to cry, break that tautness in his body, his soul. But she knew he could not. All those years meant to him, he said, was the thousands of pages, surely over three, maybe over four, he had written: all those drafts, each one draining him only to be stacked in a box or filing cabinet as another draft took its place: all those pages to get the two final drafts of the two novels that had gone into ashes, into the air. He lived now in a total of fifty-eight typed pages, the three stories that lived in trains and on the desks of men he didn't know.

"Start tomorrow," she said. "On the new novel."

For a few moments he was quiet. Then he said: "I can't. It's three in the morning. I've been drinking for eight hours."

"Just a page. Or else tomorrow will be terrible. And the day after tomorrow will be worse. You can sleep late, sleep off the booze. I'll take Sharon to the beach, and when I come home you tell me you've written and run with Jack and you feel strong again."

At the beach the next day she knew he was writing and she felt good about that; she knew that last night he had known it was what he had to do; she also knew he needed her to tell him to do it. But she felt defeated too. Last night, although she had fought it, her knowledge of defeat had begun as she held him and felt that tautness which would yield to neither passion nor grief, and she had known it was his insular will that would get him going again, and would deny her a child.

When he finished the novel fourteen months ago she had started waiting for that time—she knew it would be a moment, an hour, a day, no more: perhaps only a moment of his happy assent—when she could conceive. For by this time, though he had never said it, she knew he didn't want another child. And she knew it was not because of anything as practical and as easily solved as money. It was because of the very force in him which had first attracted her, so that after two years of marriage she could think wryly: one thing has to be said about men who've found their center: they're sometimes selfish bastards. She knew he didn't want another child because he believed a baby would interfere with his work. And his believing it would probably make it true.

She knew he was being shortsighted, foolish, and selfish; she knew that, except for the day of birth itself and perhaps a day after, until her mother arrived to care for Sharon, a baby would not prevent, damage, or even interrupt one sentence of all those pages he had to write and she was happy that he wrote and glad to listen to him on those nights when he had to read them too; those pages she also resented at times, when after burning three hundred and forty-eight of them he lay in despair and the beginnings of resilience against her body she had given him more than three hundred and forty-eight times, maybe even a thousand times, and told her all the eight years meant to him were those pages. And she resented them when she knew they would keep her from having a second child; she wanted a son; and it would do no good, she knew, to assure him that he would not lose sleep, that she would get up with the baby in the night.

Because that really wasn't why he didn't want a baby; he probably thought it was; but it wasn't. So if she told him how simple it would be, he still wouldn't want to do it. Because, whether he knew it or not, he was keeping himself in reserve. He had the life he wanted: his teaching schedule gave him free mornings; he had to prepare for classes but he taught novels he knew well and could skim; he had summers off, he had a friend, Jack Linhart, to talk, drink, and run with; he had a woman and a child he loved, and all he wanted now was to write better than he'd ever written before, and it was that he saved himself for. They had never talked about any of this, but she knew it all. She almost felt the same way about her life; but she wanted a son. So she had waited for him to sell his novel, knowing that would be for him a time of exuberance and power, a time out of the fearful drudgery and isolation of his work, and in that spirit he would give her a child. Now she had to wait again.

In the winter and into the spring when snow melted first around the trunks of trees, and the ice on the Merrimack broke into chunks that floated seaward, and the river climbed and rushed, there was a girl. She came uninvited in Christmas season to a party that Edith spent a day preparing; her escort was uninvited too, a law student, a boring one, who came with a married couple who were invited. Later Edith would think of him: if he had to crash the party he should at least have been man enough to keep the girl he crashed with. Her name was Jeanne, she was from France, she was visiting friends in Boston. That was all she was doing: visiting. Edith did not know what part of France she was from nor what she did when she was there. Probably Jeanne told her that night while they stood for perhaps a quarter of an hour in the middle of the room and voices, sipping their drinks, nodding at each other, talking the way two very attractive women will talk at a party: Edith speaking and even answering while her real focus was on Jeanne's short black hair, her sensuous, indolent lips, her brown and mischievous eyes. Edith had talked with the law student long enough—less than a quarter of an hour—to know he wasn't Jeanne's lover and couldn't be; his confidence was still young, wistful, and vulnerable; and there was an impatience, a demand, about the amatory currents she felt flowing from Jeanne. She remarked all of this and recalled nothing they talked about. They parted like two friendly but competing hunters after meeting in the woods. For the rest of the night—while talking, while dancing—Edith watched the law student and the husbands lining up at the trough of Jeanne's accent, and she watched Jeanne's eyes, which appeared vacant until you looked closely at them and saw that they were selfish: Jeanne was watching herself.

And Edith watched Hank, and listened to him. Early in their marriage she had learned to do that. His intimacy with her was private; at their table and in their bed they talked; his intimacy with men was public, and when he was with them he spoke mostly to them, looked mostly at them, and she knew there were times when he was unaware that she or any other woman was in the room. She had long ago stopped resenting this; she had watched the other wives sitting together and talking to one another; she had watched them sit listening while couples were at a dinner table and the women couldn't group so they ate and listened to the men. Usually men who talked to women were trying to make love with them, and she could sense the other men's resentment at this distraction, as if during a hand of poker a man had left the table to phone his mistress. Of course she was able to talk at parties; she wasn't shy and no man had ever intentionally made her feel he was not interested in what she had to say; but willy-nilly they patronized her. As they listened to her she could sense their courtesy, their impatience for her to finish so they could speak again to their comrades. If she had simply given in to that patronizing, stopped talking because she was a woman, she might have become bitter. But she went further: she watched the men, and saw that it wasn't a matter of their not being interested in women. They weren't interested in each other either. At least not in what they said, their ideas; the ideas and witticisms were instead the equipment of friendly, even loving, competition, as for men with different interests were the bowling ball, the putter, the tennis racket. But it went deeper than that too: she finally saw that. Hank needed and loved men, and when he loved them it was because of what they thought and how they lived. He did not measure women that way; he measured them by their sexuality and good sense. He and his friends talked with one another because it was the only way they could show their love; they might reach out and take a woman's hand and stroke it while they leaned forward, talking to men; and their conversations were fields of mutual praise. It no longer bothered her. She knew that some women writhed under these conversations; they were usually women whose husbands rarely spoke to them with the intensity and attention they gave to men.

But that night, listening to Hank, she was frightened and angry. He and Jeanne were watching each other. He talked to the men but he was really talking to her; at first Edith thought he was showing off; but it was worse, more fearful: he was being received and he knew it and that is what gave his voice its exuberant lilt. His eyes met Jeanne's over a shoulder, over the rim of a lifted glass. When Jeanne left with the law student and the invited couple, Edith and Hank told them goodbye at the door. It was only the second time that night Edith and Jeanne had looked at each other and spoken; they smiled and voiced amenities; a drunken husband lurched into the group; his arm groped for Jeanne's waist and his head plunged downward to kiss her. She quickly cocked her head away, caught the kiss lightly on her cheek, almost dodged it completely. For an instant her eyes were impatient. Then that was gone. Tilted away from the husband's muttering face she was looking at Hank. In her eyes Edith saw his passion. She reached out and put an arm about his waist; without looking at him or Jeanne she said goodnight to the law student and the couple. As the four of them went down the walk, shrugging against the cold, she could not look at Jeanne's back and hair; she watched the law student and wished him the disaster of bad grades. Be a bank teller, you bastard.

She did not see Jeanne again. In the flesh, that is. For now she saw her in dreams: not those of sleep which she could forget but her waking dreams. In the mornings Hank went to his office at school to write; at noon he and Jack ran and then ate lunch; he taught all afternoon and then went to the health club for a sauna with Jack and afterward they stopped for a drink; at seven he came home. On Tuesdays and Thursdays he didn't have classes but he spent the afternoon at school in conferences with students; on Saturday mornings he wrote in his office and, because he was free of students that day, he often worked into the middle of the afternoon then called Jack to say he was ready for the run, the sauna, the drinks. For the first time in her marriage Edith thought about how long and how often he was away from home. As she helped Sharon with her boots she saw Jeanne's brown eyes; they were attacking her; they were laughing at her; they sledded down the hill with her and Sharon.

When she became certain that Hank was Jeanne's lover she could not trust her certainty. In the enclosed days of winter she imagined too much. Like a spy, she looked for only one thing, and she could not tell if the wariness in his eyes and voice were truly there; making love with him she felt a distance in his touch, another concern in his heart; passionately she threw herself against that distance and wondered all the time if it existed only in her own quiet and fearful heart. Several times, after drinks at a party, she nearly asked Jack if Hank was always at school when he said he was. At home on Tuesday and Thursday and Saturday afternoons she wanted to call him. One Thursday she did. He didn't answer his office phone; it was a small school and the switchboard operator said if she saw him she'd tell him to call home. Edith was telling Sharon to get her coat, they would go to school to see Daddy, when he phoned. She asked him if he wanted to see a movie that night. He said they had seen everything playing in town and if she wanted to go to Boston he'd rather wait until the weekend. She said that was fine.

In April he and Jack talked about baseball and watched it on television and he started smoking Parliaments. She asked him why. They were milder, he said. He looked directly at her but she sensed he was forcing himself to, testing himself. For months she had imagined his infidelity and fought her imagination with the absence of evidence. Now she had that: she knew it was irrational but it was just rational enough to release the demons: they absorbed her: they gave her certainty. She remembered Jeanne holding a Parliament, waiting for one of the husbands to light it.

She lasted three days. On a Thursday afternoon she called the school every hour, feeling the vulnerability of this final prideless crumbling, making her voice as casual as possible to the switchboard operator, even saying once it was nothing important, just something she wanted him to pick up on the way home, and when he got home at seven carrying a damp towel and smelling faintly of gin she knew he had got back in time for the sauna with Jack and had spent the afternoon in Jeanne's bed. She waited until after dinner, when Sharon was in bed. He sat at the kitchen table, talking to her while she cleaned the kitchen. It was a ritual of theirs. She asked him for a drink. Usually she didn't drink after dinner, and he was surprised. Then he said he'd join her. He gave her the bourbon then sat at the table again.

"Are you having an affair with that phony French bitch?"

He sipped his drink, looked at her, and said: "Yes."

The talk lasted for days. That night it ended at three in the morning after, straddling him, she made love with him and fell into a sleep whose every moment, next morning, she believed she remembered. She had slept four hours. When she woke to the news on the radio she felt she had not slept at all, that her mind had continued the talk with sleeping Hank. She did not want to get up. In bed she smoked while Hank showered and shaved. At breakfast he did not read the paper. He spoke to Sharon and watched Edith. She did not eat. When he was ready to leave, he leaned down and kissed her and said he loved her and they would talk again that night.

All day she knew what madness was, or she believed she was at least tasting it and at times she yearned for the entire feast. While she did her work and made lunch for Sharon and talked to her and put her to bed with a coloring book and tried to read the newspaper and then a magazine, she could not stop the voices in her mind: some of it repeated from last night, some drawn up from what she believed she had heard and spoken in her sleep, some in anticipation of tonight, living tonight before it was there, so that at two in the afternoon she was already at midnight and

time was nothing but how much pain she could feel at once.
When Sharon had been in bed for an hour without sleeping
Edith took her for a walk and tried to listen to her and say yes
and no and I don't know, what do you think? and even heard
most of what Sharon said and all the time the voices would not
stop. All last night while awake and sleeping and all day she had
believed it was because Jeanne was pretty and Hank was a
man. Like any cliché, it was easy to live with until she tried to;
now she began to realize how little she knew about Hank and
how much she suspected and feared, and that night after dinner
which she mostly drank she tucked in Sharon and came down to
the kitchen and began asking questions. He told her he would
stop seeing Jeanne and there was nothing more to talk about;
he spoke of privacy. But she had to know everything he felt;
she persisted, she harried, and finally he told her she'd better be
as tough as her questions were, because she was going to get
the answers.

Which were: he did not believe in monogamy. Fidelity, she
said. You see? he said. You distort it. He was a faithful husband.
He had been discreet, kept his affair secret, had not risked her
losing face. He loved her and had taken nothing from her. She
accused him of having a double standard and he said no; no, she
was as free as she was before she met him. She asked him how
long he had felt this way, had he always been like this or was it
just some French bullshit he had picked up this winter. He had
always felt this way. By now she could not weep. Nor rage
either. All she could feel and say was: Why didn't I ever know
any of this? You never asked, he said.

It was, she thought, like something bitter from Mother Goose:
the woman made the child, the child made the roof, the roof
made the woman, and the child went away. Always she had done
her housework quickly and easily; by ten-thirty on most mornings she had done what had to be done. She was not one of those
women whose domesticity became an obsession; it was work that
she neither liked nor disliked and, when other women com-
plained, she was puzzled and amused and secretly believed their

frustration had little to do with scraping plates or pushing a vacuum cleaner over a rug. Now in April and May an act of will got
her out of bed in the morning. The air in the house was against
her: it seemed wet and gray and heavy, heavier than fog, and she
pushed through it to the bathroom where she sat staring at the
floor or shower curtain long after she was done; then she moved
to the kitchen and as she prepared breakfast the air pushed down
on her arms and against her body. *I am beating eggs,* she said to
herself, and she looked down at the fork in her hand, yolk dripping from the tines into the eggs as their swirling ceased and
they lay still in the bowl. *I am beating eggs.* Then she jabbed the
fork in again. At breakfast Hank read the paper. Edith talked to
Sharon and ate because she had to, because it was morning, it
was time to eat, and she glanced at Hank's face over the newspaper, listened to the crunching of his teeth on toast, and told herself: *I am talking to Sharon.* She kept her voice sweet, motherly,
attentive.

Then breakfast was over and she was again struck by the seductive waves of paralysis that had washed over her in bed, and
she stayed at the table. Hank kissed her (she turned her lips to
him, they met his, she did not kiss him) and went to the college.
She read the paper and drank coffee and smoked while Sharon
played with toast. She felt she would fall asleep at the table; Hank
would return in the afternoon to find her sleeping there among
the plates and cups and glasses while Sharon played alone in a
ditch somewhere down the road. So once again she rose through
an act of will, watched Sharon brushing her teeth (*I am watching
. . .*), sent her to the cartoons on television, and then slowly,
longing for sleep, she washed the skillet and saucepan (*always
scramble eggs in a saucepan,* her mother had told her; *they stand
deeper than in a skillet and they'll cook softer*) and scraped the
plates and put them and the glasses and cups and silverware in
the dishwasher.

Then she carried the vacuum cleaner upstairs and made the
bed Hank had left after she had, and as she leaned over to tuck in
the sheet she wanted to give in to the lean, to collapse in slow
motion face down on the half-made bed and lie there until—

there had been times in her life when she wanted to sleep until
something ended. Unmarried in Iowa, when she missed her period she wanted to sleep until she knew whether she was or not.
Now *until* meant nothing. No matter how often or how long she
slept she would wake to the same house, the same heavy air that
worked against her every move. She made Sharon's bed and
started the vacuum cleaner. Always she had done that quickly,
not well enough for her mother's eye, but her mother was a
Windex housekeeper: a house was not done unless the windows
were so clean you couldn't tell whether they were open or closed;
but her mother had a cleaning woman. The vacuum cleaner in-
terfered with the cartoons and Sharon came up to tell her and
Edith said she wouldn't be long and told Sharon to put on her
bathing suit—it was a nice day and they would go to the beach.
But the cleaning took her longer than it had before, when she
had moved quickly from room to room, without lethargy or
boredom but a sense of anticipation, the way she felt when she
did other work which required neither skill nor concentration,
like chopping onions and grating cheese for a meal she truly
wanted to cook.

Now, while Sharon went downstairs again and made lemonade
and poured it in the thermos and came upstairs and went down
again and came up and said yes there was a little mess and went
downstairs and wiped it up, Edith pushed the vacuum cleaner
and herself through the rooms and down the hall, and went
downstairs and started in the living room while Sharon's voice
tugged at her as strongly as hands gripping her clothes, and she
clamped her teeth on the sudden shrieks that rose in her throat
and told herself: *Don't: she's not the problem;* and she thought of
the women in supermarkets and on the street, dragging and
herding and all but cursing their children along (one day she had
seen a woman kick her small son's rump as she pulled him into a
drugstore), and she thought of the women at parties, at dinners,
or on blankets at the beach while they watched their children in
the waves, saying: *I'm so damned bored with talking to children all
day—no,* she told herself, *she's not the problem.* Finally she fin-

ished her work, yet she felt none of the relief she had felt before; the air in the house was like water now as she moved through it up the stairs to the bedroom, where she undressed and put on her bathing suit. Taking Sharon's hand and the windbreakers and thermos and blanket, she left the house and blinked in the late morning sun and wondered near-prayerfully when this would end, this dread disconnection between herself and what she was doing. At night making love with Hank she thought of him with Jeanne, and her heart, which she thought was beyond breaking, broke again, quickly, easily, as if there weren't much to break anymore, and fell into mute and dreary anger, the dead end of love's grief.

In the long sunlit evenings and the nights of May the talk was sometimes philosophical, sometimes dark and painful, drawing from him details about him and Jeanne; she believed if she possessed the details she would dispossess Jeanne of Hank's love. But she knew that wasn't her only reason. Obsessed by her pain, she had to plunge more deeply into it, feel all of it again and again. But most of the talk was abstract, and most of it was by Hank. When she spoke of divorce he calmly told her they had a loving, intimate marriage. They were, he said, simply experiencing an honest and healthful breakthrough. She listened to him talk about the unnatural boundaries of lifelong monogamy. He remained always calm. Cold, she thought. She could no longer find his heart.

At times she hated him. Watching him talk she saw his life: with his work he created his own harmony, and then he used the people he loved to relax with. Probably it was not exploitative; probably it was the best he could do. And it was harmony she had lost. Until now her marriage had been a circle, like its gold symbol on her finger. Wherever she went she was still inside it. It had a safe, gentle circumference, and mortality and the other perils lay outside of it. Often now while Hank slept she lay awake and tried to pray. She wanted to fall in live with God. She wanted His fingers to touch her days, to restore meaning to those simple tasks which now drained her spirit. On those nights when she tried to pray she longed to leave the world: her actions would appear secular but they would be her communion with God. Cleaning the house would be an act of forgiveness and patience under His warm eyes. But she knew it was no use: she had belief, but not faith: she could not bring God under her roof and into her life. He awaited her death.

Nightly and fearfully now, as though Hank's adulterous heart had opened a breach and let it in to stalk her, she thought of death. One night they went with Jack and Terry Linhart to Boston to hear Judy Collins. The concert hall was filled and darkened and she sat in the sensate, audible silence of listening people and watched Judy under the spotlight in a long lavender gown, her hair falling over one shoulder as she lowered her face over the guitar. Soon Edith could not hear the words of the songs. Sadly she gazed at Judy's face, and listened to the voice, and thought of the voice going out to the ears of all those people, all those strangers, and she thought how ephemeral was a human voice, and how death not only absorbed the words in the air, but absorbed as well the act of making the words, and the time it took to say them. She saw Judy as a small bird singing on a wire, and above her the hawk circled. She remembered reading once of an old man who had been working for twenty-five years sculpting, out of a granite mountain in South Dakota, a 563-foot-high statue of Chief Crazy Horse. She thought of Hank and the novel he was writing now, and as she sat beside him her soul withered away from him and she hoped he would fail, she hoped he would burn this one too: she saw herself helping him, placing alternate pages in the fire. Staring at the face above the lavender gown she strained to receive the words and notes into her body.

She had never lied to Hank and now everything was a lie. Beneath the cooking of a roast, the still affectionate chatting at dinner, the touch of their flesh, was the fact of her afternoons ten miles away in a New Hampshire woods where, on a blanket among shading pines and hemlocks, she lay in sin-quickened heat with Jack Linhart. Her days were delightfully strange, she thought. Hank's betrayal had removed her from the actions that were her life; she had performed them like a weary and disheartened dancer. Now, glancing at Hank reading, she took clothes from the laundry basket at her feet and folded them on the couch, and the folding of a warm towel was a manifestation of her deceit. And, watching him across the room, she felt her separation from him taking shape, filling the space between them like a stone. Within herself she stroked and treasured her lover. She knew she was doing the same to the self she had lost in April.

There was a price to pay. When there had been nothing to lie about in their marriage and she had not lied, she had always felt nestled with Hank; but with everyone else, even her closest friends, she had been aware of that core of her being that no one knew. Now she felt that with Hank. With Jack she recognized yet leaped into their passionate lie: they were rarely together more than twice a week; apart, she longed for him, talked to him in her mind, and vengefully saw him behind her closed eyes as she moved beneath Hank. When she was with Jack their passion burned and distorted their focus. For two hours on the blanket they made love again and again, they made love too much, pushing their bodies to consume the yearning they had borne and to delay the yearning that was waiting. Sometimes under the trees she felt like tired meat. The quiet air which she had broken in the first hour with moans now absorbed only their heavy breath. At those moments she saw with detached clarity that they were both helpless, perhaps even foolish. Jack wanted to escape his marriage; she wanted to live with hers; they drove north to the woods and made love. Then they dressed and drove back to what had brought them there.

This was the first time in her life she had committed herself to sin, and there were times when she felt her secret was venomous. Lying beside Terry at the beach she felt more adulterous than when she lay with Jack, and she believed her sun-lulled conversation was somehow poisoning her friend. When she held Sharon, salty and cold-skinned from the sea, she felt her sin flowing with the warmth of her body into the small wet breast. But more often she was proud. She was able to sin and love at the same time. She was more attentive to Sharon than she had been in April. She did not have to struggle to listen to her, to talk to her. She felt cleansed. And looking at Terry's long red hair as she bent over a child, she felt both close to her yet distant. She did not believe women truly had friends among themselves; school friendships dissolved into marriages; married women thought they had friends until they got divorced and discovered other women were only wives drawn together by their husbands. As much as she and Terry were together, they were not really intimate; they instinctively watched each other. She was certain that Terry would do what she was doing. A few weeks ago she would not have known that. She was proud that she knew it now.

With Hank she loved her lie. She kept it like a fire: some evenings after an afternoon with Jack she elaborately fanned it, looking into Hank's eyes and talking of places she had gone while the sitter stayed with Sharon; at other times she let it burn low, was evasive about how she had spent her day, and when the two couples were together she bantered with Jack, teased him. Once Jack left his pack of Luckies in her car and she brought them home and smoked them. Hank noticed but said nothing. When two cigarettes remained in the pack she put it on the coffee table and left it there. One night she purposely made a mistake: after dinner, while Hank watched a ball game on television, she drank gin while she cleaned the kitchen. She had drunk gin and tonic before dinner and wine with the flounder and now she put tonic in the gin, but not much. From the living room came the announcer's voice, and now and then Hank spoke. She hated his voice; she knew she did not hate him; if she did, she would be able to act, to leave him. She hated his voice tonight because he was talking to ballplayers on the screen and because there was no pain in it while in the kitchen her own voice keened without sound and she worked slowly and finished her drink and mixed another, the gin now doing what she had wanted it to: dissolving all happiness, all peace, all hope for it with Hank and all memory of it with Jack, even the memory of that very afternoon under the trees. Gin-saddened, she felt beyond tears, at the bottom of some abyss where there was no emotion save the quivering knees and fluttering stomach and cold-shrouded heart that told her she was finished. She took the drink into the living room and stood at the door and watched him looking at the screen over his lifted can of beer. He glanced at her, then back at the screen. One hand fingered the pack of Luckies on the table, but he did not take one.

"I wish you hadn't stopped smoking," she said. "Sometimes I think you did it so you'd outlive me."

He looked at her, told her with his eyes that she was drunk, and turned back to the game.

"I've been having an affair with Jack." He looked at her, his eyes unchanged, perhaps a bit more interested; nothing more. His lips showed nothing, except that she thought they seemed ready to smile. "We go up to the woods in New Hampshire in the afternoons. Usually twice a week. I like it. I started it. I went after him, at a party. I told him about Jeanne. I kept after him. I knew he was available because he's unhappy with Terry. For a while he was worried about you but I told him you wouldn't mind anyway. He's still your friend, if that worries you. Probably more yours than mine. You don't even look surprised. I suppose you'll tell me you've known it all the time."

"It wasn't too hard to pick up."

"So it really wasn't French bullshit. I used to want another child. A son. I wouldn't want to now: have a baby in this."

"Come here."

For a few moments, leaning against the doorjamb, she thought of going upstairs and packing her clothes and driving away. The impulse was rooted only in the blur of gin. She knew she would get no farther than the closet where her clothes hung. She walked to the couch and sat beside him. He put his arm around her; for a while she sat rigidly, then she closed her eyes and eased against him and rested her head on his shoulder.

In December after the summer which Hank called the summer of truth, when Edith's affair with Jack Linhart had both started and ended, Hank sold his novel. On a Saturday night they had a celebration party. It was a large party, and some of Hank's students came. His girl friend came with them. Edith had phoned Peter at the radio station Friday and invited him, had assured him it was all right, but he had said he was an old-fashioned guilt-ridden adulterer, and could not handle it. She told him she would see him Sunday afternoon.

The girl friend was nineteen years old and her name was Debbie. She was taller than Edith, she wore suede boots, and she had long blonde hair. She believed she was a secret from everyone but Edith. At the party she drank carefully (only wine), was discreet with Hank, and spent much time talking with Edith, who watched the face that seemed never to have borne pain, and thought: These Goddamn young girls don't care what they do anymore. Hank had said she was a good student. Edith assumed that meant the girl agreed with what he said and told it back to him in different words. What else could come out of a face so untouched? Bland and evil at the same time. Debbie was able to believe it when Hank told her Edith was not jealous. Sometimes Debbie stayed with Sharon while Hank and Edith went out. Hank drove her back to the dormitory; on those nights, by some rule of his own, he did not make love with Debbie. A bit drunk, standing in the kitchen with the girl, Edith glanced at her large breasts stretching the burgundy sweater. How ripe she must be, this young piece. Her nipples thrust against the cashmere. They made love in the car. Hank could not afford motels like Peter could. When Edith was in the car she felt she was in their bed. She looked at the breasts.

"I always wanted big ones," she murmured.

The girl blushed and took a cigarette from her purse.

"Hank hasn't started smoking again," Edith said. "It's amazing."

"I didn't know he ever did."

"Until last summer. He wants to live a long time. He wants to publish ten books."

Edith studied the girl's eyes. They were brown, and showed

nothing. A student. Couldn't she understand what she was hearing? That she had come without history into not history, that in a year or more or less she would be gone with her little heart broken or, more than likely, her cold little heart intact, her eyes and lips intact, having given nothing and received less: a memory for Hank to smile over in a moment of a spring afternoon. But then Edith looked away from the eyes. None of this mattered to the girl. Not the parentheses of time, not that blank space between them that one had to fill. It was Edith who would lose. Perhaps the next generation of students would be named Betty or Mary Ann. Well into his forties Hank would be attractive to them. Each year he would pluck what he needed. Salaried and tenured adultery. She would watch them come into her home like ghosts of each other. Sharon would like their attention, as she did now. Edith was twenty-seven. She had ten more years, perhaps thirteen; fifteen. Her looks would be gone. The girls would come with their loose breasts under her roof, and brassiered she would watch them, talk with them. It would not matter to Hank where they had come from and where they were going. He would write books.

She could not read it: the one he sold, the one she had urged him that summer night to begin next day, helping him give birth to it while she gave up a son. When he finished it a month ago and sent it to the agent he gave her the carbon and left her alone with it; it was a Saturday and he went to Jack's to watch football. She tried all afternoon. He needed her to like it; she knew that. He only pretended to care about what she thought of other books or movies. But handing her the manuscript he had boyishly lowered his eyes, and then left. He left because he could not be in the house with her while she read it. When she had read the other one, the one he burned, he had paced about the house and lawn and returned often to watch her face, to see what his work was doing to it. This time he knew better. All of that was in his eyes and voice when he said with such vulnerability that for a moment she wanted to hold him with infinite forgiveness: "I think I'll go to Jack's and watch the game."

She tried to recall that vulnerability as she read. But she could not. His prose was objective, concrete, precise. The voice of the book was the voice of the man who last spring and summer had spoken of monogamy, absolved and encouraged her adultery, and in the fall announced that he was having an affair with Debbie. Through the early chapters she was angry. She pushed herself on. Mostly she skimmed. Then she grew sad: this was the way she had wanted it when she first loved him: he would bring her his work and he would need her praise and before anyone else read it the work would be consummated between them. Now she could not read it through the glaze of pain that covered the pages. She skimmed, and when he returned in the evening she greeted him with an awed and tender voice, with brightened eyes; she held him tightly and told him it was a wonderful novel and she thought of how far she had come with this man, how frequent and convincing were her performances.

He wanted to talk about it; he was relieved and joyful; he wanted to hear everything she felt. That was easy enough: they talked for two hours while she cooked and they ate; he would believe afterward that she had talked to him about his book; she had not. Recalling what she skimmed she mentioned a scene or passage, let him interrupt her, and then let him talk about it. Now it would be published, and he would write another. Looking at Debbie she wondered if Peter would leave his wife and marry her. She had not thought of that before; and now, with images in her mind of herself and Peter and Sharon driving away, she knew too clearly what she had known from the beginning: that she did not love Peter Jackman. All adultery is a symptom, she thought. She watched Debbie, who was talking about Hank's novel; she had read it after Edith. Hank brought to his adultery the protocol of a professional. Who *was* this girl? What was she *do*ing? Did she put herself to sleep in the dormitory with visions of herself and Hank driving away? In her eyes Edith found nothing; she could have been peering through the windows of a darkened cellar.

"I'm going to circulate," she said.

In the living room she found Jack, and took his hand. Looking at his eyes she saw their summer and his longing and she touched his cheek and beard and recalled the sun over his shoulder and her hot closed eyes. He did not love Terry but he could not hurt her, nor leave his children, and he was faithful now, he drank too much, and often he talked long and with embittered anger about things of no importance.

"I hope there was *some*thing good," she said. "In last summer."

"There was." He pressed her hand.

"Doesn't Hank's girl look pretty tonight?" she said.

"I hate the little bitch."

"So do I."

Once in Iowa, while Edith was washing clothes at a launderette, a dreary place of graduate students reading, Mann juxtaposed with Tide, and stout wives with curlers in their hair, a place she gladly abandoned when she married Hank and moved into the house with her own washer and dryer, she met a young wife who was from a city in the south. Her husband was a student and he worked nights as a motel clerk. Because they found one for sixty dollars a month, they lived in a farmhouse far from town, far from anyone. From her window at night, across the flat and treeless land, she could see the lights of her closest neighbor, a mile and a half away. She had a small child, a daughter. She had never lived in the country and the farmers liked to tell her frightening stories. While she was getting mail from the box at the road they stopped their tractors and talked to her, these large sunburned farmers who she said had grown to resemble the hogs they raised. They told her of hogs eating drunks and children who fell into the pens. And they told her a year ago during the long bad winter a man had hanged himself in the barn of the house she lived in; he had lived there alone, and he was buried in town.

So at night, while her husband was at the motel desk, the woman was afraid. When she was ready for bed she forced her-

self to turn off all the downstairs lights, though she wanted to
leave every light burning, sleep as if in bright afternoon; then she
climbed the stairs and turned out the hall light too, for she was
trying to train the child to sleep in the dark. Then she would go
to bed and, if she had read long enough, was sleepy enough,
she'd go to sleep soon; but always fear was there and if she woke
in the night—her bladder, a sound from the child, a lone and rare
car on the road in front of the house—she lay terrified in the
dark which spoke to her, touched her. In those first wakeful moments she thought she was afraid of the dark itself, that if she dis-
pelled it with light her fear would subside. But she did not turn
on the light. And as she lay there she found that within the darkness were spaces of safety. She was not afraid of her room. She
lay there a while longer and thought of other rooms. She was not
afraid of her child's room. Or the bathroom. Or the hall, the
stairs, the living room. It was the kitchen. The shadowed corner
between the refrigerator and the cupboard. She did not actually
believe someone was crouched there. But it was that corner that
she feared. She lay in bed seeing it more clearly than she could
see her own darkened room. Then she rose from the bed and, in
the dark, went downstairs to the kitchen and stood facing the
dark corner, staring at it. She stared at it until she was not afraid;
then she went upstairs and slept.

On other nights she was afraid of other places. Sometimes it
was the attic, and she climbed the stairs into the stale air, past the
dusty window, and stood in the center of the room among boxes
and cardboard barrels and knew that a running mouse would
send her shouting down the stairs and vowed that it would not.
The basement was worse: it was cool and damp, its ceiling was
low, and no matter where she stood there was always a space she
couldn't see: behind the furnace in the middle of the floor, behind
the columns supporting the ceiling. Worst of all was the barn: on
some nights she woke and saw its interior, a dread place even in
daylight, with its beams. She did not know which one he had
used; she knew he had climbed out on one of them, tied the rope,
put the noose around his neck, and jumped. On some nights she
had to leave her bed and go out there. It was autumn then and

she only had to put on her robe and shoes. Crossing the lawn, approaching the wide dark open door, she was not afraid she would see him: she was afraid that as she entered the barn she would look up at the beam he had used and she would know it was the beam he had used.

Driving home Sunday night Edith thought of the woman— she could not remember her name, only her story—caught as an adult in the fears of childhood: for it was not the hanged man's ghost she feared; she did not believe in ghosts. It was the dark. A certain dark place on a certain night. She had gone to the place and looked at what she feared. But there was something incomplete about the story, something Edith had not thought of until now: the woman had looked at the place where that night her fear took shape. But she had not discovered what she was afraid of.

In daylight while Hank and Sharon were sledding Edith had driven to the bar to meet Peter. They had gone to the motel while the December sun that stayed low and skirting was already down. When he drove her back to the bar she did not want to leave him and drive home in the night. She kissed him and held him tightly. She wanted to go in for a drink but she didn't ask, for she knew he was late now; he had to return to his wife. His marriage was falling slowly, like a feather. He thought his wife had a lover (she had had others), but they kept their affairs secret from each other. Or tried to. Or pretended to. Edith knew they were merely getting by with flimsy deception while they avoided the final confrontation. Edith had never met Norma, or seen her. In the motels Peter talked about her. She released him and got out of the car and crossed the parking lot in the dark.

She buckled her seatbelt and turned on the radio and cautiously joined the traffic on the highway. But it was not a wreck she afraid of. The music was bad: repetitious rock from a station for teenagers. It was the only station she could get and she left it on. She had a thirty-minute drive and she did not know why, for the first time in her adult life, she was afraid of being alone in the dark. She had been afraid from the beginning: the first night she left Peter at a parking lot outside a bar and drove home; and now when Sharon was asleep and Hank was out she was afraid in the house and one night alone she heard the washing machine stop in the basement but she could not go down there and put the clothes in the dryer. Sometimes on gray afternoons she was frightened and she would go to the room where Sharon was and sit with her. Once when Sharon was at a birthday party she fell asleep in the late afternoon and woke alone with dusk at the windows and fled through the house turning on lights and Peter's disc-jockey program and fire for the teakettle. Now she was driving on a lovely country road through woods and white hills shimmering under the moon. But she watched only the slick dark road. She thought of the beach and the long blue afternoons and evenings of summer. She thought of grilling three steaks in the back yard. She and Hank and Sharon would be sunburned, their bodies warm and smelling of the sea. They would eat at the picnic table in the seven o'clock sun.

She hoped Hank would be awake when she got home. He would look up from his book, his eyes amused and arrogant as they always were when she returned from her nights. She hoped he was awake. For if he was already asleep she would in silence ascend the stairs and undress in the dark and lie beside him unable to sleep and she would feel the house enclosing and caressing her with some fear she could not name.

3

BEFORE JOE RITCHIE was dying they lay together in the cool nights of spring and he talked. His virginal, long-stored and (he told her) near-atrophied passion leaped and quivered inside her; during the lulls he talked with the effusion of a man who had lived forty years without being intimate with a woman. Which was, he said, pretty much a case of having never been intimate with anyone at all. It was why he left the priesthood. Edith looked beyond the foot of the bed and above the chest of drawers at the silhouette of the hanging crucifix while he told her of what he called his failures, and the yearnings they caused.

He said he had never doubted. When he consecrated he knew that he held the body, the blood. He did not feel proud or particularly humble either; just awed. It was happening in his two lifted hands (and he lifted them above his large and naked chest in the dark), his two hands, of his body; yet at the same time it was not of his body. He knew some priests who doubted. Their eyes were troubled, sometimes furtive. They kept busy: some were athletic, and did that; some read a lot, and others were active in the parish: organized and supervised fairs, started discussion groups, youth groups, pre-Cana groups, married groups, counseled, made sick calls, jail calls, anything to keep them from themselves. Some entered the service, became chaplains. One of them was reported lost at sea. He had been flying with a navy pilot, from a carrier. The poor bastard, Joe said. You know what I think? He wanted to be with that pilot, so he could be around certainty. Watch the man and the machine. A chaplain in an airplane. When I got the word I thought: That's it: in the destructive element immerse, you poor bastard.

Joe had loved the Eucharist since he was a boy; it was why he became a priest. Some went to the seminary to be pastors and bishops; they didn't know it, but it was why they went, and in the seminary they were like young officers. Some, he said, went to pad and shelter their neuroses—or give direction to them. They had a joke then, the young students with their fresh and hopeful faces: behind every Irish priest there's an Irish mother wringing her hands. But most became priests because they wanted to live their lives with God; they had, as the phrase went, a vocation. There were only two vocations, the church taught: the religious life or marriage. Tell that to Hank, she said; he'd sneer at one and laugh at the other. Which would he sneer at? Joe said. I don't really know, she said.

It was a difficult vocation because it demanded a marriage of sorts with a God who showed himself only through the volition, action, imagination, and the resultant faith of the priest himself; when he failed to create and complete this union with God he was thrust back upon himself and his loneliness. For a long time the Eucharist worked for Joe. It was the high point of his day, when he consecrated and ate and drank. The trouble was it happened early in the morning. He rose and said mass and the day was over, but it was only beginning. That was what he realized or admitted in his mid-thirties: that the morning consecration completed him but it didn't last; there was no other act during the day that gave him that completion, made him feel an action of his performed in time and mortality had transcended both and been received by a God who knew his name.

Of course while performing the tasks of a parish priest he gained the sense of accomplishment which even a conscripted soldier could feel at the end of a chore. Sometimes the reward was simply that the job was over: that he had smiled and chatted through two and a half hours of bingo without displaying his weariness that bordered on panic. But with another duty came a reward that was insidious: he knew that he was a good speaker, that his sermons were better than those of the pastor and the two younger priests. One of the younger priests should have been excused altogether from speaking to gathered people. He lacked intelligence, imagination, and style; with sweaty brow he spoke stiffly of old and superfluous truths he had learned as a student. When he was done, he left the pulpit and with great relief and concentration worked through the ritual, toward the moment when he would raise the host. When he did this, and looked up at the Eucharist in his hands, his face was no longer that of the misfit in the pulpit; his jaw was solemn, his eyes firm. Joe pitied him for his lack of talent, for his anxiety each Sunday, for his awareness of each blank face, each shifting body in the church, and his knowledge that what he said was ineffectual and dull.

Yet he also envied the young priest. In the pulpit Joe loved the sound of his own voice: the graceful flow of his words, his imagery, his timing, and the tenor reaches of his passion; his eyes engaged and swept and recorded for his delight the upturned and attentive faces. At the end of his homily he descended from the pulpit, his head lowered, his face set in the seriousness of a man who has just perceived truth. His pose continued as he faced the congregation for the Credo and the prayers of petition; it continued as he ascended the three steps to the altar and began the offertory and prepared to consecrate. In his struggle to rid himself of the pose, he assumed another: he acted like a priest who was about to hold the body of Christ in his hands, while all the time, even as he raised the host and then the chalice, his heart swelled and beat with love for himself. On the other six days, at the sparsely attended week-day masses without sermons, he broke the silence of the early mornings only with prayers, and unaware of the daily communicants, the same people usually, most of them old women who smelled of sleep and cleanliness and time, he was absorbed by the ritual, the ritual became him, and in the privacy of his soul he ate the body and drank the blood; he ascended; and then his day was over.

The remaining hours were dutiful, and he accepted them with a commitment that nearly always lacked emotion. After a few years he began to yearn; for months, perhaps a year or more, he did not know what he yearned for. Perhaps he was afraid to know. At night he drank more; sometimes the gin curbed his longings that still he wouldn't name; but usually, with drinking, he grew sad. He did not get drunk, so in the morning he woke without hangover or lapse of memory, and recalling last night's gloom he wondered at its source, as though he were trying to understand not himself but a close friend. One night he did drink too much, alone, the pastor and the two younger priests long asleep, Joe going down the hall to the kitchen with less and less caution, the cracking sound of the ice tray in his hands nothing compared to the sound that only he could hear: his monologue with himself; and it was so intense that he felt anyone who passed the kitchen door would hear the voice that resounded in his skull.

In the morning he did not recall what he talked about while he drank. He woke dehydrated and remorseful, his mind so dissipated that he had to talk himself through each step of his preparation for the day, for if he didn't focus carefully on buttoning his shirt, tying his shoes, brushing his teeth, he might fall again into the shards of last night. His sleep had been heavy and drunken, his dreams anxious. He was thankful that he could not recall them. He wished he could not recall what he did as he got into bed: lying on his side he had hugged a pillow to his breast, and holding it in both arms had left consciousness saying to himself, to the pillow, to God, and perhaps aloud: I must have a woman. Leaving the rectory, crossing the lawn to the church in the cool morning, where he would say mass not for the old ladies but for himself, he vowed that he would not get drunk again.

It was not his holding the pillow that frightened him; nor was it the words he had spoken either aloud or within his soul: it was the fearful and ascendant freedom he had felt as he listened to and saw the words. There was dew on the grass beneath his feet; he stopped and looked down at the flecks of it on his polished black shoes. He stood for a moment, a slight cool breeze touching his flesh, the early warmth of the sun on his hair and face, and he felt a loving and plaintive union with all those alive and dead who had at one time in their lives, through drink or rage or passion, suddenly made the statement whose result they had both feared and hoped for and had therefore long suppressed. He imagined a multitude of voices and pained and determined faces, leaping into separation and solitude and fear and hope. His hand rose to his hair, gray in his thirties. He walked on to the church. As he put on his vestments he looked down at the sleepy altar boy, a child. He wanted to touch him but was afraid to. He spoke gently to the boy, touched him with words. They filed into the church, and the old women and a young couple who were engaged and one old man rose.

There were ten of them. With his gin-dried mouth he voiced the prayers while his anticipatory heart beat toward that decision he knew he would one day reach, and had been reaching for some time, as though his soul had taken its own direction while his body and voice moved through the work of the parish. When the ten filed up to receive communion and he placed the host on their tongues and smelled their mouths and bodies and clothes, the sterile old ones and the young couple smelling washed as though for a date, the boy of after-shave lotion, the girl of scented soap, he studied each face for a sign. The couple were too young. In the wrinkled faces of the old he could see only an accumulation of time, of experience; he could not tell whether, beneath those faces, there was a vague recollection of a rewarding life or weary and muted self-contempt because of moments denied, choices run from. He could not tell whether any of them had reached and then denied or followed an admission like the one that gin had drawn from him the night before. Their tongues wet his fingers. He watched them with the dread, excitement, and vulnerability of a man who knows his life is about to change.

After that he stayed sober. The gin had done its work. Before dinner he approached the bottle conspiratorially, held it and looked at it as though it contained a benevolent yet demanding genie. He did not even have to drink carefully. He did not have to drink at all. He drank to achieve a warm nimbus for his secret that soon he would bare to the pastor. In the weeks that followed his drunken night he gathered up some of his past, looked at it as he had not when it was his present, and smiling at himself he saw that he had been in trouble, and the deepest trouble had been his not knowing that he was in trouble. He saw that while he was delivering his sermons he had been proud, yes; perhaps that wasn't even sinful; perhaps it was natural, even good; but the pride was no longer significant. The real trap of his sermons was that while he spoke he had acted out, soberly and with no sense of desperation, the same yearning that had made him cling to the pillow while drunk. For he realized now that beneath his sermons, even possibly at the source of them, was an abiding desire to expose his soul with all his strengths and vanities and weaknesses to another human being. And, further, the other human being was a woman.

Studying himself from his new distance he learned that while he had scanned the congregation he had of course noted the men's faces; but as attentive, as impressed, as they might be, he brushed them aside, and his eyes moved on to the faces of women. He spoke to them. It was never one face. He saw in all those eyes of all those ages the female reception he had to have: grandmothers and widows and matrons and young wives and young girls all formed a composite woman who loved him.

She came to the confessional too, where he sat profiled to the face behind the veiled window, one hand supporting his forehead and shielding his eyes. He sat and listened to the woman's voice. He had the reputation of being an understanding confessor; he had been told this by many of those people who when speaking to a priest were compelled to talk shop; not theirs: his. Go to Father Ritchie, the women told him at parish gatherings; that's what they all say, Father. He sat and listened to the woman's voice. Usually the sins were not important; and even when they were he began to sense that the woman and the ritual of confession had nothing to do with the woman and her sin. Often the sins of men were pragmatic and calculated and had to do with money; their adulteries were restive lapses from their responsibilities as husbands and fathers, and they confessed them that way, some adding the assurance that they loved their wives, their children. Some men confessed not working at their jobs as hard as they could, and giving too little time to their children. Theirs was a world of responsible action; their sins were what they considered violations of that responsibility.

But the women lived in a mysterious and amoral region which both amused and attracted Joe. Their sins were instinctual. They raged at husbands or children; they fornicated or committed adultery; the closest they came to pragmatic sin was birth control, and few of them confessed that anymore. It was not celibate lust that made Joe particularly curious about their sexual sins: it was the vision these sins gave him of their natures. Sometimes he wondered if they were capable of sinning at all. Husbands whispered of one-night stands, and in their voices Joe could hear self-reproach that was rooted in how they saw themselves as part of the world. But not so with the women. In passion they had made love. There was no other context for the act. It had nothing to do with their husbands or their children; Joe never said it in the confessional but it was clear to him that it had nothing to do with God either. He began to see God and the church and those activities that he thought of as the world—education, business, politics—as male and serious, perhaps comically so; while women were their own temples and walked cryptic, oblivious, and brooding across the earth. Behind the veil their voices whispered without remorse. Their confessions were a distant and dutiful salute to the rules and patterns of men. He sat and listened to the woman's voice.

And his reputation was real: he was indeed understanding and kind, but not for God, not for the sacrament that demanded of him empathy and compassion as God might have; or Christ. For it was not God he loved, it was Christ: God in the flesh that each morning he touched and ate, making his willful and faithful connection with what he could neither touch nor see. But his awareness of his duty to imitate Christ was not the source of his virtues as a confessor. Now, as he prepared to leave the priesthood, he saw that he had given kindness and compassion and understanding because he had wanted to expose that part of himself, real or false, to a faceless nameless woman who would at least know his name because it hung outside the confessional door. And he understood why on that hungover morning he had wanted to touch the altar boy but had been afraid to, though until then his hands had instinctively gone out to children, to touch, to caress; on that morning he had been afraid he would not stop at a touch; that he would embrace the boy, fiercely, like a father.

He did not lose his faith in the Eucharist. After leaving the priesthood he had daily gone to mass and received what he knew was the body and blood of Christ. He knew it, he told Edith, in the simplest and perhaps most profound way: most profound, he said, because he believed that faith had no more to do with intellect than love did; that touching her he knew he loved her and loving her he touched her; and that his flesh knew God through touch as it had to; that there was no other way it could; that bread and wine becoming body and blood was neither miracle nor mystery, but natural, for it happened within the leap of the heart of man toward the heart of God, a leap caused by the awareness of death. Like us, he had said. Like us what? she said, lying beside him last spring, his seed swimming in her, thinking of her Episcopal childhood, she and her family Christian by skin color and pragmatic in belief. When we make love, he said. We do it in the face of death. (And this was in the spring, before he knew.) Our bodies aren't just meat then; they become statement too; they become spirit. If we can do that with each other then why can't we do it with God, and he with us? I don't know, she said; I've never thought about it. Don't, he said; it's too simple.

After they became lovers he continued going to daily mass but he stopped receiving communion. She offered to stop seeing him, to let him confess and return to his sacrament. He told her no. It was not that he believed he was sinning with her; it was that he didn't know. And if indeed he were living in sin it was too complex for him to enter a confessional and simply murmur the word *adultery;* too complex for him to burden just any priest with, in any confessional. He recognized this as pride: the sinner assuming the anonymous confessor would be unable to understand and unwilling to grapple with the extent and perhaps even the exonerating circumstances of the sin, but would instead have to retreat and cling to the word *adultery* and the divine law forbidding it. So he did not confess. And there were times at daily mass when he nearly joined the others and received communion, because he felt that he could, that it would be all right. But he did not trust what he felt: in his love for Edith he was untroubled and happy but he did not trust himself enough to believe he could only be happy within the grace of God. It could be, he told her, that his long and celibate need for earthly love now satisfied, he had chosen to complete himself outside the corridor leading to God; that he was not really a spiritual man but was capable of, if not turning his back on God, at least glancing off to one side and keeping that glance fixed for as long as he and Edith loved. So he did not receive, even though at times he felt that he could.

If she were not married he was certain he would receive communion daily while remaining her lover because, although he knew it was rarely true, he maintained and was committed to the belief that making love could parallel and even merge with the impetus and completion of the Eucharist. Else why make love at all, he said, except for meat in meat, making ourselves meat, drawing our circle of mortality not around each other but around our own vain and separate hearts. But if she were free to love him, each act between them would become a sacrament, each act a sign of their growing union in the face of God and death, freed of their now-imposed limitations on commitment and risk and hope. Because he believed in love, he said. With all his heart he believed in it, saw it as a microcosm of the Eucharist which in turn was a microcosm of the earth-rooted love he must feel for God in order to live with certainty as a man. And like his love for God, his love for her had little to do with the emotion which at times pulsated and quivered in his breast so fiercely that he had to make love with her in order to bear it; but it had more to do with the acts themselves, and love finally was a series of gestures with escalating and enduring commitments.

So if she were free to love him he could receive communion too, take part without contradiction in that gesture too. And if their adultery were the classic variety involving cuckoldry he would know quite simply it was a sin, because for his own needs he would be inflicting pain on a man who loved his wife. But since her marriage was not in his eyes a marriage at all but an arrangement which allowed Hank to indulge his impulses within the shelter of roof, woman, and child which apparently he also needed, the sin—if it existed—was hard to define. So that finally his reason for not receiving communion was his involvement in a marriage he felt was base, perhaps even sordid; and, in love as he was, he reeked or at least smelled faintly of sin, which again he could neither define nor locate; and indeed it could be Hank's sin he carried about with him and shared. Which is why he asked her to marry him.

"It's obvious you love Hank," he said.

"Yes," she said, her head on his bare shoulder; then she touched his face, stroked it.

"If you didn't love him you would divorce him, because you could keep Sharon. But your love for him contradicts its purpose. It empties you without filling you, it dissipates you, you'll grow old in pieces."

"But if I were divorced you couldn't be married in the church. What about your Eucharist? Would you give that up?"

"I'd receive every day," he said. "Who would know? I'd go to mass and receive the Eucharist like any other man."

"I don't think you're a Catholic at all."

"If I'm not, then I don't know what I am."

4

SHE WAKES frightened beside Joe and looks in the gray light at the clock on the bedside table—six-forty. Joe is sleeping on his back, his mouth open; his face seems to have paled and shrunk or sagged during the night, and his shallow breath is liquid. She quietly gets out of bed. Her heart still beats with fright. This is the first time she has ever spent the night with Joe, or with any of her lovers; always the unspoken agreement with Hank was that for the last part of the night and the breakfast hour of the morning the family would be together under one roof; sometimes she had come home as late as four in the morning and gotten into bed beside Hank, who slept; always when he came home late she was awake and always she pretended she was asleep.

She dresses quickly, watching Joe's face and thinking of Sharon sleeping and hoping she will sleep for another half-hour; although if she wakes and comes down to the kitchen before Edith gets home, Edith can explain that she has been to the store. Yet she knows that discovery by Sharon is not what she really fears, that it will probably be another seven years before Sharon begins to see what she and Hank are doing. At the thought of seven more years of this her fear is instantly replaced by a rush of despair that tightens her jaws in resignation. Then she shakes her head, shakes away the image of those twenty-eight seasons until Sharon is fifteen, and continues to dress; again she is afraid. She needs a cigarette and goes to the kitchen for one; at the kitchen table she writes a note telling Joe she will be back later in the morning. She plans to clean his apartment but does not tell him in the note, which she leaves propped against the bedside clock so he will see it when he wakes and will not have to call her name or get up to see if she is still with him. She writes only that she will be back later and that she loves him. She assumes it is true that she loves him, but for a long time now it has been difficult to sort out her feelings and understand them.

As now, driving home, and knowing it is neither discovery by Sharon nor rebuke by Hank that makes her grip on the wheel so firm and anxious that the muscles of her arms tire from the tension. For she knows Hank will not be disturbed. He likes Joe and will understand why she had to stay the night; although, on the road now, in the pale blue start of the day, her decision to sleep with Joe seems distant and unnecessary, an impulse born in the hyperbole of bourbon and night. She wishes she had gone home after Joe was asleep. But if she is home in time to cook breakfast, Hank will not be angry. So why, then, driving through the streets of a town that she now thinks of as her true home, does she feel like a fugitive? She doesn't know.

And yet the feeling persists through breakfast, even though

she is in luck: when she enters the kitchen she hears the shower upstairs; she brings a glass of orange juice upstairs, stopping in her room long enough to hang up her coat and change her sweater and pants; then she goes to Sharon's room. Sharon sleeps on her back, the long brown hair spread on the pillow, strands of it lying on her upturned cheek; her lips are slightly parted and she seems to be frowning at a dream. The room smells of childhood: the neutral and neuter scents of bedclothes and carpet and wood, and Edith recalls the odors of Joe's apartment, and of Joe. She sits on the side of the bed, pausing to see if her weight will stir Sharon from the dream and sleep. After a while she touches Sharon's cheek; Sharon wakes so quickly, near startled, that Edith is saddened. She likes to watch Sharon wake with the insouciance of a baby, and she regrets her having to get up early and hurry to school. Sharon pushes up on her elbows, half-rising from the bed while her brown eyes are blinking at the morning. Edith kisses her and gives her the juice. Sharon blinks, looks about the room, and asks what time it is.

"There's plenty of time," Edith says. "Would you like pancakes?"

Sharon gulps the juice and says yes, then pushes back the covers and is waiting for Edith to get up so she can swing her feet to the floor. Edith kisses her again before leaving the room. In the hall she is drawn to the sound of the shower behind her, needs to say something to Hank, but doesn't know what it is; with both loss and relief she keeps going down the hall and the stairs, into the kitchen.

Hank and Sharon come down together; by this time Edith has made coffee, brought the *Boston Globe* in from the front steps and laid it at Hank's place; the bacon is frying in the iron skillet, the pancake batter is mixed, and the electric skillet is heated. Her eyes meet Hank's. He does not kiss her good-morning before sitting down; that's no longer unusual but this morning the absence of a kiss strikes her like a mild but intended slap. They tell each other good-morning. Since that summer three years ago she has felt with him, after returning from a lover, a variety of emotions which seem unrelated: vengeance, affection, weariness, and sometimes the strange and frightening lust of collusive sin. At times she has also felt shy, and that is how she feels this morning as he props the paper on the milk pitcher, then withdraws it as Sharon lifts the pitcher and pours into her glass. Edith's shyness is no different from what it would be if she and Hank were new lovers, only hours new, and this was the first morning she had waked in his house and as she cooked breakfast her eyes and heart reached out to him to see if this morning he was with her as he was last night. He looks over the paper at her, and his eyes ask about Joe. She shrugs then shakes her head, but she is not thinking of Joe, and the tears that cloud her eyes are not for him either. She pours small discs of batter into the skillet, and turns the bacon. Out of her vision Hank mumbles something to the paper. She breathes the smells of the batter, the bacon, the coffee.

When Hank and Sharon have left, Edith starts her work. There is not much to do, but still she does not take time to read the paper. When she has finished in the kitchen she looks at the guest room, the dining room, and the living room. They are all right; she vacuumed yesterday. She could dust the bookshelves in the living room but she decides they can wait. She goes upstairs; Sharon has made her bed, and Edith smooths it and then makes the other bed where the blankets on her side are still tucked in. The bathroom is clean and smells of Hank's after-shave lotion. He has left hair in the bathtub and whiskers in the lavatory; she picks these up with toilet paper. She would like a shower but she wants to flee from this house. She decides to shower anyway; perhaps the hot water and warm soft lather will calm her. But under the spray she is the same, and she washes quickly and very soon is leaving the house, carrying the vacuum cleaner. On the icy sidewalk she slips and falls hard on her rump. For a moment she sits there, hoping no one has seen her; she feels helpless to do everything she must do; early, the day is demanding more of her than she can give, and she does not believe she can deal with it, or with tomorrow, or the days after that either. She slowly stands up. In the car, with the seatbelt buckled around her heavy coat, she turns clumsily to look behind her as she backs out of the driveway.

At Joe's she moves with short strides up the sidewalk, balancing herself against the weight of the vacuum cleaner. She doesn't knock, because he may be sleeping still. But he is not. As she pushes open the front door she sees him sitting at the kitchen table, wearing the black turtleneck. He smiles and starts to rise, but instead turns his chair to face her and watches her as, leaving the vacuum cleaner, she goes down the hall and kisses him, noting as she lowers her face his weary pallor and the ghost in his eyes. In spite of that and the taste of mouthwash that tells her he has vomited again, she no longer feels like a fugitive. She doesn't understand this, because the feeling began when she woke beside him and therefore it seems that being with him again would not lift it from her. This confuses and frustrates her: when her feelings enter a terrain she neither controls nor understands she thinks they may take her even further, even into madness. She hugs Joe and tells him she has come to clean his apartment; he protests, but he is pleased.

He follows her to the living room and sits on the couch. But after a while, as she works, he lies down, resting his head on a cushion against the arm of the couch. Quietly he watches her. She watches the path of the vacuum cleaner, the clean swath approaching the layers and fluffs of dust. She feels the touch of his eyes, and what is behind them. When she is finished she moves to the bedroom and again he follows her; he lies on the bed, which he has made. For a while she works in a warm patch of sunlight from the window. She looks out at the bright snow and the woods beyond: the spread and reaching branches of elms and birches and maples and tamaracks are bare; there are pines and hemlocks green in the sun. She almost stops working. Her impulse is to throw herself against the window, cover it with her body, and scream in the impotent rage of grief. But she does not break the rhythm of her work; she continues to push the vacuum cleaner over the carpet, while behind her he watches the push and pull of her arms, the bending of her body, the movement of her legs.

When she has vacuumed and dusted the apartment and cleaned the bathtub and lavatory she drinks coffee at the kitchen table while he sits across from her drinking nothing, then with apology in his voice and eyes he says: "I called the doctor this morning. He said he'd come see me, but I told him I'd go to the office."

She puts down her coffee cup.

"I'll drive you."

He nods. Looking at him, her heart is pierced more deeply and painfully than she had predicted: she knows with all her futile and yearning body that they will never make love again, that last night's rushed and silent love was their last, and that except to pack his toilet articles and books for the final watch in the hospital, he will not return to his apartment she has cleaned.

It is night, she is in her bed again, and now Hank turns to her, his hand moving up her leg, sliding her nightgown upward, and she opens her legs, the old easy opening to the hand that has touched her for ten years; but when the nightgown reaches her hips she does not lift them to allow it to slip farther up her body. She is thinking of this afternoon when the priest came to the room and she had to leave. She nodded at the priest, perhaps spoke to him, but did not see him, would not recognize him if she saw him again, and she left and walked down the corridor to the sunporch and stood at the windows that gave back her reflection, for outside the late afternoon of the day she cleaned Joe's apartment was already dark and the streetlights and the houses across the parking lot were lighted. She smoked while on the hospital bed Joe confessed his sins, told the priest about her, about the two of them, all the slow nights and hurried afternoons, and she felt isolated as she had when, months ago, he had begun to die while, healthy, she loved him.

Since breakfast her only contact with Hank and Sharon was calling a sitter to be waiting when Sharon got home, and calling

Hank at the college to tell him she was at the hospital and ask him to feed Sharon. Those two phone calls kept her anchored in herself, but the third set her adrift and she felt that way still on the sunporch: Joe had asked her to, and she had phoned the rectory and told a priest whose name she didn't hear that her friend was dying, that he was an ex-priest, that he wanted to confess and receive communion and the last sacrament. Then she waited on the sunporch while Joe in confession told her goodbye. She felt neither anger not bitterness but a vulnerability that made her cross her arms over her breasts and draw her sweater closer about her shoulders, though the room was warm. She felt the need to move, to pace the floor, but she could not. She gazed at her reflection in the window without seeing it and gazed at the streetlights and the lighted windows beyond the parking lot and the cars of those who visited without seeing them either, as inside Joe finally confessed to the priest, any priest from any rectory. It did not take long, the confession and communion and the last anointing, not long at all before the priest emerged and walked briskly down the corridor in his black overcoat. Then she went in and sat on the edge of the bed and thought again that tomorrow she must bring flowers, must give to this room scent and spirit, and he took her hand.

"Did he understand everything?" she said.

He smiled. "I realized he didn't have to. It's something I'd forgotten with all my thinking: it's what ritual is for: nobody has to understand. The knowledge is in the ritual. Anyone can listen to the words. So I just used the simple words."

"You called us adultery?"

"That's what I called us," he said, and drew her face down to his chest.

Now she feels that touch more than she feels Hank's, and she reaches down and takes his wrist, stopping the hand, neither squeezing nor pushing, just a slight pressure of resistance and his hand is gone.

"I should be with him," she says. "There's a chair in the room where I could sleep. They'd let me: the nurses. It would be a help for them. He's drugged and he's sleeping on his back. He could vomit and drown. Tomorrow night I'll stay there. I'll come home first and cook dinner and stay till Sharon goes to bed. Then I'll go back to the hospital. I'll do that till he dies."

"I don't want you to."

She looks at him, then looks away. His hand moves to her leg again, moves up, and when she touches it resisting, it moves away and settles on her breast.

"Don't," she says. "I don't want to make love with you."

"You're grieving."

His voice is gentle and seductive, then he shifts and tries to embrace her but she pushes with her hands against his chest and closing her eyes she shakes her head.

"Don't," she says. "Just please don't. It doesn't mean anything anymore. It's my fault too. But it's over, Hank. It's because he's dying, yes—" She opens her eyes and looks past her pushing hands at his face and she feels and shares his pain and dismay; and loving him she closes her eyes. "But you're dying too. I can feel it in your chest just like I could feel it when I rubbed him when he hurt. And so am I: that's what we lost sight of."

His chest still leans against her hands, and he grips her shoulders. Then he moves away and lies on his back.

"We'll talk tomorrow," he says. "I don't trust this kind of talk at night."

"It's the best time for it," she says, and she wants to touch him just once, gently and quickly, his arm or wrist or hand; but she does not.

In late afternoon while snowclouds gather, the priest who yesterday heard Joe's confession and gave him the last sacrament comes with the Eucharist, and this time Edith can stay. By now Hank is teaching his last class of the day and Sharon is home with the sitter. Tonight at dinner Sharon will ask as she did this morning: Is your friend dead yet? Edith has told her his name is Mr. Ritchie but Sharon has never seen him and so cannot put a name on a space in her mind; calling him *your friend* she can imagine Joe existing in the world through the eyes of her mother. At breakfast Hank watched them talking; when Edith looked at him, his eyes shifted to the newspaper.

When the priest knocks and enters, Edith is sitting in a chair at the foot of the bed, a large leather chair, the one she will sleep in tonight; she nearly lowers her eyes, averts her face; yet she looks at him. He glances at her and nods. If he thinks of her as the woman in yesterday's confession there is no sign in his face, which is young: he is in his early thirties. Yet his face looks younger, and there is about it a boyish vulnerability which his seriousness doesn't hide. She guesses that he is easily set off balance, is prone to concern about trifles: that caught making a clumsy remark he will be anxious for the rest of the evening. He does not remove his overcoat, which is open. He moves to the bed, his back to her now, and places a purple stole around his neck. His hands are concealed from her; then they move toward Joe's face, the left hand cupped beneath the right hand which with thumb and forefinger holds the white disc.

"The body of Christ," he says.

"Amen," Joe says.

She watches Joe as he closes his eyes and extends his tongue and takes the disc into his mouth. His eyes remain closed; he chews slowly; then he swallows. The priest stands for a moment, watching him. Then with his right palm he touches Joe's forehead, and leaves the room. Edith goes to the bed, stis on its edge, takes Joe's hand and looks at his closed eyes and lips. She wants to hold him hard, feel his ribs against hers, has the urge to fleshless insert her ribs within his, mesh them. Gently she lowers her face to his chest, and he strokes her hair. Still he has not opened his eyes. His stroke on her hair is lighter and slower, and then it stops; his hands rest on her head, and he sleeps. She does not move. She watches as his mouth opens and she listens to the near gurgling of his breath.

She does not move. In her mind she speaks to him, telling him what she is waiting to tell him when he wakes again, what she has been waiting all day to tell him but has not because once she says it to Joe she knows it will be true, as true as it was last night. There are still two months of the cold and early sunsets of winter left, the long season of waiting, and the edges of grief which began last summer when he started to die are far from over, yet she must act: looking now at the yellow roses on the bedside table she it telling Hank goodbye, feeling that goodbye in her womb and heart, a grief that will last, she knows, longer than her grieving for Joe. When the snow is melted from his grave it will be falling still in her soul as it is now while she recalls images and voices of her ten years with Hank and quietly now she weeps, not for Joe or Sharon or Hank, but for herself; and she wishes with all her splintered heart that she and Hank could be as they once were and she longs to touch him, to cry on his broad chest, and with each wish and each image her womb and heart toll their goodbye, forcing her on into the pain that waits for her, so that now she is weeping not quietly but with shuddering sobs she cannot control, and Joe wakes and opens his eyes and touches her wet cheeks and mouth. For a while she lets him do this. Then she stops crying. She kisses him, then wipes her face on the sheet and sits up and smiles at him. Holding his hand and keeping all nuances of fear and grief from her voice, because she wants him to know he has done this for her, and she wants him to be happy about it, she says: "I'm divorcing Hank."

He smiles and touches her cheek and she strokes his cool hand.

Finding a Girl in America

Sorrow is one of the vibrations

that prove the fact of living.

ANTOINE DE SAINT EXUPÉRY,
Wind, Sand and Stars

for Suzanne and Nicole

ON AN OCTOBER night, lying in bed with a nineteen-year-old girl and tequila and grapefruit juice, thirty-five-year-old Hank Allison gets the story. They lie naked, under the sheet and one light blanket, their shoulders propped by pillows so they can drink. Lori's body is long; Hank is not a tall man, and she is perhaps a half inch taller; when she wears high-heeled boots and lowers her face to kiss him, he tells her she is like a swan bending to eat. Knowing he is foolish, he still wishes she were shorter; he has joked with Jack Linhart about this, and once Jack told him: *Hell with it: just stick out that big chest of yours and swagger down the road with that pretty girl.* Hank never wishes he were taller.

Tonight they have gone to Boston for a movie and dinner, and at the Casa Romero, their favorite restaurant, they started with margaritas but as they ate appetizers of Jalapeño and grilled cheese on tortillas, of baked cheese and sausage, they became cheerful about the movie and food and what they would order next, and switched to shots of tequila chased with Superior. They ate a lot and left the restaurant high though not drunk; then Hank bought a six-pack of San Miguel for the forty-five minute drive home, enough for one cassette of Willie Nelson and part of one by Kristofferson, Hank doing most of the talking, while a sober part of himself told him not to, reminded him that he must always control his talking with Lori; for he loves her and he knows that with him, as with everyone else, she feels and thinks much that she cannot say. He guesses her mother has something

217

to do with this, a talk-crackling woman who keeps her husband and three daughters generally quiet, who is good-looking and knows it and works at it, and is a flirt and, Hank believes from the bare evidence Lori so often murmurs in his bed, more than that. But he does not work hard at discovering why it is so difficult for Lori to give the world, even him, her heart in words. He believes some mysterious balance of power exists between lovers, and if he ever fully understands the bonds that tie her tongue, and if he tells her about them, tries to help her cut them, he will no longer be her lover. He settles for the virtues he sees in her, and waits for her to see them herself. Often she talks of her childhood; she cannot remember her father ever kissing or hugging her; she loves him, and she knows he loves her too. He just does not touch.

Until they got back to his apartment and took salty dogs to bed, Hank believed they would make love. He thought of her long body under him. But, his heart ready, his member was dull, numb, its small capacity for drink long passed. So Hank parted her legs and lowered his face: when she came he felt he had too: the best way to share a woman's orgasm, the only way to use all his senses: looking over the mound at her face between breasts, touching with hands and tongue, the lovely taste and smell, and he heard not only her moan-breaths but his tongue on her, and her hands' soft timpani against his face.

Now he lies peacefully against the pillows; the drinks on his desk beside the bed are still half-full, and he hands one to Lori. Sometimes he takes a drag from her cigarette, though he remembers this is the way to undo his quitting nine years ago when he faced how long it took him to write, and how long he would have to live to write the ten novels he had set as his goal. He is nearly finished the second draft of his third. Lori is talking about Monica. Something in her voice alerts him. She and Lori were friends. Perhaps he is going to learn something new; perhaps Monica was unfaithful while she was still here, when she was his student and they were furtive lovers, as he and Lori are now. He catches a small alcoholic slip Lori makes: No, I can't, she says, in the midst of a sentence which seems to need no restraint.

"You can't what?"

"Nothing."

"Tell me."

"I promised Monica I wouldn't."

"When I tell a friend a secret, I know he'll tell his wife or woman. That's the way it is."

"It'll hurt you."

"How can anything about Monica hurt me? I haven't seen her in over a year."

"It will."

"It can't. Not now."

"You remember when she came down that weekend? Last October? You cooked dinner for the three of us."

"Shrimp scampi. We got drunk on hot sake."

"Before dinner she and I went to the liquor store. She kept talking about this guy she'd met in art class."

"Tommy."

"She didn't say it. But I knew she was screwing him then. I could tell she wanted me to know. It was her eyes. The way she'd smile. And I got pissed at her but I didn't say anything. I loved her and I'd never had a friend who had two lovers at once and I thought she was a bitch. I was starting to love you too, and I hated knowing she was going to hurt you, and I couldn't see why she even came to spend the weekend with you."

"So she was screwing him before she told me it was over. Well, I should have known. She talked about him enough: his drawings anyway."

"That wasn't it. She was pregnant. She found out after she broke up with you." He has never heard Lori's voice so plaintive except when she speaks of her parents. "You know how Monica is. She went hysterical; she phoned me at school every night, she phoned her parents, she went to three doctors. Two in Maine and one in New York. They all placed it at the same time: it was yours. By that time she was two months pregnant. Her father took her in and they had it done."

An image comes to Hank: he sees his daughter, Sharon, thirteen, breast-points under her sweater: she is standing in his kitchen, hair dark and long; she is chopping celery at the counter for their weekly meal. He pulls Lori's cheek to his chest and strokes her hair.

"I'm all right," he says. "I had to know. I know if I didn't know I'd never know I didn't know; but I hate not knowing. I don't want to die not knowing everything about my life. You had to tell me. Who else would? You know I have to know. I'm all right. Shit. Shit that bitch. I could have—it would have been born in spring—I would have had all summer off—I could have taken it. I can raise a kid—I'm no Goddamn—I have to piss—"

He leaves the bed so quickly that he feels, barely, her head drop as his chest jerks from beneath it. He hurries down the hall, stands pissing, then as suddenly and uncontrollably as vomiting he is crying; and as with vomiting he has no self, he is only the helpless and weak host of these sounds and jerks and tears, and he places both palms on the wall in front of him, standing, moaning; the tears stop, his chest heaves, he groans, then tears come again as from some place so deep inside him that it has never been touched, even by pain. Lori stands naked beside him. She is trying to pull his arm from its push against the wall; she is trying to hold him and is crying too and saying something but he can only hear her comforting tone like wind-sough in trees that grew in a peaceful place he left long ago. Finally he turns to her, he will let her hold him and do what she needs to do; yet when he faces her tall firm body, still in October her summer tan lingering above and between breasts and loins, he swings his fists, pulling short each punch, pulling them enough so she does not even back away, nor lift an arm to protect herself; left right left right, short hooked blows at her womb and he hears himself saying No no no—He does not know whether he is yelling or mumbling. He only knows he is sounds and tears and death-sorrow and strong quick arms striking the air in front of Lori's womb.

Then it stops; his arms go to her shoulders, he sags, and she turns him and walks him back down the hall, her left arm around his waist, her right hand holding his arm around her shoulders.

He lies in bed and she asks if he wants a drink; he says he'd better not. She gets into bed, and holds his face to her breast.

"Seven months," he says. "That's all she had to give it. Then I could have taken it. You think I couldn't do that?"

"I know you could."

"It would be hard. Sometimes it would be terrible. I wasn't swinging at you."

"I know."

"It was just the womb."

"Monica's?"

"I don't know."

That night he dreams: it is summer, the lovely summers when he does not teach, does not have to hurry his writing and running before classes, and in the afternoons he picks up Sharon and sometimes a friend or two of hers and they go to Seabrook beach in New Hampshire; usually Jack and Terry Linhart are there with their daughter and son, and all of them put their blankets side by side and talk and doze and go into the sea, the long cooling afternoons whose passage is marked only by the slow arc of the sun, time's symbol giving timelessness instead. His dream does not begin with those details but with that tone: the blue peaceful days he teaches to earn, wakes in the dark winter mornings to write, then runs in snow and cold wind and over ice. The dream comes to him with an empty beach: he feels other people there but does not see them, only a stretch of sand down to the sea, and he and Sharon are lying on a blanket. They are talking to each other. She is on his right. Then he rolls slightly to his left to look down at the fetus beside him; he is not startled by it; he seems to have known it is there, has been there as long as he and Sharon. The dream tells him it is a girl; he loves her, loves watching her sleep curled on her side: he looks at the disproportionate head, the small arms and legs. But he is troubled. She is bright pink, as if just boiled, and he realizes he should have put lotion on her. She sleeps peacefully and he wonders if she will be all right sleeping there while he and Sharon go into the surf. He knows he will bring her every afternoon to the beach and she will sleep pink and curled beside him and Sharon and, nameless, she will not grow. His love for her becomes so tender that it changes to grief as he looks at her flesh in the sun's heat.

The dream does not wake him. But late next morning, when he does wake, it is there, as vivid as if he is having it again. He sees and feels it before he feels his headache, his hung-over dry mouth, his need to piss; before he smells the cigarette butts on the desk beside him, and the tequila traces in the glasses by the ashtray. Before he is aware of Lori's weight and smell in bed. Quietly he rises and goes to the bathroom then sneaks back into bed, not kindness but because he does not want Lori awake, and he lies with his dream. His heart needs to cry but his body cannot, it is emptied, and again he thinks it is like vomiting: the drunken nights when he suddenly wakes from a dream of nausea and goes quickly to the toilet, kneeling, gripping its seat, hanging on through the last dry heaves, then waking in the morning still sick, red splotches beside his eyes where the violence of his puking has broken vessels, and feeling that next moment he would be at the toilet again, but there is nothing left to disgorge and he simply lies in bed for hours.

But this will not pass. He will have to think. His employers at the college and his editor and publisher believe his vocations have to do with thinking. They are wrong. He rarely thinks. He works on instincts and trying to articulate them. What his instincts tell him now is that he'd better lie quietly and wait: today is Sunday and this afternoon he and Lori are taking Sharon for a walk on Plum Island. He lies there and imagines the three of them on the dunes until he senses Lori waking.

She knows what he likes when he wakes hung over and, without a word, she begins licking and caressing his nipples; his breath quickens, he feels the hung-over lust whose need is so strong it is near-desperate, as though only its climax can return him from the lethargy of his body, the spaces in his brain, and he needs it the way others need hair of the dog. Lori knows as well as he does that his need is insular, masturbatory; knows that she is ministering to him, her lips and fingers and now her mouth medicinal. But she likes it too. Yet this morning even in her soft mouth he remains soft until finally he takes her arms and gently pulls her up, rolls her onto her back, and kneels between her calves. When it is over he is still soft, and his lust is gone too.

"It wasn't tequila," he says. "This morning."

"I know."

Then he tells her his dream.

The day, when they finally leave his apartment, is crisp enough for sweaters and windbreakers, the air dry, the sky deep blue, and most of the trees still have their leaves dying in bright red and orange and yellow. It has taken them two hours to get out of the apartment: first Hank went to the bathroom, leaving a stench that shamed him, then he lay in bed while Lori went; and because he was trying to focus on anything to keep the dream away, he figured out why his girl friends, even on a crapulent morning like this one, never left a bad smell. Always they waited in bed, let him go first; then they went, bringing their boxes and bottles, and after sitting on the seat he had warmed they showered long and when they were finished, he entered a steamy room that smelled of woman: clean, powdered, whatever else they did in there. Very simple, and thoughtful too: let him go first so he would not have to wait with aching bowels while they went through the process of smell-changing; and they relied on him, going first, not to shower and shave and make them wait. It was sweetly vulpine and endearing and on another morning he would have smiled.

While he showered, Lori dressed and put on bacon. At breakfast he talked about last night's movie, about the day as it looked through the window near the table, about Plum Island's winter erosion, about the omelette, about anything, and Lori watched him with her soft brown eyes, and he knew she knew and was helpless, and he wished she didn't hurt that way, he knew the pain of being helpless with a lover, but there was nothing he could do except wish they both weren't helpless.

Driving the car, he is in love with Sharon, needs to see her, listen to her voice, touch her as they walk on the beach. At the house, Lori waits in the car, for she is shy about going in; she and Edith have talked outside, either because Edith was in the yard when they arrived or she walked with Hank and Sharon to the car and leaned over to talk to Lori at the window. Edith divorced him, and he has told Lori that she feels no jealousy or pain, but still Lori is uncomfortable. Hank understands this. He would feel the same. What he does not understand is why Lori loves him, and he prefers not to try, for he is afraid he will find no reason strong enough for him to rely on.

It is not the age of his body that makes him wonder. In the past three or four years, love handles and a bald spot have appeared, and all his running has no effect on the love handles, and he knows they are here to stay, and the bald spot will spread like a tonsure. But it isn't that. It's the fettered way he is thirty-five. When Monica left him, she flared after a night of silence when her eyes in turn glowered and sulked; she said, as they were finishing their last drinks in the bar near her college in Maine: *I want out. You worry about your writing first, your daughter second, money third, and I'm last.* All evening he had known something was coming. But he had never been broken up with so cleanly, precisely, succinctly. At once he was calm. He simply watched Monica's face. She was taut with fury. He was not. He was not even sad yet. He watched her, and waited for whatever he was going to say. He had no idea what it would be. He was simply repeating her words in his mind. Then he said: *You're right. Why should you put up with that shit?* Her fury was still there. Perhaps she wanted a fight. Yet all he felt was forgiveness for her, and futility because he had loved a woman so young.

Then he felt something else: that his forgiveness and futility were familiar, coming from foreknowledge, as if on that first night he took her to dinner in Boston and they ate soft-shelled crabs and his heart began to warm and rise, he had known it would end; that at the most he would get love's year. It ended with the four sentences in the bar, his two the last, and they drove quietly to her apartment near the campus; at the door he embraced her more tightly than he had intended, because holding her he saw images of death, hers and his years from now, neither knowing of the death of the first, the odds bad that it would be him since he had fifteen years on her and was a man. Then he gave her a gentle closed-lip kiss, and was walking back to his car before she could speak.

He put Waylon Jennings in the deck, and on the two-hour moonlit drive home he longed for a beer and did not cry. When he got to his apartment he drank a six-pack with bourbon and did cry and nearly phoned her; all that kept him from it was his will to keep their last scene together sculpted forever with him, Hank Allison Goddamnit, showing only dignity and strength and tenderness. She had seen him as he was now, on nights when writing or money or guilt and sorrow about Sharon or, often enough, all three punched him around the walls of his apartment, and he counterpunched with one hand holding a beer, the other a bourbon on the rocks. But she had never seen him like this because of her. So each time he went to the kitchen to get another beer or more bourbon and looked at the phone on the wall, he remembered how he was and what he said when she told him in the bar, and how he was at the door, and turned, sometimes lunged, away from the phone.

He drank in his bedroom, at his desk but with his back to it, and he listened to Dylan, the angry songs about women, the volume low because he rented the upstairs of a house whose owners were a retired couple sleeping beneath him, and he started his cure: he focused on every one of her flaws, and with booze and will and Dylan's hurt and angry encouragement, he multiplied them by emotion until they grew so out of proportion that he could no longer see what he had loved about her. He relived her quick temper and screaming rage, so loud and long that some nights he was afraid she was going mad, and always he had to command her to stop, squeeze her arms, tell her she would wake the couple downstairs; and her crying, never vulnerably, never seeming to need comfort, more a variation of her rage and nearly as loud, as she twisted from him and fled from room to room until again he had to hold and command; and the source of these rages and tears never defined so he could try to deal with them, these sources always just a little concrete but mostly abstract so on those nights he felt the impotence of believing she already was mad; and his impotence brought with it a detachment which in turn opened him up to shades of despair: he imagined her ten years from now, when her life would be more complicated and difficult, when it would attack her more often, with more strength. Listening to "Positively Fourth Street" he sipped the smooth Jack Daniel's and chased it with the foamy bite of beer and thought if she had stayed with him she would have so drained his energy that, after spending his nights as a shrink and a lion-tamer, he would wake peaceless and weary to face his morning's work. He recalled her mischievous face as, in front of his friends, in bars or at the beach, she pinched his love handles or kissed his bald spot. This usually did not bother him because he was in good condition, and she smoked heavily and could not run half a mile, was slender only because she was made that way, and she was young, and she dieted. And he guessed she was doing this for herself rather than to him; testing herself; actually touching his signs of age to see if she really wanted a man fifteen years older, with an ex-wife, a twelve-year-old daughter, and child support.

Beneath the teasing, though, something was in her eyes: something feral, and at times as she smiled and teased he looked into her eyes and felt a stir of fear which had nothing to do with her fingers squeezing his flesh, her lips smacking his crown. It was more like the detached fear he had once, looking at a Russell's viper in a zoo, the snake coiled asleep behind glass, and Hank read the typed card on the cage, about this lethargic snake and how one of its kind finally got Russell and his name.

He went to the kitchen, did not even look at the phone as he passed it. He was thinking of the snake, and one night Jack saying that after the one bit Russell, he wrote down the effects of the poison as it killed him; and Jack said: *You know, maybe he studied those bastards so long that finally he had to go all the way, know it all, and he just reached down and touched it* . . . In the dark bedroom which tomorrow would still be a bedroom, a dreary and hung-over place, not a study as it became most mornings, he listened to "Just Like a Woman" and thought *Maybe that's what I was doing, waiting for that bitch to give me the venom, end it between us, between me and all of them, between me and—* He stopped. It was time to finish the drinks, swallow aspirins and vitamin B and go to bed, for—had he completed the sentence in his mind—it would have concluded with some euphemism for suicide. He went to bed hating Monica; it was a satisfying hatred; it felt like the completion of a long-planned revenge.

He woke with relief, nearly happiness, nearly strength. He knew, for today, that was enough: last night's cure had worked. As it had with every young girl who left him since his divorce. They all left. One night he told Jack: *I think I'll get a fire escape up to my window, so they can just climb out while I'm taking a piss.* When Edith sent him away, he did not have a cure.

Five years ago, when all his pleas and arguments and bargains and accusations lay on the living room floor between them (he actually felt he was stepping on his own words as he paced while she sat watching), and he knew that she really wanted him to leave, he believed it was because he had been unfaithful. So his grief was coupled with injustice, for she had had lovers too; and even as Hank talked that night her newest and, she said, her last lover so long as she was married, was dying early of cancer: Joe Ritchie, an ex-priest who taught philosophy at the college where Hank worked.

When he moved to his apartment he was too sad to be angry at Edith. He tried to be. Alone at night, and while running, and watching movies, he told himself that he and Edith had lived equally. Or almost. True, he had a head start on her, had student girl friends before she caught him because he was with a woman more demanding: a woman not only his age but rich and from Paris, idling for six months with friends in Boston; a woman who laughed at him when he worried about Edith catching him. Now, at thirty-five, with eight years' distance, he saw how foolish he had been, for she was a woman of no substance: her idea of a good day was to sleep late, buy things at Bonwit Teller or Ann Taylor, and make love with Hank in the afternoon. He was young enough to be excited by her accent, so that he heard its sound more than what it said. He saw her in Boston, on Saturday afternoons, on Tuesdays and Thursdays when he was supposed to be in his office at school, he got careless, and he got caught.

When it happened he realized he had always known that someday it would: that he could not have lived uncaught his entire life, or until he outgrew his crushes that so quickly turned to passion not only for the body, for that lovely first penetration into new yielding flesh, but for the woman's soul too, a passion to know as much of her as he could before they parted (they were students; parting was graduation) and went on with their lives. Sometimes for weeks, even months, he would not notice a particular girl in class. Because while he was teaching he was aware mostly of himself: this was only partly vanity; more, it was his love of teaching, his fear of failing, so that before every class he had stage-fright, had to spend a few minutes in silence in his office or walking about the campus, letting his apprehension and passion grow inside him until, entering the classroom, those were all he felt. When he began to speak about a novel or story, it was as though another man were talking, and Hank listening. He taught three afternoons a week, had many bad days when he became confused, lost the students, and seeing their listless faces, his apprehension overcame his passion and he fearfully waited, still talking, for the fifty minutes to pass. At a week's end, if he had had two good days out of three, he was satisfied. He knew that hardly anyone hit three for three in this work. Or his best days he listened to Hank the teacher talking, and he tried to follow the ideas coming from his mouth, ideas he often didn't know he had until he heard them. So, usually, he did not notice a certain girl until she said something in class, something that halted him, made him look at her and think about what she had said. Or, while he was talking, his face sweeping the class, the windows, the ceiling, his hands busy with a pen or keys or coins, his face would suddenly stop, held by a girl whose eyes were fixed on his; sometimes he would stop speaking for a moment, lose the idea he was working on, as he looked at her. Then he would turn away, toss his keys or coin or pen in the air, catch the idea again as he caught the tossed object, and speak. Soon he would be talking to her on the campus.

In his thirties, he understood what those crushes, while he was married, had been. His profession was one of intimacy, but usually it went only from him to the faces sitting in the room. Any student who listened could know as much about him as all his friends, except those two or three truly deep ones. His crushes were rope bridges, built in haste between him and the girl. It was a need not only to give her more of what attracted her in the classroom, but to receive from her, to know her; and with the beginning of that, talking on the campus sidewalks or in his office, came the passion to know all of her. The ones he chose (or, he realized in his thirties, the ones who chose him) were girls who would have been known as promiscuous when he was in college; or even now in the seventies if they were salesclerks or cashiers and at night went to those bars where the young men who had gone to work instead of college drank and waited. But they were educated, affluent, and well-traveled; they wore denim to class, but he knew that what hung in their dormitory closets and in their closets at home cost at least half of his year's salary. He never saw those clothes until he was divorced at thirty and started taking the girls to Boston for the evening; and then he rarely saw the same dress or skirt and blouse twice; only a favorite sweater, a warm coat. While married, his lovemaking was in his car, and what he quiveringly pulled from their thighs was denim. They all took the pill, they all had what they called a healthy attitude toward sex, which meant they knew the affair with Hank, as deep and tender as it might be, so that it certainly felt like love (and, for all Hank knew, it probably was) would end with the school year in May, would resume (if she and Hank felt like it) in the fall, and would certainly end on Commencement Day.

So they made it easy for him. He was a man who planned most

days of his life. In the morning he wrote; then he ran, then he taught; then he was a husband and father. He tried to keep them all separated, and most days it worked, and he felt like three or four different men. When the affairs started, he made time for them as well. After class or instead of office hours he drove through town where the girl was walking. She entered his car as though he had offered her a ride. Even when they left town and drove north she would sit near her door until he turned onto the dirt road leading to the woods. Going back he stayed on the highway, skirted the town, approached the school from the south, and let her out several blocks away. Then he went home and hugged and kissed Sharon and Edith, and holding their bodies in the warmth of his house, he felt love only for them.

But with Jeanne in Boston he had to lie too much about where he was going and where he had been, and finally when Edith asked him one night: *Are you having an affair with that phony French bitch?* he said: *Yes.* He and Edith had met Jeanne when someone brought her to their Christmas party; Edith had not seen her since, but in April, when she asked him, he did not even wonder how she knew. He was afraid, but he was also relieved. That may have been why he didn't ask how she knew. Because it didn't matter: Edith was dealing with what she believed was an affair with a specific woman. To Hank, his admission of that one was an admission of all of them.

He was surprised that he felt relief. Then he believed he understood it: he had been deluding himself with his scheduled adulteries, as if a girl on his car seat in the woods were time in the classroom or at his desk; the years of lies to himself and Edith had been a detraction from the man he wanted and sometimes saw himself to be. So, once cornered, he held his ground and told her. It broke her heart. He wanted to comfort her, to make fraudulent promises, but he would not. He told her he loved her and wanted to live with no one else. But he would not become like most people he knew. They were afraid; and old, twenty years early. They bought houses, spoke of mortgages, repairs, children's ailments, and the weight of their bodies. As he talked she wiped from her eyes the dregs of her first heavy weeping. His own eyes were damp because of hers, and more: because of the impotence he felt, the old male-burden of having to be strong for both of them at once, to give her the assurance of his love so she could hear as a friend what he was saying: that he was what he was, that he had to be loved that way, that he could not limit the roads of his life until they narrowed down to one, leading from home to campus. She screamed at him: *You're a writer too! Isn't that enough for one man?* He said: *No. There's never enough. I don't want to have to say no to anything, not ever*—It was the most fearful moment of his marriage until the night over three years later when she told him he had to leave her and Sharon. He felt closer to her than he ever had before, now that all the lies were gone. And he knew he might lose her, right here in that April kitchen; he was sure of her love, but he was sure of her strength too. Yet he would not retreat into lies: he had to win.

He did. She stayed with him. Every night there was talk, and always there was pain. But she stayed. He built a case against monogamy, spoke of it as an abstraction with subtle and insidious roots in the economy: passion leashed so that lovers would need houses and things to put in them. He knew he was using his long apprenticeship to words, not to find truths, but to confuse and win his wife. He spoke of monogamy as unnatural. *The heart is too big for it,* he said. *Yours too.*

In May she started an affair with Jack Linhart, who no longer loved his wife Terry; or believed he no longer loved her. Hank knew: their faces, their voices, and when they were in the same room he could feel the passion and collusion between them as surely as he could smell a baking ham. He controlled his pain and jealousy, his moments of anger at Jack; he remembered the April night in the kitchen. He kept his silence and waited until the summer night Edith told him she was Jack's lover. He was gentle with her. He knew now that, within the marriage he needed and loved, he was free.

That summer he watched her. He had been her only lover till now; he watched the worry about what they were doing to their marriage leave her face, watched her face in its moments of girl-ish mischief, of vanity, of sensuality that brightened her eyes and shaped her lips, these moments coming unpredictably: as they ate dinner with Sharon, paused at the cheese counter in the super-market . . . Toward the end of the summer he made love twice with Terry, on successive nights, because he liked her, because she was pretty, because she was unhappy, and because he felt he had earned it. That ended everything. Terry told Jack about Hank. Then, desperate and drunk, Jack told Terry about Edith, said he wanted a divorce, and when Terry grieved he could not leave her: all of this in about twelve hours, and within twenty-four Edith and Terry had lunch together, and next afternoon Hank and Jack went running, and that evening, with the help of gin and their long friendship, they all gathered and charcoaled steaks. When the Linharts went home, Hank and Edith stood on the front lawn till the car turned a corner and was gone. Then Edith put her arm around his waist. *We're better off,* she said: *they're still unhappy.* He felt he was being held with all her strength; that strength he had feared last April; he was proud to be loved by her and, with some shame, he was proud of himself, for bringing her this far. That fall they both had new lovers.

When three years later she told him to leave and he tried to believe the injustice of it, he could not. For a long time he did not understand why. Then one night it came to him: he remembered her arm around his waist that summer night, and the pride he had felt, and then he knew why his tallying of her affairs meant nothing. She had not made him leave her life because he was un-faithful; she had made him leave because she was; because he had changed her. So she had made him leave because—and this struck him so hard, standing in his bedroom, he needed suddenly to lie down—he was Hank Allison.

On the morning after Monica jettisoned him, he woke with the images he had brought to bed. He had no memory, as he might have without last night's treatment, of anything about her that was intelligent or kind or witty or tender. Instead of losing a good woman, he had been saved from a bad one. He knew all this was like Novocain while the dentist drilled; but no matter. For what he had to face now was not the loss of Monica; he had to face, once again, what to do about loss itself. He put a banana, wheat germ, a raw egg, and buttermilk in the blender. He brought the drink downstairs and sat on the front steps, in the autumn sunlight. It was a Saturday, and Sharon wanted to see a movie that afternoon. Good: nearly two hours of distraction; he would like the movie, whatever it was. Before picking up Sharon he must plan his night, be sure he did not spend it alone in his apartment. If he called the Linharts and told them about Monica, they would invite him to dinner, stay up drinking with him as long as he wanted. He touched the steps. *It's these steps,* he thought. He looked up and down the street lined with old houses and old trees. *This street. This town. How the fuck can I beat geography?* A small town, and a dead one. The bright women went to other places. The ones he taught with were married. So he was left with either students or the women he knew casually in town, women he had tried talking to in bars—secretaries, waitresses, florists, beauticians—and he had enjoyed their company, but no matter how pretty and good-natured they were, how could he spend much time with a woman who thought Chekhov was something boys did in their beds at night? He remembered a night last summer drinking with Jack at a bar that was usually lined with girls, and he said: *Look at her: she's pretty, she looks sweet, she's nicely dressed, but look at that face: nothing there. Not one thought in her head.* And Jack said: *Sure she's got thoughts: thirty-eight ninety-five . . . size nine . . . partly cloudy.* Sharon was twelve. He would not move away until she was at least eighteen. He was with her every weekend, and they cooked at his apartment one night during the week. When his second book was published, an old friend offered him a job in Boston: he had thought about the bigger school, more parties with more women, even graduate students, as solemn as they were. But he would not leave Sharon. And when she was eighteen, he would be forty, twice the age of most of his students, and having lived on temporary love for six years, one limping, bloodstained son of a bitch. And if he moved then, who would want what was left of him?

He stood and climbed the stairs to his apartment and phoned the Linharts. Jack answered. When Hank told him, he said to come to dinner; early, as soon as he took Sharon home.

"Maybe I'll invite Lori," Hank said.

"Why not."

"I mean, she's just a friend. But maybe she'll keep the night from turning into a wake."

"Bring her. Just be careful. You fall in love faster than I can fry an egg. What is it with these Goddamn girls anyway? Are they afraid of something permanent? Is that it?"

"Old buddy, I think there's something about me that just scares shit out of them. Something they just can't handle."

You were all the way across the room, Monica said as soon as he came, before he had even collapsed on her, to nestle his cheek beside hers. So instead he rolled away and marvelled that she knew, that Goddamnit they always knew: his soul *had* been across the room; he had felt it against the wall behind him, opposite the foot of the bed, thinking, watching him and Monica, waiting for them to finish. Because of that, finishing had taken him a long time: erect and eager, his cock seemed attached not to his flesh but to that pondering soul back there; and since it did not seem his flesh, it did not seem to be inside Monica's either: there was a mingling of his hardness and her softness and liquid heat, but it had nothing to do with who he was for those minutes, or for who she was either. He knew it was an occupational hazard. Then, because of why it had just happened on that early Friday evening in winter when she was still his student, had two hours ago been in his class, had then walked to his apartment in cold twilight, he laughed. He had not expected to laugh, he knew it was a mistake, but he could not stop. A warning tried to stop him, to whisper *hush* to the laughter, a warning that knew not only the perils with a woman at a time like this, but the worse

peril of being so confident in a woman's love that he could believe she would love his laughter now too, and his reason for it.
She got out of bed and went to the bathroom and then the
kitchen and when she came back she had a glass of Dry Sack—
one glass, not two—and even that sign could not make him serious, for he was caught in the comic precision of what had just
happened. She pulled on leotards, slipped into a sweater that she
left unbuttoned, and brought a cigarette to bed where she lay
beside him, not touching, and the space between them and the
sound of her breathing felt to Hank not quite angry yet, not
quite subdued either.

"You were right," he said. He was still smiling. "I *was* across
the room. I can't help it. I was all right until we started; then
while we were making love I thought about what I was working
on today. I didn't want to. I never want to after I stop for the
day. And I wanted to ask you about it but I figured we'd better
finish first—"

"Oh good, Hank: oh good."

"I know, I know. But I was working on a scene about a girl
who's only made love once, say a few months ago, and then one
night she makes love twice to this guy and again in the morning,
and I wanted to know if I was right. In the scene her pussy is
sore next day; after the three times. Is that accurate?"

"Yes. You son of a bitch."

"Now wait a minute. None of this was on purpose. You think
I want my Goddamn head to start writing whenever it decides to?
It's not like being un*kind,* for Christ's sake. You think surgeons
and lawyers and whatever don't go through this too? Shit: you
came, didn't you?"

"I could do that alone."

"Well, what am I supposed to fucking *do?*"

He got out of bed and went for the bottle of sherry and
brought it back with another glass; but at the doorway to his
room, looking at her leotarded legs, the stretch of belly and chest
and the inner swell of breasts exposed by the sweater, at her wide
grim mouth concentrating on smoking, and her gray eyes look-

ing at the ceiling, he stopped and stayed at the threshold. He said softly: "Baby, what am I supposed to do? I don't believe in all this special crap about writers, you know that. We're just like everybody else. *Every*body gets distracted by their work, or whatever."

He cut himself off: he had been about to say *Housewives too,* but the word was too dangerous and, though he believed that vocation one of the hardest and most distracting of all, believed if he were one he could never relax enough to make unhindered love, he kept quiet. Monica would not be able to hear what he said; she would hear only the word *housewife,* would slip into jargon, think of labels, roles, would not be soothed. She did not look at him. She said: "You could try harder. You could concentrate more. You could even pretend, so I wouldn't feel like I was getting fucked by a dildo." She was often profane, but this took him by surprise; he felt slapped. "And you could shut up about it. And not laugh about it. And you could Goddamn not ask me your fucking questions when you stop laughing. I want a lover, not a Papermate."

The line pleased him, even cheered him a little, and he almost told her so; but again he heard his own warnings, and stopped.

"Look," he said, "let's go to Boston. To Casa Romero and have a hell of a dinner."

She stayed on his bed long enough to finish the cigarette; she occupied herself with it, held it above her face between drags and studied it as though it were worthy of concentration; watched her exhaled smoke plume and spread toward the ceiling; for all he knew (he still stood naked in the doorway) she was thinking, perhaps even about them. But he doubted it. For a girl so young, she had a lot of poses; when did they start learning them, for Christ's sake? When they still wrote their ages with one digit? She exhaled the last drag with a sigh, put the cigarette out slowly, watching its jabs against the ashtray as if this were her last one before giving them up; then quickly she put on her skirt, buttoned her sweater, pulled on her boots, slung her suede jacket over her shoulder, and walked toward him as if he were a swinging door. He turned sideways; passing, she touched neither him nor the doorjamb. *Awfully slender,* he thought. He followed her down the short hall; stood at the doorway and watched her going down the stairs; he hoped his semen was dripping into the crotch of her leotards, just to remind her that everything can't be walked away from. "Theatrical bitch," he said to her back, and shut the door.

Which six hours later he opened when she knocked and woke him. She was crying. Her kiss smelled of vermouth. She had been drinking with her roommate. She missed him. She was sorry. She loved him. He took her to bed with fear and sadness which were more distracting than this afternoon's thinking; he pretended passion and tenderness; he urged his cock *Come on come you bastard,* while all the time he felt defeat with this woman, felt it as surely as if it stood embodied behind him, with a raised sword. Some night, some day, the sword would arc swiftly down; all he could do was hang on to the good times with Monica while he waited for the blade.

Monica did, though, give him Lori. They were friends from summers in Maine, where Lori lived, and Monica's parents, from Manhattan, had a summer house. The girls met when Lori was fifteen and Monica sixteen. It was Monica who convinced Lori to enroll in the college, and to take Hank's courses. Then Monica transferred to Maine after her freshman year, because she didn't like her art teachers; but Lori came to the college anyway and saw Monica on the weekends when she drove down and stayed with Hank. He liked Lori on those weekends, he liked seeing her in his class, and some week nights they walked in town and drank beer; a few people probably thought they were lovers, but Hank was only afraid of gossip that was true, so he and Lori went to Timmy's, where students drank. And the night after Monica left him, he picked her up at the dormitory, for dinner at the Linharts. They did not become lovers until over a month later and, when they did, Hank realized it was the first time since Edith that he had made love with a woman who was already his good friend. So their transition lacked the fear and euphoria that people called romance. For Hank, it felt comfortable and safe, as though he had loved her for a long and good time.

Still, with Lori, he was careful: so careful that at times he thought all the will and control it demanded of him was finally the core of love; that for the first time he knew how to go about it. He watched her shyness, listened to it, loved it, and did not try to cure it. While he did this, he felt his love for her growing deeper, becoming a part of who he was in the world.

She was his fourth young girl since divorce. Each had lasted a year or more; with each he had been monogamous; and they had left him. None but Monica had told him why, in words he could understand. The other two had cried and talked about needing space. When the first left him he was sad, but he was all right. The loss of the second frightened him. That was when he saw his trap. Drinking with Jack, he could smile about it: for what had been spice in his married twenties was now his sustenance. Certainly, he told Jack, when he was married he had fallen in love with his girl friends, or at least had the feeling of being in love, had said the words, had the poignant times when he and the girl held each other and spoke, in the warm spring, of the end that was coming to them on the school calendar. But all those affairs had simply given him emotions which he had believed marriage, but its nature, could not give.

For the first time in his life he felt a disadvantage with women. Too often, as he looked at a young face in his apartment or across a restaurant table, he knew he had nothing to offer this girl with her waiting trust fund, this girl who had seen more of the world than he ever would; he imagined her moving all those clothes and other pelf into his apartment and, as he talked with the girl, he wished for some woman his own age, or at least twenty-five, who was not either married or one of those so badly divorced that their pain was not only infectious but also produced in them anger at all men, making him feel he was a tenuous exception who, at any moment, would not be. They met with women's groups, shrank each other's heads without a professional in the room, and came away with their anger so prodded they were like warriors. He had tried two of those and, bored and weary, had fled. Once with honey-blonde Donna, the last one, he had left a bar to enter a night of freezing rain, ten minutes to chip his windshield clear while she sat in the car; then driving home so slowly and tensely he could feel his heart beating, he said: "Probably some man froze all this fucking rain too." Perhaps because she was as frightened as he was, she gently, teasingly, said "MCP," and patted his shoulder.

He only argued with Donna once. He believed in most of what women wanted, believed women and men should work together to free themselves, believed *The Wild Palms* had said it first and as well as anyone since. Some trifles about the movement had piqued him: they had appropriated a word he loved, mostly because of its comic root, and he could no longer have the Cold War fun of calling someone a chauvinist. And, on his two marches in Washington during the Vietnam War, he had been angered by the women who took their turn on the speakers' platform and tried to equate dishwashing with being napalmed. The only important feeling he had about these women was he wished they had some joy. The night he argued with Donna he was drunk and, though he kept trying not to see the *Ms.* on her coffee table, it was finally all he could see, and he said abruptly: "Donna, just as an unknown, average, .260-hitting writer, who sometimes writes a story and tries to publish it, or a piece of a novel, I've got to say one thing: I hate totalitarian magazines whether they're called *Ms.* or *Penthouse.*"

"Totalitarian?"

"That." He picked up *Ms.* and dropped it on its cover so all he saw was an advertisement encouraging young girls to start working on lung cancer now, older women to keep at it. "They hate literature. They just want something that supports their position. It's like trying to publish in China, for Christ's sake." Then, because he was angry at magazines and nothing else, and she was suddenly an angry feminist, they fought.

The fight ended when it was over, so it wasn't serious. But one of the reasons he finally left her, chose loneliness instead, was what she read. She did not read him. This hurt him a little, but not much; mostly, he was baffled. He could not understand why she would make love with him when she was not interested in his work. Because to him, his work was the best of himself. He believed most men who were fortunate enough to have work they loved saw themselves in the same way. Yet Donna's affection was only for what he was at night, when he was relaxing from that day's work, and forgetting tomorrow's, in much the same way he saw most movies that came to town, no matter what they were. And his bantering night-self was so unimportant to him that often, at his desk in the morning, he felt he had not spent last evening with Donna; someone else had talked with her, made love with her; some old, close friend of his.

Typed on a sheet of paper, thumbtacked to the wall over his desk, was this from *Heart of Darkness: No, I don't like work. I had rather laze about and think of all the fine things that can be done. I don't like work—no man does—but I like what is in the work—the chance to find yourself. Your own reality—for yourself, not others— what no other man can ever know. They can only see the mere show, and never can tell what it really means.* A woman had to know that: simply know it, that was all. He did not need praise from her, he rarely liked to talk about his work, and he had no delusions about it: he liked most novels he read better than he liked his own. But the work was his, and its final quality did not matter so much as the hours it demanded from him. It made the passage of time concrete, measurable. It gave him confidence, not in the work itself, but in Hank Allison: after a morning at the desk he had earned his day on earth. When he did not work, except by choice, he disliked himself. If these days occurred in succession because of school work, hangovers, lack of will, sickness, he lost touch with himself, felt vague and abstract, felt himself becoming whomever he was with. So he thought Donna knew little more about him than she would if, never having met him, she came across his discarded clothing and wallet on her bedroom floor. At times this made him lonely; it also made him think of

Edith, all of her he had not known during their marriage, especially the final three polygamous years; and with no way now to undo, to soothe, to heal, he loved her and grieved for what she had suffered: the loneliness of not being fully known.

One night in Donna's bed, lying tensely beside her peaceful, her post-orgasmic flesh, in the dark yet seeing in his mind the bedroom cluttered with antique chairs and dressing table and family pictures on the wall and, resting on the mantel of the sealed fireplace, faces of her grandparents and parents and herself with two children, a son and daughter, he wondered why he was with her. He knew it was because of loneliness, but why her, with her colliding values, her liberated body which she had shared— offered actually—on their second date, lying here among the testaments of family, marriage, traditions? He suspected that her feminism existed solely because, as her marriage ended, her husband had become mean. He was behind on child support; often he broke dates with the children. Hank believed she was happy now, in these moments this night, because she had just made love, her children slept healthy down the hall, and she was lying amid her antiques and photographs of her life, on a four-poster bed that had been her great-aunt's. When he tired of trying to understand her, he said: "I don't know why you like me."

"Why *Hank.*"

Her voice was wrong: she thought he felt unloved, needed comfort. He left the bed to piss, to break the mood. When he returned and covered himself he said: "You're not interested in my work. That's me. All you see is what's left over. I don't think that's me."

"I've hurt you, and it was stupid and selfish. Bring them over tomorrow night. I'll read them in order."

"Wait." He spoke with gentle seriousness, as he did at times with Sharon, when they were discussing a problem she was having or a difference between them, and he wanted her to hear only calm father-words, and not to listen for or worry about his own emotions beneath them. "I'm not hurt. I just don't understand how you can feel for me, and know nothing at all about that part of my 'life. Maybe two-thirds of it; only about an eighth of my day, in hours, but usually two-thirds of it, which is all of it except sleeping; no matter what I'm doing, it's down there inside me, I can feel it at work; whether I'm with Sharon or you or teaching; or anything." He was about to explain that too, but veered away: some nights with Donna he had the same trouble he would have with Monica much later; but Donna either had not noticed or, more likely, because she had been with more men, she had simply understood; probably she had her own nights like that, as they moved together in that passion which, true as it was, did not totally absorb them, but existed in tandem with them.

"What about my work?" she said.

There was no edge on her voice; not yet; but he could sense the blade against whetstone in her heart. He watched her eyes, kept his voice the same, though with a twinge of impatience he felt he *was* talking to Sharon. Why was he so often comforting women? He wished he could see himself as they saw him: his face, his body, his gestures; wished he could hear the voice they heard. For now he felt like a mean lover, and he did not want to be, but maybe he was and could not do anything about it; or maybe (he hoped) he simply appeared that way. Whatever, he was sad and confused and lonely, felt lost and homeless and womanless, though he lay in bed with a good woman, a good companion; and he needed answers, or even just one, yet now he must give answers, and in a controlled and comforting voice whose demand on him clenched his fists, tightened his arms.

"It's not," he said. "You told me it wasn't. We were eating at Ten Center Street, and you said: 'It's not work; I wouldn't grace it with the name. It's just a job till I find out what I really want to do.' " He was still tense, but her face softened with his voice.

"You're right," she said.

"I also know about your job. I've listened. I can tell you your typical day. But mostly with me you talk about your children and rearing them alone and shithead Max not coming through with the money and not seeing the children when he's supposed to, because he's become a chic-freak smoking dope all day with young ass and bragging about leaving the engineering rat-race, when the truth is he was laid off with the rest of the poor bastards during the recession, and he talks about opening a bar when he can hardly afford to drink at one because he's drawing unemployment. And you mostly talk about men and women. And how everything's changed since you and Max bought this house and it's got you muddled and sad and pissed-off and you want to do something about it, for yourself and other women too if you could think of a way, but you don't know how yet. I don't mean any of this as an insult. You talk about these things because that's who you are right now, that's your struggle, and it never bores me. Because I care about you and because I'm going through my version of the same thing. Everything's changed for me too. When we were pregnant—"

"We?"

"Of course we. Not just Edith. I didn't vomit and my pants size didn't change and my breasts didn't swell and I didn't feel any pain. But it was we. It always is, unless some prick pretends it isn't."

"Like Max."

"I don't know what he felt then. You said he was different then—" He waved an arm at the dark room, was about to say *He liked all this stuff,* but did not.

"What did *you* feel?" she said.

"Guilt. Fear. I'd read *A Farewell to Arms* too recently. Three or four years earlier, but for me that was too recently." He saw in her face she did not know the book, and he was about to explain, but thought that would be a worse mistake than his mentioning it. "I was afraid she'd die. Off and on, until it was over. While she was delivering I hated my hard-on that had been so important whatever night it seemed so important and the diaphragm wasn't enough."

"Men shouldn't feel that way."

"Should and shouldn't don't have much to do with feelings.

Anyway, we got married. We were in graduate school and we didn't know any feminists. We were too busy, and our friends were other young couples who were busting their asses to pay bills and stay in school. It made sense then, graduate school: there were jobs waiting. And I saw Edith as a wife in I suppose the same way my father saw my mother. Which somewhat resembles a nineteenth-century aristocrat, I guess: some asshole out of Balzac or Tolstoy." (This time, remembering his marriage, he did not even notice that literature had moved into the bed again, like a troublesome cat.) "Well, not that bad. But bad enough. I don't think I knew it, most of the time. Or maybe I just believed I was right, *it* was right. It's the only way I had ever seen marriage. I'm not excusing myself. It gets down to this: I nearly drowned her in my shit creek till one night she found a paddle and broke it over my head. Then she shoved the handle through me. I still feel the splinters. All of which is to say I'm not just politely nodding my head when you talk about trouble between men and women. You're talking to a comrade in arms, and I lost too."

Goddamn: he had gotten off the track again, for now she held him with both arms, pulled him against her, and he let her quietly hold him a while, then he shifted, got an arm around her, pulled her head to his shoulder so he was talking to her hair, and said: "All of which got us away from the original question. You're a lovely woman. You could have as many kinds of men as you're lucky enough to meet—doctor lawyer Indian chief—so what I want to ask is, why me? A man you met at a party, you came up and said 'You have foam on your moustache,' and I licked it off and you said 'I like watching men lick beer from their moustaches.' Why in the world me?"

She turned and kissed him long, then raising her face above his, she said: "Because you're so *alive.*"

As if she had suddenly pulled the blankets from him, a chill went down his back and touched his heart, which felt now dry and withered, late autumn's leaf about to fall slowly through his body. Feeling her bones against him, he thought of her as a skeleton lying amid the antiques in the dark, a skeleton with a voice struggling for life, with words that were the rote of pain and anger from the weekly meetings of women. Then he felt like crying for her. It seemed that, compared to hers, his own life was full and complex and invigorating. He wished he knew a secret, and that he could give it to her: could lay his hand on her forehead and she would sleep and wake tomorrow with the same dreary job as a bank teller, the same mother-duties, and confusion and loneliness and the need to feel her life was something solid she was sculpting, yet with an excited spirit ready to engage the day, to kick it and claw it and gouge its eyes until it gave her the joy she deserved. But he had nothing to tell her, nothing to give. He held her quietly, for a long time. Then he rose and dressed. He never spent the night with her. She did not want the children, who were three and five, to know: nor did Hank; and it was implicit between them that since their affair had begun impetuously soon, it was tenuous, was at very best—or least—a trial affair. There would probably be another man, and another, and her children should not grow up seeing that male succession at breakfast. He leaned over and kissed her, whispered sweetly, then drove home.

The point was, finally, that Donna did not read. He guessed all men did not have to love women who were interested in their work; somehow a veterinarian could leave his work with its odors in the shower before dinner, spend his evening with a beloved woman who did not want a house pet. But he could not. Literature was what he turned to for passion and excitement, where he entered a world of questions he could not answer, so he finished a novel or poem or story feeling blessed with humility, with awe of life, with the knowledge that he knew so little about how one was supposed to live. So, better to have the company of a girl who loved literature and simply had not read much because she was young, far more exciting to listen to a girl's delight at her first reading of *Play It As It Lays* or *Fat City,* than to be with a woman in her thirties who did not read because she had chosen not to, had gone to the magazines and television.

Two nights later they went to dinner and, with coffee and brandy, sipping the courage to hurt her, he spoke about their starting too fast, becoming lovers too soon, before they really knew each other; he said their histories were very different, and being sudden lovers blurred their ability to see whether they were really—he paused, waiting for a series of concrete words besides the one word *compatible,* wanting his speech to at least sound different from the ones other men and women were hearing across the land that night. During his pause she said: "Compatible."

Then relief filled her face as quickly as pain does, the pain he had predicted, and for an instant he was hurt. Then he smiled at his fleeting pride. He was happy: she had wanted out too. Then she told him she had been three days late last week and her waiting had made her think about the two of them, she had been frightened, and had wanted to stop the affair. But not their friendship. They ordered second brandies and talked, without shyness, about their children. They split the bill, he drove her home, and they kissed goodnight at her door.

As he leaves Lori in the car in front of Edith's house he kisses her quickly, says he loves her. Edith opens the door: small body, long black hair, her eyes and mouth smiling like an old friend. He supposes that is what she is now and, because they have Sharon, in some way they are still married. Though he cannot define each scent, the house smells feminine to him. Like Donna, Edith does not let lovers stay the night, and for the same reasons. Hank knows this because, in their second year of divorce, when he could ask the question without risking too deep a wound, he did. Now he asks: "What kind of smell does a man bring into a house?"

"Bad ones."

"I smell bacon and the Sunday paper. Both neuter. But there's something female. Or non-male."

"It's your imagination. But there *has* been a drought."

"I'm sorry. What happened to what's-his-face?"

She shrugs, and for a moment the smile leaves her eyes: not sadness but resignation or perhaps foreknowledge of it, years of it. Then she looks at him more closely.

"What happened?" she says.

"Something shitty."

"With Lori?"

"No."

"Good. I think she's the one."

"Really? Why?"

"I don't know. I hope you can keep her. What is it? Work?"

"No. I'll talk to you tonight. Where's Sharon?"

"Cleaning her room. I'll get her."

She goes to the foot of the stairs and calls: "Sharon, Dad's here."

"I'm sorry about the drought," he says.

"What the hell. I should have been a teacher so I'd have more livestock to pasture with. It's all right now, did you know that? For women. A friend of mine is having an affair with one of her students. She's thirty-seven and he's nineteen."

She is not attacking him; those days are long past. He is sorry for her, knows her problem is geographical too, that she would do better in Boston. He is grateful and deeply respects her for staying here so he and Sharon can be near each other, but he can only tell her such things on the phone when he's had some drinks.

Sharon comes down in jeans and a sweater, carrying a wind-breaker. He hugs her and they kiss. Her new breasts make him uncomfortable; he rarely looks at them, and when he embraces her he doesn't know where to put them, what to do about their small insistence against him. They both kiss Edith and walk arm-in-arm to the car. Lori opens the door, and Sharon gets into the back seat.

Sharon and Lori get along well, and sometimes talk like two teen-aged friends, as if he's not there. That they are both teen-agers, one in her first year of it, the other in her last, gives Hank both a smile and a shiver. He wonders if someday he will have a girl who is Sharon's age. It could happen in five years. And who, he wonders as he drives on a country road winding east, ever started the myth that a young girl gave an older man his youth again? Not that he would want his confused youth again. But they were supposed to make you feel younger. All he knows is that with Lori he feels unattractive, balding, flabby. That she wakes with a hangover looking strong and fresh, and is; while at thirty he lost that resilience and now a bad hangover affects his day like the flu. Remembering how in his twenties he could wake six hours after closing a bar, then eat breakfast and write, he feels old. And when people glance at him and Lori while, in Boston, they walk holding hands, or enter a restaurant, he feels old. The beach is worse: he watches the lithe young men and wonders if Lori watches them too, and his knowing that most of them, probably all except the obsessively vain and those who are simply exempt by nature, will in a few years have enough flesh at their waists to fill a woman's hands, does not help. He feels old. Yet with Donna and the divorcée before her, he had felt young, too young, his spirit quickly wearied by their gravity. So, again, no answers: all he knows is that whoever spread the word about young girls had not been an older man in love with one.

Sharon and Lori are talking about school and their teachers and homework and how they discipline themselves to do it, how they choose which work to do first (Lori works in descending order, beginning with the course she likes most: Sharon does the opposite; they both end with science.) Last summer Sharon started and stopped smoking; quit when Edith kissed her just after running, and smelled Sharon's breath and hair; which she might not have, she told Hank on the phone, if her sense of smell hadn't been cleansed of her own cigarettes by an hour's run. Hank liked that: he had a notion that kids got away with smoking now because their parents didn't kiss them much; when he was a boy, he and his friends had chewed gum and rubbed lemon juice on their fingers before going home, because someone always kissed them hello. Edith talked to Sharon, and that night Hank took her to dinner and talked to her, pleaded with her, and she promised him, as she had Edith, that she was not hooked, had smoked maybe two packs, and from now on, she said, she would not give in to peer pressure. That was the night Hank and Edith started worrying about dope, talked on the phone about it, and he wondered how divorced parents who were too hurt and angry to talk to each other dealt with what their children were doing. Now, at least once a month, while he and Sharon cook dinner in his small kitchen, he mentions dope. She tells him not to worry, she's seen enough of the freaks at school, starting with their joints on the bus at seven in the morning.

He is not deeply worried about dope, because he trusts Sharon, knows she is sensible; that she tried cigarettes with her girl friends because at thirteen she wouldn't think of death; but he is as certain as he can be that, seeing the stoned and fruitless days of the young people around her, she will take care of herself.

What really worries him about Sharon has to do with him and Lori, and with him and Monica, and with the two girls before Monica. It also has to do with Edith: although her lovers have not spent the night, have probably not even used the house, by now Sharon must know Edith has had them. But he doesn't worry much about Edith, because he feels so confused, guilty, embarrassed, honest and dishonest about himself and his lovers and Sharon, that he has little energy left to worry about Edith's responsibilities. Also, he understands very little about mothers and daughters, the currents that run between them. But about Sharon he knows this: with each of his young girl friends—she did not meet Donna or the divorcée before her—she has been shy, has wanted to be their friend, more to them than her father's daughter. He has also sensed jealousy, which has disturbed him, and he doesn't know whether Sharon feels the girl is taking her mother's place, or her own, in his life. Always he has talked with her about his girl friends, and pretended they were not lovers. Yet he knows that she knows. So he is hung on his own petard: he does not want her to have lovers early, before she has grown enough to protect herself from pain. He wants to warn her that, until some vague age, a young boy will stick it in anything and say anything that will let him stick it. He doesn't know when he will tell her this. He does not want her girlhood and young womanhood to become a series of lovers, he does not want her to become cynical and casual about making love. He does not, in fact, want her to be like his girl friends. Yet, by having four whom she's known in five years, and two whom she hasn't, that is exactly the way he is showing her how to live.

Lori makes things better. When he became her friend, she had had one quick and brutal affair with a co-worker in a restaurant in Maine where they both waited tables the summer before she came to college. He hurt her physically, confused her about what she was doing with him, and after two weeks she stopped. So she was more the sort of girl he wanted Sharon to be. And Lori—shy, secretive not by choice, brooding (though it didn't appear on her smooth face; he had to look at her drooping lip-corners)—was warm and talkative with Sharon, enjoyed being with her, and Hank thought they were good for each other: Sharon, with her new breasts and menses, her sophistication that came from enduring divorce and having parents who were not always honest with her yet tried to be as often as they could, for the two purposes of helping her with divorce and preparing her to face the implacable and repetitive pains in a world that, when they were much younger, neither of them had foreseen. On the other hand Lori: with her quiet, tender father, his voice seldom heard, his presence seeming to ask permission for itself, and her loud mother whose dominance was always under a banner of concern for her daughter and, beneath that (Hank guessed), Lori's belief that her father was, had been, and would be a cuckold, and not only that but one without vengeance, neither rage nor demand nor even the retaliatory relief of some side-pussy of his own. So as Hank listens he thinks Sharon needs warm recognition from Lori, and that Lori needs to be able to talk, giggle, be silly, say whatever she wants, and from Sharon (and yes: him at the wheel beside her) she draws the peace to be able to talk without feeling that someone is standing behind her, about to clamp a hand on her shoulder and tell her she's wrong.

Wondering about Sharon and Lori gives him some respite but it is not complete. For all during the drive there is the cool hollow of sadness around his heart, and something is wrong with his body. Gravity is more intense: his head and shoulders and torso are pulled downward to the car seat. He crosses the bridge to the island, turns right into the game preserve, driving past the booth which is unmanned now that summer is over. To their right is the salt marsh, to their left dunes so high they cannot see the ocean. He parks facing a dune, and walking between Lori and Sharon, holding their hands, he starts climbing the grass-tufted slope of sand; his body is still heavy.

At the dune's top the sea breeze strikes them cool but not cold, coming over water that is deep blue, for the air is dry, and they stop. They stand deeply inhaling the air from the sea. On the crest of the dune, his eyes watering from the breeze, holding Lori's and Sharon's hands, breathing the ocean-smell he loves, Hank suddenly does not know what he will do about last year's dead fetus, last night's dream of her on the summer beach with him and Sharon; he cannot imagine the rest of his life. He sees himself growing older, writing and running and teaching, but that is all, and his tears now are not from the breeze.

"Let's go," he says, and they walk southward, releasing each other's hands so they can file between the low shrubs on the dune's top. He turns back to the girls and points at Canadian geese far out in the marsh, even their distant silhouettes looking fat, and he thinks of one roasting, the woman—who? his mother? he sees no face—bending over to open the oven door, peering in, basting. They walk quietly. He can feel them all, free of housewood and car-metal that surround most of their time, feeling the hard sand underfoot, the crisp brown shrubs scratching their pants, their eyes looking ahead and down the slopes of the dune, out at the marsh with its grass and, in places, shimmer of standing water, and its life of tiny creatures they can feel but not see; and at the ocean, choppy and white-capped, and he imagines a giant squid and killer whale struggling in a dance miles deep among mountains and valleys. For an instant he hopes Lori is at least a bit sad, then knows that is asking too much.

They walk nearly two miles, where the dune ends, and beneath them the island ends too at the river which flows through the marsh, into the sea. The river is narrow and, where it meets the sea, the water is lake-gentle. It is shallow and, in low tide, Hank and Sharon have waded out to a long sandbar opposite the river's mouth. Hank goes down a steep, winding path, and they move slowly. At the bottom they cross the short distance of sand and watch the end of the river, and look southeast where the coast below them curves sharply out to sea. They turn and walk up the beach, the sand cool and soft. He is walking slightly ahead of them, holding back just enough to be with them and still alone; for he feels something else behind him too, so strongly that his impulse is to turn and confront it before it leaps on him. He wants to run until his body feels light again. They move closer to the beach and walk beside washed-up kelp and green seaweed. He stops and turns to Lori and Sharon. Their faces are wind-pink, their hair blows across cheeks and eyes.

"I don't know where the car is," he says. "But I know a restaurant it can get us to."

Sharon points at the dune.

"On the other side," she says.

"Oh. I thought I parked it in the surf."

"It's *right* over there."

"No."

He looks at the dune.

"You want to bet?"

"Not with you. You'd bet a dinner at the Copley against a hamburger at Wendy's."

"Okay. What's the Copley?"

"A place I'm not taking you. Lori and I go Dutch."

"That expensive, huh?"

"We go everywhere Dutch. You can't tell me that part of the dune looks different."

"See the lifeguard tower?"

He looks north behind him, perhaps a half-mile away. Sharon talks to his back.

"When we climbed the dune I looked that way and saw it."
He looks at her. "If you're right, I'll buy you a meal."
"You already said you'd do that."
"Right. Let's climb, ladies."
He leads them up and, at the top, they see the car to the south.
"I was a bit off," Sharon says.
"No more than a hundred yards."

The restaurant is nearby, on the mainland road that curves away from the island; and it is there, seated and facing Sharon and Lori, that whatever pursued him on the beach strikes him: lands howling on his back. He can do nothing about it but look at Sharon's cheerful face while he feels, in the empty chair beside him, the daughter salined or vacuumed from Monica a year ago. The waitress is large and smiling, a New England country woman with big, strong-looking hands, and she asks if they'd like something to drink. Sharon wants a Shirley Temple, Lori wants a margarita, and Hank wants to be drunk. But he is wary. When his spirit is low, when he can barely feel it at all, just something damp and flat lying over his guts, when even speaking and eating demand effort, and he wants to lie down and let the world spin while he yearns for days of unconsciousness, he does not drink. The only cure then is a long run. It does not destroy what is attacking him, but it restores his spirit, and he can move into the world again, look at people, touch them, talk. Only once in his life it has not worked: the day after Edith told him to leave. He would like to run now. Whatever leaped on his back has settled there, more like a deadly snake than a mad dog. He must be still and quiet. He remembers one of his favorite scenes in literature, in Kipling: "Rikki-Tikki-Tavi," when Nagaina the mother cobra comes to the veranda where the family is eating, coiled and raised to strike the small boy, the three of them—father, mother, son—statues at their breakfast table.

"A mongoose," he says.
"He'll ask me how to make that one."
"It comes with a cobra egg in its mouth." She is looking down at him, her eyes amused yet holding on to caution too, perhaps

anger, waiting to see if this is harassment or friendly joking. "It's the last egg in the nest. He's killed the others. He comes up behind the cobra and she turns on him just long enough for the father to reach over the table and grab his son and pull him away."

"Sounds like a good one," she says. "Must start with rum and keep building."

She is smiling now, and he is ashamed, for he sees in her quickly tender eyes that she knows something is wrong.

"I'm sorry," he says.

"For what? I like a good story. If we had cobras around here I swear to God I'd go live up ten flights of stairs in Boston and never see grass or stars again. You going to drink that?"

"I'll have a Coke with a wedge of lime."

"So that's a mongoose. I think I'll call it that, see what he comes up with. Now I like Jackson. But he's his own man behind the bar. Any time—*every* time—somebody orders a sombrero, he says 'What do you think this is, a dairy bar?' Doesn't matter who they are. He makes them, but he always says that. Won't make a frozen daiquiri. Nobody orders them anyway. Maybe five-six a year. He just looks at them and says 'Too much trouble; I'll quit my job first. Young guy came in the other night and ordered a flintlock. Ever hear of that one?"

"No."

"Neither did Jackson. He said, Go home and watch Daniel Boone, and he went to the other end of the bar till finally the guy goes down there and asks can he have a beer. Jackson looks at him a while then opens up the bottle and says, You want a glass with that or a powder horn?"

Hank keeps smiling, thinking that on another day he would stay here for hours, drinking long after his meal, so he could banter with this woman with the crinkles at her eyes and the large hands he guesses have held many a happy man. He could get into his country-western mood and find songs on the jukebox and ask about her children and wonder how many heartbreaks she had given and received.

"Better just tell him Coke then," he says. "You order a mongoose and he'll send me the snake."

"He's a bit of one himself. Coke with a wedge," and she is gone. He looks at Lori. She understands, and he glances away from her, down at the red paper placemat. When the waitress brings their drinks, they order food, taking a long time because Sharon cannot decide and the waitress, who is not busy this early in the afternoon, enjoys helping her, calls her Honey, tells her the veal cutlet is really pork tenderloin but it's good anyway, the fisherman's platter is too big but if she doesn't stuff on the fries she might eat most of the fish, with maybe some help from the mongoose-drinker. Sharon orders a sirloin, and Hank is glad: he wants to watch her eating meat.

When it comes he does watch, eating his haddock without pleasure or attention: Sharon is hungry and she forks and cuts fast, and he watches the brown and pink bite go into her mouth, watches her lips close on it and her jaws working and the delight on her face. He remembers the smell of the sea, the feel of her hand in his, the sound of her breath beside him. *Life,* he thinks, and imagines the taste of steak in her mouth, the meat becoming part of her, and as his heart celebrates these pleasures it grieves, for he can see only the flesh now, Sharon's, and the flesh of the world: its terrain and its seasons of golden and red, then white, then mud and rain and green, and the blue and green months with their sun burning then tanning her skin. All trials of the spirit seem nothing compared to this: his grave and shameful talk with Monica and her parents, Monica's tears and seven more months of gestation, his taking the girl home, blanket-wrapped on his lap on the plane: cries in the night and diapers, formula and his impatience and frustration and anger as he powdered the pink peach of her girlhood, staying home with her at night and finding babysitters so he could teach—all this goes through his mind like blown ashes, for he can only feel the flesh: Sharon's and his and the daughter in the chair beside him: she is a small child now, has lived long enough to love the sun on her face and the taste of steak. And for the first time in his life he understands that grief is not of the mind but the body. He can dull his mind, knock it out with booze and sleeping pills. But he can do nothing about his pierced body as he watches Sharon eat, can do nothing about its pieces sitting beside him in the body of a daughter, nor about the part of it that was torn from him last October, that seems still to live wherever they dumped it in the hospital in New York. He offers Sharon dessert. The waitress says the apple pie is hot and homemade, just out of the oven. Sharon orders it with vanilla ice cream, and Hank watches her mouth open wide for the cold-hot bites, and hears the sea waves again, and sees the long rubbery brown kelp washed up on the sand.

He does not phone Edith that night because Lori stays with him. She ought to go back to the dormitory: Friday night she walked to his house with clothes and books in a knapsack, and if she goes back now she can say she spent the weekend in Boston. If anyone asks. No one does, because her friends know where she is. Tomorrow she will have to wake at six while the students are still sleeping and no one is at work except the kitchen staff and one security guard who might see her walking from the direction of Hank's apartment, not the bus stop. The security guard and kitchen staff are not interested; even if they were, their gossip doesn't travel upward to the administration; student, secretarial, and faculty gossip does. Lori and Hank have been doing this for nearly a year, with a near-celibate respite last summer when, except for her one day off a week, they saw each other in Maine, after she had finished waitressing for the night. The drive from his apartment was only an hour, but he decided, grinning at himself, that it meant he truly loved her, that he had not just turned to her during the school year because he was lonely. He had not done anything so adolescent since he had been one: at ten he met her in the restaurant, they went to a bar for a couple of hours, then to her house for coffee in the kitchen, talking quietly while her parents slept; they kissed goodnight for a long time, then he drove home. He did not even consider making love in the car, told her if he did that, hair would grow on his bald spot, his love handles would disappear, and he'd probably get pimples. Some nights her family, or part of it, was at the restaurant, and they all went out together: father, mother, and one or both of her sisters home for a weekend. Hank liked her father, though he was hard to talk with, for he rarely spoke; Lori's mother did most of that, and the two sisters did most of the rest. Everyone pretended Hank and Lori were friends, not lovers, and although Hank wanted it that way, it made him uncomfortable, increased his guilt around Lori's father, and kept him fairly quiet. Often he wanted to take Mr. Meadows aside and tell him he and Lori were lovers and that he loved her and was not using her. He felt none of this with Mrs. Meadows, perhaps because as father of a daughter he imagined Mr. Meadows's concern. Hank danced with all the women in the family and the mother was foxier on the floor than her daughters. She told Hank how pretty she was by joking about how old she was, about her lost figure (the body he held was as firm as Lori's); she asked if he wanted to go to the parking lot for some fresh air, smiling in a way that made him believe and disbelieve the invitation; she did not ask what he was doing with Lori, but when she talked about Lori she looked at him, as they danced, with various expressions: interrogation, dislike, and, most disconcerting of all, jealousy and lasciviousness. On Lori's day off each week she drove down to Hank's, telling her mother the beach was better there, sand instead of rocks; she needed to get out of town for a day; Hank did all that driving back and forth and she owed him one day of visiting him; told her mother all sorts of surface truths her mother did not believe, and on that day they made love and after dinner she drove home again.

Hank does not call Edith Sunday night because he does not know whether or not his turning to her will hurt Lori, and he does not have the energy to ask her. When he realizes that is the only reason, he then wonders if he has the energy to love. He does not remember the woman he was with, or the specific causes, or even the season or calendar year, but he remembers feeling like this before, and he is frightened by its familiarity, its reminder that so much of his life demands energy. He imagines poverty, hunger, oppression, exile, imprisonment: all those lives out there whose suffering is so much worse than his, their endurance so superior, that his own battles could earn only their scorn. He knows all this is true, but it doesn't help, and he makes a salty dog for Lori and, after hesitating, one for himself. Halfway through his drink, as they lie propped on the bed—he has no chairs except the one at his desk—watching *All in the Family,* he decides not to have a second drink. He has become mute, as if the day-long downward-pulling heaviness of his body is trying to paralyze him. So he holds Lori's hand. At nine they undress and get under the covers and watch *The New Centurions.* When George C. Scott kills himself, they wipe their eyes; when Stacey Keach dies, they wipe them again, and Lori says: "Shit." Hank wishes he had armed enemies and a .38 and a riot gun. He thinks he would rather fight that way than by watching television and staying sober and trying to speak. He goes through the apartment turning out lights, then gets into bed and tightly holds Lori.

"I still can't," he says.

"I know."

He wants to tell her—and in fact he does in his mind—how much he loves her, how grateful he is that she was with him all day, quietly knowing his pain, and that as bad as it was, the day would have been worse without her; that she might even have given him and Sharon the day, for without her he might not have been able to get out of bed this morning. But silence has him and the only way he can break it is with tears as deep and wrenching as last night's, and he will not go through that again, does not know if he can bear that emptying again and afterward have something left over for whatever it is he has to do.

Sometime in the night he dreams of him and Sharon lying on the blanket at the beach, the fetus curled pink and sweetly beside him, and asleep he knows as if awake that he is dreaming, that in the morning he will wake with it.

Monday night he eats a sandwich, standing in the kitchen by the telephone, and calls Jack and asks him to go out for a drink after dinner. Then he phones Edith. When she asks what happened he starts to tell her but can only repeat *I* three times and say *Monica;* then he is crying and cursing his tears and slapping the wall with his hand. Edith tells him to take his time (they *are* forever married, he thinks) and finally with her comforting he stops crying and tells the whole story in one long sentence, and Edith says: "That little bitch. She didn't even let you *know? I* could have taken it. I would have taken your baby."

"*I* would have."

"You would?"

"You're Goddamned right. I didn't even get a fucking shot at it. That's why she didn't let me know. She knew I'd have fought it."

"You keep surprising me. That's what happens in marriage, right? People keep changing."

"Who says I changed?"

"I just didn't know you felt that way."

"I never had to before."

"I'm sorry, baby. I never did like that girl. Too much mischief in those eyes."

"It was worse than that."

"Too many lies deciding which would come out first."

"That's her."

"I really would have taken it. If things had gotten bad for you."

"I know."

"Is there anything I can do?"

"Forgive me."

"For what?"

"Everything."

"You are. Sharon was happy when she came home yesterday."

Hank's drinks are bourbon, beer, gin and tequila, and he knows where each will take him. Bourbon will keep him in the same mood he's in when he starts to drink; beer does the same. Either of them, if he drinks enough, will sharpen his focus on his mood, but will not change it, nor take it too far. So they are reliable drinks when he is feeling either good or bad. He has never had a depressed or mean tequila drunk; it always brings him up, and he likes to use it most when he is relaxed and happy after a good day's work. He can also trust it when he is sad. He likes gin rickeys, and his favorite drink is a martini, but he does not trust gin, and drinks it very carefully: it is unpredictable, can take him any place, can suddenly—when he happily began an evening—tap some anger or sorrow he did not even know he had. Since meeting Lori, who loves tequila, he has been replacing the juniper with the cactus.

Tonight, with Jack, he drank gin rickeys, and it is not until he is lying in bed and remembering the fight he has just won that he can actually see it. Timmy's is a neighborhood bar, long and narrow, with only a restroom for men. Beyond its wall is the restaurant, with booths on both sides and one line of tables in the middle; the waitresses in there get drinks through a half door behind the bartender; when customers are in the dining room, the door is kept closed on the noise from the bar. Students rarely drink on the bar side; they stay in the dining room.

Tonight the bar was lined with regulars, working men whose ages are in every decade between twenty and seventy. Two stangers, men in their mid-twenties, stood beside Hank. Their hands were tough, dirty-fingernailed, and their faces confident. Hank noticed this because he was trying to guess what they did for a living. Some of the young men who drank at Timmy's were out of work and drawing unemployment and it showed in their eyes. After the second drink Jack said: "It's either woman-trouble or work-trouble. Which one?"

"Neither."

"It's got to be. It's always one or the other, with a man. Or money."

"Nope."

"Jesus. Are we here to talk about it?"

"No, just to shoot the shit."

Johnny McCarthy brought their drinks: in his mid-twenties, he is working his way through law school; yet always behind the

bar, even when he is taking exams, he is merry; he boxed for
Notre Dame five or six years ago and looks and moves as though
he still could. Hank paid for the round, heard "nigger" beside
him, missed the rest of the young man's sentence, and asked Jack
if he ran today.

"No, I got fucked into a meeting. Did you?"

"Just a short one by the campus. Let's run Kenoza tomorrow."

"Good."

"I'll pick you up."

The talk to his right was louder, and he tried not to hear it as
he and Jack talked about teaching, punctuated once by the man
bumping his right side, an accident probably but no apology for
it; then more talk until he heard "Lee" and, still listening to Jack
and talking to him, he also listened to blond big-shouldered cocky
asshole on his right cursing Hank's favorite man on the Red Sox,
that smooth pitcher, that competitor. In his bed he cannot count
the gin rickeys or the time that passed before he heard "Lee,"
then turned and no longer saw the broad shoulders. Drunk, he
felt big and strong and fast and, most of all, an anger that had to
be released, an anger so intense that it felt like hatred too. As a
grown man he had come close to fighting several times, in bars,
but he never had because always, just short of saying the final
words that would do it, he had images of the consequences: it was
not fear of being hurt; he had played football in high school and
was not unduly afraid of pain; it was the image of the fight's end:
the bartender, usually a friend, sober and disgusted as he ejected
Hank; or, worse, cops, sober and solemn and ready for a little action themselves, and he could not get past those images of dig-
nity-loss, of shame, of being pulled up from the floor where he
rolled and fought like a dog. So always he had stopped, had felt
like a coward till next morning when he was glad he had stopped.
But this time he turned to the man and said: "You don't know
what the fuck you're talking about."

The man stepped back to give himself room.

"What's that?"

"Lee's the best clutch pitcher on the staff."

"Fucking loudmouth spaceman is what he is."

"Oh that's it. I thought I heard nigger a while back. You don't like what he *says*, is that it?" He could feel rather than hear the silence in the bar, could hear Johnny across the bar talking to him, urging, his voice soft and friendly. "It's bussing, is that it? You don't like Lee because he's for bussing? Pissed you off when he didn't like the war?"

"Fuck *him*. I was *in* Nam, motherfucker, and I don't want to fucking hear you again: you drink with that other cunt you're with."

"I'm glad you didn't get killed over there," Hank said, his voice low, surprising him, and he turned away, nodded at Johnny, then he reached for his glass, confused, too many images now—and in his bed smiling he can understand it: dead children and women and scared soldiers and dead soldiers; and in Washington he and Jack quietly crying as they watched the veterans march, old eyes and mouths on their young bodies or what was left of some of them: the legless black with his right arm raised as a friend pushed his wheelchair, the empty sleeves, empty trouser-legs on that cold Inauguration Day; in his bed he can understand it: the man had given him a glimpse of what might have been his long suffering in Vietnam, for a moment he had become a man instead of an asshole with a voice. Then Hank surprised himself again: his rage came back, and into his drink he said: "Fuck you anyway."

They were standing side by side, nearly touching: they turned together, Hank's left fist already swinging, and his right followed it, coming up from below and behind his waist; then he seemed to be watching himself from the noise and grasping hands around him, felt the hands slipping from him as he kept swinging, and the self he was watching was calm and existed in a circle of silence, as if he were a hurricane watching its own eye. The man was off-balance from Hank's first two punches, so he could not get his feet and body set, and all his blows on Hank's arms, ribs, side of the head, came while going backward and trying to plant his feet and get his weight forward; and Hank drove inside and with short punches went for the blood at the nose and mouth. Then the man was against the wall, and Hank felt lifted and thrown though his feet did not leave the floor; the small of his back was pressed against the bar's edge, his arms spread and held to the bar by each wrist in Johnny's tight hands. Then it was Jack holding his wrists, talking to him, and over Jack's shoulder he watched Johnny push aside the two regulars holding the man against the wall. The man's friend was there, yelling, cursing. Johnny turned to him, one hand on the blond's chest, and said: "I'm sick of this shit. Open your mouth again and you'll look like your friend there." Then he turned to Jack: "Will you get Hank the fuck *out* of here."

Then he was outside, arm-in-arm with Jack, and he was laughing.

"Are you all right?"

He could feel Jack trembling; he was trembling too.

"I feel *great*," he said.

"You tore his ass. You crazy bastard, I didn't know you could fight."

"I can't," Hank said, sagging from Jack's arm as he laughed. "I just did, that's all."

He is awake a long time but it is excitement and when finally he sleeps he is still happy. The dream is familiar now: it comes earlier than usual, or Hank feels that it does, and next morning at ten he wakes to that and much more. He is grateful the sun is coming in; it doesn't help, but a gray sky would be worse: he lies thinking of Johnny's anger last night, and he wonders who the man is, and hopes that somewhere he is lying with a gentle woman who last night washed his cuts. Then he is sad. It has been this way all his life, as long as he can remember, even with bullies in grade school, and he has never understood it: he can hate a man, want to hurt him or see him hurt; but if he imagines the man going home to a woman (as the bullies went to their mothers) he is sad. He imagines the man last night entering his apartment, the woman hurrying to his face, the man vulnerable with her as he is with no one else, as he can be with no one else, loving her as she washes each cut—*Does that hurt? Yes*—the man becoming a boy again as she gently cleans him, knowing this is the deepest part of himself beneath all the layers of growing up and being a man among men and soldiering: this—and he can show it only to her, and she is the only one in his life who can love it.

"I hope he finds me and beats shit out of me," Hank says aloud. Then he can smile: he does not want the shit beat out of him. He drives to Jack's house. In the car, when Hank tells him how he feels now, Jack says: "Fuck that guy; he wanted a fight all night. And after school we'll go see Johnny. He'll start laughing as soon as he sees you." Immediately Hank knows this is true. He wonders what men without friends do on the day after they've been drunken assholes.

At Lake Kenoza he parks at the city tennis courts and locks his wallet and their windbreakers in the car. They start slowly, running on a dirt road, in the open still, the sun warm on Hank's face: he looks at the large pond to his left. The purple loose-strife is gone now; in summer it grows bright purple among the reeds near the pond. The road curves around the pond, which is separated from the lake by a finger of tree-grown earth. As they leave the pond they enter the woods, the road sun-dappled now, deeply rutted, so he has to keep glancing down at it as he also watches the lake to his left; the road is close to it, just up the slope from its bank lapped by waves in the breeze; to his right the earth rises, thick with trees. He and Jack talk while they run.

He wishes Lori ran. He has never had a woman who did. Edith started after their marriage ended. Running is the most intimate part of his friendship with Jack. Hank does not understand precisely why this is true. Perhaps it has something to do with the rhythm of their feet and breath. But there is more: it is, Hank thinks, setting free the flesh: as they approach the bend marking the second mile, the road staying by the lake and moving deeper into the woods which rise farther and farther to their right, he is no longer distracted by anything: he sees the lake and road and woods and Jack's swinging arms and reaching legs as he could never see them if he were simply walking, or standing still. It is this: even in lovemaking the body can become a voyeur of its own pleasure. But in the willful exertion of running, nothing can distract the flesh from itself.

Which is why he waits for the long hill that comes at the middle of their nearly six-mile run. They are close to it now, and are both afraid of it, and know this about each other. The road climbs away from the lake and they go up it, then leave it, onto a dirt trail dropping to the lake again. Here the lake's bank is sheer, there are rocks at its base, pebbles on the sand; to the right is the slope of the hill, steep, covered brown with pine needles, nearly all its trees are pines, and looking up there Hank cannot see the top of the hill or even the sky; always here he thinks of *For Whom the Bell Tolls*, sees Robert Jordan and Anselmo in the opening pages, lying up there among the pines. The trail often rises and falls, and then it goes down and to the right and up and they are on it: the long curving deceptive hill. It took Hank nearly a year to stop believing the next crest was the last one: short of breath, legs hurting, he looks up the road which is so steep and long that he cannot see beyond the next crest; he has never counted them, or the curves between them; he does not want to know. He prefers to run knowing only that it will get worse; and by doing this he always has that weary beat of joy when he sees that finally, a quarter of a mile or so ahead, is the top.

"Monet again," Jack says.

Hank looks past him, down the hill; between the pines he can see sweat-blurred flashes of the lake; but it is the sun on the trees he's looking at. Jack is right; the sun touches the trees like Monet. Now they run harder, to reach the top, end the pain, and slowly the road levels and they shorten their strides: fast dry breaths, and Jack shakes his hand; they are at the center of the top of the hill, and suddenly, shaking Jack's hand and running beside him, Hank sees the dream again; the hill has not worked, he has run out of cures, and he releases Jack's hand and shouts through his own gasping: "I can't get cafucking*thar*sis—"

Going downhill now, watching the road so he won't turn an ankle in a rut, he tells Jack about Monica; and the dream, which is with him now as he talks past trees and lake, talks all the way out of the woods into the sunlight where finally he stops talking for their last sprint to the tennis courts, the car, the water fountain.

"Marry Lori," Jack says, as he bends toward the fountain; he walks away gargling, then spits out the water and returns. "The fucking country's gone crazy," he says. "Marry her."

Lori worries too much. Sometimes she thinks if she could stop worrying about so many parts of her life, and focus on her few real problems, there would be an end to those times, which are coming at least weekly now so she is afraid of an ulcer, when she is eating and it seems her food drops onto tense muscles and lies there undigested and after the meal it is still there and she is nauseated; and she could stop smoking so much; and she could stop staring at her school work at night instead of doing it; and she could ask questions in class, and could say what she was thinking when the teacher tried to start a discussion, instead of sitting there with her stomach tightening and feeling sorry for him because no one else is talking either. She could talk to her friends at school, girls and boys; she talks to them now, but usually only about what they are saying; she doesn't think they even realize this, but she knows it is why they like her and think of her as sweet and kind, their faces warm when she joins them at a table in the dining room or snack bar; but they don't know any of her secrets, and they are good friends who would listen, so it is her fault. She has been able to talk to Hank, so he knows more about her than anyone, but still she has not talked to him enough. She suspects though—and this makes her feel safely loved—that he understands more about her than she has told him.

Yet on the one night, two weeks ago, when she tried to separate her smaller problems from her essential ones, made parallel lists on a legal pad, she found that they were all connected, so the vertical lists, beginning with *my stomach* in the left column and *career* in the right column, became a letter to herself. As she wrote it she was both excited and frightened: excited because she was beginning to see herself, and lovingly, on the paper on her desk; and frightened because she did not know where the writing was taking her; and because it might take her no place at all, might end on the very next page, in mid-sentence— Her first line was: *My name is Lori Meadows.* She wrote that she was nineteen years old, would be twenty in January, was a sophomore in college and was screwed up. But as soon as those two words appeared on the yellow page, she did not believe them. She was a C student. That was in her file in the registrar's office: 2.4 next to her name. Her mother said she would never get to graduate school like that. Lori always nodded, always said *I know I know I'll bring it up.* She never asked her mother what she was supposed to study in graduate school. She was all right, she wrote, except when she thought about the future. She liked going to her classes and sometimes she even came out excited; but then at night she could not study. Hank told her it was easy: she only had to spend two or three hours on school nights going over the notes from that day's classes and reading the assignments, she would be free by nine every night, and when exams came there would be no cramming, no all-nighters, all she would have to do was go over the notes again and the passages she had marked in the books. She loved the books. She loved owning them, and the way they looked on the shelves in her small room. But at night she didn't want to open them. Hank said he studied that way all through college and was on the dean's list every semester. But he was smarter than she was, and she worried about that too. But maybe that wasn't it. He was writing then; before he got out of college he wrote a novel and burned it. She would have to ask him if he studied like that so he'd have time to write, or if that was just the way he did things.

She didn't have any reason to study like that except to make grades and she didn't know what to make grades for except so she wouldn't feel like a dumb shit, and so her mother wouldn't start in on her. So at night she talked with people or went to Hank's. At least she didn't smoke dope. She didn't smoke it at all, but she was thinking of those who just went to their rooms and turned on the stereo and smoked themselves to sleep. Often in February, or even before Christmas, they packed their things and went home. In the morning she woke in panic because she hadn't done her work. Last year she got a D in biology because she couldn't memorize, but she liked the classes. But she couldn't memorize. She just didn't. She got Bs last year in Hank's literature courses because she had a crush on him and she liked the stories and novels he assigned and she could write about them on tests. And she'd probably get a B or A in his Chekhov course this fall. Maybe it was love last year, not a crush. They were drinking friends then, in September, and often she went drinking with him and Monica and sometimes just she and Hank walked down to Timmy's and sat in a booth in the dining room. She could talk to him then too. But she fell in love with him when he started taking her out after Monica, and when he made love with her so gently the first time and she came for the first time with a man, but if she hadn't had the crush she wouldn't have fallen in love holding hands on Boylston Street and stopping in the bookstore and making love that night, so maybe it was called a crush when you were in love without touching.

She didn't understand about school. She was not lazy. She worked hard learning to ride and won three cups for jumping before she was fifteen and then she stopped riding except for fun. Some girls stayed with horses, at a certain age, and they didn't change after that; they didn't go for boys. At least the girls she had known. She worked hard at the restaurant last summer and the summer before. She knew everything about those two summers, the work and what she had read and the beach and her friends, loving her quiet father and loving her mother too, wishing she and her father could talk and touch, watching him, wondering what he thought, what pictures were in his mind when she entered a room and he looked up at her, and his face loved her;

and wishing she could talk to her mother instead of just listen to the words that seemed to come as long as her mother was awake, like a radio left on; but this radio was dangerous, sometimes it was witty, sometimes cheerful, sometimes just small talk, but each day there were always other things, nearly always subtle, sometimes even with a smile: warnings, reprimands, disapprovals, threats, most of them general, having to do with things as vague as growth, the future, love, being a woman. None of these was vague but they were when her mother talked about them: cryptic, her voice implying more than the words; her mother never spoke as if, in the world, there was a plan. And when Lori listened closely enough to this she heard or felt she heard the real cause: some brittle disappointment in her mother's voice, and she wanted to say *Are you unhappy Mother? What is it you want? What is it you want for me?*

For they had never had any real trouble. Lori had avoided dope because the first time she smoked it she didn't like it, she only got very sleepy and very hungry at once and was suddenly asleep at the party; and she was afraid to swallow anything, did not want something down in her stomach where she could not throw it away. She was obedient, and had always been. She was pretty, as her sisters were. She had a notion, which she didn't want, that if she were not pretty, her mother would not forgive her for that. They had never really quarrelled. She had watched her mother flirt with boys who came for her or her sisters, and with men, in front of her father; had watched her father's face, not quite grim, mostly calm. She knew her mother needed to flirt, see her effect on the boys who blushed and the men who did not. Her mother flirted with Hank too, but when he wasn't there she frowned when Lori spoke of him. *He's too old for you,* she said. *We're just friends. What kind of friends? I get lonely at school; he's good to talk to. This is summer. He's still my friend.* Wishing she could say *I'm in love* and *What does too old mean? That he'll die first? I could drown tomorrow.* She had told Hank. He said *It's not age. It's money. If I were a doctor or a Republican senator she'd bring us coffee in bed.*

She did not know if her mother did more than flirt. But all

through the years there were times when her mother would go away, tell husband and daughters she needed a vacation, and she would go to Mexico, or the Caribbean, and return a week or two later with a tan and presents for everyone; and when Lori was fifteen she realized that for at least two years she had been trying not to wonder what a flirtatious, pretty and slender woman did alone at Puerto Vallarta, Martinique . . . Now the words on the legal pad told her exactly what her mother did and she understood why her father was even gentler than usual as he cooked for the three daughters while his wife screwed men she had met hours before. Why did her mother need that? It frightened her, as though it were an illness that ran in the women in the family, and she was ashamed that there were men walking the earth who had screwed her mother, who might crazily someday even meet her, realize she was the daughter of that six-day woman winters ago, and how could her mother do that to her— to them?

She did not know why she made love to Blake summer before last; could remember, as she wrote, moments in the restaurant when they smiled at each other as they hurried with trays, and then drank at the bar when the kitchen closed and they were done for the night. It was simply, she knew now, the camaraderie of people working together, an assurance that they were not really carriers of trays, smiling servants, charming targets of well-mannered abuse. He could have been a woman. Then at the night's end, after their drinks, Lori and the woman would have separated, as they would at the summer's end; by the time the leaves fell they would fondly think of each other, in their separate schools, as summer friends, waitress friends. But because he was a man, that affinity of co-workers, especially those with menial jobs, grew to passion and all its tributaries of humor and tenderness and wanting to know and be known; and she was eighteen, the last virgin among her friends and in her home; the last virgin on the block, her sisters teased.

It was August, she had been working all summer, school was coming. Blake was going back to Illinois, it seemed time: time to complete or begin or both, and there was tequila and cheer, the very sound of her laugh seeming different to her, something of freedom in it; there was the dirt path near the cliff's edge over the sea and rocky beach, and tenderly she walked with him and tenderly she kissed him and went to the earth with him and was not afraid, was ready, here on the cliff she had walked as a child, so much better than in a dormitory, waves slapping rocks as if they knew she was up there between them and the moving clouds and moon and stars. Then she was afraid: the slow tenderness of the walk was gone with her clothes he removed too quickly; she lay waiting, her eyes shut, listening to his clothes sliding from his skin, then too soon he was in her, big and she was tight, and everything was fast and painful and she cried, not only that night but every night after work, not because it always hurt, but because she couldn't tell him how to make it better and finally after two weeks when the summer was ending and he came, then rolled away and sat naked looking at the sea while beside him she lay softly crying, he said: *You're screwed up.* She said nothing. She got up fast and dressed and was on the path before he called to her to wait. She did not. She walked faster. But she knew he could catch up with her, so she crouched behind a pine tree, heard him coming, watched him trot past. Then she left the tree and sat near the cliff's edge and watched the ocean, listening. When she was certain she heard only wind and waves, she rose and walked down the path.

She did not want to walk the four miles home. She went to a bar where she knew her girl friends would be. She found their table; they waved and beckoned as she went to them. Monica was there. They had pitchers of beer and were laughing and on the bandstand a group was singing like Crosby Stills Nash and Young: the same songs, the same style. Her friends were talking to her: she was smiling, talking, accepting a mug. But she was angry. She did not know why and it made her feel unpredictable and moody like her mother, and guilty because her friends had not hurt her, it was Blake, yet he was only a shard of pain inside her anger. Yet writing about it over a year later she understood, and was delighted at the understanding till she paused and put her pen in her mouth and sucked on it and wondered if tonight she could have understood this without Hank. Had he taught her to see? She felt diminished. Her long-time voice with its long-time epithet whispered at her spine: *You're a dumb shit.* Then she was angry. At herself. It was Chekhov, that wonderful man dead too young; his story, when the old doctor said: *Why do you hate freedom so?* Chekhov who wrote about the perils, even the evil, of mediocrity. Hank merely assigned the stories and talked about them. And wasn't that really why she was in school? She stopped writing. Made a dash, indented. Wrote about the bar again, her friends, her anger, or else she would forget and she must get that down quickly because she had started to discover something else and if she didn't get back to the bar now she might never.

It was the people singing, and her friends' clapping praise. While she sat with the pains of Blake's attacks: the one with his cock, the one with his tongue, the one with his heart. And her friends were listening to four boys in their early twenties who were content to imitate someone else. While her betrayal on the cliff called for poetry or an act of revenge. Up *there.* On *that* cliff, where in the brightest daylight of sun on ocean she had lain beside her sisters; where she and her friends had gone with sandwiches and apples in the days of dirty hands and knees, up *there* she had tried for love and felt nothing but that cruel cock— And she walked down alone, with some bravery against pain, with some pride in her bravery, and re-entered a lowland of laughter and mediocrity, where she could never explain what had happened up there above the sea. The guitars and voices taunted her: the safe musicians who practiced to albums. Her friends' laughter drained her.

But what was that before? The anger, the *You dumb shit* voice— Yes: Hank. It was Chekhov. And first of all, she had no way of knowing whether tonight's understanding of her anger in that bar over a year ago came from reading Chekhov. But it didn't matter. What if she had learned from reading, even from hearing Hank talk about Chekhov? That didn't mean she was too dumb to understand her own life without someone else's help. It meant she was getting smarter. Now she wrote with joy, with love for herself in the world. Wasn't that what she was in school for? To enter classrooms and to hear? And if that made her understand her life better, wasn't that enough and wasn't that why she could not study for the grades for the graduate school which would give her a job she could not even imagine and therefore could not imagine the graduate school either? Wasn't she in fact an intelligent young woman trying to learn how to live, and if no profession pulled at her, if she could not see herself with a desk and office and clothes and manners to match them, that only meant she was like most people. This fall Hank talking in class about "The Kiss" and what people had to endure when they had jobs instead of vocations; Ryabovich, with his dull career, existing more in the daydreams he constructed from the accidental kiss than he did in the saddle of his horse.

She wanted to phone Hank and tell him but she did not want to stop writing, and now it was time to write about Hank anyway. Already she was with her second lover and she had tried not to think about the future but it kept talking to her anyway at times when she was alone, but she would not talk back, would not give words to her fear, but now her pen moved fast because her monologue with her future had been there for some time and she knew every word of it though she had refused, by going to sleep or going to talk to someone, ever to listen to it. Already two lovers and she wished she could cancel the first and, if she and Hank broke up, there would be a third and she would be going the way of her sisters who had recovered, she thought, too many times from too many lovers, were growing tougher through repeated pain; were growing, she thought, cynical; and when they visited home, they talked about love but never permanent love anymore, and all the time she *knew* but wouldn't say because they still talked to her like a baby sister and because she didn't want to loosen what she saw as a fragile hold on their lives, she knew what they needed was marriage. Two lovers were enough. Three seemed deadly. If she could not stay with the third, it seemed the next numbers were all the same, whether four or fifteen: some path of failure, some sequence of repetitions that would change her, take her further and further from the Lori she was beginning to love tonight.

And now here was Hank on a sunny October Saturday, having for the first time since she had known him cancelled his day with Sharon, walking beside her, on his back a nylon knapsack he said held wine and their lunch, a blanket folded over his left arm, his right arm loosely around her waist as they walked on his running road she had never seen except in her mind when he talked about it. And he was happy, his boyish happiness that she loved, for the first time since last Saturday night when she told him about Monica because she could not hide from him any longer something she knew he would want to know. Tuesday night she had gone to his apartment and he told her of his fight Monday and that he and Jack had just been to Timmy's where he had apologized to Johnny and bought the bar a round, and he said Jack had been right. Johnny had grinned and said: *The middleweight champ of Timmy's* as soon as he walked in; and he told her about running with Jack and how it hadn't worked. She slept with him that night and Wednesday and Thursday and Friday, and he held her and talked. He did not tell her he still couldn't make love. He did not even mention it. During those four nights she felt he was talking to spirits, different ones who kept appearing above them where he gazed, felt that he was struggling with some, agreeing with others, and lying beside him she was watching a strange play.

He said Jack was right. The country had gone fucking crazy. He said I'll bet ninety percent of abortions are because somebody's making love with somebody they shouldn't. So were too many people. So had he, for too long. But no more. Things were screwed up and the women had lost again. A sexual revolution and a liberation movement and look what it got them. Guys didn't carry rubbers anymore. Women were expected to be on

the pill or have an IUD and expected also to have their hearts as
ready as their wombs. And women were even less free than before, except for the roundheels, and there were more of them
around now but he didn't know any men who took them any
more seriously than the roundheels from the old days of rubbers
in the wallet and slow courting. Goddamn. The others (*Like you,*
he said to Lori) are trapped. Used to be a young woman when
they were called girls could date different guys and nobody had a
hold on her, could date three guys in one weekend; by the end of
a year in college she might have dated six, ten, any number, gone
places, had fun, been herself. Now girls are supposed to fuck.
Most students don't even date: just go to the dormitory room
and drink and smoke dope and get laid. Guy doesn't even have to
work for it. But then he's got the girl. Unless she's a roundheel,
and nobody gives a shit about them. But the good ones. Like
you. What they do is go through some little marriages. First one
breaks up, then there's another guy. Same thing. Three days or
three room-visits or whatever later, and they're lovers. Somebody else meets her, wants to take her to Boston to hear some
music, see a play, she can't. Boy friend says no. Can't blame him;
she'd say no if he wanted to take somebody to hear some music.
Girl gets out of college and what she's had is two or three monogamous affairs, even shared the same room. Call that freedom?
Men win again. Girls have to make sure they don't get pregnant,
they have to make love, have to stay faithful. Some revolution.
Some liberation. And everybody's so fucking happy, you noticed
that? Jack is right, Goddamnit; Jack is right. He's glad now they
stuck it out. He and Terry. He said I've got a good friend who's
also my wife and I've got two good children, and the three of
them make the house a good nest, and I sit and look out the window at the parade going by: some of my students are marching
and some of my buddies, men and women, and the drum ma-
jorette is Aphrodite and she's pissed off and she's leading that
parade to some bad place. I don't think it's the Styx either. It's
some place where their cocks will stay hard and their pussies wet,
some big open field with brown grass and not one tree, and no-

body's going to say anything funny there. Nobody'll laugh. All you'll hear is pants and grunts. Maybe Aphrodite will laugh, I don't know. But I don't think she's that mean. Just a trifle pissed-off at all this trifling around.

"It's beautiful," Lori says, as they enter the woods and she can see the lake.

"This is the first time I've walked it," Hank says.

"It is? You've never brought a woman here?"

"No. Not even Sharon."

"Why?"

"Never thought about it. When I think of this place I think of running. I've never even been here after it snows. Too slippery."

"Not for walking. With boots."

"No."

"Can we come here in winter?"

"Sure."

He moves his arm from her waist and takes her hand. They walk slowly. An hour passes before they start up the long hill; he looks down the slope at sun on the pines, and their needles on the earth, at boulders, and the lake between branches. At the top he says: "Blackberries grow here."

"Do you and Jack ever pick them?"

"We say we will. But when we get to the top we just sort of look at them as we gasp on by."

He turns left into the woods, and they climb again, a short slope above the road; then they are out of the trees, standing on a wide green hill, looking down and beyond at the Merrimack valley, the distant winding river, and farms and cleared earth; surrounding all the houses and fields, and bordering the river, are the red and yellow autumn trees. He unfolds the blanket and she helps him spread it on the grass. He takes off the pack and brings out a bottle of claret, deviled eggs wrapped in foil, a half-gallon jug of apple cider, two apples, a pound of Jarlsberg cheese, Syrian bread, and a summer sausage. She is smiling.

"Cider?"

She nods and takes the jug from him and he watches the muscle in her forearm as she holds it up and drinks, watching her throat moving, her small mouth. When she hands him the jug he drinks, then opens the wine with a corkscrew from the pack. "I didn't bother with glasses." They pass the bottle. She lightly kisses him and says: "You went to a lot of trouble. I thought you'd just buy a couple of subs."

They eat quietly, looking at the valley. Then Hank lies on his back while Lori sits smoking. When she puts out the cigarette she returns it to her pack.

"That does it," he says.

"What?"

"Anybody who'd take a stinking butt home instead of leaving it here ought to be loved forever."

She lies beside him, rests her head on his right shoulder, and he says: "I think when we started making love I wasn't in love with you. I felt like you were one of my best friends, and I needed someone to keep me going. I figured you'd be like the other young ones, give me a year, maybe a little more, then move on. But I chose that over staring at my walls at night. I wasn't thinking much about you. Then after a few months I didn't have to think about you anyway, because I was in love, so I knew I wasn't going to hurt you. I figured you'd leave me, and I'd just take a day at a time till you did. Like I did with Monica. I should never have made love with Monica. I haven't had the dream since Monday after the fight—"

"—She shouldn't have made love with you."

"Same thing. I can't do that again. Ever. With anyone. Unless both of us are ready for whatever happens. No more playing with semen and womb if getting pregnant means solitude and death instead of living. And that's all I mean: living. Nobody's got to do a merry dance, have the faulty rubber bronzed. But living. Worry; hope the rabbit doesn't die; keep the Tampax ready; get drunk when the rabbit dies; but laugh too. So I can't make love with you. I'm going to court you. And if someday you say you'll marry me, then it'll be all right, and—"

"—It's all right now."

She kisses him, the small mouth, the slow tongue that always feels to him shy and trusting. Then she pulls him so his breast covers hers and she holds his face up and says: "I want to finish college." She smiles. "For the fun of it. But we're engaged."

"That's almost three years. What if we get pregnant?"

"Then we'll get married and I'll go to school till the baby comes and I'll finish later, when I can."

"You've thought about it before?"

"Yes."

"For how long?"

"I don't know. But longer than you."

"Are you going to tell your folks?"

"Sure."

"They won't like it."

"She won't. My father won't mind."

"We might as well do it in the old scared-shitless way: drive up there together and tell them."

"I'd like that."

"Do you want a ring?"

"No. Something else."

"What?"

"I don't know. We'll find something."

"I like this. So next Saturday we go to Boston and find something. And we don't know what it is. But it'll mean we're getting married."

"Yes."

"And that night we go to your folks' for dinner and we say we have a little announcement to make."

"Yes."

"And your mother will hate it but she'll try not to show it. And your father will blush and grin and shake my hand."

"Maybe he'll even hug me."

"And for three years your mother will hope some rich guy steals you from me, and your father will just go on about his business."

"That's it." Then she presses both palms against his jaw and says: "And we're never going to get a divorce. And we're not going to have American children. We're going to bring them up the way you and Edith were."

"Look what that got us."

"A good daughter."

"You really think she's all right?"

"Man, that chick's got her shit together," she says, then she is laughing and he tries to kiss her as she turns away with her laughter and when it stops she says: "Clean tongues and clean lungs and no Monicas and Blakes. That's how we'll bring them up. Let's make love."

"The Trojan warriors are at home."

"You really *did* think you'd have to court me. Then let's go home."

He kisses her once, then kneels, uncorks the wine bottle, holds it to her lips while she raises her head to swallow; then he drinks and returns the cork and puts the bottle in the pack. As he stands and slips his arms through the straps, Lori shakes out the blanket, and they fold it.

"Can I keep this in my room at school?"

"Sure."

She rests it over her arm and takes his hand and looks down at the valley. Then she turns to the woods, and quietly they leave the hill and go down through the trees to the road above the lake.

"It took us a long time to get here," she says. "Did you say this is the halfway point?"

"Right about where we're standing."

"We didn't walk very fast. It'll be quicker, going back."

"It always is," he says, and starts walking.

ABOUT THE AUTHOR

Andre Dubus is the author of *The Times Are Never So Bad*, *Finding a Girl In America*, *Adultery & Other Choices*, *Separate Flights*, and *The Lieutenant*. He has also been a Marine Corps Captain, a Guggenheim Fellow, and a member of the Writers' Workshop at the University of Iowa. He lives in Bradford, Massachusetts.